Pelagia and the Black Monk

BORIS AKUNIN

D0715050

PHOENIX

A PHOENIX PAPERBACK

First published in Great Britain in 2007
by Weidenfeld & Nicolson
This paperback edition published in 2008
by Phoenix,
an imprint of Orion Books Ltd,
Orion House, 5 Upper St Martin's Lane,
London WC2H 9EA

An Hachette Livre UK company

First published in Russian as *Pelagiya i chorny monakh*
by Zakharov Publishers, Moscow, Russia and
Edizioni Frassinelli, Milan, Italy
All rights reserved.

Published by arrangement with Linda Michaels Limited,
International Literary Agents.

1 3 5 7 9 10 8 6 4 2

Copyright © Boris Akunin 2001
Translation © Andrew Bromfield 2007

A CIP catalogue record for this book
is available from the British Library.

ISBN 978-0-7538-2375-0

Printed and bound in Great Britain
by Clays Ltd, St Ives plc

The Orion Publishing Group's policy is to use papers
that are natural, renewable and recyclable products and
made from wood grown in sustainable forests. The logging
and manufacturing processes are expected to conform to
the environmental regulations of the country of origin.

www.orionbooks.co.uk

Prologue

[*The square on to which the windows of the district court looked out was already almost completely empty by this hour in the early evening. Two mongrels were yelping lazily at each other beside a street lamp, a boy in a cloth jacket and blacked boots was hopping over a puddle on one leg. But from the far end of the square, where it runs into Malaya Kupecheskaya Street, there came the resounding clop-clop of hooves over cobblestones, the rumble of wheels and the jingle of harness. This combined noise approached at a spanking pace, and soon it was possible to make out a lathered pair of piebald greys pulling along a sprung carriage. Standing on the box, waving a whip, was a dusty monk in a black cassock that fluttered behind him in the wind, and his head was uncovered, so that his long locks were tousled and tangled; and then it became clear that the forehead of this terrible coachman was covered in blood and his eyes were bulging out of his very head. The small number of people in the street who saw this sight all froze in amazement.*

Approaching the court building, the monk pulled back on the reins, halting the dashing horses, jumped to the ground and shouted to Pelagia.

Pelagia turned back quickly towards the Bishop. Mitrofanii had not seen the strange monk or heard his shout, but he immediately sensed that something was wrong. He pushed the correspondent aside gently but firmly and . . .]

The Appearance of Basilisk

... several long strides brought him to the side the nun. Glancing out of the window and seeing the lathered horses and the dishevelled monk, he knitted his bushy brows sternly.

'He shouted to me: "Mother, disaster! He's here already? Where's His Reverence?"' Pelagia told the Bishop in a low voice.

At the word 'disaster' Mitrofanii nodded in satisfaction, as if he had been expecting nothing less from this interminably long day that seemed determined never to end. He beckoned with his finger to the tattered and dusty messenger (the general manner and loud shouting of this monk who had arrived in such a rush from God only knew where left no doubt that he was precisely a messenger, and one bearing bad tidings) – as if to say: Right, come up here and we'll take a look at you.

With a rapid bow to the Bishop that reached almost down to the ground the monk dropped the reins and dashed into the court building, elbowing aside the public on their way out after the trial. The appearance of this servant of God, with his head uncovered and his forehead scratched and bleeding, was so unusual that people glanced round at him, some in curiosity, others in alarm. The tumultuous discussion of the recently concluded hearing and its remarkable verdict was suddenly broken off. It looked as though some new remarkable Event was in the offing or had even, perhaps, already taken place.

Such is always the way of things in quiet backwaters like our peaceful town of Zavolzhsk: five or ten years of peace and quiet and drowsy torpor, and then suddenly one hurricane blast following another, bending the very bell towers down to the ground.

The ominous herald ran up the white-marble staircase. On the upper landing, below the scales held aloft by blind-eyed Justice, he hesitated for a moment, uncertain which way to turn, to the right or the left, but immediately spotted the knot of correspondents from Russia's two capital cities and the two figures in black robes, one large and one small, in the far corner of the recreation area: the Reverend Mitrofanii and, beside him, the sister in spectacles who had been standing at the window.

The monk's massive boots roused a thunderous echo as he dashed across the floor towards the Bishop, howling to him from a distance: 'My lord, he's here! Close by already! Coming after me! Huge and black!'

The journalists from St Petersburg and Moscow, including some genuine luminaries of this profession, who had come to Zavolzhsk for the sensational trial, stared in bewilderment at this wild-looking figure in a cassock.

'Who's coming? Who's black?' His Grace thundered. 'Speak clearly. Who are you? Where from?'

'The humble monk Antipa from Ararat,' the agitated fellow said with a hasty bow, reaching up to remove his skullcap, but it wasn't there – he had lost it somewhere. 'Basilisk is coming – who else! He himself, our patron! He has come forth from the hermitage. Your Reverence, order the bells to be rung and the icons to be brought out! St John's prophecy is being fulfilled! "For lo, I come soon, and bring vengeance with me, to render unto each according to his deeds!" It is the end,' he howled, 'the end of everything!'

The big-city types didn't seem concerned – they weren't frightened by the news of the end of the world, they just pricked up their ears and moved a little closer to the monk – but the courthouse cleaner, who had already begun pushing his broom along the corridor, froze on the spot when he heard

3

this terrible cry, dropping his implement of labour and crossing himself hastily.

The herald of the Apocalypse was too anguished and terrified to say anything else coherent – he began shaking all over and tears began coursing down over his stark white face and his beard.

As always in critical situations, His Grace demonstrated a most efficacious decisiveness. Following the ancient precept according to which the best remedy for hysterics is a good hard slap, Mitrofanii gave the sobbing man two resounding blows to the cheeks with his weighty hand, and the monk immediately stopped shaking and howling. His eyes went blank and he hiccuped. Then, building on his success, the Bishop seized the messenger by the collar and dragged him towards the nearest door, which led into the court archives. Pelagia gave a pitiful gasp at the sound of the slaps and then trotted after them.

The archivist was just settling down to enjoy some tea following the conclusion of the court session, but the Bishop merely glanced at him with one eyebrow raised and the court official disappeared in a flash. The three ecclesiastics were left alone in the government office.

The Bishop sat the sobbing Antipa down on a chair and thrust the barely begun glass of tea under his nose: Take that, drink it. He waited while the monk took a drink with his teeth rattling against the glass, and wetted his constricted throat, then asked impatiently: 'Well, what has happened over there in Ararat? Tell me.'

The correspondents were left facing a locked door. They stood there for a while, repeating the mysterious words 'Basilisk' and 'Ararat' over and over again, and then gradually began to disperse, still in a state of total perplexity. That was natural enough – they were all strangers, people who knew nothing of our Zavolzhian holy places and legends. Local people would have understood straight away.

However, since our readers may include some outsiders who have never been to the province of Zavolzhie, or might never even have heard of it, before recounting the conversation that ensued in the archive room we will provide several explanations which, while they might appear excessively lengthy, are nonetheless essential to an understanding of the narrative that follows.

Where would be the most appropriate place to start?

Probably with Ararat – or rather, New Ararat, a famous monastery located in the far north of our extensive but little-populated province. There, on the forested islands amidst the waters of the Blue Lake, which in its dimensions resembles a sea (that is what the simple folk call it: the Blue Sea), from ancient times holy monks have taken refuge from the vanity and malice of the world. There have been times when the monastery fell into decline and neglect, so that only a small handful of anchorites were left living in isolated cells and hermitages across the entire archipelago, but it never became completely extinct, not even during the Time of Troubles.

There was one special reason for this tenacious grasp on life, and it goes by the name of Basilisk's Hermitage – but we shall tell you about that a little further on, for the hermitage has always led an existence almost separate from the actual monastery itself. In the nineteenth century, under the influence of the beneficial conditions of our calm and peaceful times, the monastery has blossomed quite magnificently – initially owing to the fashion for northern holy places that became widespread among well-to-do pilgrims, and in very recent times thanks to the efforts of the present archimandrite, Father Vitalii II, who bears that title because in the last century the monastery had another father superior with the same name.

This exceptional servant of the Church has raised New Ararat to unprecedented heights of prosperity. When he was instructed to take charge of the quiet island monastery, the reverend father rightly decided that fashion was a fickle creature and, before she could turn the gaze of her favour to some other, no less venerable monastery, he needed to extract as much benefit as possible from the flow of donations.

He began by replacing the former monastery hotel, which was dilapidated and poorly maintained, with a new one, opening a splendid eating house with dishes for the fasts, and organising boat rides round the waterways and bays, so that the well-to-do visitors would be in no hurry to depart from those blessed shores, which in their beauty, the freshness of their air and their natural serenity are in no wise inferior to the finest Finnish resorts. And then, by the skilful expenditure of the surplus funds accumulated in this manner, he set about gradually establishing a complex and highly profitable local economy, with mechanised farms, an icon-painting factory, a fishing flotilla, smoking sheds and even a small hardware factory that produced the finest bolts and catches in the whole of Russia. He also built a water main, and even a railway from the quayside to the warehouses. Some of the more experienced monks complained that life in New Ararat had become unredemptive, but their voices had a fearful ring and their complaint hardly even filtered through to the outside world at all, being drowned out by the cheerful clatter of the intensive construction work. On the main island of Canaan the father superior erected numerous new buildings and churches, which were most impressive in terms of their size and magnificence though, in the opinion of connoisseurs of architecture, they were not always distinguished by impeccable elegance.

A few years ago a special government commission, led by the Minister of Trade and Industry himself, the highly intelligent Count Litte, came to investigate the New Ararat 'economic miracle' and see whether the experience of such successful development could be adopted for the good of the whole empire.

It transpired that it could not. On returning to the capital, the Count reported to the sovereign that Father Vitalii was an adept of a dubious economic theory, which assumed that a country's true wealth does not lie in its natural resources but in the industry of its population. It was easy for the archimandrite – he had a population of a special kind: monks who performed all the labour as works of penance, and without any salary. When a worker like that stood by his butter-making machine, say, or his metal-working lathe, he wasn't thinking about his family or his bottle of vodka – he was getting on with saving his soul. That was why the product was of such high quality and cheaper than competitors could even dream of.

This economic model was definitely of no use to the Russian state, but within the limits of the archipelago entrusted to Father Vitalii's care it brought forth truly remarkable fruits. Indeed, in some respects the monastery, with all its settlements, farmsteads and utilities, resembled a small state – not a fully sovereign one, but one that was at least completely self-governing and exclusively accountable to the provincial bishop His Grace Mitrofanii.

Under Father Vitalii the number of monks and lay brothers on the islands grew to one and a half thousand, and the population of the central estate which, in addition to the holy brothers, was also home to a large number of hired workers and their entire households, was large enough to rival a district town, especially if you counted the pilgrims who, despite the father superior's concerns, continued to stream in – in fact the volume of the stream increased several times over. And now, when the economy of the monastery was firmly established, the reverend father would have been quite happy to manage without the pilgrims, who only distracted him from his urgent work in administering the New Ararat community (for among their numbers there were important and influential people who required special attention); but there was nothing that he could do on that score. People came on foot and by other means from far away, and then they sailed across the immense Blue Lake on the monastery's steamboat, not in order to take a look at the zealous pastor's industrial achievements, but to bend the knee at the holy places of New Ararat, including the foremost among them, Basilisk's Hermitage.

This latter site was actually absolutely inaccessible to visitors, since it was located on a small forested rock that bore the name of Outskirts Island, located directly opposite Canaan – not, however, facing the inhabited side, but the deserted one. The pilgrims who came to New Ararat were in the habit of going down on their knees at the water's edge and gazing reverently at the little island that was the dwelling place of holy ascetics who prayed for the whole of mankind.

However, let us now speak at greater length, as promised, about Basilisk's Hermitage and its legendary founder.

A long, long time ago, about six hundred or perhaps even eight hundred years ago (the chronology of the 'Life of Saint Basilisk' is somewhat confused), a hermit was wandering through a remote forest. All that we know about him for certain is that he was called Basilisk and was no longer young in years; that he had lived a hard life, which had been exceptional for its lack of righteousness at the beginning, but in his declining years he had seen the light of true repentance and been illuminated by the thirst for Salvation. In expiation of his earlier years lived in transgression of the moral law, the monk had taken a vow to walk round the whole world until he found the place where he could serve the Lord best. Sometimes in some devout monastery or, on the contrary, in the midst of godless pagans, it had seemed to him that this was it, the place where the humble servant of God Basilisk should stay; but soon the elderly monk would be overtaken by doubt – what if someone else who stayed there might serve the Almighty equally well? – and, driven by this thought, which was undoubtedly sent down to him from on high, the monk had continued on his way, never finding that which he sought.

But then one day, when he parted the thick branches of a fir grove, he saw blue water before him, extending away from the very edge of the forest towards the grey, lowering sky and merging into it. Basilisk had never seen so much water before, and in his simple-mindedness taking this phenomenon for a great miracle from the Lord, he bent his knee and prayed until darkness fell, and then for a long time in the dark.

And the monk had a vision. A fiery finger clove the sky into two halves, so that one became bright and the other became black, and plunged into the waters, setting them heaving and frothing. And a voice of thunder spoke to Basilisk: 'Seek no more. Go to the place that has been shown. It is a place that is close to Me. Serve Me not among men and their vanity but in the midst of silence, and in a year I shall call you to Myself.'

In his salutary simple-heartedness the monk did not even think to doubt the possibility of fulfilling this strange demand to walk into the middle of the sea, but set off straight away, and though the water bowed and sagged beneath his weight, it held him up, which did not greatly surprise Basilisk, for he recalled Christ walking on the water in the Gospels. He walked on and on, reciting the Credo in Russian for a whole night, and a whole day, and in the evening he began to feel afraid that he would not find the place that the finger had indicated to him in the middle of this watery wilderness. And then the monk was granted a second miracle in a row – something that does not happen often, even in the lives of the saints.

When darkness fell, he saw a small spark of light in the distance and turned towards it, and a short while later he saw that it was a pine tree blazing on the top of a hill, and the hill rose straight up out of the water, and behind it there was more land, lower and broader (that was the present-day Canaan, the main island of the archipelago).

And Basilisk made his home in a cave under the scorched pine. He lived there for a while in total silence and incessant inward prayer, and a year later the Lord did as he had promised and summoned the repentant sinner to Himself and gave him a place beside His Throne. The hermitage and monastery that subsequently sprang up nearby were named New Ararat in commemoration of the mountain that had remained towering alone above the waters when 'the depths stirred and the heavens opened' and had saved the lives of the righteous.

The 'Life' omits to mention how Basilisk's successors came to learn about the Miracle of the Finger, if the hermit maintained such a rigorous silence, but let us be indulgent towards ancient tradition. We can also make a concession to the scepticism of a rationalistic age and accept that the holy founder of the hermitage did not reach the islands by walking miraculously across the water, but on some kind of raft or, say, in a hollowed-out log – let it be so. But here is a fact that is indisputable, attested to by many generations and confirmable, if you should so wish, by documentary evidence: none of the ascetics who have settled in the underground cells of Basilisk's Hermitage have ever waited long for God to summon them to Himself. After six months, a year, or at the most a year and a half, all of the select few thirsting for salvation have achieved their heart's desire and, leaving behind a small heap of dusty bones, have soared aloft from the kingdom of earth to that other, Heavenly Kingdom. And it is not at all a matter of a meagre diet or the severity of the climate. There are, after all, many other hermitages where the hermits have performed even greater feats of asceticism and mortified the flesh more fervently, but God has been less quick to grant them his pardon and take them to Himself.

And so the rumour spread that of all places on earth, Basilisk's Hermitage was the very closest to God, located on the very outskirts of the Kingdom of Heaven – which is the reason for its other name of Outskirts Island. On visiting the archipelago for the first time, some people used to think the island was given that name because of its closeness to Canaan, where all the churches stand and the archimandrite lives. But this little island was not close to the archimandrite; it was close to God.

The hermitage has always been inhabited by three especially distinguished monks, and there has never been any greater honour for the monks of New Ararat than to complete their earthly journey in the caves there, on the bones of the righteous men who have preceded them.

Of course, not all of the brotherhood have always thirsted

fervently after a rapid ascent to that Other Kingdom, because even among monks there are many to whom the earthly life appears more attractive than the next one. Nonetheless, there has never been any shortage of volunteers; on the contrary, there has always been a long queue of avid applicants, and just as there must be in any queue, there have been quarrels, disputes and serious intrigues, so impatient have certain monks been to cross the narrow channel that separates Canaan from Outskirts Island as soon as possible.

One of the three ascetics was regarded as senior and given the rank of abbot. He was the only one whom the hermitage rules permitted to open his mouth and speak – but not to say more than six words, which had to come directly from Holy Writ, and another one or two, which could be chosen freely; these latter words usually conveyed the basic sense of what was said. They say that in olden times the abbot was not even permitted this much, but after the monastery on Canaan was revived, the hermits no longer wasted time on gathering meagre food to eat – berries, roots and worms (nothing else that was edible had ever been found on Outskirts Island as long as it had existed) – but received everything they needed from the monastery. So now the holy hermits whiled away the time carving cedar-wood rosaries, for which the pilgrims paid the monastery good money – sometimes as much as thirty roubles for a single string.

A boat landed on Outskirts Island once a day, to collect the rosaries and deliver necessities. The head of the hermitage came out to meet the boat and recited a brief quotation that contained a request, usually of a practical nature: to deliver certain food supplies or medicines, or shoes, or a warm blanket. Let us assume that the abbot said: 'And unto him he did give *a blanket,*' or, 'And now let there be brought *pear-water.*' The beginnings of these utterances are taken from the Book of Genesis, where Isaac addresses his son Esau, and the final two words have been added to express what is urgently needed. The boatman remembered what had been said and conveyed it word for word to the father steward and the father cellarer, and they tried to penetrate its meaning – sometimes unsuccessfully. Take, for instance, the aforementioned 'pear-water'. They say that one day the hermitage's abbot indicated one of the other monks with his staff and declared darkly: 'All his innards did pour forth.' The senior monks leafed through Holy Writ for a long time and eventually found these strange words in the Acts of the Apostles, in the passage describing the suicide of the contemptible Judas, and were greatly alarmed, thinking that the ascetic must have committed the very worst of mortal sins and laid hands on himself. For three days they tolled the bells, observed the strictest possible fast and offered up prayers to be purged of the pollution of sin; but then it turned out that the venerable monk had simply suffered a bout of diarrhoea and the abbot had been asking for him to be sent some pear liquor.

When the senior hermit told the boatman: 'Today dost Thou release Thy servant,' it meant that one of the hermits had been admitted into the presence of the Lord, and then someone would be chosen from the queue to fill the vacancy that had become available. Sometimes the fateful words were not spoken by the abbot, but by one of the other two unspeaking brothers. In that way the monastery learned that the former elder had been summoned to his Bright Dwelling in Heaven and from henceforth the hermitage had a new steward.

On one occasion, about a hundred years ago, a bear that had swum from the furthest islands fell on one of the ascetics and began tearing the unfortunate soul's flesh. He began crying out, 'Brothers! Brothers!' The other two came running up and drove the beast away with their staffs, but after that they refused to live with the man who had broken the vow of silence and sent him away to the monastery, as a result of which the exile fell into a mournful state and soon died without ever opening his mouth again, but whether he was admitted into the Radiant Sight of the Lord or is now dwelling among the sinful souls, no one can say.

What else can be said about the hermits? They wore black vestments, which took the form of a coarsely woven sack, belted round with string. The cowl that the ascetics wore was narrow and pulled down over the entire face, with the edges sewn together in a sign of their total isolation from worldly vanity. Two holes were made in this pointed hood for the eyes. If the pilgrims praying on the shore of Canaan happened to see one of the holy ascetics on the little island (which happened extremely rarely and was regarded as an exceptional piece of luck), the sight that met their observant eyes was of a shapeless black sack slowly meandering between the mossy boulders – as if it were not a man at all, but some kind of disembodied shadow.

And now that we have told you everything about New Ararat and the hermitage and Saint Basilisk, it is time to return to the courthouse archive room, where His Grace Mitrofanii has already begun interrogating the New Ararat monk Antipa.

'Something's not right over in the hermitage; our people have been saying so for a long time.' (These were the words with which Brother Antipa began his incredible story after he had calmed down somewhat, thanks to the slapping and the tea.) 'At Transfiguration, when it was nearly night, Agapii the novice went out on to the spit to wash the senior brothers' underwear. Suddenly he saw something that looked like a kind of shadow on the water near Outskirts Island. Well, what does a shadow mean – you can see all sorts of things when it's getting dark. Agapii just crossed himself and carried on rinsing out the smalls. But then he thought he heard a quiet sound above the water. He looked up, and Holy Mother of God! – there was a black shadow hanging above the waves without seeming to touch them, and he could hear words, but not clearly. All Agapii could make out was: "I curse" and "Basilisk", but that was more than enough for him. He abandoned the things he'd been washing, ran back to the brothers' cells as fast as his legs would carry him and started shouting, saying that Basilisk had returned, full of wrath, and he was cursing everyone.

'Agapii's a foolish boy; he hasn't been at Ararat for long, so no one believed him, and for the underclothes he'd left behind, which were washed away by the waves, the father assistant healer gave his ears a good pulling. But after that the dark shadow began appearing to some of the other brothers: first to Father Ilarii, a most venerable and restrained senior monk, then to Brother Melchisedek, and after that to Brother Diamid – every time at night, when there was a moon. Everybody heard different words: some heard a curse, some heard an admonition, and some couldn't make anything out at all – it depended on which way the wind was blowing – but they all saw the same thing, and they kissed the icon in front of Revered Father Vitalii to swear to it: someone dressed in black vestments down to his heels and a sharp-pointed cowl, like the monks on the island wear, floating above the waves, intoning words and raising his finger threateningly.

'After making enquiries about the miraculous events the archimandrite scolded the brothers roundly. He said, "I know you whisperers: one fool blurts out something and the others are only too happy to ring the bells and spread the news. It's true what they say: monks are worse tittle-tattles than gossipy old women." He rebuked them in all sorts of other ways and then strictly forbade anyone to go after dark to the side of Canaan where the Lenten Spit stretches out towards Outskirts Island.'

His Grace interrupted the monk's story at this point: 'Yes, I remember. Father Vitalii wrote to me about the stupid rumours and complained about the monks' weak-wittedness. In his opinion, it comes from idleness and inactivity, and so he asked my blessing to involve the entire brotherhood up to the rank of hieromonk in work useful to the community. I gave my blessing.'

Sister Pelagia took advantage of the break in the story to ask quickly: 'Tell me, brother, approximately how many *sazhens* is it from the place where Basilisk has been seen to Outskirts

Island? And does the spit stretch out far into the water? And another thing: where exactly was the shadow floating – right beside the hermitage or some distance away from it?'

Antipa blinked and gaped at this highly inquisitive nun, but he answered the questions: 'From the spit to Outskirts Island would be about fifty *sazhens*. And as for our patron, before me the others only saw him in the distance; they couldn't make him out clearly from our shore. But Basilisk came up really close to me, about from here to that picture.' And he pointed to a photographic portrait of the Governor of Zavolzhie on the opposite wall, which was about fifteen paces away.

'Not just "some kind of shadow", but Saint Basilisk himself?' the Bishop roared at the monk in a thunderous voice, and clutched his own beard in his fist, which was the way he expressed his mounting irritation. 'Vitalii's right! You monks are worse than market women!'

Antipa cringed at these terrible words, pulling his head down into his shoulders, and was unable to carry on speaking, so that Pelagia was obliged to come to his assistance. She straightened her steel-rimmed spectacles, tucked away a rebellious lock of ginger hair under her vernicle and said reproachfully: 'Your Grace, you're always talking about the harmfulness of hasty conclusions. Why not listen to the holy father without interrupting?'

That made Antipa even more frightened, he was certain that such insolence would make the prelate absolutely furious, but Mitrofanii did not grow angry with the sister and the glint of fury in his eyes faded.

He waved his hand at the monk. 'Go on. But mind, no lies now.' And so the story was continued, though its telling was somewhat burdened by the lengthy excuses that the terrified Antipa felt obliged to include.

'I'll tell you why I disobeyed the archimandrite's order. It's my calling to work as a herbalist and treat the brothers who think it a sin to visit a secular doctor. And you know the way it is with us monastery herbalists – every herb has to be gathered on the day of a special saint. Lenten Spit, opposite the hermitage, has an area where more herbs grow than anywhere else on the whole of Canaan. Hard-wort, good for overindulgence in wine, grows there under the patronage of Saint Vonifatii; and there's flock-weed, good for lascivious passion, under the patronage of holy Saint Fomaida; and pouch-weed, good for protecting against evil enchantment, under the patronage of Saint Kiprian, and many other healing plants. Because of the prohibition, I'd already failed to gather joint-weed or gem-weed, which have to be pulled with the night dew still on them. And on holy Saint Eufimia's day – she guards against the shaking sickness – the late whisper-wort flowers, and it can only be gathered on a single night in the whole year. How could I miss it? And so I disobeyed.

'As soon as all the brothers had gone off to sleep I crept out into the yard, past the fence and across the open field to the Farewell Chapel, where the hermits are locked up before they're put in the hermitage – the Lenten Spit is close by there. At first I was afraid and I kept crossing myself and looking around, but then it passed and I felt braver. Late whisper-wort is hard to find; it takes practice and a lot of effort. It was dark, of course, but I had an oil lamp with me. I covered one side of it with a rag so that no one would see it. I was crawling along on my hands and knees, pulling off the flowers, and I'd forgotten completely about the archimandrite and Saint Basilisk. I reached the very edge of the bank of earth, after that there was nothing but water and a few rocks sticking up. I was just going to turn back. Suddenly I heard it, out of the darkness . . .'

The monk turned pale at the terrible memory; his breath came faster and his teeth started chattering, and Pelagia poured him some boiled water from the samovar.

'Thank you, little sister . . . Suddenly this voice came out of the darkness, quiet but penetrating, and I could hear every word clearly: "Go. Tell everyone." I turned towards the lake, and I was so terrified that I dropped the lamp and my bag for collecting herbs. I saw a vague, thin figure just above the surface of the water, as if someone was standing on a rock. Only there weren't any rocks there. Suddenly ... Suddenly there was an unearthly glow, bright, a lot brighter than the glow from the gas lamps that shine in our streets in New Ararat. And then he appeared before me perfectly clearly: a black monk in a cassock, with light pouring out from behind his back, standing right there on the water – the small waves were splashing under his feet. "Go," he said. "Tell them. It shall be cursed." He pointed to Outskirts Island with his finger as he spoke. And then he took a step towards me right across the water – and then another, and another. I screamed and waved my hands in the air, I turned and ran as fast as I could ...'

The monk began sobbing and wiped his nose with his sleeve. Pelagia sighed and patted the poor soul on the head, and at that Antipa went completely to pieces.

'I ran to the father archimandrite, and he only swore crudely at me – he didn't believe me,' the monk complained. 'He locked me in the punishment cell, on bread and water. I was in there for four days, shaking and praying the whole day long, my insides all shrivelled up. When I came out, I was staggering. And there was a new work of penance waiting for me from the father superior: I had to take a boat from Canaan to Ukatai, the most distant of the islands, and live there from then on, at the viper nursery.'

'Why is there a viper nursery?' Mitrofanii asked in amazement.

'The archimandrite's doctor, Donat Savvich Korovin, thought of it. A man with a cunning mind, His Reverence listens to him. He said the Germans are paying good money for viper venom nowadays, so let's breed the snakes. We squeeze the venom out of their repulsive jaws and send it off to the land of Germany. Ugh!' said Antipa, spitting angrily and crossing his mouth in order not to be defiled, and then he reached under his cassock with his hand. 'Only the most experienced and godly-wise of the senior monks met together in secret and told me not to go to Ukatai but to flee from Ararat without permission and come to Your Grace and tell you everything that I had seen and heard. And they gave me a letter to bring with me. Here it is.'

The Bishop took the grey sheet of paper with a frown, set his pince-nez on his nose and began to read. Pelagia peeped over his shoulder without standing on ceremony.

Our most Reverend and Just Lord!

We, the undernamed monks of the New Ararat Communal Monastery, fall at Your Grace's feet in humility, imploring you in your great wisdom not to turn your archpastoral wrath upon us for our wilfulness and audaciousness. If we have dared to disobey our most reverend archimandrite, then it is not out of obstinacy, but only out of the fear of God and the zeal to serve him. The labour of this earthly life is but a fleeting dream, and men are subject to empty fancies, but everything that Brother Antipa will relate to Your Grace is the absolute truth, for he is a monk known among us as a truthful and generous-hearted brother who is not inclined to vain dreaming. And also all of us who have signed this letter have seen the same thing as he did, although not as closely.

Father Vitalii has hardened his heart against us and will not listen to us, but meanwhile there is confusion and vacillation among the brothers, and we are also afraid: what can this oppressive sign mean? Why does Saint Basilisk, the protector of this glorious monastery, raise his finger in threat and lay a curse on his own most holy hermitage? And the words 'it shall be cursed' – what do they mean? Were they spoken of the hermitage, of the monastery, or perhaps with a wider meaning of which we of little wit are afraid even to think? Only to Your Grace is there granted the possibility of expounding these terrible visions. Therefore we implore you, most just lord, do not order us

18

or Brother Antipa to be punished, but pour forth on this terrible event the light of your wisdom.

Imploring your holy prayers and bowing low before you, we remain your unworthy brothers in prayer and your sinful servants.

Hieromonk Ilariii
Hieromonk Melchisedek
Monk Diomid

'Father Ilarii wrote it,' Antipa explained respectfully. 'A very learned man, an academic. If he had wanted, he could have been a father superior or someone even higher, but instead of that he works to save his soul with us and dreams of getting to Basilisk's Hermitage, he's the first in the queue. And now such a bitter disappointment for him...'

'I know Ilarii,' Mitrofanii said with a nod, examining the request. 'I remember him. Not stupid, with sincere faith, only very fervent.'

The Bishop removed his pince-nez and looked the messenger over, sizing him up. 'But why do you look so tattered, my son? And why have you no hat? You didn't drive your horses all the way from Ararat, surely? That would hardly be possible across the water, unless, of course, you can walk on water like Basilisk.'

No doubt the Bishop was hoping to raise the monk's spirits and lead him into the calmer state of mind required for a more detailed conversation, but the result was the direct opposite.

Antipa suddenly leapt up out of his chair, ran over to the narrow window of the archive room and began gazing out, muttering incoherently: 'Oh Lord, how could I have forgotten! He's probably already here, in the town! Holy Mother of God, save us and protect us!' He turned to the Bishop and began jabbering: 'I came through the forest, hurrying to get to you. As soon as I got off the ship in Sineozersk the police officer gave me his carriage, so that I could get to Zavolzhsk as quickly as possible. They'd already heard about Basilisk's appearance in Sineozersk. And just as I was approaching your town, there *he* was, above the trees!'

'Who do you mean by *he*?' Mitrofanii exclaimed angrily.

'Basilisk himself! He must have set out after me, taking huge seven-league strides or moving through the air! Black and huge, looking over the tops of the trees with his great goggling eyes! I drove the horses on hard. The branches were lashing my face, the wind was whistling, but I kept driving them on. I wanted to warn you that he was already close!'

The quick-witted Pelagia was the first to guess what was the matter. 'He's talking about the statue, Father. About Yermak Timofeich.'

At this point I ought to explain that two years previously, on the orders of the Governor, Anton Antonovich von Haggenau, a majestic monument entitled 'Yermak Timofeich bringing the good news to the East' had been erected on the high bank of the River. This monument, the largest in the entire region of the River, is now an object of great pride in our town, which has nothing else to boast of to its distinguished neighbours Nizhny Novgorod, Kazan and Samara. Every locality needs to have its own reason to feel proud, after all. And now we have ours.

There are some historians who believe that Yermak Timofeich began his famous Siberian campaign, to which the empire is indebted for the greater part of its vast landholdings, from our very own district. And the bronze giant was erected in order to commemorate this. This major commission was entrusted to a certain Zavolzhsk sculptor, perhaps not as gifted as some sculptors in the capital, but a true patriot of the region and a very good man in general, greatly loved by all Zavolzhians for his breadth of spirit and goodness of heart. The sculptor had given the conqueror of Siberia a helmet that looked rather like a *klobuk*, or monk's headgear, and it was this that had led poor Brother Antipa, who was not familiar with our latest innovations, into his superstitious error.

But that was nothing! The previous autumn, when the captain of a tug pulling along a string of barges full of Astrakhan watermelons had sailed out from round a bend in the river and seen the goggle-eyed idol standing on top of the steep bank, he had taken such a fright that he ran his entire flotilla aground on a shoal, and for several weeks afterwards green-striped spheres could be seen bobbing up and down in the River, hurrying back downstream to their native parts. And that, note, was a river captain, so what was to be expected from a wretched monk?

Having explained Antipa's mistake to him and more or less calmed him down, Mitrofanii sent the monk to the diocesan hotel to await a decision on his fate. It was clear that the fugitive could not be returned to the stern archimandrite of New Ararat and a place would have to be found for him in some other monastery.

When the Bishop and his spiritual daughter were left alone together, His Grace asked: 'Well, what do you think of this gibberish?'

'I believe him,' Pelagia replied without hesitation. 'I looked in Brother Antipa's eyes and he's not lying. He described what he saw and didn't add anything.'

His Grace knitted his brows, suppressing his feeling of annoyance. He said guardedly: 'You said that deliberately to tease me. You don't believe in any ghosts, I know you too well for that.' But then he immediately realised that he had fallen into a trap set by his cunning assistant and wagged a threatening finger at her. 'Ah, what you meant was that he himself believes in his own ravings. He thought he saw something, for which the scientific name is a hallucination, and he took it for something that really happened. Is that it?'

'No, Father, that's not it,' the nun sighed. 'He's a straight-forward man and not foolish or, as it said in the letter, "not inclined to vain dreaming". People like that don't have hallucinations – they don't have enough imagination. I think that someone really did appear to him and speak to him. And then,

Antipa is not the only one who has seen this Black Monk; there are other eyewitnesses too.'

Patience had never ranked high among the provincial primate's virtues and, to judge from the crimson colour that flooded Mitrofanii's high forehead and cheeks, what little he had was now exhausted. 'And have you forgotten about mutual suggestion, examples of which are so common in monasteries?' he exploded. 'Do you remember when the devil started appearing to the sisters in the Mariinsky Convent? First to one, then to another and then to all the rest? They described him in fine detail and repeated words that honest nuns could not possibly have learned anywhere. You were the one who suggested sending a neuropsychological doctor to the convent that time!'

'That was quite different – ordinary female hysterics. But this time the testimony comes from experienced senior monks,' the nun objected. 'There is unrest at New Ararat, and it will not end well. Rumours about the Black Monk have already reached Zavolzhsk. We ought to investigate.'

'Investigate what? What? Or do you really believe in ghosts? For shame, Pelagia, it's all superstition! It's eight hundred years now since Saint Basilisk passed on, and he has no reason to go cruising over the waves around the island and frightening empty-headed monks!'

Pelagia bowed humbly, as if acknowledging that the Bishop had a perfect right to his wrath, but there was little humility in her voice, and even less in her words: 'That is your limitation as a male speaking, Your Grace. In their judgements men rely too excessively on their sight and the other five senses.'

'Four,' Mitrofanii corrected her.

'No, Your Grace, five. Not everything that exists in the world can be detected by sight, hearing, touch, smell and taste. There is another sense that has no name, which is given to us so that we might feel God's world not only with our bodies but with our souls. And it is strange that I, a plain nun weak in mind and spirit, am obliged to explain this to you. Have you not spoken of this sense numerous times in your sermons and in private conversations?'

'I had in mind faith and the moral measure that is given to every man from God! But what you are expounding to me is some kind of fairy mirage!'

'Then let it be a fairy mirage,' the nun said with a stubborn shake of her head. 'Around and within our world there is another one, invisible, and perhaps even more than one. We women feel this more clearly than men, because we are not afraid to feel it. Surely, Your Grace, you would not deny that there are some places that cheer and illuminate the soul (God's churches are usually built there) and there are some that make it shudder? There is no reason for it; you simply start walking more quickly and cross yourself. I always used to run past the Black Ravine, like that, with a chill shudder. And then what happened? That was the very spot where they found the canon!'

This argument adduced by Pelagia as if it were quite irrefutable requires an explanation. Two years previously a treasure trove had been found under the Black Ravine, located half a verst from Zavolzhsk: an old bronze mortar stuffed with gold coins and semi-precious stones – evidently it had lain in the ground since the times when Pugachev's 'general' Chika Zarubin, later raised by the pretender to the rank of count, used to roam these parts. Plenty of blood and tears must have been spilled in collecting together such a treasure. (Let us note, by the way, that this was the very money that had been used to erect on that very same spot the magnificent monument that had frightened Brother Antipa half to death.)

But the argument about the canon failed to convince His Grace. Mitrofanii merely flapped his hand dismissively: 'Ah, your chilly shudder was just imagination.'

The prelate and his spiritual daughter carried on arguing like this for a long time, until they almost had a serious quarrel. Therefore we shall omit the end of the argument about superstition and move on straight away to its practical conclusion, which did not emerge in the court archives room, but in the episcopal residence, during the drinking of tea to celebrate a happy event.

The tea had been arranged for the following day in honour of the successful outcome of the court case. In addition to Pelagia, His Grace had invited another of his spiritual children, the assistant district public prosecutor Matvei Bentsionovich Berdichevsky, who had also played a part in achieving the triumph of justice. There was a bottle of sweet communion wine standing on the table beside the samovar, and in addition there was a genuine abundance of sweet things: spice cakes, and candied fruit, and all sorts of jam, and the inevitable apple marshmallows of which the Bishop was so exceedingly fond.

They sat in the refectory, where there were copies of Mitrofanii's two favourite icons hanging on the walls: the wonder-working 'Softening of Vicious Hearts' and the little-known 'Judas Kissing Christ the Saviour', both magnificently painted, with expensive silver settings. His Grace had not simply placed them here by chance, but for a purpose – to remind himself of the most important aspects of the Christian faith: forgiveness for all and the Lord's acceptance of any soul, even the most debased, because there are no souls that have absolutely no hope of salvation. Owing to his passionate character, the Bishop was inclined to forget about these things, especially forgiveness for all: he acknowledged this sin in himself and strove to overcome it.

They spoke for a while about the trial that had just finished, recalling all of its twists and turns, and then about the imminent addition to Berdichevsky's family – the father-to-be was concerned that the child would be the thirteenth, and the Bishop laughed at the lawyer, claiming that neophyte converts like him always made the very worst obscurantists, and he rebuked Matvei Berdichevsky for his superstition, which was so shameful for an enlightened man.

From the subject of superstition the conversation naturally

turned to the Black Monk. It should be noted that the first to bring up the mysterious phenomenon was none other than the assistant public prosecutor, who, as we recall, had not been present at the explanation in the archive room and did not even know about it.

It turned out that the entire town was already talking about the way the monk from New Ararat had raced along the streets. Everyone also knew about Basilisk's appearance and the menacing omens. As he whipped his horses on, Brother Antipa had very nearly run over a cat belonging to an influential member of Zavolzhsk society, Olympiada Savelievna Shestago, but he had just carried on shouting all sorts of alarming things: 'Flee, Orthodox believers!' 'Basilisk is coming!' and so forth, as well as demanding to be told where he could find the Bishop.

It turned out that Sister Pelagia had been right the day before: after what had happened it was impossible not to take action. His Grace, having cooled off after his annoyance of the previous day, no longer took issue with that, but there was disagreement among the three revellers concerning what measures should be taken.

Mitrofanii ascribed all of his numerous successes in the field of archpastoral endeavour to the Lord, humbly acknowledging that he was only the visible instrument of a Power that acted invisibly, and when he spoke he was an absolute fatalist who loved to repeat: 'If it is pleasing to God, then it is certain to happen, but if it is not pleasing to God, then I have no need of it.' But in practice he was guided more by the maxim 'Hope in God, but make no blunders yourself', and it must be admitted that he rarely blundered and did not trouble the Lord excessively.

It need hardly be said that the Bishop was immediately fired with enthusiasm to go to New Ararat himself, in order to bring people to their senses and put an end to this business (he absolutely refused to allow the probability of anything genuinely mystical and saw the Basilisk phenomenon as either a case of mass insanity or a piece of chicanery perpetrated by someone or other).

The cautious Matvei Berdichevsky tried to persuade the Bishop not to go. He expressed the opinion that rumours were dangerous and hard to lay to rest. You couldn't stop everyone's mouth. Administrative intervention in such cases was about as effective as dousing a fire with kerosene – it only made the fire blaze even more fiercely. Berdichevsky's proposal was as follows: under no circumstances should His Grace go to the islands or give the slightest impression that anything out of the ordinary was happening there, but he should secretly send to New Ararat a sensible and tactful official, who would get to the bottom of everything, find the source of the rumours and present an exhaustive report. It was clear that by a 'sensible official' Berdichevsky meant himself and he was demonstrating yet again his constant readiness to forget about all current business and even his family responsibilities, if only he could be of service to his spiritual mentor.

As for Pelagia – while agreeing with Berdichevsky that an episcopal inspection would be inappropriate for the case, the nun could not see any point either in sending a lay person to the islands since, in the first place, he would not be able to understand the subtleties of monastery life and monkish psychology, and in the second place ... But no, we had better quote this second argument verbatim, so that the polemicist's own conscience may bear its full weight.

'In matters concerning incomprehensible phenomena that cause trepidation to the soul, men are too categorical,' Pelagia declared, clicking away rapidly with her knitting needles – after her third glass of tea she had taken out her knitting without asking the Bishop's permission. 'Men have no curiosity about anything that they regard as unimportant, but the unimportant often conceals the most essential. When something has to be built or, even better, demolished, then men have no equals. But if patience, understanding and possibly even compassion are required, then it is best to entrust the business to a woman.'

'But at the first sight of a ghost a woman will faint away or, even worse, have a fit of hysterics,' the Bishop teased the nun. 'And nothing useful will come of it.'

Pelagia looked at the row of stitches that had gone awry and sighed, but she didn't unknit it – let it come out whatever way it would.

'A woman will never faint or fall into hysterics if there's no man there,' she said. 'All women's fainting, hysterics and weepiness were invented by men. You want to think of us as weak and helpless, and so we adapt to suit you. The best thing for this business, Father, would be for you to give me your blessing to take two or three weeks' leave. I could go to Canaan, pray at the local holy places and at the same time see what kind of ghost it is they have floating over the water there. Sister Apollinaria and Sister Ambrosia could take care of my girls in the college for the time being. One can take gymnastics and the other literature, and everything would work out very well.'

'It can't be done,' said His Grace, interrupting his spiritual daughter with evident satisfaction. 'Or have you forgotten, Pelagia, that nuns are not allowed into Ararat?'

That immediately shut the nun up. And it was true that, under the strict rules of New Ararat, nuns and female novices were forbidden to travel to the islands. It was an ancient ruling, three hundred years old, but it was still rigorously observed.

It had not always been like that. In the old days there had been a nuns' convent standing beside the monks' monastery, but this propinquity had given rise to various temptations and indecent incidents, and therefore when the Patriarch Nikon, concerned to restore the honour of the monastic estate, made the monastery rules stricter everywhere, the New Ararat Convent was abolished and nuns forbidden to show their faces on the Blue Lake. The laity could come to pray, and many of them did, but the brides of Christ could not – there were other shrines for them.

Pelagia seemed on the point of making some objection to Mitrofanii, but she glanced at Berdichevsky and said nothing.

And so this discussion of the Black Monk begun by a triumvirate of the three most intelligent people in the province of Zavolzhie ran into a dead end.

The difficulty was resolved, as usually happened in such cases, by His Grace Mitrofanii – and in his typical paradoxical manner. The Bishop had an entire theory about the usefulness of paradoxes, which possess the property of overturning the excessively unwieldy constructions of human reason while at the same time revealing unexpected and sometimes shorter routes to the solution of problematical tasks. He simply loved to disconcert the person he was talking to with a surprising phrase or outlandish decision, after first assuming an air of great wisdom and intense concentration. And likewise now, when the arguments had been exhausted without leading to any conclusion and a depressed silence had set in, the Bishop wrinkled up his white forehead into three vertical folds, knitted his eyebrows together and began counting off his sandalwood rosary beads with his remarkably white and well-tended fingers. (Mitrofanii paid emphatic attention to the care of his hands and hardly ever appeared outside without silk gloves. He explained this by saying that a cleric who touched the eucharistic bread and wine should treat his hands with the greatest possible respect.)

His Grace remained sitting like that for about a minute and then opened his blue eyes, which sparkled brightly, and said in a tone that brooked no contradiction: 'Alyosha Lentochkin will go.'

Matvei Bentsionovich Berdichevsky and Pelagia simply gasped.

It would have been hard, even with a special effort, to imagine a more paradoxical nominee for the secret investigation of a highly delicate internal Church matter.

Alexei Stepanovich Lentochkin was still young in years, with cheeks that were still plump and pink, and so behind his back many people called him by the affectionately familiar name of

Alyosha – indeed, many even called him that to his face, and he did not take offence. He had appeared in our town only recently, but had immediately become one of the Bishop's circle of especial favourites.

There were, however, perfectly understandable grounds for this, since Alexei Lentochkin was the son of an old comrade of the Bishop, who, as we know, had served as a cavalry officer before he took monastic vows. This fellow-officer of Mitrofanii's had died as a major in the last Turkish war, leaving a widow with two small children – a daughter and a son – and almost no means of support at all.

The little boy Alyoshenka had grown up to be very bright, so that at the age of eleven he could easily perform integral calculus, and by the age of twenty he promised to become an absolute genius in the area of natural science or mathematics.

The Lentochkins did not live in Zavolzhsk but in the large university town of K——, which also stood on the River, but further downstream, so that when the time came for Alyosha to choose his place of higher study he was not only accepted at the local university without payment of any fees, he was even given a personal grant, so that he could study and develop his talent to the glory of his native city. Without a grant he would not have been able to attend university, even without paying for it, because his family had no money at all.

As he approached the age of twenty-three, with only a short time remaining to the end of his course, Alexei Stepanovich Lentochkin was definitely all set to become a new Evariste Gaulois or Michael Faraday, as everyone around him acknowledged and he himself was not shy of saying. Indeed, in addition to his great abilities, the youth also possessed an extremely high opinion of himself, which is not unusual among talents that mature early. He was disrespectful to authorities, insolent, sharp-tongued and overbearing – all of those qualities which, as is well known, prevented Evariste Gaulois from attaining a mature age and astounding the world with the full brilliance of his highly promising genius.

No, Alexei Lentochkin was not killed in a duel like the young Frenchman, but he became embroiled in a certain business that turned out badly for him.

One day he dared to disagree with an assessment of one of his essays on either chemistry or physics, an assessment penned by the hand of none other than Serafim Vikentievich Nosachevsky, a leading light of Russian science who was also a Privy Counsellor and the vice-chancellor of the university in K——. In his assessment this highly experienced scientist had failed to express sufficient admiration of Lentochkin's conclusions, and this had thrown the gifted student into a fury. The young man had added a highly impertinent remark to Nosachevsky's comments and sent the notebook containing the essay back to him.

The scientist was terribly offended (the remark had cast doubt on the discoveries that he had made, and on the value of His Excellency's contribution to science in general) and he used his administrative authority to have the impudent rogue's personal grant rescinded.

Alexei Lentochkin's wild act had, of course, been quite outrageous but, bearing in mind the student's youth and undoubted talent, Nosachevsky could have limited himself to a less severe punishment. Losing the grant meant that Lentochkin would have to leave the university and take some kind of job – even as an accountant in a shipping line – as a matter of urgency, and that would mean the end of all his great dreams, he could bury them all.

The cruelty of the vice-chancellor's verdict was condemned by many, and there were some who urged Lentochkin to go and apologise, saying that although Nosachevsky was stern, he did not bear grudges, but the young student's pride would not allow him to do it. Instead he chose a different path, imagining himself to be a knight joining battle with a dragon. And he dealt the perfidious beast a fatal blow. The revenge he took was so comprehensive that the Privy Counsellor was obliged ...

But let us not run ahead of ourselves. This is a story that deserves to be told properly, from the beginning.

Serafim Vikentievich Nosachevsky had one weakness, which was known to the entire city: he was a martyr to voluptuousness. This high priest of science, although he was already advanced in years, could not see a pretty little face or a curling lock above a dainty ear without instantly being transformed into a cloven-hoofed satyr, and in this matter he made no distinction between respectable ladies and demi-mondaines of the very lowest sort. If this immoral behaviour was forgiven by society in K——, it was only out of respect for the city's leading light of scholarship, and also because Nosachevsky did not make a show of his escapades and sensibly kept them private.

This was the Achilles heel at which our young Paris struck the fatal blow.

Alyosha was wonderfully good-looking, but with a beauty that was not so much manly as girlish: curly-haired, with thick eyebrows and long, elegantly curved eyelashes, with a peachy fuzz on his ruddy cheeks – in short, he was one of those good-lookers who do not age for a very long time, retaining a fresh complexion and smooth skin until about the age of forty, but thereafter rapidly beginning to shrivel and wrinkle, like an apple that has been bitten and then forgotten.

Alyosha's age was not so great, but he appeared even younger than he really was – a genuine page Cherubino from the *Marriage of Figaro*. Therefore, when he dressed up in his sister's best party dress, donned a sumptuous wig, glued on a beauty spot and painted his lips with lipstick, he made such a convincing she-devil that the lustful Serafim Vikentievich could not possibly fail to notice her, especially since the seductive wench was always strolling, as if by design, in the vicinity of His Excellency's town house.

Nosachevsky sent his butler out to the pretty stroller, and he reported that the mamselle was indeed a streetwalker, but a very choosy one, and she took her strolls along Paris Street not in order to earn money but for the sake of exercise. Then the satyr ordered his servant to lace him into his corset immediately, put on his satin waistcoat and velvet frock coat with the gold sparkles and set out to conduct negotiations in person.

The enchanting girl laughed and shot Serafim Vikentievich Nosachevsky seductive glances from her glittering eyes over the top of her fan, but she refused to go to him and soon took her leave, having completely turned the man of science's head.

He stayed at home for two days without once going out, always gazing out of the window in case the nymph appeared again.

And she did appear – on the third day. This time she submitted to his blandishments, that is, to the promise of a sapphire ring in addition to two hundred roubles. But she set one condition: her admirer had to rent the very finest apartment in the Sans-Souci Hotel – a luxurious establishment, but one with a somewhat dubious reputation – and arrive for the rendezvous at ten o'clock that evening. Nosachevsky happily agreed to all of this, and at five minutes to ten he was already knocking at the door of the apartment he had rented in advance, clutching an absolutely huge bouquet of roses.

The drawing room was lit by two candles and smelled of oriental incense. The tall, slim figure in white first reached out its arms to the vice-chancellor, then immediately pulled back with a laugh and began flirting gently with Nosachevsky, who was consumed with passion. She ran playfully round the table until Serafim Vikentievich was completely out of breath and begged for mercy, and then she delivered her ultimatum: he must unquestioningly obey all of his conqueror's instructions.

His Excellency gladly capitulated, especially since the conditions sounded so seductive: the beauty would undress her lover with her own hands and lead him into the boudoir.

Trembling in sweet anticipation, Nosachevsky allowed her light, fleeting fingers to remove all of his clothes. He did not resist, even when the fantasist blindfolded him with a headscarf, put a lace cap on his head and bound his rheumatic knee with a pink bandage.

'Let us proceed into the abode of dreams, my little duckling,' the perfidious temptress whispered, and began nudging the blind vice-chancellor towards the bedroom.

He heard the door squeak as it opened, and then he received a rather powerful push in the back, so hard that he ran forward several steps and almost fell. The door slammed shut behind him.

'Sweety-pie!' Nosachevsky called out, bewildered. 'Lovey-dove! Where are you?'

The reply was a thunderous chorus of laughter from a dozen coarse male voices, and then a discordant choir began bellowing:

> We have a welcome visitor,
> Serafim Vikentievich, our dear friend!

And that was followed by a truly hideous refrain, complete with mewing and howling:

> Serafima, Sima, Sima,
> Sima, Sima, Sima,
> Sima, Sima, Sima, Sima,
> Serafima, drain your glass!

Horrified, Nosachevsky tore off his blindfold and saw before him some of the most dissolute desperadoes among the students at the university of K——, sitting in a row on the vast bed à la Louis Quinze, insolently surveying their mentor's shameful nakedness and guzzling expensive champagne straight from the bottle – they had already devoured the fruits and chocolate.

It was only then that the miserable vice-chancellor realised he had fallen victim to a conspiracy. Nosachevsky dashed to the door and began tugging at the handle, but he couldn't open it – the vengeful Alyosha had locked it from the other side.

The hooting and shouting brought the hotel corridor staff running in through the service door, followed by a police constable from the street. All in all, it was quite the most abominable scandal one could possibly imagine.

That is to say, in the official sense there was no scandal, because the awkward incident was hushed up, but already on the following day the city of K—— and the whole of K—— province knew about the Privy Counsellor's 'benefit performance', complete with all the shocking details, which, as is the way with these things, had been considerably exaggerated.

Nosachevsky voluntarily submitted his resignation and left K——, for it was quite impossible for him to stay there. In the middle of some highly serious, even scholarly discussion, his interlocutor would suddenly start turning crimson, puffing out his cheeks and clearing his throat loudly in order to suppress his laughter – he was clearly picturing the vice-chancellor without his Order of St Anne, wearing nothing but a lacy mob cap and a pink bandage.

This business also had other sad consequences for Serafim Vikentievich. Not only did he completely lose all interest in the fair sex from that time on, he also acquired an unattractive tremor of the head and a nervous tick in his eye, and his former scientific brilliance disappeared without trace.

But the joker did not get away with his prank scot-free. Naturally, everyone immediately learned who had played such a vicious joke on the vice-chancellor (Alexei Stepanovich and his comrades took no great pains to conceal who was the instigator of the prank) and the provincial authorities made it clear to the former student that it would be best for him to change his place of residence.

That was when his inconsolable mother wrote to our reverend Bishop, imploring him to take Major Lentochkin's wayward offspring under his pastoral supervision in Zavolzhsk, arrange some kind of work for him and wean him away from his nonsense and mischief.

Mitrofanii had agreed – initially in memory of his comrade-in-arms; but later, when he had come to know Alexei Lentochkin better, he was truly glad to have such an interesting charge.

Lentochkin junior had captured the stern Bishop's affection with his reckless daring and his total disdain for his own position, which depended in every respect on His Grace. In Alexei Stepanovich, things that Mitrofanii would never have suffered from anyone else – including disrespect and even open mockery – not only failed to anger the Bishop, they merely amused him, and perhaps even inspired his admiration.

Let us start with the fact that Alyosha was a non-believer – and not just one of those agnostics who are now a penny a dozen among the educated classes, so that almost anyone you ask replies: 'I can allow the possible existence of a Supreme Reason, but I cannot entirely vouch for it.' Oh no, he was an absolutely out-and-out, thoroughgoing atheist. At his very first meeting with His Grace at the episcopal residence, right there in the icon room, under the radiant gaze of the evangelists, the holy saints and the female martyrs, the young man and Mitrofanii had had an argument about the omniscience and grace of the Lord, which had ended with the Bishop throwing the blasphemer out on his ear. But when Mitrofanii had cooled off, he had ordered Lentochkin to be sent for again, regaled him with clear broth and pies and spoken to him in a different manner – one that was cheerful and friendly. He had found the young man an appropriate position as a junior consistory auditor, lodged him with a good, conscientious landlady and told him to feel at home in the episcopal chambers, an invitation of which Lentochkin, who had not yet managed to make any acquaintances in Zavolzhsk, had taken full advantage without the slightest ceremony: he dined there, spent hours in the Bishop's library and even chatted with Mitrofanii about all manner of things. Very many people would have regarded it as a great good fortune to listen to what the Bishop said, for his speech was always not only instructive but also highly delightful to the ear, but Lentochkin for the most part held forth himself – and Mitrofanii did not object or interrupt but listened with evident enjoyment.

There can be no doubt that this friendship took hold because the Bishop ranked sharpness of wit and independence of thought more highly than almost all other human qualities, and Lentochkin possessed these particular characteristics in the highest degree. Sister Pelagia, who took a dislike to Alexei Stepanovich Lentochkin from the very beginning (for, after all, the feeling of envy is sometimes encountered among individuals of the monastic calling), said that Mitrofanii's partiality to the boy was also motivated by his competitive spirit – he wanted to crack this hard nut, to awaken him to Faith. When the nun accused the Bishop of vain pride, he did not argue with her, but he justified himself by saying that it was not a great sin and to some extent it was even excused by Holy Scripture, for it was written: 'I say unto you, there shall be greater rejoicing over one sinner who repents than over ninety-nine righteous who are in no need of repentance.'

But it seems to us that in addition to this praiseworthy aspiration – meaning the salvation of a human soul – there was another, psychological reason of which His Grace himself was probably not even aware. While his vocation as a monk had deprived him of the sweet burden of fatherhood, Mitrofanii had still not entirely overcome the corresponding emotional impulse, and while to a certain extent Pelagia had taken the place of his daughter, the position of a son had remained vacant until Alexei Stepanovich appeared. The perceptive Matvei Berdichevsky, himself an experienced father with numerous children, was the first to draw Sister Pelagia's attention to this possible reason for His Grace's exceptional partiality for the impertinent youth, and although deep in his heart, of course, he was stung, he was able to summon up enough irony to joke: 'The Bishop might have been glad to regard me as his son, but then he would have had to accept a dozen grandchildren into the bargain, and not many men are brave enough to attempt such a heroic feat.'

When they were in each other's company, Mitrofanii and Alyosha resembled most of all (we beg the reader's forgiveness for such a disrespectful comparison) a big old dog with a frisky puppy who gambols round his parent, sometimes grabbing him by the ear, sometimes trying to clamber up on him, sometimes snapping at his nose with his sharp little teeth; for a certain time the giant bears this pestering uncomplainingly, but when the puppy gets too carried away, he will growl at him gently or press him to the floor with his mighty paw, but gently, so as not to crush him.

On the day following the portentous tea party Mitrofanii had to leave for one of his outlying deaneries on urgent business, but the Bishop did not forget his decision, and on his return he summoned Alexei Stepanovich Lentochkin; but even before that he sent for Berdichevsky and Pelagia to explain his reasoning to them, this time without any shade of paradox.

'There is a double logic to sending Lentochkin,' the Bishop told his advisers. 'Firstly, it is best for the matter in hand if these chimeras are dealt with not by a person who has leanings towards mysticism (at this point His Grace cast a sideways glance at his spiritual daughter), but by someone who holds a thoroughly unabashed sceptical and even material view of the world. Alexei Stepanovich's character is such that his natural inclination is to get straight to the bottom of any strange phenomenon and he takes nothing on trust. He is intelligent, resourceful and also extremely impudent, which may prove useful in the present case. And secondly,' said Mitrofanii, raising one finger in the air, 'I believe that this mission will not be without benefit to the envoy himself. Let him see that there are people – and many of them – to whom spiritual things are dearer than those of the flesh. Let him breathe the fresh air of a holy monastery for a while. They do say that the air in Ararat has a special quality: it sets your whole chest vibrating deliciously, as if you are breathing everything bad out of yourself and breathing in heavenly ambrosia.'

The Bishop lowered his eyes and added in a quieter voice, as if he were speaking reluctantly: 'He is a lively boy, full of curiosity, but he lacks the strong core that only Faith gives to a man. Someone less talented, with less lively feelings, might perhaps get by anyway, but without God Alyosha is doomed for certain.'

Berdichevsky and Pelagia exchanged furtive glances, instantly concluding an unspoken agreement not to contradict the Bishop – it would have been disrespectful, not to mention cruel.

Soon after this Alexei Lentochkin arrived, still not suspecting what far-reaching plans the Bishop had in mind for him.

After greeting everyone present, Lentochkin tossed his head of chestnut curls, which reached almost down to his shoulders, and enquired jocularly: 'Why have you convened your entire inquisition, Torquemada? What torment have you devised for the heretic now?'

As we have already said, the youth's wit was exceptionally keen – he had realised immediately that there was some special purpose to this meeting and he had also spotted the special expressions on their faces. And as for 'Torquemada', that was Alexei Stepanovich's little joke – calling Father Mitrofanii by the name of some figure from Church history: either Cardinal Richelieu, or Arch-Priest Avvakum or someone else, depending on the way the conversation turned and the Bishop's mood, which on occasion did indeed seem to express the stern political philosophy of the French statesman, and the passionate fury of the schismatic martyr, and the menace of the Castilian exterminator of spiritual pollution.

Mitrofanii did not smile at the joke. Speaking with emphatic coolness, he told Lentochkin about the alarming manifestations at New Ararat and explained the meaning of the young man's mission to him tersely, concluding as follows: 'According to his job description, a consistorial auditor is not only responsible for the accounts but also for other diocesan business that requires special verification. So go and verify this. I am counting on you.'

At first Lentochkin listened to the story of the Black Monk wandering across the waves with incredulous amazement, as if he were afraid that some joke was being played on him, and twice he even made caustic remarks; but then he realised that the conversation was serious and stopped playing the comic, although he occasionally raised one eyebrow with a certain playfulness.

When he had heard everything, Alexei Lentochkin shook his head and seemed to have understood the 'double logic' underlying his patron's decision. He smiled with his plump lips, making wonderful dimples appear on his ruddy cheeks, and spread his hands wide in admiration.

'Well, you are a cunning one, Bishop of Auton. Killing two birds with one stone, are we? Do you wish to know my opinion about these mysteries? What *I* think is that—'

'"I" is a very short word,' His Grace interrupted the boy – being compared with Talleyrand was even less to his taste than being likened to the Grand Inquisitor.

'But one used by the Lord himself,' Lentochkin retorted spryly.

Mitrofanii frowned to let the joker know that he was going too far. He blessed the youth with the sign of the cross and said quietly: 'Go. And may the Lord watch over you.'

PART ONE

The Canaan Expeditions

THE FIRST EXPEDITION
The Adventures of the Comic

Alexei Stepanovich Lentochkin's preparations did not take long and he left on his secret expedition two days after the conversation with His Grace, after having received strict instructions to send reports on his progress at least once every three days.

Taking into account the wait for the steamer in Sinieozersk and the subsequent voyage across the lake, the journey to New Ararat took four days, and the first letter arrived after exactly one week; in other words, it seemed that, for all his nihilistic attitude, Alyosha was a reliable envoy who carried out his instructions to the letter.

His Grace was very pleased with the report's punctual arrival and the report itself, but pleased most of all because he had not been mistaken in the boy. He summoned Berdichevsky and Sister Pelagia and read out the report to them, although he occasionally frowned at the insufferable rollicking freedom of the style.

Alexei Stepanovich Lentochkin's first letter

To Roland's most glorious Archbishop Turpin from his faithful paladin, sent to do battle with enchanters and Saracens,

> O pastor of great wisdom and sternness,
> Terror of deep-rooted superstitions,

Luminary of faith and loving kindness,
Defender of orphans and lash of the proud!
At your feet do I humbly cast down
My simple and artless tale.
Ah-oo!

As, shaking on a creaking wagon,
I struggled through the kingdom of Zavolzhsk,
And on that mournful road did count
Fifteen thousand, one hundred and one
Ruts and also potholes deep,
Many a time there came to me
Bad thoughts about Your Grace's person
And I did utter sacrilegious words.
Ah-oo!

But when the Blue Sea's sacred waters
Did glitter brightly in the distance far,
Conquered by this captivating landscape,
Straightway did I forget my hardships,
And prayed as I was borne across
On the smoke-puffing, snow-white vessel
Named for the good Saint Basilisk.
Ah-oo!

Through the long, moonlit, chilly night
I shivered 'neath my meagre blanket
And when I tried to close my eyes in sleep,
My fragile dreams were forthwith interrupted
By the captain's wild swearing rant,
The devout chanting of the sailors' prayers
And the bell's booming hourly chime.

And so, to switch from exhausting versification to
delightfully welcome prose, I disembarked on the quayside

in New Ararat short of sleep and as bad-tempered as the devil. Oh, forgive me, father – it just slipped out, and if I cross it out now, it will look untidy, and you don't like that, so to hell with the devil, let him be.

To tell the truth, in addition to the sounds of the ship, I was also prevented from sleeping by the book that you placed in my basket, together with the incomparable episcopal curd rolls, as you saw me off, adding in a most innocent voice: 'Pay no attention to the title, Alyosha, and don't worry, it's not religious reading, just a little novel – to help you pass the time on the journey.' Oh most perfidious of the priests of Babylon!

The title – *The Possessed* – and the substantial thickness of the 'little novel' really did frighten me at first, and I only started reading it on the steamer, to the sound of the waves splashing and the seagulls calling. In one night I read it halfway through, and I think I have understood why you slipped me this inarticulate but inspired treatise masquerading as belles-lettres. Not, of course, because of that senseless rogue Petrusha Verkhovensky and those caricatured Carbonari who are his comrades, but for the sake of Stavrogin, in whose example you no doubt perceive my own fatal danger: to play the *Übermensch* and end up as a buffoon or, in your terminology, 'to doom my immortal soul'.

A shot wide of the mark, *éminence*. There is a fundamental difference between the Byronic Mr Stavrogin and myself. He acts outrageously because he believes in god (I can just see how you have wrinkled up your brow at this point – very well then, let it be 'in God') and he feels offended with Him: Why will You not turn Your paternal gaze on a naughty child like me, why do You not rebuke me or crush me under Your foot? Hey there! Where are You? Wake up! Or else I might start imagining You don't even exist. Stavrogin is bored with the company of ordinary people; what he wants is the supreme Interlocutor. But, unlike Dostoevsky's defiler of little girls and seducer of idiots, I do not believe either in God or god, and that is my firm position. Human company is quite sufficient for me.

Your earlier literary hint was closer to the mark, when you made me a present of Count Tolstoy's composition *War and Peace* for my saint's day. I am more like Bolkonsky – not, of course, in terms of his lordliness but in sharing an interest in Bonapartism. I am twenty-four now, and there is still no sign of my Toulon; in fact there is not even a distant prospect of it. Tolstoy's prince developed such exorbitant vanity owing to his full belly and blasé attitude for, after all, Fortune had simply given him every imaginable sweet morsel in her possession – noble status, wealth, beauty – all by right of birth, so that he had nothing else left to wish for except to become the people's idol. But I, by contrast, come from the estate of the half-starved and envious, which, by the way, makes me much more like Napoleon than Tolstoy's aristocrat is and improves my chances of an emperor's crown. But, joking aside, it is more difficult for a man with a full belly to scramble up to the height of a Bonaparte than for a hungry man, because a full belly inclines a man not to nimble climbing but to philosophising and peaceful dreaming.

But I have got carried away. What you expect from me is not lofty verbiage about literature, but a spy's report about your patrimonial estate that has been engulfed in turmoil and discord.

Let me hasten to reassure Your Reverence. As is usually the case, the site of the trouble appears far more frightening from the distance than from close up. Sitting in Zavolzhsk, one might imagine that in New Ararat everyone talks of nothing but the Black Monk and the normal flow of life has been totally mesmerised.

Nothing of the sort. Life here pulsates and gurgles in livelier fashion than in your provincial capital, and so far I have not heard any gossip at all about your Saint Dracula, that is, *entschuldigen*, Saint Basilisk.

At first I found New Ararat disappointing, since on the morning of my arrival the lake was covered by low clouds, which were pouring a repulsive cold rain down on to the islands, and the landscape I saw from the deck of the steamship was all 'wet-mouse' colour: slimy grey bell towers with a terrible resemblance to enema tubes and the dejected roofs of the small town.

Mindful of the fact that all my expenses will be paid out of your abundant treasure houses, I ordered the porter to take me to the very best local hotel, which bears the proud name of Noah's Ark. I had been expecting to see some kind of gloomy log structure dimly lit with icon lamps, but I was pleasantly surprised. The hotel is fitted out in a perfectly European fashion: the room has a bathroom, mirrors and moulding on the ceiling.

The majority of the guests consists of gentlewomen already of a platonic age from St Petersburg and Moscow, but in the evening, in the coffee shop on the ground floor, I saw a veritable Princess Lointaine such as is not to be found in quiet Zavolzhsk. I do not know if the like has ever happened before in the global history of relations between the sexes, but I fell in love with the beautiful stranger on the spot, from behind, even before she turned round. Picture to yourself, my pious pastor, a slim figure in an exquisite dress of black silk, a wide-brimmed hat with ostrich feathers and a delicate, supple neck, quite blinding in its perfection, looking like a tapering alabaster column.

Sensing my gaze, the Princess turned to present me with her profile, which I could not make out clearly, since Her Majesty's face was half-covered with a hazy veil, but what I did see was enough: a slim nose with the very slightest of aquiline curves, eyes with a moist glint ... You are familiar with that female peculiarity (ah, but no, how could you be, with your celibate status!) of surveying an extremely broad sector of the immediate vicinity with the edge of their vision without actually turning round very far. A man would have to twist round his entire neck and his shoulders, but a charming creature such as this one merely turns her eye a little to the side and sees everything she needs in an instant.

I am sure that the Princess made out all the details of my modest (oh, very well – let it be immodest) person. And note, she did not turn away immediately, but first she gently touched her throat and only then turned the regal back of her head to me once again. Oh, how much that gesture means, that spontaneous raising of the fingers to the source of the breath!

Ah yes, I forgot to mention that the beauty was sitting in the coffee shop alone – you must admit that this is not entirely usual, and it intrigued me too. She might possibly have been waiting for someone, or perhaps she was simply looking out of the window at the square. Inspired by those fingers, my secret allies, I bent all my mathematical abilities to solving the problem of how best to strike up an acquaintance with this Circe of New Ararat, but I had no time to complete the integral calculation. She suddenly rose abruptly to her feet, dropped a silver coin on the table and walked out quickly, casting another swift, coal-black glance at me from behind her half-veil. The waiter told me that this lady often comes to the coffee shop. That means I will have another chance, I thought, and for lack of other employment I began imagining all sorts of seductive scenes, about which you, as a man of the Church, do not need to know.

I had better share with you my impressions of the island.

Well, this is a really strange place to which you have sent me, rabbi. The central square, on which the hotel stands, seems to have been cut out of some Baden-Baden or other with a pair of scissors: brightly painted stone houses two or three storeys high, clean people strolling about everywhere, almost as bright in the evening as it is during the day. And everywhere there are establishments that could hardly be more worldly; I would even call them vain in the biblical sense, with quite incredible names: a restaurant serving meat in abundance called Balshazzar's Feast, a hairdresser's called Delilah, a souvenir shop called Gifts of the Magi, a bank called The Widow's Mite and more in the same vein. But only a few minutes' walk away from the square you find yourself back on the banks of the Neva shortly after the foundation of our consumptive capital, in 1704: workers running about with barrows, hammering stakes into the swampy ground, sawing logs, digging pits. All with beards and black cassocks, but with their sleeves rolled up and wearing oil-cloth aprons – the veritable realisation of the revolutionary dream of making the parasitical estate of clerics perform socially useful work.

Several times a day, in the most unexpected places, you come across the lord and master of this entire ant army, the archimandrite Vitalii II (*sic*!), who really does look like Peter the Great: long and lanky, menacing, impetuous, striding along so vigorously that his cassock balloons up around him and his retinue can hardly keep up behind. Not a priest, but a canon-ball, blasted from a canon. I would love to set you, Monk Peresvet of Kulikovo, against him one to one, and see who would come off best. I would probably bet on you anyway – the archimandrite may be more rapid-firing, but your calibre is heavier.

Here on the islands they seem to have mastered the art, previously unheard of in Russia, of making money out of everything and even out of nothing. It is usually entirely the other way round here: the more gold ore or diamonds there are lying around under our feet, the more ruinous the losses; but here, no sooner did Vitalii decide to put the useless stony ground on the Cape of Righteousness to good use than it was discovered that the stones there are not ordinary, but holy, for they were watered with the blood of the holy martyrs who were put to the sword three hundred years ago by the cut-throats of the Swedish Count Delagardi. The stones really do have a reddish-brownish colour, only I suspect it is not from blood but because they are impregnated with manganese. But then, that is not important; what is important is that now the pilgrims themselves chip pieces off the boulders and carry them away. There is a special monk standing there with a mattock and a pair of scales. If you want to use the mattock – pay fifteen kopecks. If you want to take the sacred stone away with you – weigh it and take it, it costs ninety-nine kopecks a pound. And so Vitalii's useless plot of land is gradually cleared, and the monastery coffers profit in the process. What a splendid arrangement!

Or take the water. An entire regiment of monks pours the local well water into bottles, seals the bottles with caps and glues on labels that say 'New Ararat Holy Water, blessed by the Reverend Father Vitalii', after which this H_2O is shipped wholesale to the mainland – to Peter and especially to devout Moscow. Meanwhile in Ararat, for the convenience of the pilgrims, they have constructed a wonder of wonders, a miracle of miracles, which is called the Automatic Holy Water Dispensers. These cunning machines, the invention of local Edisons, are located in a wooden pavilion. When someone drops a five-kopeck coin into the slot, it falls on a valve, a shutter opens and the holy water pours out into a mug. There is also a more expensive version, for ten kopecks, in which raspberry syrup is added to the water in a kind of special 'triple blessing'. They say that in summer there is a queue for this place, but I have come at a bad time – from mid-autumn the pavilion is closed so that this cunning technology will not be damaged by the night frosts. But never mind, sooner or later Vitalii will come up with the idea of installing a steam generator inside the dispensers to warm them, and then they will bring forth fruit in winter too.

But that is nothing when one considers that the archimandrite has leased out several *desyatines* of the finest land outside the town for use as a private psychiatric clinic, for which he receives fifty, or perhaps even seventy thousand roubles a year. This doleful establishment is owned by a certain Donat Korovin, from the same Korovin family that owns half the mines and factories in the Urals. And so the good doctor's cousins drink the blood and sweat of the brothers in Christ, but Donat Savvich Korovin, on the contrary, heals wounded souls. They do say, though, that he only accepts a select few into his miraculous hospital, only those patients whose insanity this millionaire Aesculapius finds interesting from the scientific point of view.

I have seen his clinic. No walls, no locks, nothing but grassy meadows, little groves of trees, little dolls' houses, pagodas and pergolas, ponds and streams, conservatories – a heavenly spot. I wouldn't mind a week or two of that kind of treatment myself. Korovin's method is extremely advanced, even revolutionary for the field of psychiatry. They come to him from Switzerland and even – oh, *horribile dictu*! – from Vienna itself to learn. Well, perhaps not to learn, rather simply out of curiosity, but it is still flattering even so.

Korovin's method is revolutionary in that he does not keep his patients under lock and key, as has been the custom in civilised countries since olden times: they are entirely at liberty to go where they will. This lends the crowd on the streets of New Ararat a certain risqué variety: one is hard put to tell which of the people one meets are normal and have come to the islands to pray, purge their souls and drink the holy water, and which of them are Korovin's crazy clients. Sometimes, it is true, there is no need to puzzle over this question. For example, I had barely disembarked from the steamer when I was approached by one highly colourful character. Imagine a man with a big bushy beard but with his moustache shaved completely off, a folded umbrella under his arm (ah, I remember, it was still spitting with that repulsive icy rain), a beret in the Doctor Faustus style on his head, and on his nose a huge pair of spectacles with immensely thick violet lenses.

This Faust or, rather, Captain Fracasse, stared at me in a most unceremonious manner, fiddled with some little metal levers on the frame of his spectacles and muttered in a highly agitated tone of voice: 'Ai-ai! The rib cage – aura in the cold grey-green range, the forehead hot and crimson. Very, very dangerous. Take especial care of your reason.' Then he turned to my cabin-mate, a portly gentleman who is a barrister from Moscow, and said something equally revolting to him: 'And you have a reddish-brown emanation from the left cerebral hemisphere. Do not drink wine and do not eat fatty foods, otherwise you will be keeping an appointment with the Grim Reaper.' It was not the lawyer's first time in Ararat; he comes here to relish the freshly smoked local salmon and the monastery's cranberry vodka, drink the holy digestive water and breathe the bracing air. The Noah's Ark Hotel was his recommendation. My Cicero reacted to the strange prophecy by the violet Fracasse with absolute imperturbability and explained to me about the psychiatric clinic, adding: 'Don't you worry, Monsieur Lentochkin, Donat Savvich doesn't have any violent patients.'

That very day, as I was dining in the grill-restaurant The Burnt Offering, I fell into conversation with a certain curious gentleman who was also connected with Korovin's clinic. You are familiar with my theory that reinforcing the body with calories while the eyes and the brain are left unoccupied is a simple waste of time, and therefore I was eating my grilled zander with my eyes glued to your novel. Suddenly a man of rather noble appearance approached my table and said: 'Pray forgive me, sir, for distracting you from the double pleasure of consuming both bodily and spiritual nourishment, but I happened to notice the name of the writer on the spine of your book. So you are reading a work by Mr Dostoevsky?' The direct manner in which he addressed me was atoned for by such a pleasant, disarming smile that it was quite impossible to be angry. 'Yes,' I replied, 'it is the novel *The Possessed*. Have you read it?' At that he quite literally began trembling all over and his cheek twitched in a highly amusing fashion. 'No,' he said, 'I have not read it, but I have heard a lot about it. Here on the island there is a library and a bookshop, but the archimandrite will not give his blessing to the sale of worldly books. Of course, from his point of view he is quite right, but I do miss good novels and new plays so badly.'

One thing led to another and we began talking. He took a seat at my table and soon he was telling me the story of his life, which was quite unusual. His name was Lev Nikolaevich, and it was quite clear that he was a fine individual who would never hurt a fly or say a bad word about anyone. As you know, I myself am not like that, and I am not fond of pious hypocrites, but somehow I found this Lev Nikolaevich interesting.

He immediately confessed quite frankly that he used to live in Korovin's hospital, having been brought there from St Petersburg in an extremely serious condition, almost completely out of his mind following some terrible series of shocks, all memory of which had now been completely erased from his mind. The doctor said that that was for the best, there was no point in raking over the past and what he needed to do now was to build his life over again from the beginning. Lev Nikolaevich is completely well already, but he does not wish to leave Canaan. He has grown attached to Korovin, and he feels afraid of the world. He said so in as many words: 'I'm afraid of the world, in case it breaks me again. But it's calm and peaceful here. God's beauty all around and all the people are very good too. To live on the mainland, you have to be strong – strong enough to bear the entire weight of the world and not be bowed by it. It is a great man who can repeat after Jesus: "The yoke is my blessing, and my burden is light." But then it is also written: "An unbearable burden must not be laid upon the weak." I am weak, it is better for me to live on the island.' He is an original character in general, this former resident of St Petersburg. It would be interesting for you to have a talk with him; you would like each other. But the reason I am telling you about Lev Nikolaevich is that your 'Possessed' are now in his possession. So I shall never know how Verkhovensky's conspiracy turned out. It's a pity, of course, but Lev Nikolaevich was looking at the book with such desperate longing – I could see he wanted to ask for it, but he didn't dare. Well, I gave it to him. In any case, I have no free time for reading novels, I have been sent here as the Holy Inquisition's exorcist.

Do not think, O Sheikh-ul-Islam, that all I do here is sit around in restaurants and coffee houses and gaze at the Princess Lointaine (O, my delight, where are you?). I have already clambered all over this island of Canaan and examined Outskirts Island from every side through binoculars – I very nearly tumbled out of the boat. I have seen all three of the hermits emerge from their burrows for their daily constitutional. They are bent over double and can scarcely hobble along – more like moles than human beings. I can boast of the fact that the abbot (he has a white border to his cowl) has favoured me with his most holy attention – he threatened me with his crutch to make sure I didn't sail too close.

I have discovered that the head mole is called Israel, and the story of his life is highly intriguing. Before taking monastic vows he was the kind of rich and idle aristocrat who, for lack of anything useful to occupy their time, take up some kind of *hobby*, devoting themselves passionately to their chosen whimsy and spending their entire lives and fortunes on it. This man had chosen a passion that is not particularly rare, but is the most engrossing of all – he collected women, and he applied himself so keenly to this activity that a certain retired vice-chancellor of my acquaintance would seem like a genuine seraph in comparison. This latter-day Don Juan's thirst for new knowledge was supposedly so insatiable that he compiled a geographical atlas of comparative female anatomy, for which purpose he took special voyages of voluptuousness to various countries, including such exotic destinations as Annam, the kingdom of Hawaii and Darkest Africa. And the number of highly respectable matrons he seduced and haughty young maidens he perverted within the borders of our own Orthodox fatherland is beyond all count, because he possessed some special talent for casting a spell on female hearts. Reputation plays a great part in this matter too. Ladies will not even spare a glance for some common drab bay, but the moment the news spreads that he is a dangerous seducer, they will immediately discover something in him that is attractive and even irresistible: the eyes, the hands or, if he has no outstanding features at all, they will invent some kind of magnetic aura.

Ah, but I am only grumbling out of jealousy. To live one's life like the holy man Israel's would not be half bad: plough your way wildly through all the lush years and then, when you get bored with it all and your health gets a bit shaky, rush to save your immortal soul – and with the same intense passion that you used to put into sinning. Only the debt to the Heavenly Moneylender that the father superior has run up is too great – Israel has already been stuck in this hallway to Heaven for two years and buried six of his cohabitants, but he still cannot pay it off. They say that no one else has overstayed his allotted span on Outskirts Island by so much in the last eighty years – so you can see what a great sinner he is.

On that note I conclude the discourse required of me

and call down upon your luminous personage, O sovereign lord, the blessings of Allah.

Slave of the Lamp Alexei Lentochkin

PS And now that you have finally decided that in this letter I shall do no more than amuse you with idle gossip about the local curiosities here, I shall move on to the actual matter in hand.

Know then, O most wise of the wisest, that I almost have the solution to the riddle of your Black Monk in the bag. Yes, indeed. And it seems likely that this solution will prove to be highly comical. That is to say, I already understand what the actual trick consists of; all that is unclear is who is amusing himself by playing the part of Basilisk, and to what end. But I shall obtain the answers to these questions today, because all the signs are that there will be a clear moon tonight.

My routine for these last three days has been as follows: in the morning I have slept late and then launched into my expeditions by land and sea, and with the onset of darkness I have settled to wait in ambush on the Lenten Spit, which extends out in the direction of Outskirts Island. I have not observed any supernatural events, but that is probably because the nights have been pitch-black with no moon and, as we know, the holy saint prefers celestial illumination. For lack of any other occupation, I have spent some time jumping from one rock to another and rowing backwards and forwards in a 'rocker' (that is a small kind of boat they make here that I have rented from a local resident), hoping to find out if it is possible to balance on one of the boulders so that you appear to be standing on the water. It is perfectly possible to balance on a boulder, but it is quite impossible to move even two or three steps. Having become convinced of this, I was inclined to think that in their fright the monks have simply imagined the walking on water. Then, on the third night – that is, yesterday – I discovered a certain highly suggestive detail that has made everything clear. But for now – mum's the word.

The effect will be more spectacular if I write and tell you the full story all at once, and that will happen no later than tomorrow. In two hours, as soon as it gets dark and the moon rises, I shall set out for my duel with the phantom. And since doing battle with the world beyond always carries the danger of death or, in the very best case, the loss of reason, I am prudently dispatching this letter in advance by the evening packet boat. Now pine in suspense until tomorrow's post, Archbishop of Rheims; languish in your curiosity and impatience.

> Girding on his sword of damask steel
> And donning his stout hauberk of chain mail,
> See the audacious warrior of good
> Prepare to face the insuperable giant.
> And if his fate in this ferocious battle
> Should be to sacrifice his valiant head,
> Remember him, Your Reverence, in a word of prayer,
> And you, bright Princess of the coffee shop,
> Water the hero's body with your tears.
> Ah-oo!

So that was the letter. At first Matvei Berdichevsky and Pelagia listened with a smile – they were amused by the comparison of His Grace to Turpin, the Archbishop of Rheims, the indefatigable exterminator of Moors and comrade-in-arms of Roland of Ronceval. But by the end of this verbose epistle the faces of the nun and the assistant public prosecutor both wore puzzled expressions, and Berdichevsky even called Lentochkin a rotten so-and-so for his posturing. They decided definitely not to succumb to Alyosha's attempted provocation or to indulge in any speculation concerning the mysterious hints contained in the postscript, but to wait for the following day's delivery from New Ararat and then discuss everything in detail.

But the post that arrived the following day did not include the promised letter from Lentochkin. Nor did it arrive on the second day, or the third. His Grace became extremely alarmed and began wondering if he ought to write to Father Vitalii about his missing emissary, and the only reason he did not was that it would have been awkward to have to admit to the archimandrite that Alexei Lentochkin had been sent to Ararat unbeknownst to the monastery's father superior.

On the seventh day, just when Mitrofanii, haggard and tormented by insomnia, was on the verge of setting out for the Blue Lake in person (the Bishop was so fearful for Alyosha that he was no longer concerned about the diplomatic complications), the letter finally arrived, but it was quite different in kind from the first. The Bishop once again summoned his advisers and read them the epistle he had received but, unlike the previous occasion, he seemed puzzled rather than pleased. On this occasion Alyosha went straight to the business in hand, without any introductory remarks or exhortations.

Alexei Stepanovich Lentochkin's second letter

I realise that I am quite impossibly late with this continuation, but there are serious grounds for that. Precisely *serious* grounds, not humorous ones. The Black Monk is no trick played by some adroit swindler, as I assumed at first; this is something different. But so far I have not been able to understand exactly what.

I had better tell you everything that has happened in the right order. First, to avoid any confusion and, secondly, because I need to clarify for myself how it all happened, what came first and what came later. Because my head is spinning.

After sending off my last letter to you and eating a hearty supper (was that really only a week ago? It feels like months or even years), I set out for Lenten Spit as if I were on my way to a jolly picnic, savouring in advance the cunning trap in which I would catch the presumptive hoaxer who had decided to frighten the peace-loving monks. I took up my position between two large boulders in a spot I had noted earlier, settling in with every possible comfort. I spread out the blanket I had brought with me from the hotel; I had tea with rum splashing in my Thermos flask and a bundle of small cakes from the remarkable local confectioner's The Temptation of St Antony. I sat there, enjoying my snack and chuckling to myself as I waited for the moon to rise. The lake was as dark as could be, you couldn't have spotted a water-sprite – if there had happened to be one – and Outskirts Island was no more than a vague outline.

But then a yellow stripe of moonlight appeared on the smooth surface of the water, the colour of the night changed from an inky-black monotone to a shimmering gleam and the darkness shrank away to the edges of the sky, leaving the moon enthroned on high at its centre. And at that very instant, right in front of me, a black silhouette appeared, partly blocking out the pale disc of the lamp of night. I am prepared to swear on anything at all that only a second before it had not been there, and then suddenly there it was – elongated, with a pointed top, swaying slightly. And not exactly in the place I had been expecting it, where a flat rock protruded only slightly above the water, but a little to one side, where there were no rocks at all.

At first I was simply astounded. Where could he have come from? It had been dark before the moon rose, but not so dark that I could have failed to see a man only a dozen paces away!

According to my plan, the moment 'Basilisk' appeared, I should have emerged from my hiding place, wearing a long cloak with a hood, very similar to the hermit's own robes, and howled in a sepulchral voice: 'I am the blessed Saint Basilisk! Go to hell, you impostor!' – I imagined that in that way I would scare the scarecrow, so that he would tumble off his rock into the water.

But at the sight of the black figure that seemed to be hanging above the surface of the lake, something happened to me – an absolutely specific, physiological reaction. I felt an unaccountable cold sensation run across my skin and while my arms and legs didn't exactly lose the power of movement (I remember quite clearly setting the Thermos flask down on the ground and feeling my icy forehead with my hand), they moved slowly and reluctantly, as if I were under water. I have never felt anything like it before in my life.

Light began streaming out from behind the silent silhouette, light far brighter than that of the moon. No, I can't describe it very well, because 'streaming' is not the right expression, and I don't know how to explain it any better. A moment earlier there was nothing except the moonlight, and then it was as if the entire world had been lit up so brightly that I had to screw up my eyes and shield them with my hand.

I was almost deafened by the pounding of the blood in my ears, but I still heard four words quite distinctly, even though they were spoken very quietly: 'Not salvation, but decay' – and the black figure gestured towards Outskirts Island. Then, when it began moving straight towards me over the water, the numb torpor fell away and I took to my heels in a most shameful fashion, I believe I was even sobbing as I ran. See what a bold paladin you have chosen for yourself, O short-sighted prince of the Church!

Afterwards, when I had run as far as the chapel, I felt ashamed. If this was, after all, some especially cunning hoax, I could not allow myself to be made a fool of, I told myself. And if it was not a hoax . . . Well, then the Lord God existed, the world was created in seven days, there were angels flying in the sky and the lamps of heaven rotated round the Earth. Since all of that was quite impossible, Basilisk could not exist either. Having reached this conclusion, I strode off with the utmost determination in the direction I had come from and arrived back at the spit; but there was no longer any mysterious glow or black silhouette to be seen. I walked up and down the shoreline, stamping my feet loudly to keep up my courage and whistling a song about a priest who had a dog. When I had finally convinced myself of the unshakably material nature of the world, I retrieved the Thermos flask and hotel property and came back to the Ark.

But I decided not to write a report until I had seen Basilisk again and made absolutely certain either that he was a hoaxer's trick or that I had lost my mind and the best place for me was in Dr Korovin's clinic.

As ill luck would have it, the next two nights were overcast. I strolled round the streets of Ararat, which now seemed so tedious, drank fizzy holy water and Jamaican coffee and read all sorts of nonsense in the monastery's reading hall just to pass the time. During this period of enforced idleness my nerves were tormented so badly with the agonising anticipation and my mental arguments with myself that on the eve of the expedition my courage almost deserted me completely. However, it was not possible to let such an opportunity slip, so I took a decision that seemed to me as wise as any of Solomon's.

I have already mentioned in my last letter the barrister from Moscow who is a devotee of smoked salmon and fresh air. His name is Kubovsky, and he has been coming to Canaan every autumn for several years. They say that November is an especially fine month here. We had taken rooms in the same hotel and dined together a few times, when he had eaten and drunk about five times as much as myself (and my appetite is far from poor, as your chef and my benefactor, Kuzma Savelievich, can testify). I thought

61

Kubovsky to be a man of sober, even clinical cast of mind, without the slightest interest in the supernatural. For instance, he was inclined to explain absolutely all the manifestations of human psychology exclusively from the viewpoint of the ingestion, digestion and evacuation of food. If he saw me, for instance, in a state of pensiveness while I was considering the mystery of the Black Monk, he would say: 'Hey, my dear fellow, what you need is a bit of something spicy, and then your melancholy will disappear.' Or if I pointed out from a distance the romantic lady who had almost distracted me from your mission (ah, Princess Lointaine, how can I think of you now?), Kubovsky would shake his head and say: 'Ah, look how pale she is, the poor soul. No doubt she eats food that is not nutritious, and not enough of it, and that makes the stomach sluggish and causes constipation. A bit of sturgeon with cranberry syrup is good for that, and then, of course, a little glass of Italian grappa or French calvados. That will bring the bowels back to life.' Well, anyway, you can see the sort of man he is. And so I had the idea of taking him with me under the guise of a night-time promenade for the sake of the digestion. First, I thought that if I had company I would not be so frightened and secondly, if Basilisk was a hallucination, the barrister would not see him. And thirdly, if it was some kind of circus trick, a prosaic man like him would never fall for it. I deliberately did not warn my companion in advance, in order to maintain the purity of the experiment.

And that was clearly a mistake, for which I now feel guilty.

Everything happened exactly as it had the previous time. I deliberately seated Kubovsky with his face towards Outskirts Island and sat down with my own eyes glued to the same spot. There was nobody there, nobody and nothing – there is absolutely no doubt about that. But no sooner did the moon break through the thin clouds than the familiar phantom appeared on the water and was almost immediately shrouded in a blinding radiance.

I didn't hear any voice this time, because my cynic – who was just about to despatch a chocolate bon-bon into his mouth – began yelling loudly in a wild voice and went dashing away from the spot with the most surprising agility. I could not keep up with him (oh yes, the very instant that repulsive, deathlike chill crept across my skin, all of my determination evaporated) and I probably would not have caught up with him before the outskirts of the town if halfway there Kubovsky had not suddenly fallen flat on his face. I squatted down beside him and saw that he was wheezing and rolling his eyes, showing no desire to leap up and run on ...

He died. Not there on the road, but in the morning, in the monastery's infirmary. A cerebral haemorrhage. In other words, the Grim Reaper that the violet-eyed Faust warned him about had come calling after all.

What do you think, Your Reverence: who was it that killed the poor glutton – I or the Black Monk? Even if it was the monk, I am still an accomplice.

When the infirmary monks (all wearing beards, with white coats over their black cassocks) had taken the dead man away to the ice room, I set out straight away for Dr Korovin's clinic and, although it was still early in the morning, I demanded an immediate meeting with this leading light of neuropsychological medicine. At first they absolutely refused to let me through without a recommendation from anyone, but you know me: if necessary, I will creep through the eye of a needle. I had two questions for the medical luminary. The first was: Is a group visual and auditory hallucination possible? The second was: Have I lost my mind?

Korovin dealt with the second question first, and it was an hour later before he answered it. He asked me questions about my daddy and mummy and various ancestors going all the way back to my great-grandfather Pantaleimon Lentochkin, who died of alcohol poisoning. Then he shone a light into my eyes, tapped on my joints with a little hammer and made me draw geometrical shapes. Finally he declared: 'You are perfectly well, only in a state of severe, almost hysteroid fright. Well then, now I can listen to what you have to say about the hallucination.' I told him. He listened to everything very closely, nodding, and then propounded the following explanation, which at the time I found entirely satisfactory.

'During the autumn nights here on the islands,' said Korovin, 'the exceptionally high level of ozone in the air and the effect of light reflected from the surface of the water frequently give rise to various kinds of optical illusion. Sometimes, especially when the moon is shining, a black pillar can be seen moving across the lake, and a poetically or religiously inclined sensibility might well be reminded of a monk in hermit's dress. In actual fact it is merely a small waterspout.' 'What?' I asked incredulously. 'A waterspout – a small one, that is. It can be very localised: still air all around, but at one spot some whimsical trick of atmospheric pressure suddenly produces a flow of air, and a rather rapid one too. It can pick up fallen leaves and fine litter from the shore of the lake, swirl them round, twist them into a cone – and there you have your Black Monk. Especially if you were already expecting to see him.'

I left the doctor feeling completely reassured, apart from my regret for the ill-fated Kubovsky, but the further I moved away from the clinic, the louder the voice of inner doubt became. What about the unearthly light? And the words that I had heard so clearly? And it couldn't possibly have been a waterspout – it had moved slowly, no more than a few paces, and its outlines had really been very distinct.

Subsequent events confirmed that waterspouts and the

ozone level in the air had nothing at all to do with the business.

Having destroyed one life, Basilisk seemed suddenly to cast off his shackles and break free of the bounds of Lenten Spit.

The following night he appeared to Brother Kleopa, the boatman, who is the only person in New Ararat allowed to visit Basilisk's Hermitage: once a day he ferries necessities to the hermits and collects the rosary beads that they have made. That night, when Kleopa was making his way back to the monastery from some friend's house, Basilisk appeared before him just beside the monks' graveyard. He gave the boatman a mighty shove in the chest that sent him tumbling to the ground and forbade him in a thunderous voice to take his boat to Outskirts Island, because 'the place is cursed'.

The impact of this sensational news was lessened somewhat by the general knowledge of Brother Kleopa's intemperance with regard to wine – he had been walking back to his cell tipsy on that night too. Even the eyewitness himself could not swear that he had not imagined seeing the saint. Nonetheless the rumour immediately spread throughout the whole of Canaan.

And then, two nights after that, an event occurred that could not be doubted, one that had very grave, even tragic consequences.

The spectre had failed to frighten Brother Kleopa, since he sailed to the hermitage by the light of day, and by the time the night came and the Black Monk appeared he was usually already intoxicated and not afraid of anything. But there is another person who often visited the strait separating Canaan from Outskirts Island – a buoy-keeper whose duties include setting out the spar buoys in the channel, which were frequently shifted by the current and the wind. This buoy-keeper is not a monk, but a layman. He lives in a small log hut on the north side of Canaan, which is almost uninhabited, with his heavily pregnant young wife. Or rather, they used to live there, since now the hut stands empty.

The day before yesterday the buoy-keeper and his wife were woken by a loud knocking on the window. In the moonlight pouring in through the glass they saw a black cowl and immediately realised who was there. Their midnight visitor shook a threatening finger at the husband and wife, who were frozen in terror, and then he drew something on the glass with that selfsame finger, making a horrible scraping sound (it turned out later that it was a cross – the old kind, with two extra crosspieces set at an angle).

Then the spectre disappeared, but the woman suffered a miscarriage because of the shock, and while her husband went running to fetch help, she bled to death. The buoy-keeper told the monastery authorities about the nocturnal vision and set about making two coffins: one for his wife and the other for himself; for he said quite definitely that he did not wish to go on living. That evening he got into his boat, rowed out into open water, tied a stone round his neck and threw himself overboard – many people on the shore saw it. They searched for the drowned man but failed to find him, and so the second coffin remained unused.

The town has changed beyond recognition now. That is to say, during the day it is still as populous as ever – none of the pilgrims are in any hurry to leave the island, since people's curiosity and fascination with things mystical are stronger than their prudence and fear, but by night the streets are completely deserted. Bad things are said about Basilisk's Hermitage. They say there is no place worse than one that used to be blessed, but has *turned bad* – whether it is an abandoned church or a defiled graveyard, and especially a hermitage intended for salvation through repentance. The opinion is gaining ground among the holy brothers and the local population that they should heed these warnings from the monastery's patron and remove the hermits from Outskirts Island – for fear of angering the Black Monk even more.

The archimandrite led a procession bearing icons right across Canaan and sprinkled the buoy-keeper's hut with holy water, but even so no one goes to that place now. I, by the way, have visited it (but in the morning, when the sun was shining). I have seen the notorious cross scraped on the window pane and even touched it with my finger.

Please do not believe, great sorcerer Merlin, that your knight's courage has failed completely. I am ready to concede the possibility that the universe does not consist exclusively of physical matter, but this signifies not so much capitulation as a change of methodology. Apparently I shall have to doff one suit of armour and don another. But I do not intend to surrender and I am not yet asking for your help.

Your Lancelot of the Lake

This letter, so remarkable in every respect, produced different impressions on the three individuals consulting on it.

'He's putting a brave face on things, but he's really scared to death,' said the Bishop. 'I know from my own experience how terrifying it is when the whole world is turned upside down. Only for me it was all the other way round: ever since I was a child I had believed that the world was ruled by the spirit, and when I suspected for the first time that there was no God, and nothing but matter existed, I became depressed, I had a feeling of hopelessness. That was when I became a monk, in order to turn everything the right way up again.'

'What?' said Berdichevsky, amazed. 'You mean that *you* once had doubts like that? And I thought that ...'

He stopped in confusion.

'That you were the only one?' said Mitrofanii, completing Berdichevsky's thought with a wry laugh. 'And that I am full of nothing but holy certainty? No, Matvei, only the dull of intellect have nothing but holy certainty inside them, but a thinking man is visited with grievous temptations and trials. It is not he who is not tempted that is blessed, but he who overcomes. The soul of a man who never doubts anything is dead.'

'Then do you believe in all these wonders, Father?' asked Pelagia, looking up from her knitting. 'In the ghost, the walking on water and all the rest of it? That's not what you said before.'

'What does the boy mean by changing his armour?' His Grace mused pensively as if he had not heard her. 'It's not clear ... Ah, how fascinating and multifarious in meaning are the ways of the Lord!'

But Pelagia chose to express an opinion of a psychological nature: 'I had assumed from the previous letter that your emissary had become infatuated with that seductive lady and forgotten about the task you set him, and that that was the reason for the gap in the correspondence. But this time she is only mentioned once, in passing. I don't know if what Alexei Stepanovich writes about the spectre is true, but it is absolutely clear that the young man really has suffered some extremely powerful shock. Otherwise he would never have forgotten such an attractive individual.'

'Women always have only one thing on their minds,' the prelate said with a frown of annoyance. 'You always exaggerate the extent of your influence on men. There are more mysterious riddles in the world than romantic strangers wearing veils. Oh, the boy needs to be rescued. He needs help, even if he says he doesn't want it.'

At this point Matvei Berdichevsky, who had listened to the reasoning of the Bishop and his spiritual daughter with his eyebrows raised in astonishment, could hold back no longer. 'Are you serious? Really, Father, I am surprised at you! Have you really taken this cock-and-bull nonsense at face value? Why, Lentochkin is pulling the wool over your eyes, making fools of you in the most shameful manner possible! Of course he has spent all these days trailing around after his "princess", and now he is inventing fairy tales to amuse himself at our expense. It's perfectly obvious! There's just one thing I can't understand: how could you, with your knowledge of people, have sent a dissolute raw youth on such a responsible mission?'

The logic and common sense of what the assistant district public prosecutor said was so clear that Mitrofanii was actually embarrassed, and although Pelagia shook her head, she made no attempt to argue.

That was how they parted, without having taken any decision, and so precious time was lost, as became clear two days later when a third letter arrived. The autumn rains had turned the roads to quagmires and the post coach was seriously delayed, so that the envelope was only delivered to the Bishop as night was approaching. In spite of this, His Grace immediately sent for Berdichevsky and Pelagia.

Alexei Stephanovich Lentochkin's third letter

Eureka! The method has been found!

The most difficult thing was to abandon the materialistic system of coordinates, the two-dimensionality of which is erroneous. It ignores the third dimension, which I shall provisionally call mystical – I am sure that in time some other, less emotional term will be found for it. But first I need to devise a system for conducting research and techniques of measurement. Modern science does not concern itself with this area at all, being completely in agreement with your adored Ecclesiastes, who said: 'The crooked cannot be made straight and the non-existent cannot be counted.' But then Galileo, the founding father of scientific progress, took a different view. He formulated the scientist's primary article of faith as follows: 'Measure everything that is subject to measurement and render measurable that which is not.'

So what is needed is to render the mystical measurable.

Materialistic science may not acknowledge this goal, but before the Age of Reason began there was another, magical science which attempted for centuries to quantify that which is usually called supernatural. And as far I am aware, it achieved some progress in this field of endeavour!

It is this original premise, which I hit upon only two days ago, that has led me to the solution of the problem. I believe I have already mentioned in a letter that the monastery has a library with a collection of numerous books, old and new, on religious matters. I had been there before, passing the time for lack of anything else to do by leafing through some 'Spiritual Alphabet' by Ioann Lestvichkin and Efrem Sirin, or the 'Lives of the Holy Fathers of New Ararat', but now I set about searching with a specific purpose in mind.

And what do you think? On the second day – that is, yesterday – I found a book published in 1747, a translation from the Latin: 'On the Propitiation of Good Spirits and the Overcoming of Evil Spirits'. When I started reading it, I was thrilled! It was exactly what I needed! The precise thing! (This coincidence, by the way, is another proof of the reality of the mystical dimension.)

In this old book it is written in black on white: 'And should an incorporeal spirit leave behind it anywhere a corporeal (that is, in modern terms, material) reminder of itself, then this sign is like a tail, by seizing which the spirit can be caught and pulled out of the incorporeal realm into this world.' I shall not relate the verbose and naïve reasoning about the fallibility of Satan who, unlike the omnipresent Lord, sometimes makes errors and therefore can be and should be defeated, but go straight to the heart of the matter.

And so, if a certain essential being belonging to the mystical dimension has in its rashness left behind some substantial mark of its presence in our material world, then this physical trace can be used by someone to draw the phantom into the corporeal world perceived by our sense organs. That is the most important point!

A little further on, several pages of the treatise are devoted to a detailed description of how to go about doing this.

At exactly midnight, when the third dimension coincides with the first two, which is obviously why time is transformed at that point (that is, in the earthly sense it, as it were, stands still), you have to stand facing the sign and pronounce the words of the magical formula: 'Come, unholy spirit (or "blessed spirit", as the case requires) to the trace that you have left, according to the agreement between Gabriel and the Evil One.' As he says this, the person summoning the spirit must be completely naked and not wearing any rings or a cross round his neck or any other extraneous items, for at the moment of transformation even the very smallest of these becomes heavy and impedes the movements of the body.

The formula not only compels the imprudent spirit to appear immediately before his summoner, it also preserves the latter from danger. And if the spirit should, even so, attempt to take its revenge (of course, this only happens with evil spirits and, to judge from all that we know, Basilisk belongs to the category of good spirits), then it is possible to defend yourself against an attack with the simple exclamation: '*Credo, credo, Domine!*' (I assume that the Russian 'I believe, I believe, O Lord!' will serve as well – after all, it is not the sounds that matter, but the meaning.)

I have a material sign – the cross drawn on the window of the buoy-keeper's hut. At night there is not a soul anywhere near the place, so I shall not shock anyone with

71

my nakedness (and anyway, I can go inside first and then get undressed). I have committed the magical formula to memory, and the prayer is not hard to remember either.

So let us try it – after all, nothing ventured, nothing gained. In the very worst case, I shall make myself appear a stupid blockhead – but it does not matter, I am not afraid of that.

If it does not work, I shall carry on searching for a way to render measurable what cannot be measured.

I shall go tonight. Think of me kindly, father. And if anything should happen, let me be remembered occasionally in your prayers,

Yours with love and respect,
Alyosha Lentochkin

Someone must go to New Ararat, and immediately – the Bishop announced that as the decision he had already taken after careful consideration, without even giving his advisers a chance to comment. However, Berdichevsky and Pelagia seemed so perplexed that they were not really sure what to say.

While he was waiting for them to arrive, Mitrofanii had already resolved everything for himself.

'The boy has completely lost his way in the fog,' he said. 'I repent; it is my fault. I wanted to open his spiritual eyes, but the sudden flash of light has proved too bright for him – it has blinded him completely. Alyosha must be brought back from there, forcibly if necessary – that is the first thing; and then we can get to the bottom of the miraculous happenings at New Ararat. What's required is a man with a military cast of mind: a man of determination, with no fancy ideas or superfluous imagination. You, Matvei, are not suited.'

Matvei Bentsionovich Berdichevsky most certainly did not consider himself a man of a military cast of mind, but even so he felt slightly offended. 'And who is this man of yours without any imagination, Your Grace?' he enquired with the very slightest hint of acrimony in his voice, certain that the Bishop was thinking of himself.

The reply was unexpected: 'Don't you go thinking that it is me. I am a man of the Church and might not prove resistant to mystical impressions. If Lentochkin has not been able to resist . . .' – and Mitrofanii shook his head, as if he were marvelling yet again at the fragility of Alyosha's nihilism. 'Lagrange will go.'

At first sight this decision was no less surprising than the previous one, when the Bishop had made up his mind to send a young atheist to deal with internal Church matters.

That is to say, on the one hand the police chief of Zavolzhie, Felix Stanislavovich Lagrange, might have seemed, by virtue of his official position, an entirely appropriate candidate for carrying out a rapid and decisive operation, but that was only if one did not know the background to the situation; and the background included the fact that Colonel Lagrange was in His Grace's debt – in fact not very long before he had almost found himself in court as a consequence of certain rather indecorous goings-on. However, just recently Lagrange had been almost forgiven and had even begun going to the Bishop for confession. We may assume that here Mitrofanii's ambition, which we have already mentioned, had come into play once again, the Bishop being driven less by concern for the pastoral care of enlightened souls than by the hope of evoking a response from those that were calloused and deaf.

Berdichevsky opened his mouth to protest, but immediately shut it again when the thought occurred to him that at second glance the choice that had just been announced did not look so very bad after all, because . . . But that was exactly what the Bishop went on to explain.

'Felix Stanislavovich comes to me for confession, but he does it exactly as if he were going on watch or trooping the colour, as if he were simply carrying out standing orders. He reports to me in meticulous detail on how many times he has used obscene language and which whores he has visited, receives absolution for his sins, clicks his spurs together, then does a quick about-face and marches off at the double. He is one of that rare breed of people who have absolutely no need of faith. But then,' Mitrofanii added with a smile, 'the colonel would probably take great offence if anyone were to call him a materialist – he would most likely slap their face for it. And he is an efficient soldier, he knows police business and is a man of exceptional bravery. I shall summon him tomorrow and ask him to go – he won't refuse.'

And that was what the Bishop did. He summoned Lagrange and gave him his instructions and, of course, it never even entered the police chief's head to be obstinate – he accepted His Grace's wishes implicitly, as he would have accepted instructions from the Governor or the director of the police department. He promised to set out first thing in the morning, as soon as he had handed over current business to his deputy.

But even sooner than that, that very same evening, a special courier delivered a new letter from New Ararat that shocked and astounded the Bishop, Berdichevsky and Pelagia, while at the same time explaining a great deal.

But then why should we attempt to explain in our own words, when that will only confuse matters? Here is the document itself. As they say, any comment is superfluous.

Reverend Bishop,

I am not certain that you are in fact the person to whom this letter should be addressed, but there is no one here who knows the place of residence or family circumstances of the young man who was staying at the Noah's Ark Hotel under the name of Alexei Stepanovich Lentochkin. On the table in the room that he occupied, an envelope was discovered bearing the words 'To His Reverence Father Mitrofanii, the Episcopal Residence, Zavolzhsk', with a blank piece of paper lying beside it, as if Lentochkin was intending to write you a letter but had not had enough time to do so. Therefore I am writing to Your Grace in the hope that you know this youth and will be able to inform his relatives of the misfortune that has befallen him and provide me with any details in your possession concerning his life hitherto, since this is of great importance in selecting the correct method of treatment.

Mr Lentochkin (if that is his real name) is suffering from an extremely acute form of mental disturbance that excludes any possibility of transporting him off the island. At dawn this morning he came dashing into the psychiatric clinic that I run in such a lamentable state that I have been obliged to keep him here. He does not reply to any questions but keeps mumbling, over and over again: '*Credo, credo, Domine,*' from time to time declaiming incoherent, entirely delirious monologues. Apart from the obvious inadvisability of moving the patient from place to place, as a medical man I find the nature of his mania interesting. I assume that you have heard about my clinic, but you might possibly not know that I do not undertake the treatment of absolutely any mental malady but only those that have been little studied by the science of psychiatry. Lentochkin is precisely such a case.

I will not burden you with all the sad details, since I am still not absolutely certain that you are acquainted with my new patient. In view of the religious theme of his ravings (which are obscure and almost totally incoherent), one might easily assume that Lentochkin had decided to write to the provincial bishop just as others in my care write to His Highness the Emperor of Russia, the Pope of Rome or the Emperor of China.

However, if you do happen to know how to contact Lentochkin's relatives, please do not delay. I know from experience that with very few exceptions the condition of patients of his kind deteriorates very rapidly and soon leads to a fatal outcome.

I remain Your Reverence's most respectful servant,
Donat Savvich Korovin, Doctor of Medicine

THE SECOND EXPEDITION
The Adventures of the Man of Courage

This deplorable new turn of events (it was, indeed, rather surprising that it had not actually been foreseen by such very clever people) gave rise to a new quarrel about who should go, but eventually the Bishop insisted on his original choice and the chief of police was dispatched to New Ararat. This outcome was, however, preceded by a sharp argument between Mitrofanii and Sister Pelagia – on the question of Lagrange, Berdichevsky maintained his neutrality and therefore said nothing for most of the time.

The argument concerned the Gordian Knot. It began with the prelate comparing Lagrange to the resolute Alexander who, finding himself unable to untie the intricate knot, had found an excellent way out of his awkward situation by simply slicing it in two with his sword. In His Grace's opinion that was exactly how Lagrange would act if he were to find himself in difficulties: as a military man he would not capitulate in the face of any baffling conundrum, but tackle it head on, which could prove to be the most effective approach in a complicated case such as this.

'And in general,' said the Bishop, 'it seems to me that the more complex and confused a situation, the easier the way out of it.'

'Oh, how mistaken you are, Father!' Pelagia exclaimed in great agitation. 'Those are extremely dangerous words! If you, the wisest and kindest of all the people I know, can reason like that, then what is to be expected from the earthly rulers of men? They are in any case inclined to reach for their swords in the face of the slightest difficulty. Slicing the Gordian Knot in two was a deed of no great merit; any fool could have done it. After Alexander's heroic exploit there was simply one less wonder left in the world!'

Mitrofanii was about to object, but the nun began fluttering her hands at him and the pastor stared in astonishment at his spiritual daughter, for he had never known her to behave so disrespectfully before.

'There are no simple ways out of complicated situations! You must know that!' the nun exclaimed heatedly. 'And your military men do nothing but destroy and ruin! Where tact, caution and patience are required, they go barging in with their boots, sabres and cannons, and make such a mess of things that afterwards the process of healing, repairing and general patching up is long and painful.'

The Bishop was astonished: 'Do you mean to say you think soldiers are not necessary at all?'

'No, of course they are – when an enemy has attacked and the fatherland has to be defended. But they can't be trusted with anything else! Not even civil matters, let alone spiritual ones! But here in Russia military men are trusted to deal with absolutely anything at all! A sabre is a useless instrument for repairing a fault in a delicate mechanism. And sending your colonel to Ararat is like letting an elephant loose in a china shop!'

'Never mind,' Mitrofanii interrupted, taking offence for the estate of the military. 'Hannibal conquered the Alps on elephants! Yes, Felix Stanislavovich won't stand for any nonsense. If he has to turn the islands upside down, he'll find me the villain who drove Alyosha into the madhouse. Ghost or no ghost – it's all the same to Lagrange. And there's an end of it. Go now, Pelagia. I will not change my decision.' And he turned away, so angry that he did not even bless the nun in farewell.

The steamship *St Basilisk* slapped the paddles of its wheels against the dark water with brisk efficiency as it sailed across the Blue Lake. The impressive-looking gentleman with a good complexion standing on the upper deck was wearing a check three-piece woollen suit, white spats and an English cap with ear-flaps, and he was absorbed in studying his own reflection in the window of one of the cabins. The panoramic view of the bay wreathed in evening mist and the twinkling lights of Sineozersk held no attraction for this passenger – he had his back towards the lyrical landscape. He turned this way and that to make sure that his jacket sat well on him, fingered the remarkable curls of his moustache and was satisfied. Naturally, a blue uniform jacket embroidered with gold would be a hundred times better, he thought to himself, but a real man looked well enough even in civilian clothes.

He was not able to continue admiring himself, however, because a light came on in the cabin. That is, first a narrow crack appeared in the darkness and rapidly expanded into an illuminated rectangle, and then a silhouette appeared, outlined against it; then the rectangle disappeared (as the door to the corridor was closed), but a second later the gas burner sprang to life. An attractive young woman removed her hand from the small control lever, took off her hat and cast an absent-minded glance at herself in the mirror.

The passenger with the moustache did not even think of leaving – on the contrary, he moved even closer to the pane of glass and examined the lady's slim figure with the attentive eye of a connoisseur.

At this point the inhabitant of the cabin finally turned towards the window and noticed the gentleman peeping in. Her eyebrows shot up and her lips moved – we must assume that she gasped 'Ah!' or made some other expression of the same kind.

The handsome gentleman was not in the least embarrassed; in fact, he raised his cap politely and bowed. The lady moved her lips soundlessly again, this time for longer, but though her words were inaudible outside, it was not difficult to guess their meaning: 'What can I do for you, sir?'

Instead of replying or, even better, going away, the passenger rapped insistently on the glass with his knuckles. When the female traveller, intrigued, lowered the window frame, he said in a clear, resonant voice: 'Felix Stanislavovich Lagrange. Pardon my directness, madam – I am a soldier, you see – but at the sight of you I suddenly felt as if you and I were all alone on this ship. Just the two of us, and not another soul. Now isn't that a strange thing?'

The lady blushed and was about to close the window without speaking, but after glancing more closely at the soldier's attract-ive face, and especially at his round, extraordinarily intense eyes, she seemed suddenly to become thoughtful, and the moment for demonstrating intransigence was missed.

Shortly thereafter the colonel and his new acquaintance were already sitting in the ship's saloon, surrounded by pilgrims (an entirely and exclusively respectable crowd), drinking champagne cup and making conversation.

In fact it was Natalya Genrikhovna (that was the lady's name) who did most of the talking, and the chief of police hardly even opened his mouth, because at the first stage of a new acquaintance that was superfluous – he merely smiled mys-teriously into his scented moustache and gazed adoringly at his companion.

With her cheeks glowing pink, the lady, who was the wife of a St Petersburg newspaper publisher, told him that she had grown weary of the vain bustle of life in the capital and decided to cleanse her soul, which was why she had set out on this trip to the holy island.

'You know, Felix Stanislavovich, there suddenly comes a moment in life when you feel things cannot go on as they are any longer,' Natalya Genrikhovna told him in a confidential tone. 'You have to stop and look around, listen to the silence and understand what is most important about yourself. That is why I came alone – in order to be quiet and to listen. And also to beg the Lord's forgiveness for all my sins, both voluntary and involuntary. Do you understand me?'

The colonel raised his eyebrows expressively: Oh, yes!

An hour later they were strolling along the deck and, in order to shelter his companion from the fresh wind, Lagrange reduced the distance between his strong, manly shoulder and Natalya Genrikhovna's delicate one to an entirely insignificant gap.

When the *St Basilisk* emerged from the mouth of the bay into a wide, black, open expanse, the wind suddenly acquired a keen edge, the white-toothed waves began slapping angrily against the side of the ship and from time to time the colonel was obliged to catch hold of the lady round the waist, and every time his hand lingered longer against her gently yielding side.

Sailor monks holding up the hems of their cassocks ran around the deck, securing the dancing lifeboats and muttering prayers in a habitual murmur. On the bridge they could see the massive figure of the captain, also wearing a cassock, but with a peaked leather cap on his head and a broad leather belt round his hips. The captain was shouting into a megaphone in a hoarse bass voice: 'Porfirii, may you choke on unction! Cast on two hitches!'

At the stern, where the wind was blowing less furiously, the strolling couple halted. Natalya Genrikhovna surveyed the boundless expanse of stormy water and the lowering, grey-black sky and shuddered.

'My God, how frightening it is! As if we'd fallen into a hole between time and space!'

Lagrange realised the moment had come to launch a full frontal offensive. A frightened woman was like an enemy cowed by a blast of grapeshot. He conducted his attack brilliantly. Lowering his voice to a trembling baritone, he said: 'I am really quite terribly lonely. And you know, sometimes I long for understanding, warmth and ... affection, yes, that's it – ordinary, simple human affection.' He lowered his forehead on to the lady's shoulder, which required him to bend his knees slightly, and heaved a sigh.

'That ... that wasn't the reason I decided to make the trip to Ararat,' Natalya Genrikhovna whispered, disconcerted, making as if to push Felix Stanislavovich's head away, but at the same time running her fingers through his thick hair. 'Not to commit new sins, but to pray for the forgiveness of the old ones . . .'

'Then you can ask forgiveness for everything all at once,' said the colonel, adducing an argument of irrefutable logic.

Five minutes later they were kissing in the dark cabin – in a purely romantic fashion as yet, but the police chief's fingers had already identified the disposition of buttons on Natalya Genrikhovna's dress and even stealthily unfastened the upper one . . .

In the middle of the night Felix Stanislavovich Lagrange was woken by a powerful jolt. Raising himself up on one elbow, he saw a pair of frightened eyes – a woman's eyes – close beside him. Although the narrow bed was not designed for two, the colonel had been sleeping very soundly indeed, as he always did, and if he had been woken, the blow must have been a serious one.

'What is it?' asked Lagrange, still half-asleep and not remembering where he was; but he immediately glanced towards the door. 'Your husband?'

The lady (what was her name?) said in a low, breathy voice: 'We're sinking . . .'

The colonel shook his head briskly and then, fully awake at last, he heard the roaring of the storm and felt the hull of the ship shuddering so violently that it seemed strange the lovers had not yet been thrown out of their bed.

'Pagan freaks!' he heard the captain roar somewhere above him. 'Bestial Sadducees, may Moloch have the lot of you, you vipers!'

On every side – from out on deck and in the lower cabins – he could hear the despairing shouts and weeping of terrified passengers.

Natalya Genrikhovna (yes, that was what her name was) said with profound conviction: 'This is the reward for my blasphemy – for sinning on the way to a holy monastery.' And she burst into pitiful, hopeless tears.

Lagrange patted her wet cheek reassuringly and got dressed quickly, military fashion.

'Where are you going?' his pilgrim lover asked in horror, but the door had already slammed shut behind him.

Half a minute later the colonel was out on the boat deck. Holding his cap on with his hand to prevent it from taking flight, he summed the situation up in a jiffy. The situation was decidedly of the water-closet variety.

The captain was dashing round the deckhouse, trying in vain to make half a dozen sailors, who were down on their knees praying, get to their feet. Felix Stanislavovich could make out some of the words: 'In Thy mercy do we seek refuge, Virgin Mother . . .' The wheel in the deckhouse was twirling this way and that as if it were drunk, and the steamship was hurtling on, ploughing headlong through the huge, towering waves on its way to God only knew where.

'Why have you abandoned the helm, Lord Nelson?' Lagrange yelled to the captain.

The captain swung his huge fist through the air. 'I can't turn it on my own! This ship's a heap of junk; it can't hold its course in a high sea! I told the archimandrite! This rust-bucket was made for taking young ladies on rides along the Neva, but this is the Blue Sea! We're being carried on to Devil's Rock; there are shoals there!'

At that very moment the steamship gave a sudden jerk and stopped dead in its tracks. The police chief and the captain were both flung against the wall of the deckhouse and they almost fell. The ship shifted a little and began slowly turning round its own axis.

'That's it, we're aground!' the captain shouted in despair. 'Unless we can turn the bow into the waves, in a quarter of an hour we'll heel over and that'll be the end – we'll be done for! Oh, those blockheaded peasants' – he raised a threatening hand in the direction of his praying crew – 'I should give them a good thrashing, but I can't, I've taken a vow of non-violence!'

Lagrange wrinkled up his brow in intense concentration. 'And if they get a good thrashing, then what?'

'Everyone heaves on the cable, and we can bring her round. But what point is there now!' The captain threw his hands up in the air, then went down on his knees himself and began intoning in a nasal voice: 'Accept, O Lord, the soul of Thy servant, whose hope is set in Thee, our God the Creator and Sustainer . . .'

'Heave on a cable?' the colonel asked brusquely. 'Why, we can get that done soon enough.'

He walked up to the nearest monk, leaned down over him and said emphatically: 'Right then, up you get, Father, or I'll knock your Eucharist round the back of your head.'

The praying man failed to heed the warning. Then Lagrange jerked him to his feet and in two ticks put his violent intention into effect. He left the holy man spitting out bloody saliva in amazement and immediately set about the next one. In less than a minute all the deckhands had been restored to a state of complete subordination.

'Now what is it we have to pull on?' Lagrange asked the captain, who was stunned by his efficient initiative.

And everything was all right; God is merciful; they all heaved together and swung the bow round in the right direction. No one was drowned.

As they were saying goodbye, with the ship already standing at the quayside in New Ararat, Brother Jonah (that was the captain's name) clung on to Felix Stanislavovich's hand for a long time with his own claw of iron.

'Give up your job,' Jonah boomed, gazing into the colonel's face with the bright-blue eyes that were set so strikingly in his own broad, coarse features. 'Come and be my first mate. We'll have a grand time sailing together. Things can get pretty interesting here on the Blue Sea – you've seen that for yourself. And you'll be saving your soul at the same time.'

'If it weren't for the female passengers,' said the colonel, stroking his moustache, because just at that moment Natalya

Genrikhovna had come out to the gangway, with a stern expression on her face and wearing a severe black headscarf instead of her frivolous hat. The porter following her down the slope was carrying an entire pyramid of suitcases, bags and boxes, managing somehow to balance this entire ancient-Egyptian structure on his head. The lady pilgrim halted, crossed herself with broad, sweeping gestures and bowed from the waist to this splendid town – or, rather, to its illuminated quayside, because it was evening and New Ararat itself could not be seen: the *St Basilisk* had been stuck on the shoal for half a day while it waited for the tug and had only reached the island very late, when it was already dark.

Lagrange bowed gallantly to his accomplice in romantic adventure, but she had evidently already prepared herself for spiritual enlightenment and purgation, and she simply strode on by, without even turning her head to look at the colonel.

Ah, women, Lagrange thought to himself with a smile of complete understanding and respect for the lady's redemptive state of mind.

'All right, Father, we'll meet again on my return voyage. I think that will be in two or three days; it's hardly going to be any longer than that. Since you believe that by then the weather will have sett—' he said, turning back to face the captain, and stopped short, because Brother Jonah was staring off into the darkness and his face had changed quite strikingly: it had become enraptured and strangely perplexed at the same time, as if the bold captain had heard the fateful song of a siren or spied a young maiden running over the waves – a sign to sailors that their sorrows will soon be forgotten and good fortune is coming their way.

Following the direction of the strangely silent captain's gaze, Lagrange did indeed see a supple young female silhouette, only it was not slipping along between the foaming crests of the waves but standing absolutely still under a lamp post on the quayside. The young lady raised a finger and beckoned the captain peremptorily, and he set off towards the gangway, moving like a sleepwalker, without even glancing round at the man who would not be his first mate.

Being curious both by constitution and by virtue of his job, as well as naturally passionate and attracted to female beauty, Felix Lagrange picked up his yellow travelling bag of patent pig's skin and set off, following stealthily in the captain's footsteps or – as sailors say – in his wake. Intuition and experience told the colonel that, with such a marvellous figure and assured bearing, the waiting woman's face was bound to be beautiful. But he had to make sure, did he not?

'Hello, Lidia Evgenievna,' Jonah boomed timidly as he approached the lady.

She reached out an imperious hand in a long grey glove – but not, as it turned out, to be kissed or shaken.

'Did you bring it?' she asked.

The captain took something very small out from inside the front of his monk's robe and laid it on the slim palm, but the colonel had no chance to see what it was, because at that moment the lady turned her face towards him and raised her veil with a gentle movement of her hand – evidently in order to take a better look at the stranger. Two seconds, or perhaps three, were all the time she needed, but that briefest possible period was also long enough for Lagrange to be struck dumb.

Oh! The chief of police clutched at his tight collar. Those immense, fathomless eyes, with that strange glimmer! Those hollows below the cheekbones! And that curve of the eyelashes! And that mournful hint of shadow beside those defenceless lips! Damnation!

Lagrange shouldered aside the bison-like Brother Jonah and raised his cap. 'My lady, I am here for the first time, I know nobody and nothing. I have come to pray at the holy places. Please help a man who has suffered terribly and advise me where the most heinous of sinners should direct his steps first. To the monastery? To Basilisk's Hermitage? Or, perhaps, to some shrine? And incidentally, allow me to introduce myself:

Felix Stanislavovich Lagrange, former cavalry colonel.'

The beautiful lady's face was already half-concealed again behind the light, flimsy gauze, but he saw her lovely mouth twist into a disdainful grimace below the edge of the veil. Paying absolutely no attention to the police chief's cunning and psychologically faultless approach, the young woman whom the captain had called Lidia Evgenievna put the small bundle in her handbag, turned gracefully on her heels and walked away. Brother Jonah heaved a deep sigh and Lagrange began blinking rapidly.

This is unheard of, thought Lagrange. First that nanny goat from St Petersburg hadn't even bothered to say goodbye to him, and now he had to suffer this humiliation!

Disconcerted, the colonel took a convenient little mirror out of the pocket of his waistcoat and checked to see whether anything off-putting could possibly have happened to his face – a sudden nervous eczema, a pimple or, God forbid, a string of snot dangling from his nose. But no, Felix Stanislavovich Lagrange's appearance was as handsome and agreeable as always: that manly chin and resolute mouth, that magnificent moustache and moderately proportioned, perfectly clean nose.

The colonel's mood was finally ruined completely by some short little idiot in a beret wearing gigantic dark glasses. First he blocked Lagrange's path, then fiddled with the frame of his clownish oculars for some reason and finally muttered: 'Perhaps this one? Red – that's good. But the head! Crimson! No, he won't do!' And then he cast any pretence at civil behaviour to the four winds and began waving his hands angrily at the colonel. 'Go on, get away! What are you standing there for? Numbskull! Blockhead!'

What a town!

The Noah's Ark Hotel, about which the colonel had heard from His Grace Mitrofanii, was good, except for the prices. It was really quite incredible: six roubles for a room! Naturally, the colonel had been provided with a certain sum from the

Bishop's personal fund, quite adequate to cover even such an extravagant billet as this one, but the chief of police decided to draw on the resourcefulness that was so essentially typical of his character. He signed the guest book, thereby indicating his firm intention to take a room for at least three days, and then, after finding fault with the view from the window, did not stay in the Ark at all, but sought out a more economical lodging for himself. Rooms in the Refuge of the Lowly cost the guests only a rouble a night – in other words, he would make a clear profit of five roubles a day. Father Mitrofanii wasn't the kind of individual to go delving into petty details, and if some day, when the accounts were being checked, the consistory inspector should go poking his nose into the matter, then there was the entry in the book: F. S. Lagrange had been at Noah's Ark and left his mark, and all the rest was sheer nonsensical conjecture.

The following morning, after spending the night in a tiny room with a view of the blank brick wall of the monastery's fish-smoking shed, the chief of police drank tea and immediately set out to reconnoitre. The information that His Grace had received from Alexei Stepanovich Lentochkin needed to be thoroughly checked, for it raised doubts about absolutely everything – and in the first place about the character of the emissary himself, whom the colonel knew slightly and personally thought of as a 'skitter-bug'. And now, as if it were not enough to be a frivolous and irresponsible character who ought to have been kept under police surveillance following the outrageous events in K——, Lentochkin had decided to go insane as well. But who could tell exactly when his reason had become clouded – perhaps he'd arrived in Ararat already totally barmy, and this entire business was a load of raving nonsense!

Lagrange armed himself with a map of New Ararat, divided the town up into squares and two hours later he had combed every one of them thoroughly, keeping his ears and his eyes open and jotting down anything worthy of interest in a special little notebook.

Beside a little fountain of medicinal water he found several respectable-looking pilgrims of a rather advanced age talking in low voices, discussing the night just past, which had turned out bright, although the moon was already well on the wane.

'He's been seen again,' a gentleman in a grey top hat with a mourning band of black crêpe was saying in a voice of hushed mystery. 'Psoi Timofeevich was watching through a telescope, from the Conception bell tower. He didn't risk going any closer.'

'And what did he see?' asked his listeners, moving closer.

'You know what he saw. *Him*. Walking along over the waves. Then the moon went behind a cloud, and when it came out again, he was gone ...' The narrator crossed himself and all the others followed his example.

'Psoi Tim.,' Lagrange jotted down, so that he could locate the eyewitness later and question him. However, in the course of his reconnaissance he heard talk of the previous night's water-walking not just once but quite a number of times. It turned out that, in addition to the unknown Psoi Timofeevich, several other bold fellows had been observing from a safe distance, and they had all seen something; one of them even asserted that the Black Monk had not walked, but *rushed* along above the water. Another had actually seen a pair of webbed wings, like a bat's, behind Basilisk's back (and we all know who has those).

In the Fatted Calf chop house the chief of police heard an argument between two elderly ladies about whether the buoy-keeper's wife and the infant she had miscarried ought to have been buried in hallowed ground, and whether the monastery cemetery might be defiled in some way as a result. After all, *he* had been seen by the fence two days ago – one of the women who made the communion bread had got such a terrible fright that she was still stuttering and stammering. They eventually agreed that the buoy-keeper's wife was all right, but the unchristened fruit of her womb ought to have been burned and the ashes scattered to the wind.

Later, some of the senior, grey-bearded brothers from the monastery were sitting on a bench in a square overlooking the lake and discoursing in low, decorous voices about how any doubtfulness in matters of faith led to wavering and temptation, and one old monk, to whom the others listened with particular attention, called for Basilisk's Hermitage to be closed for a while, in order to see whether the monastery's patron would calm down, and said that if, after all this, he stopped his rampaging, it meant that Outskirts Island was a bad place, possibly even cursed, and it should be left uninhabited.

The colonel stood behind the bench for a while, pretending to be admiring the starry sky (for basic astronomical reasons there was no moon that night). Then he walked on.

He heard all sorts of other things too. Apparently, Basilisk had been seen at night not only on the water and by the graveyard, but even in Ararat itself. Near the old Church of Ss. Kosma and Damian (which had burned down), on the monastery wall, in the Gethsemane Grotto. And every time the Black Monk appeared to anyone he had pointed a monitory finger in the direction of Outskirts Island.

And so it turned out that the 'skitter-bug's' exposition of the facts had not been a lie after all. Certain phenomena, the meaning and significance of which had yet to be established, had indeed occurred. The first task of the investigation could be considered complete.

Further investigative activities were planned in the following sequence: take testimony from Dr Korovin and interrogate the insane Lentochkin – provided, of course, that he had not already become totally inarticulate – and then, after that, having collected all the preliminary information, set up an ambush on Lenten Spit, arrest the phantom without fail and establish his true identity.

In short it was all not so very difficult. Felix Stanislavovich had unraveled more cunning tangles in his time.

The hour was already too late for a visit to the clinic, and the colonel turned back towards the Refuge of the Lowly, now not so much listening to the conversation of the people he met as simply observing the mores of New Ararat.

Lagrange definitely liked the town. A clean, decent, sober place. No tramps, no beggars (who would let them on to the steamer so that they could get to the island?), no one dressed in patched rags to insult the eye. Simple people, non-ecclesiastics – fishermen and artisans – dressed cleanly and respectably; women in white headscarves with round faces and well-nourished bodies. All the street lamps lit and working properly, pavements made of smoothly planed planks, good-quality roadways surfaced with oak tiles, without a single chip in them anywhere. You probably couldn't find such an exemplary town anywhere else in Russia.

The colonel also found New Ararat interesting for another, exclusively professional reason. As a settlement that had grown out of the suburbs of a monastery and was located on Church land, the town was not included in any administrative district; it was under the direct governance of the archimandrite and therefore lacked the usual administrative structures. From the provincial statistics Lagrange knew that there were never any crimes or untoward incidents of any kind on the islands. He wanted to find out how they managed here without any police or bureaucrats or firemen.

The answer to the last question was not long in coming – it was almost as if someone had deliberately decided to arrange a demonstration for the police chief of Zavolzhsk.

As he was walking across the town's main square, Lagrange heard a noise – people shouting and bells ringing frantically – and he saw some boys running somewhere as hard as they could, with intensely serious expressions on their faces. Drawing in the night air with a nose that was highly sensitive to extraordinary events, he caught the smell of smoke and realised there was a fire.

He followed the boys, lengthening his stride. After he turned one corner, and then another, there it was, blazing like a scarlet bush that had blossomed in the darkness – the Unleavened

Bread Pavilion, a wooden construction in a pseudo-classical style. It was blazing furiously, unstoppably – some sparks from the brazier must have found their way into the wrong place and the cook had failed to notice. There he was in his white cap and leather apron, and two kitchen boys with him, all running round the burning bush, waving their hands in the air. But there was no point in waving like that: the establishment was done for; there was no way to put the blaze out – the colonel could see that straight away, with his experienced eye. The danger was that it might leap across to the next house. Ah, what was needed here was a fire pump.

And then immediately, the very moment he had the thought, he heard a ringing of bells, a clatter of hooves and a cheerful jangling of harness from round the corner, and two teams of horses came hurtling out on to the street illuminated by the blaze.

The first was a dashing threesome of blacks drawing a carriage in which an extremely tall, emaciated monk was standing erect, wearing a purple skullcap and a pectoral cross with precious stones (the archimandrite himself, Lagrange immediately guessed from the cross). Hurrying along behind it came a team of six sorrel horses, drawing the very latest fire engine, far more modern than anything that had ever been seen in Zavolzhsk. Seated in state on this monster with gleaming copper flanks were seven monks in polished helmets, holding gaffs, picks and axes.

The reverend archimandrite leapt down on to the ground while his carriage was still moving and began issuing commands in stentorian tones, and the firemen carried them out with a precision that the colonel found simply delightful.

In an instant they had rolled out the tarpaulin hose and attached the pump to the water barrel. Then, first of all, they gave the next building, which had not yet caught fire, a good dousing, and only after that turned their attention to the Unleavened Bread Pavilion.

In less than half an hour a genuinely serious danger had

been completely eliminated. The monks dragged out the charred beams with their gaffs as the damp, subdued embers steamed; Father Vitalii, looking like a victorious general in the middle of a battlefield covered with bodies, was sternly interrogating the downcast cook.

A fine priest, well done there, Lagrange thought approvingly. A pity you didn't go in for a military career; you'd have made a fine regimental commander. Or something even higher than that – a divisional general.

His question about the police was answered too. While the fire was still blazing away, a platoon of strapping monks wearing cassocks shorter than usual, boots and white armbands, appeared out of nowhere. They were commanded by a sturdy-looking hieromonk who looked the very picture of a local police inspector. And hanging on his belt each of them had an impressive-looking rubber truncheon – that most humane invention from the New World, so excellent in absolutely every respect: hit some ruffian across the head with one of those things and it wouldn't knock his brains out, but it would certainly give him something to think about.

In a jiffy the police monks had surrounded the huge blaze and moved back the crowd, for which the truncheons were not required, since the idle onlookers heeded the appeals of the guardians of public order without a murmur.

Now Lagrange understood how order was maintained on the islands and why there were no crimes. If only I had some fine fellows like that, he thought enviously.

As he made his way back to his night's lodging through the quiet, rapidly emptying streets, he was visited by a fit of inspiration: under the impression of what he had just seen, the colonel conceived the thrilling idea of a total reorganisation of the gendarmerie and the police. If only he could establish some order of monastic knights, like the Teutonic Order, to provide a firm foundation for the entire structure of Russian statehood, Felix Lagrange thought fancifully. Accept only the very finest servicemen, devoted to the Emperor and his throne, make them take a vow of sobriety, unquestioning obedience to their commander, poverty and celibacy. A vow of total chastity was probably not required, but it would be a good thing if they were not married – it would avoid a lot of problems. Of course, police constables and even low-ranking officers would not necessarily have to be members of the association, but only those who had taken the vow would be able to rise to a high position in the hierarchy. Then the true kingdom of order and the dictatorship of rigorous legality would be made manifest on earth!

The colonel became so carried away with his great ideas, the clattering of his heels on the oak surface of the street was so sweet in his ears, that he almost walked right past the Refuge of the Lowly (which would not have been hard to do in the dark, for the sign offering rooms was lit only by the dim glow of the stars).

The helpful attendant tore himself way from his well-thumbed book, undoubtedly on some divine theme, cast a reproachful look at the guest over the top of his iron-rimmed spectacles, pursed his lips and said: 'You had a visitor.'

'What kind of visitor?' Lagrange asked in surprise.

'A female one,' the pious attendant informed him. 'In a large hat, with netting over her face. She did not look the prayerful type.'

It was her! thought Lagrange the moment he heard about the 'netting'. His manly heart began pounding rapidly.

But how had she found out where he was staying?

The police master immediately answered his own question. It was a small town, after all, there were not many hotels, and he was a fine figure of a man. It had not been hard to find him.

'Who is this lady, do you know?' he asked, leaning down towards the attendant. 'What is her name?'

He almost decided to put ten kopecks, or even fifteen, on the counter, but instead he hammered on it with his fist. 'Well!'

The attendant gave the remarkably tough fist a respectful look, the reproach in his eyes faded and he began speaking in a more respectful tone of voice. 'I don't know that, sir. I have come across her around the town, indeed, but this is the first time she has called in here, sir.'

That was easy to believe – what would such a beautiful and elegant lady be doing in a dive like this?

'But she did leave a note for you. Here it is, sir.'

The colonel grabbed the narrow sealed envelope and sniffed it. It had a heady, spicy aroma that provoked a languid palpitation in Felix Stanislavovich's nostrils.

There were only two words: 'Midnight. Sinai.'

What was the meaning?

His sweetly melting heart immediately gave the police chief his answer: it was the time and place of a rendezvous. Well, the time was clear enough – zero hundred hours precisely. But what was 'Sinai'? Apparently some kind of allegorical term.

Think, Lagrange told himself – after all, hadn't His Excellency the Governor told him: 'I am amazed, Colonel, at the speed with which your mind works'? But the most important thing was that there was only three-quarters of an hour left until midnight.

'Sinai, Sinai, where should I try ...' he sang pensively to himself, to the tune of the popular chansonette 'The Bouquet of Love'.

The attendant, still digesting the impression made by the police chief's fist, enquired solicitously: 'Is sir interested in seeing Sinai? There's no point, I'm afraid. There's no one there at this hour. St Nicholas's Chapel is closed; you won't be able to get in before tomorrow.'

It turned out that Sinai was not the holy mountain where Moses conversed with the Lord – or, rather, not only that mountain, but also one of the well-known sights of New Ararat, a steep cliff overlooking the lake, where people prayed to St Nicholas the Blessed.

The regal terseness of the note was impressive. No words like 'I will wait' or 'come', or even an explanation of what 'Sinai' was. Just an absolutely unshakable certainty that he would understand everything and immediately come running to the summons. And she had only looked at him for a moment. Oh, the goddess!

Having ascertained how to get to Sinai (it lay a little over a verst to the west of the monastery), Felix Lagrange set out for his midnight tryst.

The colonel's heart was fluttering in sweet anticipation, and if his rapture was clouded by anything at all, it was only shame for the wretched cheapness of the Refuge. On the way he thought up the idea of saying that he was travelling incognito, on a secret mission, but not going into the details. It would be even better without any details, more mysterious.

The streets of New Ararat were totally deserted by night. All the way to the monastery the only living creature that Lagrange met was a cat, and that was a black one. The colonel walked past the white walls of the monastery, past the church set above its gates, and came to the edge of the forest. For about a quarter of an hour he strode up a slight incline along a broad, well-trampled path, and then the trees parted to reveal a hill with a small, sharp-pointed tower standing on it, beyond which there was nothing but the black sky sprinkled with stars. Lagrange scampered up the hill with a brisk stride and stopped: immediately beyond the chapel the ground fell away in a steep cliff. At its bottom, far below, the water splashed against round boulders that gleamed wetly, and beyond that lay the boundless expanse of the Blue Lake, its immense surface shimmering and heaving.

Not a bad view, thought Lagrange, and he took off his cap – not out of reverence for the grandeur of nature, but so that his English headgear would not be blown off by the wind.

But where was she? Could she have played a joke on him after all?

No! A slim figure detached itself from the wooden beams

of the wall and slowly came towards him, the ostrich feathers above the crown of its hat swaying and the veil in front of its face floating in the air like a delicate cobweb. An arm in a long glove (not grey like the last time, but white) was raised to hold the brim of the hat. Those white, floating arms were the only things he could see clearly, for the mysterious lady's black dress merged into the darkness.

'You are strong, I realised that immediately from your face,' the young woman said without any preliminaries, speaking in a low, chesty voice that set Lagrange trembling strangely. 'There are so many weak men nowadays, your sex is degenerating. Soon, in a hundred or two hundred years, men will be indistinguishable from women. But you are not like that. Or am I mistaken?'

'No!' the chief of police exclaimed vehemently. 'You are not mistaken in the least! However ...'

'Did you say "however"?' the mysterious stranger interrupted him. 'Did I hear aright? That word is only used by weak men.'

Felix Stanislavovich Lagrange felt terribly afraid that now she would turn round and disappear into the darkness. 'I meant to say "wherever"; it was a mere slip of the tongue in my excitement,' he replied quickly. 'Wherever my guiding star leads, I follow, and it has led me to this island and told my heart that here it will finally meet the one it has been dreaming of all these long—'

'I have no time now for such meaningless pleasantries,' the beautiful creature interrupted him again, and the weak light of the stars reflected in her eyes was intensified many times over, setting them glimmering and sparkling. 'I am in a state of despair, and that is the only reason why I am appealing for help to a complete stranger. It is just that back there, on the quayside, I thought that ... that ...' Her magical voice trembled, and all the gallant tirades that Lagrange had prepared in advance were driven clean out of his head.

'What?' he whispered. 'Tell me, what did you think? In God's name!'

'. . . That you could save me,' she said in a barely audible voice, waving her hand smoothly through the air. The circle that her white arm traced through the blackness reminded Lagrange of a wounded bird flapping its wing.

Greatly agitated, he exclaimed: 'I do not know what misfortune has befallen you, but – on the word of an officer – I will do anything! Anything! Tell me about it.'

'And you will not be afraid?' she asked with a searching glance into his face. 'No, I see. You are brave.' Then she suddenly turned away, and there was her delicate white neck, right in front of the colonel's eyes.

Lagrange longed to press his lips against it, but he did not dare. So much for being brave.

'There is a certain man . . . a terrible man, a genuine monster. He is the curse of my entire life.' The young woman spoke slowly, as if every word cost her an effort. 'I will not tell you his name yet; I do not know you well enough . . . Just tell me if I can count on you.'

'No doubt about it,' the police chief replied, immediately feeling calmer. The villain, tormenting a poor girl – what an outrage! Just let Colonel Lagrange get his hands on him, and he'd turn meek as a lamb soon enough. 'Is he here, this man of yours? On the island?'

She glanced round at him, allowing Felix Stanislavovich to admire her sculpted profile. She nodded.

'Excellent, my lady. Tomorrow I have to see a local doctor, a certain Korovin, and one of his patients. But from the day after tomorrow I shall be entirely at your disposal.'

At that the young woman turned back towards Lagrange and shook her head, as if there was something she did not believe or doubted. There was a long pause (exactly how long it lasted is hard to say because, caught in that glittering gaze, Felix Lagrange froze rigid and lost all sense of time), then those tender lips moved and murmured: 'Well, then, so much the better.' She abruptly removed one glove and held out her hand to be kissed as if she were granting him a great gift.

The colonel pressed his lips against the fragrant, surprisingly hot skin. The physical contact set his head spinning as giddily as if he had drunk twenty litres of hot punch.

'Enough,' said the lady, and once again Lagrange did not dare disobey. He even took a step back. Would you believe it!

'What ... What is your name?' he asked, gasping for breath.

'Lidia Evgenievna,' she replied distractedly, taking a step towards the colonel and looking at something over his shoulder.

Lagrange swung round and realised that they were standing on the very edge of the sheer drop. One more step backwards and he would have gone tumbling over the cliff.

Lidia Evgenievna groaned: 'I can't stand it here any longer! There, that's where I want to go, there!' She made a sweeping gesture with her arm towards the lake, or perhaps the sky. Or perhaps the wide world that lay out of sight, beyond the dark waters?

The glove slid out of her fingers and went flying downwards, describing an elegant spiral through the air. Their shoulders touched as they leaned forward and saw it, a white spot fluttering in the wind on a rocky ledge down below.

Now will I have to climb down for it? the police chief thought with a shudder, but his fingers were already unbuttoning his jacket. 'Never mind,' Lagrange said in a cheerful voice, hoping that she would stop him. 'I'll get it back in a moment.'

'Yes, I was not mistaken in you,' said Lidia Evgenievna, nodding to herself, and after that the colonel was ready to fling himself downwards like a swallow, let alone climb. His fear had evaporated.

He began climbing down, clutching at roots and feeling for rocks and minute ledges with his feet. Twice he almost fell, but the Lord protected him. The fluttering strip of white came closer and closer. It was a good thing the glove hadn't flown all the way to the bottom but got caught halfway down the cliff.

There it was, the little darling!

Lagrange reached out for it and stuffed the silk trophy inside his shirt. It was quite a way back up to the cliff edge, but never mind: climbing up was easier than climbing down.

It was some time before he reached the top, filthy all over, soaked in sweat, wheezing and groaning. 'Here is your glove,' he declared triumphantly, gazing round.

But Lidia Evgenievna was no longer there on the hill. She had disappeared.

'So, you say you are his uncle on his mother's side?' Korovin asked, looking intently at Felix Stanislavovich but for some reason keeping his eyes on his visitor's neck. 'And it seems you work in a bank?'

Lagrange had already been hanging about in the doctor's office for almost an hour, and so far he had got absolutely nowhere. Donat Savvich Korovin had proved to be a difficult man to talk to and resistant to psychological manipulation according to the rules worked out by the finest minds of the Police Department and the Corps of Gendarmes.

Acting precisely in accordance with the very latest interrogational techniques, in the first minute of conversation the police chief had tried to establish the appropriate hierarchy and define who was the 'father' and who was the 'son'. Firmly clasping the lean, clean-shaven doctor's hand, he had looked him straight in the eye, smiled pleasantly and said: 'An excellent establishment you have here. I've heard about it, read about it, and I'm impressed. We are really fortunate that Alyosha has found himself in such reliable hands.'

He deliberately spoke the compliment in an extremely quiet voice, so that his opponent would immediately start listening carefully, mobilise the muscles of his lower neck and involuntarily lean his head forward. In addition, according to the law of mirror reflection, Korovin ought to have spoken loudly, straining his vocal cords. That would have successfully completed the first stage of the incipient relationship, with an initial psychological advantage already established.

But the doctor's skill in the art of discursive positioning was no less great than the police chief's. He must have had plenty of practice with his patients. If the conversation had not taken place on Dr Korovin's territory but in a certain severely appointed office with a portrait of His Majesty the Emperor on the wall, then the advantage would have lain with Felix Stanislavovich Lagrange, but as things were he was obliged to change tack.

When the doctor squeezed the colonel's hand energetically he did not turn his eyes away, and he replied to the complimentary words in a tone that was barely audible: 'Come now, the case is hardly fortunate.' Lagrange immediately realised that Donat Savvich would be no pushover. The host sat the visitor in an extremely comfortable but rather low armchair that was tilted backwards slightly, while he himself took a seat at the desk, so that the colonel was obliged to look up at Korovin from below. The doctor thereby immediately acquired the initiative in the dialogue.

'It's very good that you came so quickly. Well then, tell me everything as quickly as you can.'

'Tell you what?' Lagrange asked, confused.

'What? Why, your nephew's entire life, starting from the very beginning. When he began to hold his little head up, how old he was when he started to walk, at what age he stopped wetting the bed. And his family tree too, with all the details. The young man came to see me once, before the breakdown, and I questioned him on a preliminary basis, but I need to verify the data . . .'

Cursing himself for his unsuccessful choice of cover story, the police chief began fantasising as he answered a myriad idiotic questions. There was simply no way he could move on to the real business.

'Yes, I work in a bank,' he replied. 'The Volga–Caspian, as a senior clerk.'

'Aha, as a clerk,' Korovin said with a sigh, taking a *papirosa* out of a gold cigarette case with a monogram and blowing a crumb of tobacco off it. 'So where did you get that line on your neck? Just here. The kind that military men ... or gendarmes ... have from the constant contact of their uniform collars?'

Damn this doctor! He'd led him on, taunting him for the best part of an hour, forcing him to think up all sorts of rubbish about his adored nephew's chickenpox in childhood and his inclination to masturbate, when he'd already guessed everything!

Felix Stanislavovich Lagrange chuckled good-naturedly and shrugged, as if in acknowledgement of the doctor's perspicacity. Now he had to switch tactics yet again.

'All right, Mr Korovin. I can see there's no fooling you. I am not the clerk Chervyakov. I am Lagrange, the chief of police of Zavolzhsk. As you can understand, a man in my position would not become involved in trifling matters. I have come here on extremely important business, but in an unofficial capacity. This matter concerns—'

'A certain monk who goes strolling on the water at night and frightening foolish local inhabitants,' the shrewd doctor put in, blowing out a smoke ring. 'Please be so good as to inform me how this phantom has attracted the attention of your ubiquitous department? Surely you have not decided that St Baslisk is the notorious spectre with whom the Marxist gentlemen threaten the exploiters?'

Lagrange flushed scarlet, ready to put this jumped-up little doctor in his place; but just then something strange happened.

That day, unlike the one before, had turned out sunny and exceptionally warm, and therefore the windows of the doctor's office were open. The weather was quite splendid. Not a cloud in the sky, not a breath of wind, a vision of golden foliage and shimmering, trembling air. And yet one fold of the open blind suddenly swayed – only a tiny bit, but this anomaly did not escape the police chief's keen professional eye. Well, well,

Lagrange thought, making a mental note. Let's see what will happen next.

Keeping the interesting blind in sight out of the corner of his eye, he lowered his voice and said: 'No, Donat Savvich, the Black Monk in no way resembles the spectre of communism. But there is confusion and vacillation among the population, and that is already our concern.'

'So Lentochkin is a police agent?' Korovin asked with an astonished shake of his head. 'I would never have thought it. He's obviously a very capable young man and would have gone far. But now, alas, that is unlikely. I feel sorry for the boy; he is in a very, very bad way. And the worst thing of all is that I can't find a single medical precedent that is in any way similar. I have no idea how to go about treating him. And time is passing, precious time. He won't last very long as he is ...'

Finally the conversation had got round to the real point.

'What did he tell you about what happened that night?' the colonel asked, taking out his notebook.

The doctor shrugged: 'Nothing. Absolutely nothing at all. He was in no fit state to tell me anything.'

He finds me disagreeable, Lagrange noted to himself, so disagreeable that he feels no need to hide the fact ... Never mind, my dear fellow, one way or another you will tell me, there's no escaping it.

He didn't say anything out loud, but merely tapped his pencil against the paper expressively, as if to say: Carry on, I'm listening.

'Last Tuesday – that is, exactly a week ago – the doorkeeper woke me at dawn. Your "nephew" was trying to force his way into the house. He was dishevelled and scratched, with wild, staring eyes, and entirely naked.'

'How's that?' Lagrange said, unable to believe his ears. 'Entirely naked. And he walked across the island like that?'

'As naked as it is possible to be. He kept repeating the same thing over and over again: "*Credo, credo, Domine!*" Since he had already been to see me before, when ...'

The colonel nodded impatiently: I know, I know, go on.

'Ah, so that's it?' the doctor said, scratching the bridge of his nose. 'Hmm, so he had managed to report to you about his first ... Anyway, seeing the state he was in, I ordered him to be let in. But it was quite impossible. He was shouting and struggling; two orderlies couldn't drag him into the hallway. They tried putting a blanket over him – it was cold, after all – but the result was the same: he struggled and tore it off himself. In the heat of the moment they put a straitjacket on him, but he immediately started having such terrible convulsions that I ordered it to be taken off. I am opposed to forcible means of treatment in general. It took a while, quite a while, before I realised ...'

Donat Savvich Korovin removed his spectacles, wiped the lenses unhurriedly and then continued with his story.

'Well then. It took me a while to realise that I was dealing with an acute case of claustrophobia, when the patient is not only afraid of any enclosed spaces but cannot even tolerate any clothing ... I tell you, it's a very rare case; I have never come across one like it either in the textbooks or in articles. And so I kept your "nephew" here for observation. In any case, it seems to me quite impossible to send him anywhere else. In the first place, he will catch cold. And from the point of view of public morality, how can you transport someone in a state of nakedness? The pilgrims would be shocked and outraged, and the archimandrite would be none too pleased with me either.'

Colonel Lagrange wrinkled up his forehead as he digested this astonishing information. The police chief had completely stopped thinking about the restless fold of the blind (which, in any case, was no longer moving).

'But wait, Doctor ... Where are you keeping him? Outside in the open air, naked?'

Korovin gave a smug, condescending laugh and stood up. 'Come with me, Mr Senior Clerk, and you'll see for yourself.'

*

Dr Korovin's clinic was located in the very best spot on the island of Canaan, on a gentle, forested hill that rose to the north of the town. From the very beginning Lagrange had been surprised by the absence of any fences or gates. A pathway paved with bright-yellow brick wound between small meadows and groves of trees, where small houses built in a wide variety of different styles stood with some distance between them: houses built of stone, of logs, of boards; black, white and multi-coloured; with glass walls and completely without windows; with little towers and Mohammedan flat roofs – in short, a quite incredible sight. This peculiar settlement reminded the police chief somewhat of a picture from the book *The Town in the Snuffbox*, of which little Felix had been very fond in his childhood; but almost forty years had passed since then, and Lagrange's tastes had changed greatly in the meantime.

His first impression, before he had actually met Dr Korovin, had been that the care of the insane was entrusted to an even greater madman. What could the provincial guardians of order be thinking of?

But now, as he followed the doctor deeper into the hospital grounds, the colonel no longer paid any attention to the little dolls' houses; he was too busy keeping an eye on the thick bushes of hawthorn that ran along both sides of the pathway. Someone was creeping along on just behind them, and none too skilfully either, with a rustle of fallen leaves and crunching of twigs. In two bounds Lagrange could have been on the other side of that living wall and collared the heavy-footed fellow, but he decided not to hurry. They turned on to a narrow path flanked by glass hothouses containing vegetable beds, flowers and fruit trees.

Now that is praiseworthy, the colonel thought in approval, looking through the glass walls at the strawberries and oranges and even pineapples. Apparently this Korovin knew how to live in style.

The doctor halted beside the central conservatory, which looked like an ocean mirage – a lush, green tropical island soaring up above the dreary northern waters. 'There,' he said, pointing. 'Nine hundred square *sazhens* of palms, banana trees, magnolias and orchids. It cost me a hundred and forty thousand. But it's a genuine Garden of Eden.'

At this Lagrange's patience finally snapped. 'Listen here, you doctor-heal-thyself!' he exclaimed, rolling his eyes menacingly. 'Do you think I came here to admire your pretty flowers? Enough of this beating around the bush! Where's Lentochkin?'

When he was furious, Felix Stanislavovich Lagrange looked frightening. Even those hardened types, the port police constables, shivered in their shoes. But Dr Korovin didn't so much as turn a hair. 'Where is he? In there, under the glass sky, in paradise.' He pointed to the conservatory. 'He hid in there himself, the very first day. It's the only possible place for him. It's warm, and you can't see any walls or roof. If he gets hungry, he can eat some fruit or other. And there's water too, a mains pipe. You wanted to see him? Please be my guest. Only he avoids people and he might hide – it's a real jungle in there.'

'That's all right, we'll find him,' the police chief promised confidently, jerking open the door and striding into the damp, sticky heat that immediately soaked his collar through and sent a ticklish trickle of sweat running down his back.

He set off at a trot along the central passage, turning his head to the right and the left. Dr Korovin immediately fell behind.

Aha! Behind a plant with broad, spreading leaves, the name of which the colonel did not know – poisonous green, with predatory-looking red buds – he saw something flesh-coloured move.

'Alexei Stepanovich!' the chief of police called out. 'Mr Lentochkin! Wait!'

It was pointless. The broad shiny leaves swayed and he heard the light rustle of feet running away.

'Doctor, you go left, and I'll go right!' Lagrange commanded and went dashing in pursuit. He stumbled over a thick stem trailing across the ground and fell full length. And that helped – from the ground Felix Stanislavovich caught sight of the tip of a foot, protruding from behind the hairy trunk of a palm tree – no more than twelve paces away. So that's where you're hiding, is it, my little darling?

The colonel stood up, dusted off his elbows and knees and shouted: 'All right, then, Donat Savvich. If he doesn't want to, then never mind.' He moved slowly through the undergrowth, then leapt to one side and caught hold of a naked man by the shoulders.

It was him, all right, the nobleman Alexei Stepanovich Lentochkin, twenty-three years of age – no doubt about it. Wavy chestnut hair, blue eyes (staring wildly just at the moment), oval face, slim build, height two *arshins* and eight *vershoks*.

'All right, all right, don't tremble like that,' the chief of police said reassuringly to the naked madman. 'I've come from Bishop Mitrofanii to help you.'

The boy didn't struggle, he stood there quietly, but he was shuddering terribly.

'I'll just give him an injection so that he won't get violent,' Lagrange heard the doctor's voice say.

Dr Korovin turned out to have a flat metal box in his pocket. In thirty seconds the doctor had assembled a syringe and loaded it with colourless liquid; but Alyosha suddenly gave a pitiful groan and fell on the police chief's chest. He did not seem to be inclined to violence.

'I see I was mistaken and you really are his favourite uncle,' Korovin observed coolly, putting the loaded syringe away in his pocket.

'To hell with you,' said Lagrange, waving him away and stroking the curly back of the madman's head awkwardly. 'Ai-ai-ai, what a nasty fright those bad bogeymen gave us; but we'll get them back. We'll show them what for. I'll catch that Basilisk in a couple of shakes; he won't pull any tricks on me. Just let him show his face and he's done for.'

Lentochkin was still sobbing, but no longer as convulsively as before.

The colonel moved away a little and asked in a cajoling voice: 'What was it that happened, then? You know, that night? Tell me, don't be afraid.'

'Sh-sh-sh,' the youth hissed, pressing his finger to his lips. 'He'll hear.'

'Who, the Black Monk? He won't hear a thing. He sleeps during the day,' Felix Stanislavovich told him, delighted at this articulate response. 'You tell me quietly and he won't wake up.'

With a frightened glance at Korovin, the madman pressed himself up against Lagrange and whispered in his ear: 'The cross – it isn't a cross, quite the opposite. Crrrr across the glass, the walls trrrr, the ceiling sssssh, and you can't run away. The door's too small, you can't get through, and the windows are all teeny-weeny, like this.' He demonstrated with his fingers. 'Up jumps the house and hops about, the little hut on chicken legs.' Lentochkin gave a thin little laugh, but his face was immediately distorted in terror. 'There's no air! No space! Aaagh!'

He started trembling all over and began muttering: '*Credo, Domine, credo, credo, credo, credo, credo, credo, credo, credo, credo* . . .' He repeated the Latin word a hundred or even two hundred times, and it was clear that he was not going to stop soon.

Lagrange grabbed hold of the boy by the shoulders and gave him a good shaking. 'That's enough! Tell me the rest!'

'There's nothing to tell,' Lentochkin suddenly declared in a calm, rational voice. 'You go there, to the hut on chicken legs. At midnight. And you'll see it all for yourself. Only make sure you don't get squeezed, or your heart will burst. Bang – and splashes all over the place.' He folded over double, burst into laughter and started repeating a different word: 'Bang! Bang! Bang!'

'That's enough,' Dr Korovin declared sternly. 'You have an agitating effect on him, and he's weak enough as it is.'

Lagrange wiped the sweat off his neck with a handkerchief. 'What hut is that? What is he talking about?'

'I have no idea. Perfectly ordinary ravings,' the doctor replied dryly, and deftly jabbed the needle into his patient's buttock.

Lentochkin almost immediately stopped laughing, squatted down and yawned.

'That's all; let's go,' said Korovin, tugging on the colonel's sleeve. 'He'll go to sleep now.'

Lagrange left the conservatory in a state of profound thoughtfulness. It was clear that he could not expect any help from the 'skitter-bug'. His Grace's emissary had become a total and complete idiot. But never mind, he'd manage somehow on his own. It was a clear day, and that meant it would be a bright night. There would be a new moon, just right for the Black Monk. Starting in the evening he would lie in ambush on that – what was it called? – Lenten Spit. And catch the fellow red-handed just as soon as he put in an appearance. What did it matter if he was a ghost? The year before last, when Felix Stanislavovich was still in his old job in the Pri-vislensky region, he had personally arrested Stas the Blood-sucker, the Vampire of Lublin himself. He'd been a sly fellow, that monster, but Lagrange had nabbed him before he could say knife.

But before going back to Ararat, he had another piece of business to finish.

As he emerged from the tropics into the delightful cool of the north, he stood for about half a minute without moving at all, then went dashing into the bushes and dragged someone out of them, kicking and struggling, the same spy who had been stalking him along the pathway; and he must have been the person listening under the window as well – it couldn't have been anyone else.

It turned out that he already knew him. Once you'd seen someone like that you wouldn't forget them: a black beret, check raincoat, violet spectacles, bushy beard. That insolent type from the quayside.

'Who are you?' the colonel roared. 'Why were you spying?'

'We have to! Definitely! About everything!' the short little man jabbered, swallowing words and entire chunks of sentences, so that there was no discernible general sense in what he said. 'I heard! The powers that be! Sacred duty! But God knows how! There's death here, and now them. And no one, not a single person. Deaf, blind, crimson!'

'Sergei Nikolaevich, dear fellow, do calm down,' Korovin said affectionately to the shouting man. 'You'll have convulsions again. This gentleman came to see the young man who lives in the conservatory. And what did you imagine?' Then he explained to the colonel in a low voice: 'Another patient of mine, Sergei Nikolaevich Lampier. A highly talented physicist. But extremely eccentric.'

'I should say he is,' Lagrange muttered, but his iron fingers opened and released his prisoner. 'A total lunatic, and still wandering around at large. You have some damn strange ways of doing things here.'

The mentally unbalanced physicist clasped his hands together imploringly and exclaimed: 'A terrible error! I thought I was the only one! But it's not me! It's someone else! Something's wrong here! Everything's wrong! But that's not important! I need to go that way!' And he jabbed his finger off to one side. 'I need a Commission. To Paris! Masha and Toto! Let them come here! They'll see, they'll understand! Tell them all! Death! And there'll be more!'

That did it. Lagrange was sick to death of associating with idiots. He tactlessly twirled his forefinger beside his temple and walked away, but the madman still would not calm down. He overtook the colonel, ran in front of him, grabbed hold of his ludicrous spectacles with both hands and groaned in despair: 'A crimson head, crimson! Hopeless!"

In order not to waste time following the wandering course of the pathway between the low hills, the chief of police set off directly towards the monastery bell tower, the golden dome of which he could see glittering above the tree tops. He walked through a thin copse of trees, then an open meadow, then through some yellow-and-red bushes, which were followed by another meadow and then the final descent from the high ground to the plain. And so he had an excellent view of the town, the monastery, almost half of the island and the open expanse of the lake into the bargain.

There was someone sitting in an open arbour at the edge of the meadow, wearing a straw hat and a short little jacket. When he heard resolute footsteps behind him, this stranger cried out in fright and hastily covered something lying on the bench beside him with his coat.

This hasty gesture was very familiar to Lagrange from his police work. It was the way a thief caught red-handed conceals his stolen goods. He need have no hesitation in grabbing this fellow by the collar and insisting that he turn out his pockets – something incriminating was absolutely sure to turn up.

The furtive subject glanced round at the colonel and gave a gentle smile of embarrassment. 'I beg your pardon, I thought it was ... someone quite different. Ah, how awkward it would have been!'

At this point he noticed Felix Stanislavovich's glance of professional suspicion and laughed quietly. 'No doubt you thought that I'd hidden a murder weapon here, or something equally terrible. No, sir, it's a book.' And he willingly raised his coat to reveal the book beneath it: a rather thick one, in a brown-leather binding. There were only two options: either it was something obscene, or it was political. Otherwise, why hide it?

But the police chief had no time for prohibited reading matter now. 'What concern is that of mine?' he growled irritably. 'And what way is that to carry on, pestering a stranger with all sorts of nonsense ...' And he walked on to go down the path towards the town.

The talkative gentleman said to his back: 'Donat Savvich

reproaches me too, for being too importunate and pestering people. I'm sorry.'

There was not a hint of offence in the voice that pronounced those words. Lagrange stopped dead in his tracks, not because he regretted having been rude but at the sound of the doctor's name.

The colonel went back to the arbour and took a closer look at the stranger. He noted the trusting gaze of the wide blue eyes, the soft line of the lips, the childishly naïve inclination of the head with its light-coloured hair.

'You must be one of Mr Korovin's patients, then?' the chief of police asked in an extremely polite manner.

'No,' the blond man replied, again without taking the slightest offence. 'I am perfectly well now. But I used to be in Dr Korovin's care. He still keeps an eye on me even now. Gives me advice, supervises my reading. I am terribly uneducated; I've never really studied anything properly anywhere.'

Lagrange seemed to have been presented with a convenient opportunity to gather additional information about the acerbic doctor. It was clear straight away that this sissy wouldn't conceal a thing, but just come straight out with whatever he was asked for.

'Would you permit me to sit here with you for a while?' asked Lagrange, walking up the step. 'The view here is so very fine.'

'Yes, it is very fine; that's why I like it here. Just recently, when the air was particularly clear, do you know what thought occurred to me?' The light-haired man moved over to make way and laughed again. 'Put some arrant, hardened atheist here, one of those who are always demanding scientific proof of the existence of God, and show that sceptic the island and the lake. There's the proof, and no others are needed. Do you agree with me?'

Lagrange immediately expressed his passionate agreement, trying to figure out how he could exchange this theme for a more productive subject; but the verbose stranger appeared to have his own plans for the forthcoming conversation.

'Your joining me here is most timely. I have read a lot of important things in a certain novel, and I would really like to share my thoughts with someone. And I have a lot of questions too. You have a clever, energetic face. I can see straight away that you have firm opinions about everything. Tell me: which human crime do you regard as the most monstrous of all?'

After thinking for a moment and recalling the provisions of the criminal code, the police chief replied: 'State treason.'

'Oh, how similar our ways of thinking are! Just imagine, I also think there can be nothing worse than betrayal! That is, I don't mean the betrayal of a state (although breaking an oath is not a good thing, of course), but the betrayal of one person by another. Especially if someone weak has put his total trust in you. To pervert a child who has idolised you and lived only for you – that is really terrible. Or to mock some wretched creature who is oppressed by everyone and weak-minded and has believed in no one but you in the whole world. To violate trust or love must surely be worse than murder, even though it is not punished by the law. For it is the destruction of your own soul! What do you think about that?'

Lagrange wrinkled up his forehead and replied at length: 'Well, for the perversion of juveniles the law prescribes hard labour, but as far as the other everyday forms of treachery are concerned, things are a little more complicated, unless, of course, it's a matter of financial fraud. Many people, especially men, do not regard unfaithfulness in marriage as a sin at all. But even among our sex there are exceptions,' he said, brightening up as he recalled a certain spicy story. 'I had a classmate by the name of Bulkin. A more virtuous man you could never hope to meet, he absolutely adored his wife. After classes were over, all of our group would go off to Ligovka, to a bawdy house, but he would always go home – that's the kind of eccentric he was. When we graduated, he was appointed to the Baltic Squadron – the secret service, naturally.' The colonel hesitated, afraid that he had given himself away, and glanced anxiously at the other man. He need not have worried – there was not the slightest hint of a cloud on his countenance; he was still gazing at Lagrange with exactly the same calm interest as before. 'Yes, well. Naturally, then the voyages began, sometimes long ones, for months at a time. In port all the officers dashed straight to the bordello, but Bulkin sat in his cabin, showering kisses on a medallion with a portrait of his wife. He spent about a year sailing like that until he decided he'd suffered enough torment and found an excellent compromise.'

'Yes?' the blond man asked. 'But I didn't think any compromise was possible in such a case.'

'Bulkin was a bright one! Always first in our class when it came to analytical tasks!' Felix Stanislavovich exclaimed with an admiring shake of his head. 'And this is what he thought up. He found a theatre-design artist and commissioned a papier-mâché mask that was exactly like his adored wife's face; he even glued a golden-haired wig on to it. Now when they arrived in port, Bulkin was the very first into the whorehouse. He took some slag – begging your pardon – who had a face as ugly as sin (so she'd be cheaper, naturally), put the mask of his wife on her, and after that his conscience was absolutely clear. He used to say: "Perhaps I am being unfaithful in body, but not in spirit, not in the least." And he was right! In any case, his comrades used to respect him for it.'

The story Lagrange had told seemed to present the other man with some difficulty. He began blinking his sheep's eyes and spread his hands.

'Yes, I suppose that is not being entirely unfaithful ... although I don't understand very much about that kind of love ...'

All his life Felix Stanislavovich Lagrange had never been able to stand sentimental milksops, but for some reason he had taken a real liking to this eccentric. Indeed, he liked the fellow so much that, incredible as it seemed, he even lost all desire to winkle anything out of him by some devious deception. The colonel was quite amazed at himself.

Instead of interrogating the ideal informant about his suspect (for Dr Korovin had, after all, been noted down by Colonel Lagrange for special attention), the police chief suddenly began talking in a manner that was quite untypical of him.

'Tell me, sir, this is only my second day on the island … That is, strictly speaking, my first, since I arrived yesterday evening … It's a strange place, quite unlike any other. Whatever you take hold of, whatever you look at, it just evaporates, like mist. Have you been here long?'

'More than two years.'

'So you're used to it. Tell, quite frankly and clearly, what do you think about all this?'

The colonel accompanied the last two words, so indefinite and even rather strange for a man used to clear, concise formulations, with an equally vague gesture that seemed to take in the monastery, the town, the lake and something else as well.

Nonetheless, the other man understood him perfectly well.

'You mean the Black Monk?'

'Yes. Do you believe in him?'

'That many people have actually seen him? I do believe that, without the slightest doubt. It is enough to look into the eyes of the people who tell you about it. They are not lying; I can sense a lie immediately. It's a different question whether they have seen something that really exists, or only what they have been shown …'

'Been shown by whom?' Lagrange asked cautiously.

'Well, I don't know. We all – every one of us – only see what we are shown. Many things that really do exist, and which other people see, we do not; but then sometimes we are presented with something that is intended for our eyes only. Not even sometimes; it happens quite often. I used to have visions almost every day. As I now understand, that was what my illness consisted of. When someone is shown what is intended for his eyes only too often, that is probably what constitutes insanity.'

Oh brother, I can see I won't get far with you, the colonel thought in exasperation. It was time to put an end to the useless conversation – he'd wasted almost half the day already as it was. In order to garner at least something useful from this unnecessary meeting, he asked: 'Could you tell me which way Lenten Spit lies from here, where the phantom is seen most often?'

The blond man got up politely, walked across to the railings of the arbour and began showing him: 'You see the edge of the town? Beyond it there's a large field, then the fishing-boat cemetery – you can see the masts sticking up. To the left there's a white abandoned lighthouse. That reddish brown cone is the Farewell Chapel, where they hold the hermits' funeral services. And beyond that there's a narrow strip of land reaching out into the water, like a finger pointing to the island. That island is the hermitage, and the strip of land is Lenten Spit. Over there, between the chapel and the buoy-keeper's hut.'

'Hut?' the colonel asked with a frown. Could that be the one that Lentochkin had been talking about?

'Yes. Where the terrible event took place. In fact two terrible events. First with the buoy-keeper's wife, and then with that young man who came running to the clinic naked. It was there, in that hut, that he lost his reason.'

The police chief glared hard at the local man. 'How do you know it was precisely there?'

The other man turned towards him, fluttering his light eye-lashes. 'Why, it's clear. In the morning they found his clothes in the hut, all neatly folded. On a bench. And his shoes and his hat. So he must have arrived there dressed decently, as normal, and run out already totally insane, and he clearly ran straight to Donat Savvich's house without even stopping.'

It was only then that the colonel remembered Alexei Lentochkin's final letter, in which the young man had indeed mentioned the buoy-keeper's cottage and his intention of going there that night. Lagrange, however, had read that part inattentively, since it had been obvious that, by the time of his third report, Lentochkin was already as mad as a hatter and what he had written was obviously nonsense.

But now it had turned out not to be quite such absolute nonsense at all. That is, as far as the mysticism and the incantations were concerned, of course it was all wild, delirious nonsense. What was that he had said today? 'You go there, to the hut on chicken legs. At midnight. And you'll see everything for yourself. Only take care not to get squeezed, or your heart will burst.' Well, let's assume the final phrase could be attributed to his insanity, but as far as the place and the time were concerned, there was certainly something worth thinking about here.

And at that moment a certain idea began stirring in the police chief's head.

That night the plan of action had matured and taken such a perfectly rational and simple form that it had completely displaced the plan of going to Lenten Spit and standing on guard there, waiting for the rampaging Basilisk.

The final change in Lagrange's intentions had been facilitated by yet another significant circumstance: as the sun set and darkness fell over the island, it had become clear that the new moon was still as yet too small and slim, no more than a nail-paring in the sky, and it would not be able to illuminate Lenten Spit properly, which meant there was no point in lying in ambush there.

But the dilapidated hut with the eight-pointed cross scratched on the window was a different matter (when he went back to his room, the colonel had read the letter very closely indeed and committed all the details to memory). Lagrange had learned from the locals that the night when the 'skitter-bug' had visited the spot, with such sad consequences for himself, had been moonless, but that had not prevented whatever had happened from happening. So the absence of a moon was no hindrance to the business in hand.

He would arrive there exactly at midnight, as the madman

had written, pronounce the incantation and see what would happen this time. That, basically, was the entire plan.

Any other man might have been afraid to plunge headlong into such a murky enterprise with nothing to guide him in the regulations and the standing instructions, but not Colonel Felix Stanislavovich Lagrange.

As the chief of police approached the miserable hut in the pitch darkness (it was precisely five minutes to midnight), his heart was beating calmly, his hands were steady and his step was firm.

But it was not a pleasant place to be: an eagle owl hooted in the distant forest and the surface of the water seemed to give off a draught of cold, damp air and fear. Apart from that there was only an absolute, dead silence, and he could hear the pounding of his own living blood as loudly as if he had stopped his ears. Lagrange's eyes, already accustomed to the darkness, made out the crooked outline of the little log house ahead of him, and it seemed incredible to the colonel that only a few days ago a young and, no doubt, happy married couple had lived here, occupying themselves with the ordinary business of life as they waited for their first child. In this dead place nothing warm or joyful could possibly happen.

The colonel shuddered – he suddenly felt chilly, despite the woollen sweater he had put on under his jacket and waistcoat. Just in case (in case of what, damn it?), he took his Smith and Wesson out from under his arm and stuck it into his belt.

The door had been nailed shut with two boards set in a cross. The chief of police set his fingers in the crack, tugged with all his might and almost fell over, so easily did the nails slide out of the rotten wood. The silence was broken by a sickening crack and a creak, and some large bird launched itself off the roof, flapping its wings frantically.

Lagrange spotted the window immediately: a grey square against the blackness.

So, he had to go up to it, cross himself and say: 'Come, blessed spirit, to the trace that you have left, according to the agreement between Gabriel and the Evil One.' Holy Moses, he'd better not get it mixed up.

Felix Stanislavovich held out his hands and cautiously moved forward. His fingers caught the edge of something wooden, something big. A chest? A crate?

THE THIRD EXPEDITION
The Adventures of the Man of Intelligence

The news of Colonel Lagrange's suicide did not reach Zavolzhsk until three days after the terrible event itself, since there was no telegraph on the island and all messages, even those that were extremely urgent, were still delivered in the old manner – by post or special messenger.

The letters that the father superior addressed to the lay and clerical leaders of the province provided only the briefest of information on the circumstances of the fatal drama. The police chief's body had been discovered in an abandoned house previously occupied by the family of a buoy-keeper, who only a few days earlier had also laid hands on himself. But whereas on that occasion it had been possible to understand the reason for this insane and – from the viewpoint of the Church – absolutely unforgivable act, the archimandrite did not undertake to discuss, even provisionally, the reasons that had driven the chief of police to take the fatal step. He laid especial emphasis on the fact that he had not been aware of the arrival in New Ararat of a high-ranking police official (the visitor's status had only been discovered *post mortem*, during the search of his hotel room and possessions), and he requested, nay, demanded an explanation from the Governor.

The only details of the incident contained in the letter were as follows. The colonel had committed suicide by shooting himself in the chest with a revolver. There was, unfortunately, absolutely no doubt that it had indeed been suicide: the dead man had been found clutching a revolver with one bullet missing from its chamber. The lethal shot had struck the heart itself, tearing the vital organ apart, and death appeared to have been instantaneous.

The letter to Governor von Haggenau concluded at this point, but the epistle to the Bishop continued at some considerable length. The archimandrite drew His Grace's attention to the possible consequences of this shameful occurrence for the peace, calm and reputation of the holy monastery, which had already been darkened by all sorts of alarming rumours (this reserved expression was no doubt a reference to the notorious appearances of the Black Monk). By the merciful providence of God, the father superior wrote, only a small number of people knew about this misfortune: the sexton who had found the body, three of the monastery's peace-keepers (that was what Ararat's police monks were called) and the attendant at the hotel where the suicide had been staying. A vow of silence had been extracted from all of them, but even so it was doubtful whether it would be possible to keep the scandalous news entirely secret from the local inhabitants and the pilgrims. Father Vitalii's letter concluded with the words: '... I am even concerned that this formerly serene island might find itself dubbed – as proud Albion once was – "the island of suicides", for in only a short space of time the most heinous of all the mortal sins has been committed here twice.'

The Bishop blamed himself entirely for the tragedy. Suddenly aged and stooping, he told his trusted advisers: 'This is all the result of my pride and self-assurance. I listened to no one, but decided as I wanted, and not just once, but twice. First I destroyed Alyosha, and now Lagrange. And the most unbearable thing is that I have not only condemned their mortal bodies to profanation, but also their immortal souls. The soul of the first has been struck down with a grave illness, and the second has destroyed his own soul utterly. It is a hundred times worse than mere death ... I was mistaken, cruelly mistaken. I thought that a military man, with his straightforward approach and lack of fantasy, could not be affected by spiritual despair and mystical horror. But I failed to take account of the fact that when people of that character encounter phenomena that completely violate their simple, clear picture of the world, they do not bend, but break. You were right, my daughter, a thousand times right, in what you said to me about the Gordian Knot. Evidently our colonel came across a knot that he was not capable of untying. His natural pride would not permit him to retreat and so he swung his sword at the knot from the shoulder. And the name of that Gordian Knot was the world of God . . .'

At this point His Grace could contain himself no longer, and he began to cry, but since his usual presence of character did not incline him to tears – indeed, he entirely lacked the gift of weeping – the sounds that he produced were rather inelegant: first a dull groan mingled with a throaty wheezing, followed by a lengthy trumpeting of his nose into a handkerchief. But the very awkwardness of this keening for a lost soul affected the others present more powerfully than any loud sobbing: Matvei Bentsionovich began blinking rapidly and also pulled out a quite immense handkerchief, while Sister Pelagia more than made up for male niggardliness in the matter of weeping by setting up a terrible wail and dissolving in tears.

The Bishop was the first to recover his strength of mind. 'I shall pray for Felix Stanislavovich's soul. Alone, in my chapel. It is forbidden to pray for a suicide in the churches. Though he himself may have rejected God and there can be no forgiveness for him, he is still worthy of kind remembrance in prayer.'

'No forgiveness?' Pelagia sobbed. 'Not for any single suicide? Never-ever, not even after a thousand years? Can you be absolutely certain of that, Your Grace?'

'Who am I to say? That has been the Church's teaching since time immemorial.'

The nun dried her white face with its sprinkling of pale freckles and knitted her brows in intense concentration. 'But what if the burden of life has proved far more than someone can bear? If someone has an unbearable grief, or an excruciatingly painful illness, or he is tortured by merciless brutes trying to force him to commit treason? Is there no forgiveness for these people either?'

'No,' Mitrofanii replied sternly. 'And your questions come from too little faith. The Lord knows which tests each of us can bear and he does not test a single soul beyond its measure. If he sends terrible torment, it means that soul is especially strong, and strength must be tested. Such are all the holy martyrs. None of them was afraid of torture, and they did not lay hands on themselves.'

'But the holy saints are only one in a million. And then, what shall we say of those who have doomed themselves not out of fear or weakness, but for the sake of others? I remember you reading an article in the newspaper about the captain of a steamship who gave his place in the lifeboat to someone else when the ship was wrecked, and because of that he went to the bottom with the vessel. You admired his action and praised him.'

Berdichevsky sighed with a martyred air, knowing in advance how this discussion that had flared up so inopportunely would end. Pelagia would provoke His Grace's annoyance with her questions and arguments; there would be a serious quarrel and precious time would be wasted, when they ought to be talking about the business in hand.

'I did admire him – as a citizen of this earthly world; but as a cleric who is obliged to take care for the immortality of the soul, I condemn him and grieve for him.'

'I see,' said the nun, flashing a keen glance at the Bishop, and then she struck him a blow that the English would have called unsporting. 'Then what of Ivan Susanin, who voluntarily exposed himself to the Polish sabres in order to save our most august royal dynasty – do you condemn him too?'

Beginning to grow angry, Mitrofanii grabbed hold of his beard with his fingers. 'Perhaps Ivan Susanin hoped that at the last moment he would be able to escape from his enemies into the forest. If there is hope, even the very tiniest, then it is not suicide. When soldiers go into a dangerous attack, even when, as people say, they go "to certain death", every one of them is still hoping for a miracle and praying to God for one. Hope makes all the difference, hope! While hope is still alive, then so is God. And you, as a nun, should know that!'

Pelagia responded to this reproach with a humble bow, but still she did not relent. 'And Christ, when he went to the cross, did he also hope?' she asked in a quiet voice.

The Bishop did not immediately appreciate the full significance of this audacious question and merely frowned. But having understood it, he raised himself up to his full height, stamped his foot and exclaimed: 'Would you make a suicide of our Saviour? Get thee behind me, Satan! Begone!'

At this point even the nun realised that her inquisitive questioning had transgressed every permissible limit. Catching up the hem of her nun's habit and pulling her head down into her shoulders, Pelagia darted out through the door at which the monitory episcopal finger was pointed.

And so it happened that the plan of further action was determined without the participation of the stubborn nun, with just His Grace and Matvei Bentsionovich Berdichevsky speaking tête-à-tête. In addition it should be borne in mind that the deplorable fate that had overtaken both of the Bishop's chosen emissaries had deprived Mitrofanii of his customary confidence (while the quarrel with his spiritual daughter had added dejection to his state of mind), and so for most of the time Mitrofanii listened and agreed with everything, while Berdichevsky, on the contrary, although he felt genuine sympathy for his spiritual pastor, spoke more magniloquently and passionately than usual.

'We just keep talking about nothing but intricate knots,' he said, 'and it is true that in this business everything is so tangled up, it's enough to drive you crazy. But the members of my profession are not known as hair-splitters without good reason. We court officers are past masters at tangling up balls of thread and writing in incomprehensible squiggles. Sometimes we can even tie such a tight little knot that it puts the Gordius of ancient times to shame. But then there is no one who knows how to unravel these tangles better than we do. That's right, is it not?'

'Yes,' His Grace agreed with a mournful air, glancing at the door to see if Pelagia would come back.

'Well then, if that's right, then I am the one who ought to go to New Ararat. This time we have clear grounds for an entirely official investigation, even if it is a secret one. A chief of police committing suicide is no joking matter; it is no longer superstition or the workings of a hysterical imagination, it is something quite unheard of. Our governor, Anton Antonovich, will be asked to explain by the ministry, why, the Emperor himself will demand an explanation from him.'

'Yes, of course, the Governor will be asked to explain,' said Mitrofanii, nodding listlessly.

'So he will have to know what answer to give. You cannot go yourself under any circumstances – do not even think of it. Neither your bishop's title nor the provisions of the law give you any right to deal with an investigation into a criminal case of suicide.'

'Then let us go together. You will concern yourself with the secret investigation into the circumstances of Lagrange's death, and I will concern myself with the Black Monk.' The old fire flared up in Mitrofanii's eyes, and then was instantly extinguished again. 'And I'll see poor Alyosha . . .' he concluded in a cheerless voice.

'No,' snapped Berdichevsky. 'What secrecy will there be left, if I arrive in Ararat with you? We'll cause a fine commotion! Not only has the Bishop come rushing to meet the Black Monk, he's even brought the assistant provincial public prosecutor with him! It's simply ludicrous. No, Father, give me your blessing to go on my own.'

His Grace was clearly not himself that day, he was feeling downcast and had lost heart. There was something glinting suspiciously on his eyelashes again. Mitrofanii stood up and kissed the lay official on the forehead. 'You're my treasure, Matiusha. Your head is worth its weight in gold. And above all I value the fact that you are prepared to make such a sacrifice. Do you think I don't understand? Your Maria is near her time already. Go, and solve the mystery. You can see for yourself what a terrible mystery it is, so terrible that ordinary methods cannot resolve it. In the name of Christ the Lord, I implore you: take care of yourself – protect your life and your reason.'

Trying not to show how touched he was, Berdichevsky replied in gallant style: 'Never mind, Your Grace. God willing, I'll get the job done and be back in time for Masha to give birth. You know the popular saying: "The cunning Yid always has time for everything."'

But on his way home in the carriage his bravado deserted him and he felt sick at heart, and the closer he came to home, the sicker he felt. How could he tell his wife? How could he look her in the eye?

'Masha, my angel, something has come up ... An extremely important trip ... Just for a week, and there's no way I can possibly refuse ... I'll be as quick as I can, on my word of honour ...'

He was immediately ejected from her embrace and roundly abused in terms that were severe but just. He spent the night in the study, on the hard divan, but the worst thing of all was that he left in the morning without having said a proper goodbye to his wife. He kissed and blessed their children – all twelve of them – but Masha was adamant and would have none of it.

He left instructions concerning the disposal of his property in the drawer of the writing desk – just to be on the safe side, as a responsible man.

Ah, Masha, Masha, will we ever see each other again?

Remorse – that was the feeling that completely overwhelmed the assistant public prosecutor on his way to the archipelago of the Blue Lake. What had he got himself involved in by following a momentary impulse? And for what?

That is to say, what he had done it for or, rather, for whom was clear enough – for his beloved mentor and benefactor, and also in the name of establishing the truth, which was the professional duty of a servant of justice. But there was also a moral, even philosophical question: what was a man's primary responsibility – to society or to love? One pan of the scales held civic convictions, professional reputation, a man's honour and self-respect; the other held thirteen living souls – one woman and twelve children (and soon, God willing, another one would be added, a tiny new infant). If it were only himself he was risking, that would not be so bad; but those thirteen others who would be lost without him and who, if the truth were told, were dearer to him than all the other millions populating the earth, what were they guilty of? And so, whichever way you looked at things, it turned out that Matvei Berdichevsky was a traitor. If he put his family first and evaded his duty, then he would be a traitor to his principles and society. But if he honestly fulfilled his duty to society, he was a scoundrel and a Judas to his Masha and his children.

Not for the first or even the hundredth time, Berdichevsky regretted that he had chosen the path of a guardian of the law, which imposed so many restraints on an honest man. If only he worked as a barrister or a legal consultant, then he wouldn't have to suffer this torment from the moral impossibility of choice, would he?

But yes, he would, Berdichevsky told himself, and again not for the first time. Every man, even if he was not in public office and led a completely private life, inevitably encountered conflicts requiring him to choose what to sacrifice. God was certain to inflict this test on every man alive, so that he could learn his own worth and measure his shoulder against one cross or another.

He was in a foul mood, even setting aside the moral agony of the choice that he had made. The trouble was that he abhorred the very qualities that were being revealed in his own soul. Instead of dashing into the investigation on the wings of inspiration, driven on by the thirst for the truth, the assistant public prosecutor was experiencing something entirely different, a feeling tactfully referred to as trepidation, but in simple terms plain desperate cowardice.

What terrible experiences, what kind of unimaginable nightmare could it be that had driven a hard-bitten nihilist insane and made a gruff, fearless policeman shatter his own heart with a bullet? What kind of demon could have made its home there, on that accursed island? And how could an ordinary man who was very far from heroic by nature possibly do combat with such a horror?

Naturally, being an educated and progressive individual, Matvei Bentsionovich Berdichevsky did not believe in evil spirits, ghosts and so forth. But on the other hand, following Hamlet's famous maxim that 'There are more things in heaven and earth, Horatio, Than are dreamt of in your philosophy,' he could not entirely exclude the theoretical possibility of the existence of some other energies or substances, as yet undiscovered by science.

Berdichevsky sat on the deck of the steamer, huddled up miserably in his insubstantial Palmerston coat with a cape (since the investigation was secret, he had not brought his fine uniform greatcoat with him) and sighed over and over again.

No matter what the court official's glance fell on, he did not like it at all: neither the sour faces of the pilgrims sharing his journey, nor the vast, gloomy expanse of the great lake, nor the shuffling run of the glum-faced sailors. The captain was the perfect picture of a pirate, even if he was wearing a cassock – immensely tall, with a red face and a stentorian voice. What sort of expression was 'A censer up your rump'? Or 'Seed-spilling servants of Onan' – how about that?

Eventually Berdichevsky went to his cabin, lay down on his bunk bed and covered his face with the pillow. He carried on sighing for a while and then fell asleep. And he had a revolting dream.

There he was, not yet a collegiate counsellor, but still the little boy Mordka, running through the Skornyazhnaya suburb, pursued by a crowd of silent, bearded monks waving censers, with the clatter of huge boots and the hoarse breathing getting closer and closer. Then they caught up with him and knocked him down and he cried out: 'I'm an Orthodox Christian, the Bishop himself baptised me!' He tore open his shirt, but there was no cross hanging round his neck – he had dropped it somewhere. Berdichevsky began sobbing tearfully and struck the back of his head against the bulkhead. Still half-asleep, he fumbled for the cross on his chest, then drank a little water and slumped back into sleep.

In the morning the assistant public prosecutor stood on the prow of the steamship with his holdall in his hand, pale-faced and filled with noble fatalism: He would do what must be done, come what may.

The island of Canaan came drifting towards him out of the dense fog. At first there was nothing at all. Then a black, shaggy hump emerged from the milky mist – a low cliff, overgrown with scrub. Then behind it another, a bit lower, and another, and another … A long dark strip appeared, and coming from it he heard the dull rumble of bells chiming, as if they were muffled in cotton wool.

The sun was still trying to break through the dense atmosphere: in places the fog was suffused with a pink or even golden light, but that was mostly high up, closer to the sky, and down below everything was still a dull, blank grey.

As he walked down the gangway on to the almost invisible quayside Matvei Berdichevsky felt as if he were descending on to an immaterial cloud. He could hear voices shouting somewhere: 'If you want the very finest hotel, it's the Noah's Ark for you! … Rooms in the Refuge of the Lowly – any cheaper and they'd be free!' and so on in the same vein.

Berdichevsky listened for a while and then set off towards a thin, boyish voice enticing him to the Promised Land guest house. Where else should a Jew go, he thought with gentle self-irony.

A slim, shapely figure wearing a broad-rimmed hat with ostrich feathers emerged fleetingly from the matte-grey background and promptly disappeared again. He heard the rustle of a dress and the clatter of heels, and caught the sudden smell of perfume – not the 'Lily-of-the-Valley' that his Mashenka always used, but some distinctive scent, alarming and exciting. A narrow ray of sunlight suddenly struck Berdichevsky directly in the eyes, as if it had been specially aimed at him, and the fog dispersed with surprising rapidity. That is, it didn't actually disperse; it seemed to be rolled up from all four sides towards the centre, as if someone were removing a dirty tablecloth from a table in order to shake it out.

Startled by the suddenness of the change, Berdichevsky saw that he was standing in the middle of a neat and tidy street with fine stone buildings on both sides, with a roadway paved with timber and neatly planted trees. There were people strolling along the pavements and to the left, above the town, he could see the walls of a monastery – with no turrets or bell towers as yet, because the tablecloth of fog had still not risen very high above the ground.

The assistant public prosecutor looked round for the lady whose mere appearance had been enough to scatter the gloom, but only caught a brief glimpse of a sharp heel protruding from under the train of a mourning dress on the very corner of the street, and a feather swaying on a hat.

How many such fleeting encounters there are in life, Matvei Berdichevsky thought as he strode after the boy from the hotel. That which could have happened, but never will happen, will brush your cheek with its rustling wing and then fly on its way, leaving you reeling. And every day of life was a myriad of missed opportunities and twists of fate that never came to anything. There was no point in sighing over it; you had to appreciate the path that you were treading.

And so Berdichevsky's thoughts turned towards business.

He ought to begin by inspecting the police chief's things and also (at this point he shuddered mentally) the dead man's body. But even before that, he should send notes to both the archimandrite and Dr Korovin, notifying them that an investigator had arrived and demanding an immediate meeting. He could set the meeting with the former for, say, two o'clock in the afternoon, and with the latter for five.

'An entry wound the size of a kopeck coin, located between the sixth and seventh ribs, three inches below and half an inch to the left of the left nipple. An exit wound at the protruding vertebra (the seventh, I think), which has been shattered by the bullet; about the size of a five-kopeck piece. Other visible injuries include a bump one inch to the right of the crown of the head, evidently caused by convulsive blows of the head against the floor after the body had fallen ...'

Matvei Berdichevsky had never had to draw up any reports of post-mortem examinations. The province had a medical expert and a police investigator to do that, as well as the more lowly members of the public prosecutor's office. But here in New Ararat, where there was no crime, or even police as such, there was no one to whom he could delegate this terrible task. Berdichevsky was familiar with the special terminology, but he had not mastered it, and so he tried to describe everything in as much detail as possible, using his own words. From time to time he broke off to take a sip of water.

Matvei Berdichevsky had a shameful weakness – in fact, in his profession it was positively detrimental: he was terribly afraid of dead bodies, especially if one turned up that was half-decayed or mutilated. Colonel Lagrange's corpse, to give it its due, still looked more or less decent. The white, motionless features of the face had even acquired a certain expression of significance, not to say grandeur – qualities that had been quite uncharacteristic of the police chief's physiognomy when he was alive. Berdichevsky's sensitive heart was tormented far more by the cadaver of an old monk lying on the next zinc table. In the first place, the old man was completely naked, and in a man of the Church this natural human condition seemed improper. But even worse was the fact that the monk had expired in the course of a surgical operation on his abdomen, during which they had managed to cut him open and even extract some of his viscera, but they had not bothered to sew them back in again. The deputy public prosecutor had deliberately sat with his back to the nightmarish corpse, but even so he was feeling rather sick. It was best not to think about the kind of dreams he would have that night.

Berdichevsky scratched away with his pen, frequently wiping the sweat off his bald patch, although it was very far from hot in the mortuary – there was a cold draught from the half-open door of the ice room, out of which the police chief's body had been wheeled on a trolley. Eventually the most unpleasant part of the job was over. The assistant public prosecutor ordered the trolley to be wheeled back into the cold chamber and sighed in relief as he went through into the next room, where the suicide's belongings were in store.

'Where's he going?' asked the servant of the faith who followed him into the room, wiping his hands on his greasy cassock. 'Will you take him back to the World or is he going to be buried here?'

Berdichevsky did not immediately appreciate the meaning of the question. But when he realised that 'the World' was what they called the mainland here, he was struck by the picturesque quality of the monks' terminology. It was as if they lived, not on islands in a lake, but in Heaven.

'We'll take him away. When I go back, I'll collect him. Where are his things? Where are his clothes?'

The investigator did not discover anything worthy of note in the travelling bag. The only things that caught his attention were an impressive store of fixative for curling moustaches and a little Parisian album of indecent photographs – Felix Stanislavovich must have brought it to look through on his journey. At a different time and in a different place, where there were no witnesses, Matvei Berdichevsky would have leafed through the frivolous little volume himself, but just now he was not in the mood.

The investigator paid special attention to the weapon used for the suicide – a forty-five calibre Smith and Wesson revolver. He sniffed it and scraped the inside of the barrel for sooty deposit (there was some) and checked the drum (five bullets in place, one missing). Then he set it aside and started on the clothes, which were folded in a neat pile, with each item numbered. On item number three (a jacket) just below the left breast pocket there was a hole with singed edges, such as a shot at point-blank range would leave. Berdichevsky compared the hole with the holes in items number five (a waistcoat), number six (a jersey), number eight (a shirt) and number nine (an undershirt). Everything matched up perfectly. There were traces of blood visible on the shirt and undershirt and also some on the jersey.

In short, the general picture was perfectly clear. The suicide had held the gun in his left hand, with his wrist twisted a long way up. That was why the bullet had followed a course to the right and upwards. This was rather strange – it would have been far easier to grasp the handle of the long-barrelled revolver in both hands and fire the bullet directly into the heart. But then, the act itself was strange, to put it mildly; no one in his right mind would shoot a hole in himself anyway. He had probably just stuck the gun against his chest any old way and fired . . .

'And what is this?' Berdichevsky asked, lifting up a white lady's glove bearing the label 'No. 13' between his finger and thumb.

'A glove,' the servant of the faith replied indifferently.

The assistant public prosecutor sighed and formulated his question more precisely. 'What is it doing here? And why is there blood on it?'

'It was lying on his chest, under his shirt,' the monk said with a shrug. 'Worldly nonsense.'

On closer inspection the fine silk also proved to have a hole in it.

Hmm. Berdichevsky decided to refrain from drawing any conclusions concerning the glove for the time being, but he set the intriguing item on one side, together with the letters and the revolver. He put the items he required for the investigation into Lagrange's travelling bag (after all, he had to carry them in something) and left an appropriate receipt with the list.

In the next room the monk was singing something to himself in a quiet voice as he sewed up the old man's belly. Berdichevsky listened carefully and made out some of the words: 'Weeping and sobbing, always do I think of death, and see our beauty, created in the image of God, lying in the grave, defaced, hideous and inglorious . . .'

The Breguet watch in his pocket jingled: once quite loudly and twice quietly. The excellent little device, a genuine miracle of the Swiss mechanical genius, had been a gift from Father Mitrofanii for Berdichevsky's tenth wedding anniversary. The jingling signified that it was now half past one in the afternoon. It was time to visit the father superior of New Ararat.

The conversation with Father Vitalii proved to be short and unpleasant.

The archimandrite was already in a state of great annoyance when he greeted the provincial official. In fact, Berdichevsky had deliberately contrived to provoke the ruler of New Ararat by writing his letter in a peremptory tone and indicating the precise time of the meeting, on the one hand, to remind Father Vitalii that a power higher than that of the father superior was involved here and, on the other, to provoke him into speaking abruptly and without restraint – he would probably reach the truth of this business more quickly that way than by being obsequious and equivocal.

Well, Berdichevsky had certainly succeeded in provoking an abrupt response – too abrupt in fact.

The reverend father was striding impatiently to and fro in front of the porch of his residence, wearing an extremely old cassock, which for some reason was tucked up almost as high as his waist to reveal a dirty pair of tall boots, and waving a round turnip watch in his hand.

'Ah, Mr Public Prosecutor,' he exclaimed on catching sight of Berdichevsky. 'Three minutes after two. Why do you keep me waiting? Isn't that too insolent altogether?'

Berdichevsky did not reply to the cleric or even greet him. He merely jabbed his finger in the direction of the clock adorning a rather grand bell tower that appeared to have been built only recently. The minute hand of the clock had only just begun to creep towards the figure twelve. And just at that moment, as if by deliberate design, the chimes rang out – all in all, the effect was quite striking.

'I have no time for making conversation, I've got too many things to deal with!' Vitalii growled even more angrily. 'We can talk as we walk. Over that way.' He pointed towards a log-walled shed that was visible some distance away, outside the monastery wall. 'We're taking down the old pig shed and we're going to put up a new one.'

So that was the reason for the tucked-up cassock and the waders. The audience took place in a farmyard that was ankle-deep in mud and excrement – Berdichevsky's shoes and trousers were filthy in an instant.

Monks tore the shingles off the roof of the shed with gaffs, with the father superior supervising them, so that Berdichevsky had to expound the essence of his business to the sound of cracking, rumbling and shouting, and Vitalii did not even appear to be listening properly.

That alone would have been enough to make the assistant public prosecutor take a dislike to the archimandrite, but another circumstance soon increased this initial antipathy to an extreme degree. Father Vitalii rested a keen glance of a kind only too familiar to Matvei Berdichevsky on the hooked nose of this emissary from Zavolzhsk, on his gristly ears and the distinctly non-Slavic blackness of his thinning hair, and then the father superior's face assumed a distinct expression of disgust.

After listening to an explanation of the investigation into the suicide and the concern felt by the provincial authorities over the marvellous events at New Ararat, the archimandrite said darkly: 'I'm a straightforward man. Write as many complaints as you like afterwards – I'm well used to that. But don't you dare to stick your long nose into the affairs of the Church. Take the suicide. Tinker with that loathsome abomination as long as you like. But the other matter is none of your business.'

'And what do you mean by that?' asked the deputy public prosecutor, almost choking on his indignation. 'And by what right, Your Reverence, do you instruct me as to what—'

'By this right,' Father Vitalii interrupted him. 'Here on the islands I am in charge of everything, and I am also answerable for everything. Especially in matters that concern the spiritual sphere. For such matters, your national origins are inappropriate. I regard it as an affront from my superior to have sent such an investigator to Ararat. What is needed here is a sensitive, Russian heart, one that is full of faith, and not ...'

The father superior stopped without finishing what he was saying and spat. And that was the crudest insult of all.

Berdichevsky saw that things were heading towards a scandalous confrontation and he refrained from answering insult with insult.

'In the first place, holy Father, allow me to remind you that according to the Apostle Paul there is neither Jew nor Hellene, but we are all one in Christ,' he said in a quiet voice. 'And in the second place, I am an Orthodox Christian, exactly like yourself.'

The words came out with such calm dignity (although, of course, everything inside him was quaking and shuddering) that Matvei Berdichevsky even admired himself.

But what good is dignity against a rabid anti-Semite?

'Only a Russian can understand and accept our Russian faith in its entirety,' Father Vitalii hissed, twisting his lips. 'And the

Orthodox faith is especially unsuited to the heart and mind of Jewish arrogance and egotism. Get back, keep your claws off our sacred Russian beliefs! And as for your being christened, the people have a saying for that: a Jew christened is like a thief forgiven.'

So saying, the archimandrite turned his back on the assistant public prosecutor and strode off, champing through the mud, into the pig shed that was being demolished – a tall, black figure as straight as a ramrod. Berdichevsky walked out of the monastery, fuming in fury.

Because the conversation had been so brief, occupying less than ten minutes, there was a lot of time left before his next meeting, with Dr Korovin. In order not to let this time go to waste, and at the same time to calm himself by taking a little exercise, the assistant public prosecutor decided to walk round the town and familiarise himself with its distinctive topographical, institutional and other features.

It was quite remarkable: those very same streets which at first acquaintance had produced on Matvei Berdichevsky an uplifting impression of carefully tended order and cleanliness now seemed hostile and even malevolent. The new arrival's attention was caught more and more often by the grimly pursed lips of the female pilgrims, the excessive profusion of churches and chapels of every possible kind and the ethnic uniformity of the faces that he met; not a single face with swarthy skin, a hook nose, black eyes or even slanting eyes, nothing but Great Russian brown hair, grey eyes and snub noses.

Never in his life had Berdichevsky ever felt such a keen sense of hopeless isolation as here in this Orthodox paradise. But was it really paradise? A dozen strapping monks with truncheons on their belts went marching past him – a fine Eden this was. Just try living under the rule of an obscurantist and rabid Slavophile like this Father Vitalii. In the bookshops there was nothing but spiritual reading, the only newspapers available were the *Church Herald*, the *Torch of Orthodoxy* and Prince Meshchersky's *Citizen*.

No theatre, no brass band in the park and no dance hall – God forbid. But countless eating places. Eating and praying – that's all there is to this heaven of yours, Matvei Berdichevsky thought maliciously.

However, once his sense of hurt and anger at the archimandrite had abated somewhat, following his customary intellectual principle of *audiatur et altera pars*, Berdichevsky began thinking that Vitalii was not really all that far wrong about him. Yes, Matvei did suffer from intellectual pride. Yes, he was a sceptic, entirely unfitted for a simple-hearted faith. And if he was absolutely and totally frank with himself, then his religious feelings were founded entirely not on a love of Christ, whom Berdichevsky had never actually seen, but on a love of His Grace Mitrofanii. That is, if he imagined that Mordka Berdichevsky's spiritual father had not been an Orthodox bishop, but some wise sheikh or Buddhist bonze, then the collegiate counsellor would have been walking around in a turban or a conical straw hat. Only in that case, my dear sir, you would never have made any sort of career for yourself in the Russian Empire, thought Berdichevsky, castigating himself even more bitterly and sinking into a state of self-abasement.

Now his bitterness was complete, because his earthly loneliness, which was temporary and limited in space to the island of Canaan, was augmented by a metaphysical loneliness. Forgive, O Lord, my lack of faith and my doubt, the assistant public prosecutor began to pray in his fright, turning his head this way and that to see if there was a church nearby, so that he could confess his guilt as soon as possible before an image of the Saviour.

And, of course, there was one – after all, this was New Ararat, not St Petersburg. There was a small church very close, only twenty paces away; but even closer, right in front of Berdichevsky's nose, in fact, there was a large icon hanging under a sheet-metal awning on the wall of the monastery college, and not just any holy image, but the Vernicle Image of the Saviour. In this coincidence Berdichevsky discerned a sign from above, and decided not to walk to the church. He threw himself down on his knees in front of the image of the Saviour (after the farmyard his trousers were ruined in any case, and he would have to change them) and began to pray – passionately, fervently, as he had never prayed before.

O Lord, Berdichevsky begged, grant me a simple, childlike faith of the heart that will support me always and never abandon me in the face of any tests. Let me believe in the immortality of the soul and the life hereafter; let my intellectual pride be replaced by wisdom, so that I will no longer tremble constantly for my family, but be mindful of eternity, so that I might have the strength to stand firm against temptations, so that … And what with one thing and another, the prayer turned out to be a long one, for Matvei Berdichevsky had many requests to make of the Almighty, and to list them all here would be tedious.

No one interrupted the pilgrim at his prayers, no one stared at the respectable gentleman rubbing holes in the knees of his trousers in the middle of the pavement; in fact the people passing by skirted round him respectfully, for in New Ararat scenes like this were perfectly normal.

The only thing that distracted the provincial official from his efforts to purge his soul was the ringing sound of childish laughter coming from the porch of the college. There was a man wearing a soft hat sitting there, surrounded by a pack of small boys, and it was clear that he was enjoying the little scamps' company, and they were enjoying his. Several times Berdichevsky glanced round at the noise in annoyance, and he was able to note several distinctive features of this child-lover's face, which was extremely pleasant and open – even, perhaps, a little simple.

When he finally got up from his knees, wiping away his tears, the stranger came up to him, raised his hat politely and began apologising: 'I beg your pardon for the way we interrupted your prayer with our chatter. The children are constantly pestering me with questions about all sorts of things.

It's quite remarkable how little their teachers explain to them about the most important subjects. And they are afraid to ask their teachers too many questions, since the teachers here are all monks, and extremely strict. But they're not afraid of me,' the man said with a smile that made it quite clear there really was no reason for anyone to feel afraid of him. 'Pardon me for approaching you so offhandedly. You know, I am a quite exceptionally sociable individual, and you attracted me with the sincerity of your praying. You don't often see an educated man down on his knees in front of an icon, praying so fervently, with tears in his eyes. At home, perhaps, all on his own, but in the middle of the street! I have taken a great liking to you.'

Berdichevsky bowed slightly and was about to go, but instead he took a closer look at the stranger, screwed up his eyes and asked cautiously: 'E-er, would you mind, my dear sir, if I were to ask what your first name and patronymic are? Would they by any chance be Lev Nikolaevich?'

In his manners and appearance the present gentleman seemed remarkably similar to the lover of reading mentioned in Alyosha Lentochkin's letter. As an inveterate chess player, Berdichevsky had an excellent memory, and remembering a name like that – the same as Count Tolstoy's – was not difficult.

The man was surprised, but not excessively so. He looked in any case as if he constantly expected surprises from reality – and for the most part happy ones.

'Yes, that is my name. But how do you know it?'

With his soul's burden lightened by prayer Berdichevsky thought he could perceive the providence of God yet again in this chance encounter. 'You and I have a mutual acquaintance, Alexei Stepanovich Lentochkin. The young man who gave you a book, one of the works of Fyodor Dostoevsky.'

Lev Nikolaevich was once again surprised by the other man's preternatural knowledge, but once again not very greatly. 'Yes, I remember the unfortunate youth very well. Did you know that something terrible happened to him? He became mentally ill.'

Berdichevsky said nothing, but he raised his eyebrows in an expression of surprise, as if to ask: What are you saying?

'Because of the Black Monk,' said Lev Nikolaevich, lowering his voice. 'In the middle of the night he went to a little hut where there is a cross scratched on the window, and he lost his mind. He saw something there. And then afterwards, in the very same place, another man I knew slightly shot himself with a pistol. Oh, now I've blurted it out! That was supposed to be a secret,' Lev Nikolaevich exclaimed in fright. 'I was told about it in strict secrecy, I gave my word. Don't tell anyone else, all right?'

Well, well, the investigator thought to himself, and he began rubbing the bridge of his nose furiously in order to calm the excited pulsing of his blood. Well, well.

'I won't tell anyone,' he promised, pretending to give a yawn of boredom. 'But you know, I find you very likeable too, as it happens, and now it turns out that we have a mutual acquaintance. Would you perhaps care to take a cup of tea or coffee with me? We could talk a little about this and that. Perhaps even about Dostoevsky.'

'I should be delighted!' Lev Nikolaevich replied happily. 'You know, it's such a rare thing here to meet anyone who is well read and truly cultured. And then again, not everyone finds it interesting to talk with me. I'm not clever, not educated; sometimes I say ridiculous things. We could sit in the Good Samaritan. They serve an original tea there, smoked. And it's not expensive.'

He was all set to go for a talk with his new acquaintance there and then, but the Breguet in Berdichevsky's pocket jingled loudly four times and once quietly. It was already a quarter past four – what a long time he must have spent praying.

'My dearest Lev Nikolaevich, I have urgent business to attend to, which will take me two or three hours. If it were possible for us to meet after that ...' The assistant public prosecutor broke off his sentence on an interrogative note, waited for a nod and then continued. 'My name is Matvei Bentsionovich, but I will introduce myself more fully when we meet this evening. Where should I look for you?'

'Until seven I usually stroll round the town, watching the people and thinking about anything that comes into my head,' the valuable witness explained. 'At seven I take supper at the Five Loaves cookshop and then, if it's not raining and the wind is not too strong – and today, as you can see, the weather is fine – I sit on a bench somewhere, with a view over the lake. For a long time. Sometimes until about ten . . .'

'Excellent,' Berdichevsky broke in. 'Then that's where we'll meet. Name some particular spot.'

Lev Nikolaevich thought for a moment. 'Let's say on the waterfront near the Rotunda. So that you can find it easily. Will you really come?'

'You may be quite certain that I shall,' the assistant public prosecutor said with a smile.

Matvei Berdichevsky mopped his damp forehead and clutched at his heart. Mashenka was absolutely right: he ought to do gymnastics and ride a bicycle, as all enlightened people who were concerned for their physical health did. This was absurd – at the age of thirty-eight he already had a paunch, he suffered from shortness of breath and he was quite unable to dodge about so rapidly.

'Alexei Stepanovich, really, that's enough of these games!' he appealed to the tropical jungle thickets in which he had just heard the rapid rustling of unshod feet. 'It's me, Berdichevsky; you know me very well! Bishop Mitrofanii sent me to see you!' The game of hide-and-seek or catch-me-if-you-can or, more accurately, both at the same time, had been going on for quite a while, and the assistant public prosecutor was already worn out.

Donat Savvich Korovin had stayed at the door of the conservatory. He was smoking a small cigar and observing the manoeuvres of the two sides with interest. Matvei Berdichevsky had not actually seen Lentochkin's face yet, but the boy was definitely here – twice the official had caught a glimpse of a naked shoulder through the broad shiny leaves.

'Don't worry, he'll run out of breath in a moment,' said the doctor. 'He's getting weaker by the day. A week ago, when I needed to examine him, the attendants had to chase him for half an hour; they even had to bring him down from the palm trees. But two days ago fifteen minutes was enough. Yesterday it was ten. That's bad.'

He could have lent me those attendants, Berdichevsky thought angrily. He's trying to show that the provincial authorities mean nothing to an international authority like him. He took offence at the tone of my letter, just like the father superior.

However, he actually liked the doctor, unlike the father superior. The doctor was calm, businesslike and slightly sarcastic, but without being insulting. Having heard the investigator out, he had suggested quite reasonably: 'First take a look at your Lentochkin, and then we'll come back here and talk.'

But, as we have already said, taking a look at Alexei Lentochkin had proved to be far from simple.

After a few more minutes, he succeeded in driving the wild inhabitant of the jungle into a corner and then, at last, the running about came to an end. He could see a curly head of hair protruding from behind a luxuriant bush, with a pair of blue eyes goggling in fright (beyond the bush, with its scattering of unnaturally blue flowers, there was nothing but a glass wall). The boy had grown terribly thin and lost all the colour in his cheeks, Berdichevsky noticed, and his hair hung down in matted tangles.

'Don't,' Alyosha said in a whining voice. 'I'll fly away into the sky soon. He'll come to collect me. Wait a while.'

On Donat Savvich's advice Berdichevsky did not try to creep any closer to the patient, in order not to provoke a fit. He stopped, spread his arms and began as gently as he could: 'Alexei Stepanovich, I have reread your last letter, where you wrote about the magical incantation and the buoy-keeper's little house. Do you remember what happened there in that house?'

Korovin chuckled behind Berdichevsky's back. 'You're going at it very fast. You think he'll just tell you everything just like that?'

'Don't go there,' Alyosha suddenly told Berdichevsky in a thin little voice. 'It will be the end of you.'

The doctor walked up to the assistant public prosecutor and stood beside him. 'My apologies,' he whispered. 'I was wrong. You really do have some special kind of effect on him.'

Encouraged by his success, Berdichevsky took half a step forward. 'Alexei Stepanovich, my dear chap, the Bishop is so worried about you that he can't sleep. He can't forgive himself for sending you here. Let's go back to him, eh? He ordered me not to come back without you. Let's go.'

'Let's go,' Alyosha muttered.

'And we'll talk about that night?'

'We'll talk.'

Berdichevsky glanced round triumphantly at the doctor: How's that then!

Korovin frowned anxiously.

'Something incredible must have happened to you there, I suppose?' Berdichevsky said in a very quiet voice, drawing out his words like an angler paying out his line.

'Something incredible.'

'Did Basilisk appear to you?'

'Basilisk.'

'And he gave you a bad fright?'

'A bad fright.'

The doctor moved the investigator aside a little. 'Wait, will you. He's just repeating the most important words you say, can't you see that? It's a habit he has developed over the last three days. Obsessive repetition. He can't focus his attention for longer than a moment. He doesn't really hear you.'

'Alexei Stepanovich, can you hear me?' the assistant public prosecutor asked.

'Hear me,' Lentochkin repeated, making it clear that Dr Korovin was, unfortunately, right.

Matvei Berdichevsky sighed in disappointment. 'What is going to happen to him?'

'A week, two at the most, and . . .' The doctor shook his head eloquently. 'Unless, of course, a miracle happens.'

'What sort of miracle?'

'If I can discover a means of halting the disease process and reversing it. All right, let's go. You won't get anything out of him, just like your predecessor.'

Once they were back in Korovin's study, they began talking, not about poor Alexei Lentochkin but about Berdichevsky's 'predecessor' – that is, about the deceased Colonel Lagrange.

'In my line of work I have to be a good physiognomist,' said Dr Korovin, switching his gaze from Berdichevsky to the window and back. 'And I am very, very rarely mistaken about people. But I must confess that your police chief's behaviour has left me baffled. I would have guaranteed quite confidently that he was a well-balanced character with a high level of self-esteem and a primitive, object-related view of the world. People like that do not tend to commit suicide, or go insane as a result of psychological trauma. If they do away with themselves, then it is only out of a sense of total hopelessness – when they are threatened with a shameful trial, or when their noses collapse and they go blind from neglected syphilis. If they go insane, then the reason is always something vulgar and uninteresting: their superiors have passed them over for promotion, or the winning ticket in a lottery had the next number to theirs – that was what happened to a certain captain of dragoons. I would never take on a patient like your Lagrange, not for anything. It's not interesting.'

Somehow, as the conversation proceeded, without any special effort on the part of the two men the initial mutual caution and even hostility completely evaporated, until they were talking like intelligent individuals who respected each other.

Berdichevsky also went across to the window and looked at the spruce little houses where Korovin's wards lived. 'Supporting your patients must cost you a tidy sum, I suppose?'

'A little less than a quarter of a million a year. If you divide that by twenty-eight (which is the number of patients that I have), the average cost comes to approximately eight thousand, although, of course, the difference in costs is very great. Lentochkin costs me almost nothing. He lives as free as a bird. And I'm afraid he will soon take wing and "fly away into the sky",' the doctor said with a sad laugh.

Berdichevsky was astounded by this incredible figure. He exclaimed: 'Eight thousand! But that's . . .'

'You wish to say that it's madness?' Dr Korovin asked with a smile. 'More like a millionaire's whim. Other rich men spend their money on items of luxury or courtesans, but I have my own passion. It's not philanthropy, since I don't do it for mankind but for my own satisfaction. But I spend quite a lot on charity too, because of all the things this earthly life has to offer the one I value most of all is my own peace of mind and I do everything I can to avoid any pangs of conscience.'

'But doesn't it seem to you that your quarter of a million could be spent to the benefit of a far greater number of people?' asked Berdichevsky, unable to resist the riposte.

The doctor smiled again, even more good-naturedly. 'You mean the hungry and the homeless? Well, naturally, I don't forget about them. The income from the capital that I inherited amounts to half a million a year. I give away exactly half of it to charitable societies as a voluntary wealth tax or, if you like, as payment for my clear conscience, but then I do exactly as I wish with the remainder. I dine on foie gras without the slightest feeling of guilt. I want to play at doctors, so I do. With complete peace of mind. Would you really begrudge half of your income in exchange for sound sleep and harmony with your own soul?'

Matvei Berdichevsky merely shrugged, at a loss to reply to this question. There was no point in trying to explain to the millionaire about his twelve children and the payments on the bank loan for his modest house and garden.

'I spend a mere trifle on myself, twenty or thirty thousand,' Korovin continued; 'all the rest goes on my passion. Every one of my patients is a genuine treasure trove. They are all unusual, all talented; you could write a dissertation, or even a book, on any of them. I've already told you that I'm very selective and I don't take just anyone, only those for whom I feel a certain sympathy. Otherwise it's impossible to establish a bond of trust.'

He looked at the assistant public prosecutor, smiled at him in a most friendly fashion and said: 'I would probably take somebody like you. If you should happen to develop a mental illness, of course.'

'Really?' laughed Berdichevsky, feeling flattered. 'What sort of person do you think I am?'

Dr Korovin was on the point of answering, but just then his gaze turned to the window once again and he declared with a conspiratorial air: 'We'll find that out in just a moment.'

He opened the window and shouted to someone: 'Sergei Nikolaevich! Are you eavesdropping again? Ai-ai-ai. Well, tell me, do you have your remarkable glasses with you? Excellent! Then would you be so kind as to call in to see me for a minute?'

A few moments later a puny little man entered the study, wearing something like a medieval gown and a large beret and carrying a linen bag in which something was rattling.

'What's that you have there?' the doctor asked curiously, pointing to the bag.

'Samples,' the strange individual replied, looking Berdichevsky up and down. 'Minerals. From the shore. Emanational analysis. I explained it to you. But you're deaf. Who's this? What about the other?'

'Right, allow me to introduce you. Mr Berdichevsky, a guardian of law and order. He has come to investigate our mysterious goings-on. Mr Lampier, a brilliant physicist, who also happens to be my guest.'

'I see,' said the assistant public prosecutor, with a sideways glance at Korovin, and then he spoke cautiously to the 'physicist'. 'Hm-hm, pleased to meet you, very pleased. How do you do?'

'A guardian? Investigate!' the madman cried, without replying to the greeting. 'But that ... yes, yes! A long time ago! And he doesn't look like the other! Just a moment, just a moment ... Ah, where are they? Where have they gone?'

He became so agitated that Berdichevsky began feeling worried that he might pounce on him, but the doctor winked reassuringly. 'Are you looking for your remarkable spectacles? Why, there they are, in your breast pocket. I wanted to ask you to carry out a chromospectrographic inspection of this gentleman.'

'What's that?' Berdichevsky exclaimed, even more alarmed now. 'A chromo ...'

'A chromospectrographic inspection. It's one of Sergei Nikolaevich's inventions. He has discovered that every human being is surrounded by a certain emanation of energy that is invisible to the eye. The colour of this emission is determined by the condition of the internal organs, a person's level of intellectual development and even his moral qualities,' Korovin began to explain with a perfectly serious air. 'Mr Lampier's spectacles render this invisible aureole visible. And I must say that as far as physical health is concerned, Sergei Nikolaevich's emanational diagnosis is quite frequently correct.'

Meanwhile, the man had already set a huge pair of spectacles with violet lenses on his nose and aimed them at Berdichevsky.

'Good,' Lampier muttered. 'Excellent ... Not like the other one ... No crimson at all ... A hint of yellowish-green – ai-ai-ai ... But never mind, there's some orange ... The head ... I see ... The heart ... Did you know that you have a sick liver?' he suddenly asked in a perfectly normal voice, and Berdichevsky shuddered, because recently he had been getting stabbing pains in his right side, especially after supper.

The madman whisked his absurd oculars off his nose,

grabbed the investigator by the hand and started gabbling: 'A talk! Absolutely! Face to face! I've been waiting a long time, a long time! A lot of blue! That means you'll be able to understand! Immediately! To my place, my place! Oh, at last!'

He began pulling Berdichevsky after him with so much determination that the startled official barely managed to break free.

'Calm down, Sergei Nikolaevich, calm down,' said the doctor, coming to Berdichevsky's assistance. 'Matvei Bentsionovich and I will just finish talking, and then I'll send him across to your laboratory. You go there and wait.'

When his patient had gone out, muttering and waving his arms about, Donat Savvich gave the assistant public prosecutor a glance of mock horror and whispered: 'You have no more than five minutes to leave the grounds of the clinic. Otherwise Lampier will come back and you won't get rid of him that easily.'

It was good advice, and Berdichevsky decided it would be best to take it, especially since there seemed to be no point in delaying at the clinic any longer.

Matvei Berdichevsky strode along the yellow-brick road winding between the low forested hills – no doubt it was the same one that the unfortunate Lagrange had followed only a week earlier on his way from visiting Doctor Korovin. What had been going on then in the doomed police chief's soul? Had he known that he was approaching the end of his last day in this world? What had he been thinking about as he looked down at the town, the monastery, the lake?

Actually, it was not all that difficult to reconstruct Felix Stanislavovich's train of thought. It could be assumed that by the evening he had already firmly decided to make his nocturnal excursion to the mysterious hut and check what kind of evil spirit it was that had broken its way through into the human world at that spot. How very like the gallant colonel it was to go dashing in headlong, and damn the consequences.

Well then, we shall act differently, the assistant public prosecutor thought to himself, although, of course, we shall not ignore that important little house either. The very first thing we shall do is to examine it by the light of day – that is, not today, but tomorrow, because it is already getting dark, and we shall need witnesses.

And then what? Cut the pane of glass with the cross on it out of the window frame and send it to Zavolzhsk for examination.

No, that would take too long. Better summon Semyon Ivanovich here, together with three or four of the brighter police officers, to avoid having to rely on the base Vitalii and his peace-keepers. Establish twenty-four-hour observation posts in the hut and around it. And then we'll see how this demon of ours behaves.

Hmm, Berdichevsky suddenly said to himself, coming to a halt. Here I am thinking just like a regular police goon. As if I didn't understand that if there really is some kind of mystical material involved here, then the subtle thread connecting it with earthly reality could be snapped very easily. It would be exactly the same approach to the Gordian Knot that I argued against so strongly.

Even a blockhead like Lagrange, God rest his soul, had realised that supernatural phenomena can only be observed one to one, without any official witnesses or police constables. If the experiment was to be accurate, he had to do as Lentochkin described in his letter: go alone, naked and pronounce the incantation. And if nothing out of the ordinary happened, only then conduct the investigation in the usual manner, in the firm conviction that he was dealing with physical phenomena.

Matvei Berdichevsky realised that these considerations were largely a matter of theory, because nothing would make him go anywhere at night, at least not to a place where one man had gone crazy and another had shot himself through the heart.

To launch into that kind of escapade would be stupid –

ludicrous, in fact; and, above all, it would be a betrayal of his responsibility to Masha and the children.

From this consideration Berdichevsky's thoughts naturally turned to his family. He began thinking about his wife, thanks to whom his life had become complete, full of meaning and happiness. How dear and good his Masha was, especially when she was pregnant, even though at those times her eyes turned red, her eyelids were covered with broken veins and her nose stuck out just like a duck's bill. The assistant public prosecutor smiled as he recalled Masha's fondness for singing even though she had no ear for music at all, her superstitious fear of the pockmarked crescent moon and brown cockroaches, the rebellious lock of hair on the back of her head and many more of those little details that have no meaning except to one who loves.

His eldest daughter, Katyenka, had taken after her mother, thank God. Just as determined and all of a piece, always knowing what she wanted and how to get it.

His second daughter, Ludmilochka, was probably more like her father – she liked to cry a bit, she was a compassionate soul, sensitive to the beauties of nature. Life would not be easy for her. May God grant her a husband who was considerate and humane.

And his third daughter, Nastenka, promised to develop into a genuine musical talent. How fleetly her pink little fingers slid across the keys of the pianoforte! When she was a little older, he would definitely have to take her to St Petersburg and show her to Iosif Solomonovich.

This mental inventorisation of the numerous members of his family was Berdichevsky's favourite pastime, but on this occasion he failed to get as far as his fourth daughter, Lizanka. Suddenly a woman on a black horse appeared from round the bend, riding towards him, her appearance as unexpected as it was out of keeping with the languid chiming of the monastery bells and the entire dreary landscape of Canaan: Matvei Berdichevsky was stupefied.

The slim-legged stallion came trotting along the roadway, turned slightly sideways, as genuinely thoroughbred and frolicsome English horses sometimes do, and so the assistant public prosecutor had a full view of the woman riding side-saddle – from her little hat with a veil to the toes of her lacquered boots.

As she drew level with the man walking along, she looked down at him, and the piercing gaze of those black eyes, as sharp as any arrow, set the sober-minded official's heart fluttering.

It was she – there was no doubt about it! The same stranger whose mere appearance had seemed to drive the blanket of fog from the island. The hat with ostrich feathers had been replaced by a cardinal's cap of scarlet velvet, but the dress was still black, the colour of mourning, and Berdichevsky's sensitive nose also caught the familiar, dangerously exciting scent of that perfume.

Berdichevsky stopped and watched the graceful horsewoman ride by. Rather than lashing on her English stallion, she was gently stroking its gleaming crupper with her riding crop, and in her left hand she was holding a small lacy handkerchief.

Suddenly this light scrap of material broke free, swirled round in the air for a brief moment like a playful butterfly and landed on the ground at the edge of the road. The horsewoman rode on without noticing her loss or bothering to glance round at the man, who was still standing there stock-still.

Let it lie where it has fallen, Berdichevsky's reason cautioned him – or perhaps it was not even his reason, but his instinct for self-preservation. What was not meant to be should be left well alone.

But Matvei Berdichevsky's feet were already carrying him towards the fallen handkerchief. 'My lady, stop!' the investigator called out in a halting voice. 'Your handkerchief! You have dropped your handkerchief!'

He called out three times before the rider looked round. Realising what was wrong, she nodded and turned back towards him. She rode up slowly, examining this gentleman in a Palmerston coat and muddy shoes with a strange smile of enquiry or mockery.

'Thank you,' she said, pulling back on the reins, but she did not reach out her hand for the handkerchief. 'You are most kind.'

Berdichevsky held out the handkerchief, gazing avidly into the dazzling face of this lady, wondering if she was married or not. The depths of those almond-shaped eyes! That bold line to the mouth, that stubborn chin and those bitter shadows barely visible below the cheekbones.

But he had to say something. He couldn't just stand there staring. 'It's a fine cambric handkerchief . . . It would be a shame to lose it,' the assistant public prosecutor muttered, feeling himself blushing like a schoolboy.

'You have intelligent eyes. Sensitive lips. I've never seen you here before.' The horsewoman stroked her black stallion on the neck. 'Who are you?'

He told her his title without mentioning his job: 'A collegiate counsellor.'

For some reason the stranger found this amusing. 'A counsellor?' she laughed, revealing her regular white teeth. 'I could do with a counsellor just at present. Or are you merely fond of giving advice? Ah, but what difference does it make? Give me some advice, my dear collegiate counsellor: what can be done with a ruined life?'

'Whose?' Matvei Berdichevsky asked in a hoarse voice.

'Mine. And perhaps yours. Tell me, advice-giver: could you take your entire life and just strike it out, destroy it, all for the sake of one single moment? Not even a moment, but the hope of that moment, a hope that might never be realised?'

Berdichevsky babbled: 'I do not understand you . . . What you say is strange.'

But he did understand; he understood everything perfectly. The thing that could never under any circumstances happen to *him*, because his entire life flowed along an entirely different channel, was close, very close. A moment? A hope? But what about Masha?

'Do you believe in fate?' The woman on the horse was no longer smiling, her clear brow had clouded over, the crop was tapping insistently against the horse's crupper, and the black was shifting its feet nervously. 'Do you believe everything is predetermined and there are no accidental meetings?'

'I don't know . . .'

But he did know that he was almost lost, and he was already prepared to be lost completely – he even desired it. The orange stripe of the sunset protruded on both sides of the black horse, as if it had suddenly grown wings of fire.

'I believe it. I dropped my handkerchief: you picked it up. But perhaps it is not really a handkerchief at all?'

The assistant public prosecutor looked in bemusement at the scrap of cloth that he was still clutching in his fingers and thought: I am like a beggar, standing with his hand held out.

The horsewoman's voice assumed a menacing tone: 'Do you want me to turn my horse and gallop away from here? So that you will never see me again? Then you will never know whether you have tricked fate or fate has tricked you.' She jerked on the bridle, swung round and raised her riding crop.

'No!' Berdichevsky exclaimed, instantly forgetting about Masha and the twelve children, and the thirteenth still to come – so unbearable was the thought that the strange horsewoman would gallop off for ever into the gathering gloom.

'Then take hold of the stirrup, take a good, firm grip if you want to keep hold!' she ordered.

Spellbound, he grabbed the silvery bracket tight in his fist. The horsewoman gave a guttural cry, struck the black with her crop, and the horse set off at a brisk jog.

Matvei Berdichevsky ran as fast as his legs would carry him, without understanding what was happening. After about fifty or perhaps a hundred steps he stumbled, fell flat on his face and went tumbling over and over.

From out of the darkness he heard the sound of rapidly receding laughter.

'What kind of island is this?' the investigator asked himself senselessly, over and over again, as he sat in the road nursing his bruised elbow. His knuckles were skinned and bleeding too, but Matvei Berdichevsky had kept hold of the cambric handkerchief.

This unbelievable, absolutely incredible adventure clearly left the assistant public prosecutor in a disturbed state of mind. This is the only possible explanation for the fact that he completely lost track of the time and could not even remember walking back to his hotel. And when he finally did recover his senses, he discovered that he was sitting on the bed in his room and staring dull-wittedly out of the window at the segment of orange hanging in the sky – the moon was young.

He took his watch out of his waistcoat pocket with a mechanical gesture. It was one minute after ten, from which Berdichevsky concluded that he must have been brought back to reality by the chiming of his Breguet, although the sound had left no trace in his memory.

Lev Nikolaevich! He had promised to wait on the bench only until ten o'clock!

The assistant public prosecutor leapt up off the bed and ran out of his room. And he carried on running, not walking, along the street and the seafront. Passers-by glanced round at him: in sedate New Ararat a man running, especially late in the evening, was obviously a rare sight.

The chance to talk to a witness, even an important one, would not on its own have been enough to set Berdichevsky dashing along in this manner, but he suddenly felt a quite irresistible desire to see Lev Nikolaevich's serene, kind face and talk to him, simply talk to him, about something simple and important, something far more important than any investigation.

The white dome of the Rotunda, one of the local beauty

spots, was visible from a distance. The assistant public prosecutor ran all the way, arriving completely exhausted and with no hope left of finding Lev Nikolaevich still there – but there was his thin figure rising from the bench to greet the runner with a friendly wave of the hand.

Both men were absolutely delighted. Of course, Matvei Bentsionovich Berdichevsky's reaction was perfectly understandable, but Lev Nikolaevich was clearly very pleased as well.

'And I was thinking that you wouldn't come!' he exclaimed, shaking the investigator firmly by the hand. 'But I went on sitting here, just in case. And now here you are! How wonderful, how remarkable!'

It was a bright or, as poetic souls might have it, magical night. Lev Nikolaevich's eyes and his marvellous smile were so full of such amiable benevolence, and Berdichevsky's heart was in such terrible turmoil, that before he had fully recovered his breath, without any introductions or preambles, he had told this man whom he barely knew about what had happened. Matvei Berdichevsky was reticent by nature, with a shyness that was deep-rooted, and it was by no means his natural inclination to share intimate confidences, especially with strangers. But, firstly, Lev Nikolaevich somehow did not seem like a stranger to him and, secondly, his need to speak out and ease the burden of his soul was far too urgent.

Berdichevsky told Lev Nikolaevich about the mysterious horsewoman and his own fall (in both the literal sense and the moral) without concealing anything, every now and then wiping away the tears from his cheeks.

Lev Nikolaevich proved to be an ideal confidant – he listened seriously, without interrupting, and with such intense sympathy that he almost burst into tears himself.

'You are wrong to chastise yourself so!' he exclaimed as soon as Berdichevsky had finished his story. 'Really, you shouldn't! I know very little about the love between men and women, but I have been told about it, and I have read that even the most exemplary and virtuous family man can suffer something like an eclipse of the reason. After all, in the depths of his soul every man, no matter how orderly his way of thinking might be, is waiting for a miracle, and very often he thinks he has found this miracle in the form of some exceptional woman. It happens to wives too, but especially often to husbands – simply because men are more disposed to adventures. What you have told me is a mere nothing. That is, of course, I don't really mean it is nothing – I just blurted that out to reassure you; but after all, nothing happened. As far as your wife is concerned, you are entirely blameless . . .'

'No, I am guilty, guilty,' said Berdichevsky, interrupting his kind companion. 'Far more guilty than if I had got drunk and spent the night in a bawdy house. That would simply have been swinishness, physical filth, but I have been unfaithful, genuinely unfaithful! And so quickly, so easily – all in a moment!'

Lev Nikolaevich looked closely at his new acquaintance and said thoughtfully: 'No, it was not a genuine betrayal, not the most serious case.'

'Then what, in your opinion, is genuine betrayal?'

'Genuine, satanic betrayal is when you betray someone to their face, looking into their eyes, and take a special pleasure in your own baseness.'

'Hah, pleasure,' said Berdichevsky, gesturing dismissively. 'And as for baseness, I am an absolutely genuine scoundrel. I know now that I am, and I must live with that knowledge . . . Ah,' he said, rousing himself, 'if only I could atone for that moment, wash it from my soul, eh? I would submit to any test, go through any torment, if I could feel once again that I was . . .' He had been going to say 'a noble man', but he felt too ashamed and said simply: 'a man.'

'To put oneself to the test is useful, even necessary,' Lev Nikolaevich agreed. 'What I think is that—'

'Wait!' the assistant public prosecutor broke in, struck by a sudden idea. 'Wait! I know what test I must submit to! Tell me, for God's sake, tell me: where is the house in which the buoy-keeper used to live? Do you know?'

'Of course I do,' said Lev Nikolaevich, surprised. 'It's over that way, along the shoreline as far as Lenten Spit, and then to the left. About two versts from here ... but why do you want to know?'

'I'll tell you why ...' And then – that night must clearly have been special in some way – Berdichevsky revealed all the secrets of the investigation to his dear friend: he told him about Alyosha Lentochkin, and about Lagrange and, naturally, about his own mission.

His listener merely gasped and shook his head.

'I swear to you,' Matvei Bentsionovich said in conclusion, raising his hand as if he were taking the oath in court, 'that I shall set off immediately, this very moment, to that accursed hut, completely alone, wait until midnight and then go in, just as Alexei Stepanovich and Felix Stanislavovich did. I don't care if there's nothing there – if it's all nothing but superstitious nonsense. The important thing is that I shall conquer my fear and in doing so recover my self-respect!'

Lev Nikolaevich jumped to his feet and exclaimed in admiration: 'What a wonderful thing you have just said! In your place I should do exactly the same thing. Only, you know ... ' He grabbed hold of Berdichevsky's elbow impetuously. 'You must not go there alone. It's far too frightening. Take me with you. Yes, really! Let's go together, eh?' And he looked into Matvei Berdichevsky's eyes so imploringly that the investigator felt his chest constrict and fresh tears began pouring from his eyes.

'Thank you,' the assistant public prosecutor said with feeling. 'I appreciate your noble impulse, but my heart tells me I must go into that hut alone. Otherwise it will all amount to nothing, and I shall not achieve genuine atonement.' He forced himself to smile and even attempted to joke. 'And apart from that, you are a creature of such angelic appearance that the evil spirit might feel too shy to show himself before you.'

'All right, all right,' said Lev Nikolaevich, nodding. 'I won't interfere. You know, I'll just see you there and then stand on one side, well out of the way. At a distance of fifty paces, or even a hundred. But I will see you there. You won't feel so lonely, and I shall be less worried. You never know ...'

Berdichevsky was quite delighted by this idea since, on the one hand, it did not devalue the proposed trial of courage, while on the other it promised at least the illusion of a certain support. But then he immediately felt angry with himself for being so delighted.

He frowned and said: 'Not a hundred paces. Two hundred.'

They parted on the little bridge over the swift, narrow river that had no more than twenty *sazhens* left to run to the lake.

'There it is, the buoy-keeper's little house,' said Lev Nikolaevich, pointing to a dark cube with its white straw roof glinting in the moonlight. 'Are you quite sure I can't come with you?'

Berdichevsky shook his head. He did not try to say anything, because his teeth were clenched tightly together – he was afraid that if he set them free, they would start chattering shamefully.

'Well then, God be with you,' his faithful second said excitedly. 'I shall wait right here, by the Farewell Chapel. If anything happens, shout, and I'll come running straight away.'

Instead of answering, Matvei Berdichevsky put his arms awkwardly round Lev Nikolaevich's shoulders and pulled him against himself for a second; and then, with a wave of his hand, he stepped out towards the hut.

There were two minutes left until midnight, but he had no real distance to go – not even two hundred paces; a hundred and fifty at the most.

What nonsense it all is, the assistant public prosecutor thought to himself as he glanced into the hut. I know for certain that nothing is going to happen. Nothing can happen. I'll go in, stand there for a while, and then come back out, feeling like a total blockhead. It's a good thing that at least I have such a kind-hearted witness. Anyone else would have made me a public laughing stock for this – imagine the assistant provincial public prosecutor quaking in his boots on his way to keep appointments with evil spirits! Stung by his pride, the courage began to stir deep in his soul. Now he had to nurture it carefully, protect it like a small flame trembling in the wind, not allow it to go out.

'Come on then, come on then,' Berdichevsky drawled, lengthening his stride. But even so he paused in front of the crookedly boarded-up door and crossed himself, making small movements that would not be visible from behind. The idea of taking all his clothes off was absurd, of course, he decided. He couldn't remember the formula from the medieval treatise properly anyway. But that was all right; he would manage somehow without any formula. He could touch the cross scratched on the glass and say something about an agreement between the Archangel Gabriel and the Evil One. 'Come hither, blessed spirit' – wasn't that how it went? And if things started to get unpleasant, he had to shout out in Latin that he believed in the Lord, and everything would be settled quite excellently.

Joking made the investigator feel bolder. He took hold of the edge of the door and pulled, straining with all his might.

He need not have strained at all, as it turned out, for the door yielded easily. As he stepped across the creaking floor, Matvei Berdichevsky tried to determine where the window was. He froze in indecision and just at that moment the moon, which had been hidden briefly behind a cloud, lit up the vault of heaven once again, also illuminating a silvery square to his left.

The investigator turned his neck and choked on a convulsive shriek.

There was someone standing there!

Motionless, black, in a pointed cowl!

No, no, no, thought Berdichevsky, shaking his head to drive the vision away. As if the shaking were too much for it to bear, his head suddenly exploded in unbearable agony that seared through his brain. Matvei Berdichevsky's consciousness, overwhelmed, abandoned him and he saw and heard nothing more.

After some indefinite period of time the unfortunate investigator's senses returned to him, but not all of them – his vision still refused to function. Berdichevsky's eyes were open, but they could not see anything.

He listened. He heard the rapid pitter-patter of his own heart; he could even hear his eyelashes blinking, the silence was so intense. His nose inhaled a smell of dust and wood shavings. His head hurt and his body felt numb, and that meant he was alive.

But where was he? In the hut?

No. It had been dark there, but not this dark, not *absolutely* dark, as dark as in a coffin.

Berdichevsky tried to get up, and he struck something with his forehead. He moved his arms, and he could not spread his elbows. He bent his knees, and they also hit something hard.

Then the assistant public prosecutor realised that he really was lying in a closed coffin, and he began calling out.

At first not very loudly, as if he had not yet lost hope: 'A-ah! A-a-ah!'

And then with all the power of his lungs: 'A-a-a-ah!'

Once Berdichevsky had emptied his lungs of air by shouting, he broke into choking sobs. His brain, trained to think logically, took advantage of this brief respite to offer him the answer to a riddle – alas, too late. That was why Lagrange had shot himself with his left hand, from below! There was no other way he could turn the revolver inside the coffin. He had pulled out his Smith and Wesson as best he could, pointed it at his heart and fired.

Berdichevsky was overwhelmed by a fierce envy of the deceased chief of police. What a relief, what incredible happiness it would be to have a revolver with him! Just press the trigger, and the nightmare would be over for ever and ever.

Swallowing his tears, Berdichevsky muttered: 'Masha, my

little Masha, forgive me ... I have betrayed you again, and more seriously than back there, on the road! I am leaving you, abandoning you ...' But meanwhile his brain continued its work, the work that was no longer of any use to anyone.

So it was clear what had happened to Lentochkin too. After the coffin he couldn't tolerate any roofs or walls – or any restrictions of his body at all.

The sobbing suddenly stopped of its own accord – Berdichevsky had been struck by another realisation: Lentochkin had managed to get out of the coffin somehow after all. He might be insane, but he was alive! That meant there was hope!

The prayer! How could he have forgotten about the prayer!

However, the Latin that Matvei Berdichevsky thought he had swotted so thoroughly during his years in the grammar school and at university seemed to have been completely erased from his memory by the fear of death. He could not even remember the Latin for 'Lord'!

And so His Grace Mitrofanii's spiritual son began yelling in Russian: 'I believe, O Lord, I believe!'

He braced himself in the wooden box, pressing against the lid with his forehead, his hands and his knees – and a miracle happened. The top of the coffin flew off with a resounding crack and Berdichevsky sat up, gulping in air, and looked around.

He saw the same hut as before, looking strangely bright after the pitch-darkness – he could make out the stove in the corner, and even the oven fork. And the window was still where it had been; only that terrible silhouette had disappeared.

Repeatedly intoning 'I believe, O Lord, I believe,' Berdichevsky clambered over the edge of the coffin and fell heavily on to the floor: the coffin was standing on a table.

Paying no attention to the pain that racked his entire body, he began working with his elbows and knees and crawled rapidly towards the door. He tumbled over the threshold, leapt to his feet and limped towards the river.

'Lev Nikolaevich! Help! Save me!' the assistant public

prosecutor called out hoarsely, afraid to look round, in case he might see a black monk in a pointed cowl gliding above the ground after him. 'Help me! I'm going to fall!'

There was the little bridge, and there was the fence. Lev Nikolaevich had promised to wait here.

Berdichevsky dashed to the left, then to the right, but there was no one there.

It wasn't possible! Lev Nikolaevich wasn't the kind of man who would simply get up and walk away!

'Where are you?' Berdichevsky groaned. 'I'm hurt, I'm afraid!'

When the dark figure silently detached itself from the wall of the chapel, the exhausted investigator shrieked, imagining that his nightmarish pursuer had overtaken him and been waiting in ambush.

But no, to judge from the silhouette, it was Lev Nikolaevich. Sobbing, Berdichevsky went dashing towards him. 'Thank ... Thank God! I believe, O Lord, I believe! Why didn't you answer? I thought ...' As he came closer to his trusted comrade-in-arms, he mumbled: 'I ... I don't know what happened, but it was horrible ... I think I'm losing my mind! Lev Nikolaevich, dear friend, what's happening? What's wrong with me?'

At that moment his silent companion turned to face the moonlight, and Berdichevsky fell silent in confusion.

Lev Nikolaevich had undergone a strange metamorphosis. While his features were still the same, his face had changed, subtly but quite distinctly. His gentle, affectionate gaze had acquired a menacing glitter, his lips were twisted into a cruel smirk, his shoulders had straightened up and his forehead was dissected by a crease as dramatic as a scar left by a knife.

'I'll tell you what's wrong,' the unrecognisable Lev Nikolaevich hissed, twirling his finger beside his temple. 'You, my friend, have lost your mind. My God, just look at that idiotic expression on your face!'

Matvei Berdichevsky started back in fright, and Lev Nikolaevich, with his right cheek twitching rapidly, bared his remarkably white teeth and exclaimed triumphantly three times: 'Idiot! Idiot! Idiot!'

It was only then that Berdichevsky realised, with the very edge of his rapidly failing mind, that he really had gone mad, and not just a little while ago, in the hut, but earlier, much earlier. Dream and reality had become jumbled together in his sick head, so that now there was no way of telling which of the events of this terrible day had really happened and which were the ravings of his delirious reason.

The insane official pulled his head down into his shoulders and ran off along the moonlit road wherever his feet might take him, dragging one leg and repeating over and over again: 'I believe, O Lord, I believe!'

PART TWO

Mrs Lisitsyna's Pilgrimage

A Moscow Province Noblewoman

Of course, it just had to happen that immediately before the second letter from Dr Korovin arrived, in fact on the very evening before, the Bishop and Sister Pelagia had a conversation about men and women. His Grace and his spiritual daughter argued about this subject quite often, but on this occasion the pretext for their clash happened to be the question of strength and weakness. Pelagia attempted to prove that women should never have been dubbed the 'weaker sex', for it was not true, except perhaps in the matter of muscular strength, and even there it was not always true of everyone. The nun got quite carried away and even offered to run or swim in a race against the Bishop in order to see who was quicker, but she immediately came to her senses and apologised. Mitrofanii, however, was not in the least bit angry; he simply laughed.

'The two of us would make a fine sight,' said His Grace. 'Just imagine us dashing along Bolshaya Dvoryanskaya Street at full speed, with our cassocks tucked up, flinging up our heels, me with my beard flapping in the wind, you with your ginger locks fluttering about. All the people watching and crossing themselves, and us not taking the slightest bit of notice – we run as far as the river, plunge in off the cliff, and away we go, arm over arm.'

Pelagia laughed as well, but she pursued her theme relentlessly: 'There is no strong sex or weak sex. Each half of humanity is strong in some ways and weak in others. Men, of course, are more subtle in logic, which is why they are stronger in the exact sciences, but it is also their shortcoming. You men always try to make everything fit the geometry you learned at grammar school, you dismiss anything you cannot squeeze into regular forms and right angles, and therefore you lose sight of what is most important. And you are great muddle-heads, always constructing nonsensical schemes, and then suffering the dire consequences. And your pride is a great hindrance; more than anything else you are afraid of finding yourself in a ridiculous or humiliating situation. But women don't care about that; we know very well how stupid and childish that kind of fear is. We are more easily confused and misled in matters that are unimportant, but in the most important things of all, those that are truly significant, there is no logic that can delude us.'

'And what is all this leading to?' Mitrofanii asked, laughing. 'What precisely is the point of your philippic? That men are stupid and control over society should be taken away from them and given to you?'

The nun pushed the spectacles that had slid down to the tip of her nose back up with her finger. 'No, Your Grace, you are not listening to what I say! Both of the sexes are clever and stupid, strong and weak in their own way. But in different areas! And therein lies the majesty of God's plan, the meaning of love and marriage – so that the weaknesses of each person might be buttressed by the strengths of their spouses.'

However, the Bishop was not in the mood for serious conversation that day. He feigned surprise: 'Are you planning to marry then?'

'I am not talking about myself. I have a different Bridegroom, who lends me more strength than any man. What I am saying, Father, is that you are wrong to rely only on the male intellect in serious matters, that you forget about women's strength and men's weakness.'

Mitrofanii listened, chuckling into his whiskers, and that inflamed Pelagia even more. 'The worst thing of all is that condescending laugh of yours!' she said, finally exploding. 'It comes from your male arrogance, which is entirely out of place in a monk! Have you not been told: "There is no male or female sex, for you all are one in Jesus Christ"?'

'I know why you are reading me this sermon, why you are so furious,' the perspicacious pastor replied. 'You are offended because I did not send you to New Ararat. You are jealous of Matvei. What if he untangles the entire business without any help from your ginger head? And Matvei certainly will untangle it, because he is cautious, astute and *logical*.' At this point Mitrofanii stopped smiling and spoke without a trace of jocularity. 'Do I not appreciate your merits? Do I not know what sharp wits and subtle intuition you possess, how discerning you are with people? But you know yourself that a nun cannot go to Ararat. The charter of the monastery forbids it.'

'You have already mentioned that, and in Berdichevsky's presence I did not argue. Of course Sister Pelagia cannot go. But Polina Andreevna Lisitsyna certainly can.'

'Do not even think of it!' said His Grace, speaking more sternly. 'Enough! We have sinned and angered God, but it is time to call a halt. I repent, I am at fault for giving you my blessing for such an obscenity – all in the name of the search for truth and the triumph of justice. I took the sin entirely on myself. And if the Synod knew about these pranks, they would throw me out of my see; they might even defrock me. However, I have not forsworn it because I fear for my episcopal robes but because I fear for your safety. Have you forgotten that last time this play-acting almost cost you your life? It is over; Lisitsyna will not return, and let me hear no more of it!'

Their argument over the mysterious woman Lisitsyna continued for a long time, but neither could convince the other, and so they parted having agreed to differ.

The next morning, however, the post delivered a letter to His Grace from the medical psychiatrist Korovin on the island of Canaan.

The Bishop opened the envelope, read its contents, clutched at his heart and fell.

The episcopal residence was thrown into unprecedented

turmoil. Doctors came running, the Governor arrived at a gallop on an unsaddled horse, without his hat, and the marshal of the nobility came dashing into town from his country estate.

Of course, Sister Pelagia was there too. She came very quietly and sat in the reception room for a while, watching the doctors bustling about with fright in her eyes, and then seized her chance to lead the Bishop's secretary, Father Userdov, off to one side. He informed her how the catastrophe had occurred and showed her the disastrous letter about the new patient in Dr Korovin's hospital.

The nun spent the rest of the day and the whole night praying in the Bishop's icon room – not on the prie-dieu, but kneeling directly on the floor. She prayed fervently for the recovery of the sick man, whose death would be a great misfortune for the entire region and for the many people who loved the Bishop. Pelagia did not intrude in the bedchamber where the doctors were treating their patient – there were more than enough people caring for him without her, and in any case she would not have been allowed in. An entire council of physicians were practising their arcane arts on the unconscious body, and three of Russia's leading specialists in ailments of the heart were already on their way from St Petersburg, summoned by telegram.

In the morning the youngest of the doctors came out of the room, sullen and pale-faced. He approached the kneeling nun and told her: 'He is conscious and he is asking for you. Only do not be long. And for God's sake, Sister, no weeping. He must not be upset.'

Pelagia rose to her feet with difficulty, rubbed the bruises on her knees and went into the bedchamber. Mitrofanii was lying there on his high old bed with the blue canopy that was decorated with a depiction of the vault of heaven, wheezing heavily. Pelagia was astounded by the deathly pallor of the Bishop's complexion, the strange sharpness of his features and above all by the stillness that was so far out of keeping with the Bishop's energetic character.

The nun sobbed, and the angry doctor immediately cleared his throat loudly behind her back. Then Pelagia smiled fearfully and approached the bed with that pitiful, inappropriate smile on her lips.

The man lying in the bed glanced sideways at her and lowered his eyelids slightly – he had recognised her. He moved his purple lips with a struggle, but no sound emerged.

With the smile still on her face, Pelagia fell to her knees and crawled to the bed so that she could guess what he was saying from the movement of his lips.

His Grace gazed into her eyes, not with the glance of calm benediction that would have been appropriate at such a moment, but sternly, even menacingly. Summoning all his strength, he whispered three strange words: 'Don't you dare . . .'

The nun waited to see if he would say anything more, and when he did not, she nodded reassuringly, kissed the sick man's feeble hand and got to her feet. The doctor nudged her in the side as if to say: Come on now, be on your way.

Pelagia walked slowly through the rooms, whispering the words of a prayer of repentance: 'Take pity on me, O God, in Thy great mercy, and in the multitude of Thy bounties purge my iniquity, for I do know my own iniquity, and my sin against myself . . .'

The meaning of this prayer was soon revealed. From the icon room the nun did not turn into the reception room; instead she slipped into the Bishop's dark, empty study. Without the slightest hesitation she unlocked the drawer of the writing desk and took out the bronze casket in which Mitrofanii kept the personal savings that he usually spent on books and the requirements of episcopal vestments, or help for the poor – and with a steady hand she thrust the entire wad of bank notes inside her habit, leaving not a single rouble behind.

The courtyard was crowded with the carriages of well-wishers. Pelagia walked across it unhurriedly, with decorum, but the moment she turned into the garden in front of the episcopal college, she broke into an unseemly run.

She called into the cell of the head of the college and told her that at the behest of His Grace Mitrofanii she had to go away for a time, although it was not yet clear for how long, and asked her to find a replacement teacher for her lessons. Kind Sister Christina, accustomed to the sudden absences of her teacher of Russian and gymnastics, asked no questions about Pelagia's destination, but merely enquired if she had enough warm things to avoid catching cold on her journey. The nuns embraced each other shoulder to shoulder; Pelagia collected a small trunk from her room, found a cabby and ordered him to take her to the landing stage at top speed – there was less than half an hour left before the steamboat was due to leave.

At noon the following day she was already walking down the gangway on to the quayside in Nizhny Novgorod, no longer wearing her nun's habit but a modest black dress that she had taken out of the trunk. And that was only the first stage of her metamorphosis.

In her hotel the red-headed guest first asked for a pile of the latest fashion magazines to be brought to her room, then armed herself with a pencil and began copying out all sorts of abstruse phrases on to a sheet of paper: *capote écossaise*, *velvet peplos*, *wooln. talma* and more in the same vein.

Having completed this research as painstakingly as possible, spending no less than two hours on the task, Pelagia paid a visit to Nizhny Novgorod's very finest ready-made clothing emporium, Dubois et Fils, where she gave the shop assistant remarkably precise and detailed instructions, which were received with a respectful bow and put into effect without delay.

An hour and a half later, having despatched to the hotel an entire coach-load of bundles and boxes, the plunderer of the Bishop's private treasury, now decked out in that mysterious *velvet peplos* (a straight-cut dress of Utrecht velvet with no fitted bodice), committed a quite unimaginable act for a nun: she went to a *salon de coiffures* and had her short hair curled in the latest

172

Parisian style, '*joli cherubin*', which suited her oval, slightly freckled face very well.

As is the way with women, having dressed more smartly and paid some attention to her appearance, this lady from Zavolzhsk was transformed inwardly as well as outwardly. Her gait became lighter, as if she were gliding along; her shoulders straightened; her neck held her head higher, with the face inclined upwards instead of downwards. Men walking past her glanced round; two officers actually stopped – one of them even whistled, and the other reproached him: 'Fie, Michel, such manners!'

At the entrance to the office of the tourist agency Cook and Kantorovich the stylish lady was pestered by a dirty, spiteful gipsy woman, who began threatening her with inevitable disaster, nightmares and death by drowning, and demanded ten kopecks to ward off her misfortune. Pelagia was not at all alarmed by this prophetess, especially since in the none-too-distant past she had successfully evaded a watery grave, but even so she gave the witch some money – a whole rouble, not just ten kopecks – so that in future she would be more good-natured and not regard everybody as her enemy.

Inside the agency, which incorporated a shop selling travelling accessories, another one hundred and fifty roubles of the Bishop's savings was spent on two wonderful Scottish suitcases, a manicure set and a little mother-of-pearl spectacle case that could be attached to a belt (both elegant and convenient), in addition to the acquisition of a ticket to the monastery of New Ararat, which could only be reached by taking the railway to Vologda, then travelling by coach to Sineozersk and finally boarding a steamship.

'Are you going on pilgrimage?' the assistant enquired politely. 'Just the right time, madam, before the cold weather sets in. Perhaps you would like to book a hotel straight away?'

'Which do you recommend?' the traveller asked in reply.

'The mayor's wife and her daughter recently booked their journey with us. They stayed at the Holofernes' Head and were most complimentary about it.'

'The Holofernes' Head?' the lady echoed with a frown. 'Are there not any other hotels, a little less bloodthirsty, perhaps?'

'Why, of course there are. The Noah's Ark Hotel and the Promised Land boarding house. And those ladies who wish to isolate themselves completely from male company put up at the Immaculate Virgin – a most devout establishment for noble and well-to-do female pilgrims. The charges are not high, but each guest is expected to make a donation of at least a hundred roubles to the monastery treasury. Those who give three hundred or more are accorded a private audience with the archimandrite himself.'

This final item of information seemed to be of great interest to the prospective pilgrim. She opened her new *ridicule*, took out a bundle of bank notes (still quite substantial) and began counting them. The assistant followed this procedure with tactful reverence. At five hundred roubles his client stopped and put the money back into her handbag without completing her count.

'Will your servant be sharing your room or in separate accommodation?'

'How can you ask?' the lady objected, tossing her bronze curls reproachfully. 'Take a servant on a pilgrimage? Why, that's not Christian. I shall do everything myself – dress and wash, and perhaps even brush my own hair.'

'I beg your pardon. I'm afraid not everybody is quite so scrupulous, madam . . .' The clerk began scribbling on a blank form, deftly dunking his steel-nibbed pen in the inkwell. 'In whose name shall I make out the order?'

The pilgrim sighed and for some reason crossed herself. 'Write: "Polina Andreevna Lisitsyna, widow, hereditary noblewoman of the Moscow Province".'

Travel sketches

Since the heroine of our narrative, having cast off her nun's habit, has chosen to call herself by a different name, we shall also call her by it – out of respect for the conventual vocation and in order to avoid any blasphemous ambivalence. Let her be a noblewoman, and let her be Lisitsyna – after all, she should know. Especially since, to all appearances the spiritual daughter of the archpastor of Zavolzhsk felt quite as much at ease in her new persona as she had in her old one. It was easy to see that she did not find travelling wearisome – quite the contrary: it was a joy and a pleasure to her.

Riding along in the train, the young lady occasionally cast a favourable glance out of the window at the empty fields and autumnal forests, which had still not completely shed their farewell finery. In the tourist agency, as a complimentary gift to go with her various purchases, Polina Andreevna Lisitsyna had been given a fine velvet needlework bag, which was now resting cosily on her chest, and she was whiling away the time knitting a warm merino pullover, which His Grace Mitrofanii was sure to need in the cold winter season, especially after such serious problems with his heart. It was extremely complicated work, with alternating bouclé and stocking stitches and coloured inserts, and it was not going well: the stitches lay unevenly, the coloured threads were drawn too tight, completely distorting the pattern, and yet Lisitsyna herself seemed pleased with the results of her creative efforts. Every now and then she would break off and survey her clumsy handiwork with evident satisfaction.

When the traveller grew weary of her knitting, she took up

her reading, and she somehow managed to pursue this activity not only in the peaceful railway carriage, but also in a jolting omnibus. She was reading two books alternately, one of which was perfectly suited to a pilgrimage – *An Outline of Christian Morality* by Theophanes the Anchorite The other was a very strange choice – *A Textbook of Firearms Ballistics*, Part 2 – but she read it with no less care and attention.

Once on board the steamship *St Basilisk* in Sineozersk, Polina Andreevna demonstrated in full measure one of her most distinctive characteristics: irrepressible curiosity. She walked round the entire vessel, spoke with the sailors in cassocks, watched the huge paddle wheels straining against the water. She visited the engine room and listened to the engineer telling those passengers who were interested how the flywheels, the crankshafts and the boiler worked. Lisitsyna even put on her spectacles (which, following the transformation of the nun from Zavolzhsk into the hereditary noblewoman from Moscow, had been banished from the pilgrim's nose to the mother-of-pearl case) and glanced into the furnace, where the red-hot coals flashed and crackled in a most frightening fashion.

Then, together with the other curious passengers, who were all without exception male, she set out to investigate the captain's wheelhouse.

The tour had been arranged in order to demonstrate New Ararat's benevolent hospitality, which extended beyond the shores of the archipelago to include the ship that bore the name of the monastery's founder. The explanations about the fairway, the control of the steamship and the unpredictable behaviour of the winds on the Blue Lake were provided by the mate, a humble monk in a moth-eaten skullcap, but Lisitsyna found the captain, Brother Jonah, far more intriguing. He was a red-faced bandit with a thick beard and an oilskin cap, who stood at the helm in person in order to have an excuse to avoid looking at the passengers.

Despite being dressed in a cassock, this colourful individual looked so very unlike a monk that Polina Andreevna could not resist the urge to sidle a little closer and ask him: 'Tell me, holy Father, is it long since you took monastic vows?'

The hulking brute squinted down at her and said nothing, hoping she would go away. Realising that she would not, he answered her reluctantly in his rumbling voice: 'Over four years now.'

The passenger immediately moved right in under the captain's elbow so that it would be more convenient to talk. 'And who were you out in the world?'

The captain heaved a sigh that left no doubt at all that if he could have his own way, he would refuse to answer the pushy little lady's questions and march her out of the wheelhouse in a jiffy, because women had no right being in there.

'The same as I am now. A helmsman. I used to hunt whales round Spitzbergen.'

'How very interesting!' exclaimed Polina Andreevna, not embarrassed in the least by his unfriendly tone. 'That must be why they called you Jonah, I suppose? Because of the whales?'

In a genuinely heroic feat of Christian humility, the captain stretched his mouth out to both sides in an expression that was evidently intended to signify a polite smile. 'Not because of the whales – because of one whale. The beast smashed the boat to pieces with his tail and everybody drowned. I was the only one who came back up. He sucked me right into his mouth and scraped me with his great whiskers, but he can't have liked the taste of me and he spat me out again. I couldn't have been in his mouth more than half a minute, but it was long enough for me to promise that if survived, I'd go for a monk.'

'What an incredible story!' the passenger exclaimed admiringly. 'And the most amazing thing about it is that, after you were saved, you really did join a monastery. You know, many people make promises to God in a moment of despair, but afterwards very few of them actually carry them out.'

Jonah stopped imitating a smile and knitted his shaggy eyebrows in a frown. 'A promise is a promise.'

This short phrase was so full of adamantine resolution mixed with intense bitterness that Mrs Lisitsyna suddenly felt terribly sorry for the poor whaler. 'Ah, you should never have become a monk,' she said, distraught. 'The Lord would have understood and forgiven you. The monastic life should be a reward, but for you it is like a punishment. You miss your old, free life, don't you? I know seamen. Life without drink and oaths is a torment to you. And then there is the vow of celibacy . . .' The tender-hearted pilgrim finished in a low voice, as if she were talking to herself.

But the captain heard her anyway, and he gave the tactless creature a glance that made Polina Andreevna beat a rapid retreat from the wheelhouse out on to the deck, and from there to her cabin.

A Male Heaven

The captain's furious glance was explained to some extent when the *St Basilisk* moored at the New Ararat landing stage the following morning. Polina Andreevna was detained on board for a while, waiting for the porter, and she was almost the last passenger to leave the ship. Her attention was caught by a slim, elegant young lady dressed in black who was waiting impatiently for someone on the quayside. After looking the waiting woman over carefully and noting certain distinctive features of her outfit (although it was fanciful, it was somewhat *démodé* – judging from the magazines, such broad hats and boots with silver buttons were no longer being worn this season), Lisitsyna concluded that this lady was probably one of the local inhabitants. She was very good-looking, but rather pale, and the impression she made was also spoiled by a glance that was far too rapid and hostile. The native woman also studied the noble lady from Moscow, resting her gaze on the fashionable *talma*, or cape, and the ginger curls protruding from beneath the 'mischievous page-boy' cap. The stranger's beautiful face contorted in fury and she turned her face away, looking for someone on the deck.

Intrigued, Polina Andreevna walked on a few steps, then turned back and put on her spectacles and was rewarded for her prudence with an interesting scene.

Brother Jonah came out on to the gangway, saw the lady in black and stopped dead in his tracks. But no sooner did she beckon him with a brief, imperious gesture than the captain went dashing down on to the quayside, almost skipping along. Recalling the monastic vow of celibacy once again, Polina

Andreevna shook her head. She also observed another intriguing detail: as he drew level with the local woman, Jonah turned his head towards her slightly (the broad, coarse features of the captain's face were even redder than usual), but he did not stop – he only touched her hand gently. However, Mrs Lisitsyna's eyes, assisted by her spectacles, observed some small, square paper object make the transition from the former whaler's massive hand to the grey-suede glove covering the woman's slim palm – it was either a small envelope or a folded note.

Ah, the poor soul, Polina Andreevna sighed to herself and walked on, observing the holy town with interest.

The new pilgrim was extremely lucky with the weather that day. A gentle sun illuminated the golden domes of the churches and the bell towers, the white walls of the monastery and the motley-coloured roofs of the local inhabitants' houses with a placid melancholy. The new arrival especially liked the fact that in New Ararat the bright colours of autumn had not yet faded away: the trees were all warm yellows, browns and reds, and the blue of the sky was not at all November-like, whereas in Zavolzhsk, which was located much further south, the leaves had long since fallen and in the morning the puddles were covered with a crust of dirty ice.

Polina Andreevna recalled that in the wheelhouse the first mate had told them about some special 'micro-climate' on the islands, resulting from the whims of the warm currents and also, naturally, the Lord's especially favourable disposition towards this godly spot.

Before she even reached her hotel, the traveller had spied out all the unusual sights of New Ararat and formed her first impression of this peculiar town.

New Ararat appeared to Lisitsyna to be a very fine town, cleverly arranged, but at the same time strangely unfortunate, or, as she put it in her own mind, 'impoverished'. Not in terms of a lack of public amenities or poor buildings – as far as that went everything was in perfect order: the houses were very fine, mostly built of stone, the churches were numerous and magnificent (although they were very block-like; they did not reach for the heavens in that way that uplifts the soul) and the streets were a real treat for the eyes – not a speck of dirt or a single puddle. Polina Andreevna dubbed the town 'impoverished' because to her it seemed strangely joyless, and she had not expected that from a monastery so close to God.

It took the pilgrim a little time to puzzle out the reason for this state of deprivation. In fact, Mrs Lisitsyna was only struck by the answer after she had settled into her hotel. The very first thing she did there was to announce that she wished personally to present the father superior with a donation of five hundred roubles – and she was immediately granted an audience, on the very first day. The population of the Immaculate Virgin, including the staff, consisted entirely of women, and so the décor in the rooms was dominated by embroidered curtains, padded pouffes and cushions, and little benches with cloth covers – the new guest, accustomed to the simplicity of a conventual cell, disliked this mawkish display intensely. And as she emerged from this female heaven out on to the street, the contrast suddenly brought home to Polina Andreevna what was wrong with the town itself.

It was also a simulacrum of Heaven, but in this case a male one. Everything here was run by men; they did everything and arranged everything as they saw fit, with no thought for any wives, daughters or sisters, and therefore the town had turned out like a guards' barracks: spruce and neat to the point of geometrical precision, yet not the sort of place where you would want to live.

Having made this discovery, Lisitsyna began looking around her with redoubled curiosity. So this was how men would arrange life on Earth if they were given total freedom! Praying, pushing broomsticks, growing huge beards and marching in formation (Polina Andreevna had encountered a detachment of the monastery's 'peace-keepers'). Then she began feeling sorry for everyone: New Ararat, and the men, and the women. But more for the men than the women, because women could get by somehow or other without men, but if the men were left to themselves, they were certain to come to grief. They would either run riot and start behaving like animals, or fall into this kind of arid lifelessness. She didn't know which was worse.

A Kitten is Rescued

As has already been mentioned, the generous female donor had been promised an almost immediate audience with His Reverence Vitalii, and so on leaving her hotel she set out straight away in the direction of the monastery.

With its white walls and numerous domes, it could be seen from almost every point in the town, for it was located on the side of town that was elevated above the lake. From the last houses to the first structures flanking the monastery walls, most of which served some economic function, the path ran through a park laid out on the top of a rocky cliff with the indefatigable blue waves lapping gently at its foot.

As she walked along the edge of the lake, Polina Andreevna wrapped her woollen *talma* around herself more tightly, for the wind was rather cool, but she did not move deeper into the park and away from the cliff edge – the view from up there of the watery expanse was far too fine, and the gusty breeze refreshed rather than chilled her.

When she was already quite close to the boundary of the monastery itself, the ever-curious Lisitsyna saw that something unusual was going on in an open meadow which obviously served the locals as a favourite spot for walks, and she immediately turned in that direction.

At first she saw a crowd of people clustering together at the very edge of the cliff, by an old, crooked alder tree; then she heard a child crying and some other piercing, plaintive sounds that she could not quite identify. Polina Andreevna, who was familiar from her experience as a teacher with all the subtle variations of children's crying, suddenly felt alarmed, because the note of unfeigned grief in the lament was quite unmistakable.

It took the young lady no more than half a minute to grasp what was going on. In all honesty, it was a perfectly commonplace story, even somewhat comical. A little girl playing with a kitten had allowed it to climb up the tree. Clinging to the rough bark with its claws, the fluffy little beast had climbed too far and too high, and now it could not get down again. The danger of the situation was that the alder tree hung out over the sheer cliff, and the kitten was stuck on the longest and thinnest branch, with the waves splashing and foaming far below it.

It was clear straight away that the poor creature could not be saved, and that was a shame, for he was quite charming: short white fur like swan's down and round blue eyes, with a satin ribbon lovingly tied round his neck.

Lisitsyna felt even sorrier for his owner, a girl of six or seven. She was very pretty too: dressed in a clean little *sarafan*, a bright-coloured headscarf with locks of light-coloured hair peeping out from under it and little birch-bark sandals that looked as though they were made for a doll.

'Kuzya, Kuzenka!' the little child sobbed. 'Come down, you'll fall!'

Come down, indeed! The kitten was clinging to the very end of the branch with its last ounces of strength. The wind was swaying its little white body, first to the right, then to the left, and it was quite clear that soon it would shake the poor thing off altogether.

Polina Andreevna observed the sad scene with her hands pressed to her heart. She recalled an occasion not so long before when she had found herself in the same position as this little kitten and had only been saved by the benign Providence of God. Remembering that terrible night, she crossed herself and whispered a prayer – not in gratitude for her own miraculous deliverance then but for this poor doomed little creature: 'Lord God, let the little kitten live a little longer! What is such a small thing to Thee?'

She realised, of course, that it would take a miracle to save the kitten, and it was not really appropriate for Providence to squander its miracles on an instance such as this. It would be somehow lacking in sublimity – absurd, in fact.

The crowd was not standing there in silence, of course: some were comforting the little girl; others were discussing how to save the foolish little beast.

One said: 'You need to climb up, prop your foot against the branch and scoop him up with a butterfly net' – although it was quite clear that there was nowhere in the park where you could possibly lay your hands on a butterfly net. Someone else was thinking aloud to himself: 'You could lie on the branch and try to reach him, only you'd be sure to fall off. It's all very well to go risking your life for something important, but for a little animal like that . . .' And he was right, absolutely right.

Polina Andreevna was about to walk on, in order not to see the little ball of white fur go hurtling downwards with a squeal and hear the little girl's terrible scream (they could at least take her away), but just then a new character joined the small crowd, someone who looked so interesting that the *soi-disant* Moscow lady decided not to leave just yet.

The tall, lean gentleman in a foppish snow-white overcoat and equally white linen cap elbowed his way unceremoniously through the crowd towards the alder tree. Beyond the slightest shadow of a doubt, this determined individual belonged to the infamous category of 'handsome devils' to which, as we know, men are assigned not because of the classical regularity of their features (although the gentleman was really rather good-looking, in the golden-haired and blue-eyed Slavic style), but because of their general air of calm self-assurance and fascinating audacity. These two qualities, which unfailingly impress almost all women, were inscribed so distinctly in the face and manners of this elegant gentleman that all the fine ladies and common women, married women and young spinsters who happened to be in the crowd immediately began to pay him *special* attention.

In this Mrs Lisitsyna was no exception, thinking to herself:

Well now, what interesting characters you do find in Ararat! Could this one really be here on pilgrimage too?

After this, however, the new arrival began behaving in such a manner that the *special* attention he was already receiving became positively *mesmeric* (which, we might observe, is a not uncommon occurrence when 'handsome devils' put in an appearance).

Evaluating the situation at a single glance, the fine fellow unhesitatingly flung his cap down on the ground, where it was immediately followed by his fashionably tailored overcoat.

The gentleman issued instructions to one of the idle onlookers, who looked like a factory hand: 'Hey you, get up on that tree, quick march. And don't be afraid; you won't have to climb out on to the branch. When I shout "All right!" shake it with all your might.'

It was impossible not to obey someone like that. The factory hand threw his own greasy cap down at his feet, spat on his hands and climbed up.

The crowd held its breath: What was going to happen next?

Next the handsome fellow dropped his frock coat, which was also white, on to the grass, took a short run and jumped over the edge of the cliff into the bottomless abyss.

Ah!

Of course, 'bottomless abyss' is a term that is normally employed to create an impressive effect, for everyone knows that, apart from the one unique and final Abyss, all other abysses, whether on land or under water, come to an end at some point. This abyss was also by no means bottomless – perhaps about ten *sazhens* deep. But even this distance could be quite enough for someone to injure himself badly against the surface of the lake and then drown – not to mention the icy chill emanating from that leaden water.

In fact, whichever way you looked at it, it was an insane thing to do. Not heroic, but precisely insane – what reason was there here for demonstrating heroism?

With the aforementioned exclamation of 'Ah!' everybody clustered together at the edge of the sheer descent to see if the madman's blond head of hair would surface above the waves.

It did! And it started bobbing about between the startled white crests like a little lawn-tennis ball.

Then a hand emerged and waved. And a ringing voice, obligingly assisted by a following wind, shouted: 'All right.'

The apprentice shook the tree as hard as he could, and the kitten fell off with a pitiful squeal. He landed in the water about a *sazhen* away from the gentleman and a moment later was seized and held up in the air.

The people watching shouted and shrieked, quite beside themselves with delight.

The hero (a hero after all, and not a madman – that was clear from the reaction of the public) sculled through the water with his free hand until he reached the foot of the cliff, clambered out with some difficulty on to a wet boulder and set off along the very edge of the tide towards a path that was carved into the rock face. People ran down from above to meet him, ready to take him by the arms, wipe him down, embrace him.

A few minutes later the handsome fellow was at the top, greeted by general exultation. But he refused to let anyone hold him by the arms or wipe him down, let alone embrace him. He walked unaided, quite blue and shuddering from the cold, with a lock of hair sticking to his forehead. In this wet and far-from-elegant condition, he seemed even more handsome to Polina Andreevna than in his fashionable snow-white attire. (And not only to her – that much was clear from the dreamy expressions on the women's faces.)

The miraculous saviour glanced round absent-mindedly and his gaze suddenly settled on the beautiful red-headed lady regarding him with a look, less of admiration – like the other women – than of fright.

He walked up to her, still clutching the soaking wet, skinny little kitten. Looking her straight in the eye, he asked: 'Who are you?'

'Lisitsyna,' Polina Andreevna replied in a low voice.

The pupils of the hero's eyes were broad and black, and the irises around them were light-blue, with a hint of azure.

'A widow,' the woman added, without even knowing why, quailing under that gaze.

'A widow?' the gentleman repeated slowly and smiled in a special sort of way: as if Polina Andreevna were laid out in front of him on a dish, decorated with parsley and celery.

Lisitsyna took an involuntary step backwards and said: 'I have a Bridegroom.'

'Who are you, then, a widow or a bride?' the tempter laughed with a flash of white teeth. 'Ah, what does it matter?' He turned away and walked on.

Oh, how very handsome he was! Polina Andreevna felt for the little cross at her breast and clutched it tight in her fingers. But there was one thing that jarred: the hero flung the rescued kitten down at the happy little girl's feet without even looking at her or listening to her incoherent babble of gratitude.

Throwing the coat that was obligingly held up for him across his shoulders (it was no longer as brilliantly white as before), he set his cap in the appropriate cocked position on one side of his head and walked away without looking round even once.

A Dream about a Crocodile

When Lisitsyna entered the bounds of the monastery proper, she had not yet completely recovered from her alarming encounter – her face was flushed and she was still blinking guiltily. However, the stern, solemn appearance of the godly institution and the sheer abundance of monks and novices robed in black helped restore Polina Andreevna to an appropriate mood.

After walking past the main church, the block of private cells and the administration building, the pilgrim found herself in the inner section of the monastery, where there were two grand houses surrounded by beds of flowers: the father superior's residence and the hierarchical chambers – the former was where Vitalii, the father superior of New Ararat, had his quarters, the latter was intended for the accommodation of his highly placed superiors, should they wish to honour the holy places of the islands with a visit. And it should be said that such superiors visited Canaan often, both churchmen and members of the Holy Synod, and lay officials. Only the provincial prelate, who could surely have reached New Ararat more easily than visitors from Moscow or St Petersburg, had not come visiting in many a long year – not out of neglect, but quite the opposite: out of respect for the archimandrite's efficient management. His Grace was fond of saying that the negligent needed to be watched carefully, but there was no point in watching those who were efficient, and in accordance with this maxim he preferred to visit only the less well organised of the monasteries and deaneries under his jurisdiction.

Father Vitalii's lay-brother assistant asked the lady donor to wait in the reception room, where the walls were hung alternately with icons and the architectural plans of various structures. Lisitsyna bowed to the icons, examined the plans closely, pitied a stunted geranium that was struggling to grow on the window sill, and then she was summoned to His Reverence.

Father Vitalii greeted the pilgrim in friendly fashion, blessed her from his immense height and even leaned down to the ginger locks peeping out from under the headscarf to mimic a kiss, but it was quite clear that the father superior had many other matters to deal with and he wanted to be rid of his lady visitor as soon as possible.

'Is your donation for the monastery as a whole, or for some specific activity?' he asked, opening the accounts ledger and preparing to enter the widow's mite in it.

'That is entirely at Your Reverence's discretion,' Polina Andreevna replied. 'Might I be permitted to sit?'

Vitalii sighed, realising that he would not be able to avoid an edifying conversation – the widow Lisitsyna would consume a quarter of an hour of his time, if not more, for her donation.

'Please, over here,' he said, indicating an uncomfortable chair acquired especially for such occasions, with ribs running across the seat and a back with protruding spikes – it was impossible for anyone to spend more than a quarter of an hour on that inquisitor's seat.

Polina Andreevna sat down and gasped, but she did not say a word about the remarkable chair.

She briefly praised the wonderful organisation of New Ararat, the decorous propriety and sobriety of the population, the industrial innovations and magnificent buildings. The archimandrite heard her out benevolently, for when she wished Lisitsyna was very good at flattering people and gratifying their feelings. Then the visitor turned her attention to the essential business for the sake of which the five hundred roubles had been spent.

'What great assistance Your Reverence must derive from Basilisk's Hermitage! A source of such grace, attracting so many pilgrims,' she said, rejoicing for the community of New Ararat. 'There are few monasteries that possess such an invaluable treasure.'

Vitalii grimaced, contorting the round face so ill-suited to his lanky figure. 'I cannot agree with you, my daughter. Outskirts Island was a source of income to fathers superior who came before me but, to be quite honest, it causes me nothing but bother. Pilgrims come to Ararat now less for Basilisk's sake than for repose – both spiritual and corporeal. We have a genuine paradise here, a true Garden of Eden! And even without the pilgrims, thank the Lord, we are doing well. The hermitage does nothing but spread vacillation and confusion among the brethren. Can you believe that there are times when I dream of the Synod issuing a decree closing down all the hermitages and prohibiting asceticism in order to avoid violations of hierarchy and good order?' The father superior stamped his heavy foot angrily, rousing a rumbling echo from the floor. 'I can see that you are an intelligent woman with a modern cast of mind, so I am speaking to you frankly, without beating about the bush. What sanctity can there possibly be, when the abbot on Outskirts Island is an inveterate libertine! Eh, have you not heard?' Vitalii asked, observing the grimace on the face of his visitor (very possibly not occasioned by surprise, but by the discomfort of her chair). 'The holy elder Israel, formerly a lustful sensualist, a genuine Lucifer of carnality! He has outlived all the other hermits and now, by your leave, he has been the abbot of the hermitage and the chief guardian of the Blue Lake's sanctity for an entire year. The Lord simply will not gather him to Himself. And though I may be the father superior, I have no authority over this appointment, for Outskirts Island is ruled by its own charter!'

Polina Andreevna shook her head sadly in sympathy.

'So do not talk to me of Basilisk's Hermitage,' His Reverence continued, still fuming. 'Here in my monastery there is an absolute prohibition on the drinking of spirituous liquor, and for breaking it I exile the offender to Ukatai or put him in the punishment cell on bread and water; but the hermitage sets the brethren an example of drunken indulgence, and one that goes entirely unpunished, because there is nothing I can do about it.'

'Do the holy elders drink wine?' Lisitsyna asked, fluttering the eyelashes over her brown eyes.

'Oh no, the elders don't drink. But Brother Kleopa, the boatman, does, the only one allowed to go across to Outskirts Island. He is immoderate in his drinking and behaves quite scandalously almost every evening. He sings raucously – and not always songs on spiritual subjects. But I can't dismiss him, since there is no one to take his place. All the others are afraid to go anywhere near the shore, let alone across to the island. There's no punishment that will make them go!'

'But why is that?' the lady donor asked with an innocent air. 'What is so frightening about it?'

The archimandrite looked down quizzically at her. 'You mean you haven't heard?'

'About what, holy Father?'

He muttered reluctantly: 'Oh, it's rubbish. If you haven't heard yet, you will. But I tell you that the hermitage is a hotbed of raving nonsense and superstition.' He didn't tell the visitor from Moscow anything about the Black Monk – we must assume he did not want to waste any time on that.

'Are you comfortable sitting there, my daughter?' Vitalii enquired solicitously, glancing at the clock on the wall. 'The monastery furniture is rough; it is not intended for pleasure, but the mortification of the flesh.'

'Quite comfortable,' Polina Andreevna assured him, not demonstrating the slightest desire to take her leave.

Then the father superior tried an outflanking manoeuvre: 'It is almost time for lunch. Why don't you dine on our monastic cuisine with the father cellarer and father steward? I myself am not lunching today – I am very busy; but please do try it. Today is not a fast day, so they will be serving fresh-killed beef and the monastery sausages. Our beef is famous throughout

Russia. You don't need a knife to eat it; you can just break pieces off with a fork, it's so soft and crumbly. And all because my cattle never move; they live in their stalls and have the lushest grass brought to them, and they're given kvass to drink, and their sides are kneaded. You really ought to try it – you won't regret it.'

But not even the temptation of gluttony worked on this bothersome visitor. 'I thought that they didn't eat meat in monasteries, even on days when it is allowed,' said Mrs Lisitsyna, leaning back against her chair with obvious pleasure.

'In mine they do, and I see no sin in that. Shortly after I was appointed I realised that a man who eats only Lenten fare will never make a good worker – he hasn't got the strength. I feed my monks nourishing food. Eating meat is not forbidden anywhere in the Holy Scriptures, merely rationally restricted. It is written: "When the Lord shall give you meat to eat ..." and again: "And the Lord shall give you meat to eat, and you shall eat meat."'

'But don't you feel sorry to kill those poor cows and pigs?' Polina Andreevna asked reproachfully. 'After all, they are also God's creatures; they bear the spark of life within them.'

It was apparently not the first time that His Reverence had been asked this question, because he had no difficulty in finding an answer: 'I know, I know. I have heard that in Moscow and St Petersburg vegetarianism is fashionable now and many people take a keen interest in the protection of animals. They would do better to protect people. Tell me, my lady, in what way are you and I in any better position? At least cattle are cared for before they are sent to the slaughterhouse. Fattened up and pampered. And do not forget, either, that cows and pigs have no fear of death and do not even realise that they are mortal. Their life is calm and predictable, for no one will send them to be butchered before a certain age. But we humans can meet our end at any moment of our existence. We do not know what tomorrow holds for us and we must constantly prepare ourselves for sudden death. We also have our own Slaughterman, but we know very little about his rules and reasoning. What he requires of us is not fatty meat or abundant milk, but something quite different – we ourselves have no idea what exactly, and this ignorance increases our fear a hundredfold. So save your feelings of pity for people.'

His visitor listened attentively, remembering that Father Mitrofanii was also no great enthusiast of Lenten fare and liked to repeat the words of the anchorite Zosima Verkhovsky: 'Do not pursue fasting alone. God has not said anywhere: If you fast, then you are my disciples, rather, have love for each other.'

The time had come, however, to direct the conversation into a different channel, since the visit had another purpose in addition to ascertaining the archimandrite's position concerning Basilisk. 'Is it true what they say, Father, that non-believers are forbidden to come to Canaan, so that they cannot defile the holy ground? Is it true that absolutely all the inhabitants without exception are zealous devotees of the most rigorous Orthodoxy?'

'Who told you a piece of nonsense like that?' Vitalii asked in amazement. 'I have many people who are hired to work for me, and I don't go poking my nose into their souls – as long as they do their job, I'm happy. There are foreigners, adherents of different faiths, even complete atheists. You know, I am no supporter of mass proselytisation. God grant that I can preserve my own flock; I have no need of someone else's, especially one made up of mangy sheep.' And then, without any further encouragement, the archimandrite himself turned the conversation in precisely the direction required. 'I have a millionaire living here on Canaan, a man by the name of Korovin. He runs a clinic for the mentally ill. Let him; I don't get in his way. As long as he doesn't bring in any violent cases and pays promptly. He's a man without any faith in God at all; he doesn't attend church, even for the holy festival of Easter, but his money goes on work that is pleasing to God.'

His visitor flung her hands up in surprise. 'I've read about Dr Korovin's clinic!' she exclaimed. 'They say he is a genuine wizard at curing neuropsychological ailments.'

'Quite possibly.'

Vitalii squinted at the clock again.

'And I have also heard, that without a special recommendation it is quite impossible to obtain an appointment with him – he simply will not talk to you. Ah, how I wish he would see me! I am suffering such terrible torment! Tell me, Father, could you possibly give me a recommendation for the doctor?'

'No,' said His Reverence with a frown. 'It is not our custom. Apply through the usual channels, via his offices in St Petersburg or Moscow, and they will decide.'

'I have terrible visions,' Polina Andreevna complained. 'I can't sleep at night. The psychiatrists in Moscow have washed their hands of me.'

'What sort of visions do you have?' the father superior asked wearily as he saw his visitor settling even more firmly into her chair.

'Tell me, Your Reverence, have you ever happened to see a live crocodile?'

The question was so unexpected that Vitalii blinked. 'No, I haven't. Why do you ask?'

'I have. In Moscow, last Christmas. An English menagerie came to town, and like a fool, I went to see it.'

'Why do you say "like a fool"?'

'Because it's absolutely horrible! All green and lumpy, with a mouth full of huge teeth, and the heathen beast leers at you with that mouth! It's absolutely terrifying! And those little eyes, so bloodthirsty, watching you and smiling! I've never seen anything more frightening in my life! And ever since then I dream about it every night – I dream about that nightmarish smile!'

From the way that the visitor, hitherto so extremely calm and rational, suddenly became agitated and excited, it was clear that a course of neuropsychological treatment would certainly not do her any harm. After all, it so often happens that an individual who is normal in every respect and perfectly rational manifests a truly maniacal obsession over some quirky little point. Apparently the African reptile had become the subject of precisely such a mania.

After listening to her description of morbid dreams, each more nightmarish than the last (but all involving the smiling reptile), Father Vitalii surrendered: he walked across to his desk and dashed off a few lines rapidly, spattering the paper with ink.

'Very well, my daughter. Here is my recommendation. Go to see Donat Savvich. And now please forgive me, I have urgent business to attend to.'

Mrs Lisitsyna leapt to her feet, involuntarily clutching at her hindquarters where they had been tormented by the chair, and read the note, but was not satisfied.

'No, Father. What kind of recommendation is this: "Please listen to what this donor has to say and render her every possible assistance"? That's the sort of thing they write on petitions in government departments when they want to get rid of someone. Write something sterner, Father, something more insistent.'

'How do you mean, "more insistent"?'

'My dear Donat Savvich,' Polina Andreevna dictated, 'as you are well aware, I rarely burden you with requests of a personal nature, and I therefore implore you not to refuse this petition of mine. My most cordial friend and intimate spiritual collaborator, Mrs Lisitsyna, is suffering from a grave mental ailment and is in need of urgent ...'

The father superior almost baulked at 'my most cordial friend and intimate spiritual collaborator', but Lisitsyna installed herself on the chair again and began narrating yet another dream, in which she had found her deceased husband back in her cold widow's bed, but when she embraced him and kissed him, she had suddenly seen the repulsive toothy mouth grinning below the nightcap and the terrible claws ready to tear at her sides ...

The archimandrite was a stalwart man, but he could not

stand this, and he capitulated before he had even heard the end of the terrible dream. He wrote the recommendation as requested, word for word.

And so Mrs Lisitsyna's flesh had not suffered the torment of the chair in vain – now she could get down to some serious investigative work.

Interesting People

His Reverence Vitalii would have been extremely surprised if he had heard how the extravagant lady from Moscow conducted her conversation with Dr Korovin. Polina Andreevna did not tell the owner of the psychiatric clinic anything about the grinning reptile or her ambivalent dreams. At the beginning she hardly even opened her mouth at all, watching closely as the confident, clean-shaven gentleman read her letter of recommendation.

But she also looked around at the study – it was quite ordinary, with diplomas and photographs on the walls. The only unusual thing was the painting in a magnificent bronze frame hanging behind the desk: a highly convincing and detailed depiction of an octopus, with a naked human figure squirming in the grip of each of its suckered tentacles. The monster's face (if the combined head and trunk of the gigantic mollusc could be called a 'face') was remarkably reminiscent of the imperious, bespectacled features of Donat Savvich himself, although it was quite impossible to determine exactly how such a precise resemblance had been achieved, since there was no trace of caricature or artificiality to be observed in the image of this immense eight-legged denizen of the deep.

Having read the archimandrite's note, the doctor gave his visitor a curious glance over the top of his gold-rimmed spectacles.

'I have never received such an insistent communication from Father Vitalii before. Just what can your relationship to His Reverence be, for him to go to such great pains?' Donat Savvich smiled sardonically. '"Intimate spiritual collaborator" – now there's a fascinating phrase. Could there really be some romantic aspect to this? That would be rather interesting from the psychophysiological point of view – I had always categorised the father superior as the classical type of suppressed homosexual. Tell me, Mrs . . . er . . . er . . . Lisitsyna, are you really seriously ill? It says here: "Save this woman's soul, which has been tormented beyond all endurance." At first glance your soul does not appear so very badly tormented.'

Polina Andreevna, who had already formed a definite opinion about the owner of the study, gestured dismissively at the letter and laughed light-heartedly. 'You are quite right. And probably about the archimandrite, too. He cannot stand women – and I shamelessly exploited the fact in order to extort a pass into your citadel from the poor man.'

The doctor raised his eyebrows and extended the corners of his mouth slightly, as if he were also joining in the laughter – but not completely; only to a certain extent.

'And what exactly did you think I could do for you?'

'They say so many intriguing things about you in Moscow. My decision to come on pilgrimage to New Ararat was a sudden impulse; even I was taken by surprise. You know how these things happen with us women. And now I've got here, I haven't the slightest idea what to do with myself. Well, I tried praying, but I'm afraid the devotional impulse has passed. I went to take a look at the archimandrite. And I'll take a ride round the archipelago on a launch . . .' Polina Andreevna shrugged. 'But there are four days left before I take the ship back.'

The beautiful lady's frankness did not anger Korovin; in fact it seemed to amuse him.

'So I'm some kind of fairground attraction for you, am I?' he asked, smiling broadly now, not with just the corners of his mouth.

'Oh no, don't say that!' said his frivolous visitor, alarmed, and then she chortled herself. 'Well, if you are, only in the most respectful sense. No, really, I have been told absolutely miraculous things about you. I simply couldn't miss the opportunity!'

Then, having won over the doctor with her frankness, Polina continued the conversation in accordance with the standard rules for dealing with men. Law number one said: If you want a man to like you, flatter him. The more intelligent and subtle the man was, the more intelligent and subtle the flattery had to be. The cruder he was, the cruder the praise should be. Since Dr Korovin was quite clearly not a stupid man, Polina Andreevna set about weaving her lacy web in a roundabout manner.

Suddenly assuming a serious air, she said: 'I find you most intriguing. I would like to understand what kind of man you are. Why does the heir to the Korovin millions spend the best years of his life and huge sums of money on trying to cure madmen? Tell me, why did you decide to take up psychiatry? Because you were surfeited with life? Was it idle curiosity and disdain for other people? Or was it the desire to rummage in people's souls with your cold hands? If that's it, then it is certainly interesting. But I suspect that the reason might be more dramatic. I can see from your face that you are not world-weary . . . You have lively, passionate eyes. Or am I mistaken, and is that gleam nothing but curiosity?'

Let a man know that you find him infinitely interesting, that you alone can see how unique and unlike anyone else he is – in either a good or bad sense, it doesn't really matter which – that is the point of the first law. We must admit that Polina Andreevna did not really have to pretend very hard, for she believed quite sincerely that everyone was unique in his or her own way, and therefore interesting, if you looked closely enough. Especially such an unusual man as Donat Savvich Korovin.

The doctor looked at his visitor quizzically, as if he were trying to absorb the change that had taken place in her. He began speaking in a low, confidential tone: 'No, I did not take up psychiatry out of curiosity. It was more out of despair. Are you genuinely interested?'

'Very!'

'I joined the medical faculty out of youthful narcissism. Initially the department of physiology, not psychiatry. At the age of nineteen I imagined I was Fortune's favourite, a happy prince who had everything that any mortal could possibly possess, and there was only one more thing I wanted: to discover the secret of eternal or, if not eternal, then at least very long life. This is a rather common form of mania among the rich – at this very moment I have one patient of this kind, whose narcissism has developed to a pathological extent. And as for myself, twenty years ago, I dreamed of understanding the workings of my body so well that I could prolong its functioning for as long as possible. . .'

'But what diverted you from that path?' Lisitsyna exclaimed when the doctor paused briefly in his narrative.

'The same thing that usually diverts excessively rational young men from their intended trajectory in life.'

'Love?' Polina Andreevna guessed.

'Yes. Passionate, irrational, all-consuming – in short, just as love ought to be.'

'Was your love not requited?'

'Oh yes; I myself was loved no less ardently than I loved.'

'But why do you speak of it so sadly?'

'Because it was the saddest and most unusual of all the love stories I know. We were drawn irresistibly to each other, but we could not spend even a minute in each other's embrace. The moment I came within arm's length of the object of my adoration, she became seriously ill: tears poured from her eyes and her nose began streaming, she came out in a bright red rash and her temples started to throb with the unbearable agony of migraine. I only had to move away and the morbid symptoms vanished almost immediately. If I had not been studying medicine, I should probably have suspected witchcraft, but in my second year as a student I already knew about the mysterious, implacable ailment known as idiosyncratic allergy. In very many cases it is impossible to guess what causes it and even more impossible to treat it.' Donat Savvich closed his eyes, laughed and shook his head, as if he were astonished that such a thing could actually have happened to him. 'The way we suffered was indescribable. The mighty power of love drew us to each other, but my touch was fatal to the one I adored ... I read everything known to medicine about idiosyncratic allergy and realised that the chemical and biological sciences were still too imperfect and in the course of my lifetime they would not develop far enough to defeat this mechanism of the physical rejection of one body by another. That was when I decided to switch to psychiatry and devote myself to studying the structure of the human soul – and my own soul, which had played such an appalling trick on me by making me love the only woman out of all the women on earth whom I could not possibly possess.'

'And so you parted?' Polina Andreevna exclaimed, moved almost to tears by the story itself and the restrained tone in which it had been told.

'Yes. That was my decision. Eventually she married. I hope she is happy. But I, as you can see, am still single. I live for my work.'

Quick-witted as she was, Mrs Lisitsyna had not immediately realised that the cunning doctor was also playing a game with her – not a woman's game, but a man's, no less ancient and immutable in its rules. The sure means to gain access to a woman's heart is to arouse the spirit of competition in it. The best thing of all is to tell some romantic story, which must have a sad ending, about yourself, as if you are saying: See what depths of feeling I was once capable of, and possibly would be again, if only I had a worthy object of affection.

When Polina Andreevna realised what was happening, she smiled to herself in appreciation of this manoeuvre. Regardless of whether it was true or not, the story she had been told was certainly original. And in addition, the entire monologue indicated that the doctor liked his visitor, and that, say what you will, was flattering, and also useful.

'So you value your work?' Lisitsyna asked sympathetically.

'Very much. My patients are unusual people, each of them a unique individual in his own way. And uniqueness is a kind of talent.'

'In what way are they so talented? Please, do tell me!'

The red-headed visitor's round eyes opened even wider in joyful anticipation. At this point law number two came into its own: Lead the man on to the subject that interests him more than any other, and then listen properly. That is all there is to it, but how many men's hearts are won by means of this simple method! How many plain Janes and dowryless brides find themselves such fine bridegrooms that everybody is amazed at how they could possibly have come by such undeserved happiness – but the way they came by it was simply by listening.

Polina Andreevna certainly did know how to listen, raising her eyebrows when it was required, gasping occasionally and even pressing her hands to her breast, but all without the slightest exaggeration and, most importantly, without pretending, with entirely unfeigned interest.

Donat Savvich seemed to speak reluctantly at first, but such exemplary listening gradually roused his enthusiasm. 'My patients, of course, are abnormal, but that only means that they deviate from a certain average norm that is accepted by society – in other words, they are more unusual, exotic and whimsical than "normal" people. I am opposed in principle to the very concept of the "norm" as used in any comparisons in the sphere of the human psyche. Each one of us has his or her own norm. And the individual has a duty to himself to rise above this norm.'

Here Mrs Lisitsyna began nodding her head, as if the doctor had propounded a thesis that had occurred to her earlier and with which she was entirely in agreement.

'What makes human beings valuable and interesting,' Korovin continued, 'what makes them great, if you like, is that they can change for the better. Always. At any age, after any mistake, any moral lapse. The mechanism of self-improvement is embedded in our very psyche. If this mechanism is not used, it grows rusty, and then a person declines and sinks below the level of his own norm. The second cornerstone of my theory is this: every blemish, every failing in the personality is simultaneously an advantage, a high point in the landscape – all that is required is to rotate that point of the psychological relief by a hundred and eighty degrees. And here is my third fundamental principle: anyone who is suffering can be helped, and anyone who is beyond understanding *can* be understood. And when you have understood them, then you can start working with them: transforming a weak person into a strong one, a defective person into a complete one, an unhappy person into a happy one. My dear Polina Andreevna, I am not superior to my patients, I am not cleverer or better – the only difference is that I am richer, although there are some extremely wealthy people among them too.'

'You believe that every person can be helped?' his listener asked in surprise, throwing her hands up in the air. 'But surely there are aberrations that are very difficult to cure? For instance chronic alcoholism or, even worse, opium addiction!'

'In fact that's a very simple matter,' the doctor said with a condescending smile. 'That was what I began my experiments with. I have an island of my own in the Indian Ocean, a long way from the sea lanes, where I put the most hopeless alcoholics and drug addicts. There are no intoxicating substances at all to be found on the island, not for any money. In fact, money has no value there in any case. Once every three months a schooner comes from the Maldives, bringing everything the people need.'

'And don't they run away?'

'Anyone who wants to go back to the old life is free to sail away on the schooner. No one is held there by force. I don't believe in depriving a human being of the right to choose. If he wants to destroy himself, well then, that is his right. And so the real difficulty is not presented by slaves of the bottle and the hookah, but by people with anomalies to which the key is not so easy to find. I work with patients like that here, on Canaan. Sometimes successfully and sometimes – alas.' Korovin sighed. 'The person living in cottage number eighteen here is a railway telegrapher who claims that he was abducted by the inhabitants of another planet, who took him away and kept him on that planet for several years, which were much longer than years here on Earth, because the sun there is much bigger than ours.'

'Quite a subtle observation for a simple telegrapher,' Polina Andreevna remarked.

'Oh, that's nothing. You should hear him talk about that Woofer of his (that's what the planet is called) – Jonathan Swift and Jules Verne combined are no match for him! Such vivid descriptions! Such technical detail – it's quite fascinating. And the language! He is giving me lessons in the language of Woofer. I even began compiling a special glossary in order to catch him out. And would you believe it – he has never made a single mistake, he remembers all the words! And the grammar is remarkably logical, far more elegant that any earth language that I know!'

Lisitsyna clasped her hands together – she found this story about another planet so interesting. 'And how does he explain his return to Earth?'

'He says they told him straight away that they were only taking him for a while, just for a visit, and they would bring him back safe and unharmed. He also claims that a lot of visitors from Earth have been to Woofer, but they wipe most of their memories clean in order not to make things difficult for them when they return here. But my patient asked them to leave him all his memories, and now he is paying the price. By the way, remind me to tell you about another case of the caprices of memory . . .'

It was clear that Korovin had mounted his favourite hobby horse and would go on talking for some time, but the last thing Polina Andreevna wanted was for him to stop.

'He says that the Wooferians have been observing life on Earth for a very long time – centuries, in fact.'

'But why don't they show themselves?'

'From their point of view, we are still too savage. First we have to solve our own problems and stop tormenting each other. Only after that will we mature sufficiently for interplanetary contact. According to their calculations, it could happen in the year 2080, but that's only in the very best case.'

'Ah, such a long time,' Lisitsyna said, disappointed. 'You and I will not live to see it.'

Donat Savvich smiled: 'Come now, these are the ravings of a sick imagination, no matter how coherent they might be. In actual fact our telegrapher never went anywhere. He was out hunting with friends and winged a duck. He waded into the rushes for his trophy and was gone for no more than five minutes. He came back without the duck or his gun, behaving very strangely, and immediately started telling his friends about the planet Woofer. He was taken straight from the swamp to the district hospital and many months later he arrived here. I am struggling with him, struggling really hard. The important thing in his case is to punch a hole in his shell of logic, to discredit his ravings. So far I haven't managed it.'

'Ah, how very interesting,' Polina Andreevna sighed dreamily.

'It most certainly is,' the doctor said, with the air of a collector proudly demonstrating the most important treasures in his collection. 'The telegrapher does at least behave in the usual way (if you don't count the fact that he sleeps during the day and spends the whole night looking up at the stars). But you remember I mentioned a maniac who wants to live for ever, as I did in my youth? His name is Weller, in cottage number nine. He is totally obsessed with his own health and longevity. He very probably will live until 2080, when the people from the planet Woofer come to introduce themselves to us. He eats nothing but healthy food, calculating its chemical composition precisely. He lives in a room that is hermetically sealed and sterilised and always wears gloves. The only contact the staff and I have with him is through a window covered with gauze. Weller was taken into a psychiatric clinic after he voluntarily submitted to castration – he claims that every ejaculation of sperm takes away two days' worth of vital energy, which is why men live on average eight years less than women.'

'But without fresh air and exercise he won't live very long!'

'Don't worry, Weller has everything worked out. First, a complex ventilation system made according to his own drawings has been installed in the cottage. Secondly, from morning till night he does gymnastics or deep-breathing exercises, or pours hot and cold water over himself – distilled, of course. For an hour each day he takes a walk in the fresh air, with the most incredible precautions. He never touches the ground with his feet; he learned how to walk on stilts especially "to avoid breathing in the vapours of the soil". The stilts stand on the porch, outside the house, and so Weller never touches them at all unless he is wearing gloves. Weller out walking is a sight, I can tell you! Come and admire him some day between nine and ten in the morning. Completely covered in a suit of oilcloth, with a respiratory mask on his face, striding over the ground on his wooden poles: boom, boom, boom. Like the Commander's statue in Don Juan!' The doctor laughed, and Polina Andreevna gladly joined in.

'And what was it you wanted to tell me about the caprices of memory?' she asked, still smiling. 'Something else funny?'

'On the contrary: something very sad. I have a female patient here who wakes up every morning and always returns to the same day, the most terrible day of her life, when she received the news of her husband's death. On that day she screamed, fainted and lay unconscious right through the night. Every morning since then she thinks that she hasn't woken up from sleep, but come round after her fainting fit, and the terrible news only arrived the evening before. It is as if time has stopped for her, and the pain of her loss is not blunted at all. She opens her eyes in the morning and immediately there are screams, tears, hysterics . . . She has been assigned a special doctor, who tries to comfort her by making her understand that the disaster happened a long time ago – seven years ago, in fact. At first, of course, she doesn't believe him. The first half of the day is spent in presenting her with proofs and explanations. By lunch time the patient allows herself to be convinced, calms down a little and starts asking what has happened during those seven years, taking a very lively interest in everything. By the evening she is already quite calm and pacified. She goes to bed with a smile and sleeps like a little child; but in the morning she wakes up and everything starts all over again: the grief, the sobbing, the attempts at suicide. I struggle and struggle, but so far I haven't been able to do anything. The mechanism of psychological shock has been too little studied as yet; I have to grope my way forward. Working with this patient is very hard, with the same thing being repeated day after day. The doctors can never stand it for more than two or three weeks, I have to replace them . . .'

Noticing that his listener had tears in her eyes, Donat Savvich said cheerfully: 'Come now. Not all of my patients are unhappy. There is one who is perfectly happy. Do you see the picture?' The doctor pointed to the octopus that we have already mentioned.

Polina Andreevna had kept glancing at it throughout their conversation – there was something special about that canvas; it held her gaze in a firm grip, never releasing it for long.

'It is by Konon Yoshihin. Have you heard the name?'

'No. It is amazingly talented!'

'Yoshihin is a genius,' Korovin said with a nod. 'A quite genuine, unadulterated genius. You know, he is one of those artists who paint as if no painting had ever existed before them – no Raphael, no Goya, no Cézanne. Nobody at all, until Konon Yoshihin, the first artist on Earth, was born and began bringing the canvas to life beneath his brush.'

'Yoshihin? No, I don't know him.'

'Naturally. Not many people know Yoshihin – only a few gourmets of art, and they are sure that he died a long time ago. Because Konon Petrovich is totally insane; he hasn't come out of cottage number three in more than five years, and before that he spent ten years in an ordinary insane asylum where the idiot doctors who wanted to restore Yoshihin to the "norm" would not give him any paints or pencils.'

'What form does his insanity take?' asked Polina Andreevna, still looking at the octopus, and the longer she looked at it, the more it mesmerised her with its strange gaze.

'Do you remember what Pushkin said about genius and villainy being incompatible? Yoshihin's example shows that they are in fact perfectly compatible. Konon Petrovich is a spontaneous natural villain. His passion for art has obliterated every other feeling in his soul. Not straight away, but gradually. The only living creature that Yoshihin loved, and loved with passion, was his daughter, a lovely, quiet girl who lost her mother early and was slowly dying of consumption. For months he hardly left her bedside at all, except perhaps to work on a painting for an hour or two in his studio. Eventually he even moved his canvas into the child's bedroom in order not to leave her at all. He didn't eat, drink or sleep. People who saw Yoshihin in those days say that he looked absolutely awful: his hair was matted, he didn't shave and his shirt was spattered all over with paint. He was painting his daughter's portrait, knowing that it would be the last. He wouldn't let anyone into the room; he did everything himself – he gave the girl a drink, or medicine, or food, and then grabbed his brush again. And when the child's death agony began, Yoshihin fell into an absolute frenzy, not from grief, but from delight – the play of light and shade was so wonderful on the emaciated little face contorted in pain. The people gathered in the next room heard pitiful groans from behind the locked door. The dying girl was weeping and begging for water, but in vain – Yoshihin could not tear himself away from his painting. When they finally broke the door down, the little girl had already passed away, but Yoshihin had not even looked at her; he was still correcting something on his canvas. They took the daughter away to the cemetery and the father to the insane asylum. And the picture, even though it was still unfinished, was exhibited in the Paris Salon under the title "La morte triomphante" and won the gold medal.'

'The father's reason broke down under the grief and he erected defences in the form of art' – such was kind-hearted Polina Andreevna's interpretation of the story she had just heard.

'Do you think so?' Donat Savvich took off his spectacles, wiped them and put them back on again. 'But when I study Yoshihin's case, I come to the conclusion that a truly gigantic genius cannot mature completely without the necrosis of certain regions of the soul. By destroying the final remnants of human feeling within himself, including his love for his daughter, Konon Petrovich liberated himself completely for art. The things he now creates for himself in cottage number three will one day adorn the finest galleries in the world. And then who among our grateful descendants will recall the little girl who cried and died without quenching her final thirst? I have absolutely no doubt that my clinic, I myself and even the island of Canaan will only be remembered by the generations to come because a genius lived and worked here. By the way, would you like to take a look at Yoshihin and his pictures?'

Mrs Lisitsyna hesitated for a moment before answering rather uncertainly: 'Yes . . . I suppose I would.'

She thought a little longer, nodded to herself and said in a firmer voice: 'I definitely would. Take me there.'

Warm, Warmer, Hot

Before she set out to visit Dr Korovin, Lisitsyna had called in at her hotel, where she had changed her light *talma* for a long black cloak with a hood – evidently in anticipation of the coolness of evening. However, even though the sun was not bright, in the course of the day it had warmed the air quite well, and there was no need to put on the cloak for a walk round the grounds of the clinic. Polina Andreevna limited herself to throwing a scarf across her shoulders, and Korovin went just as he was, in his waistcoat and frock coat.

Cottage number three stood on the very edge of the pine-forested hill that Korovin rented from the monastery. With its smoothly plastered white walls the cottage did not strike Polina Andreevna as being in any way remarkable, especially in comparison with the other cottages, many of which were quite astounding in their quaint whimsicality.

'All the magic here is inside,' Donat Savvich explained. 'Yoshihin is not concerned about what his dwelling looks like from the outside, and anyway, as I told you, he never comes out.'

They walked in without knocking. It became clear why a little later: the artist would not have heard them anyway, and if he had heard, he would not have answered.

Polina saw that the cottage consisted of one room with five large windows – one in each wall and another in the ceiling. There was no furniture at all to be seen in the studio: Yoshihin probably ate and slept right there on the floor.

However, before the visitor could take a good look at the

contents of the room, her attention was captured by the walls and the ceiling of this peculiar dwelling. All the internal surfaces, apart from the floor and the windows, were covered with canvas, almost all of which had been painted with oil paints. The ceiling was a painting of the night sky, so precise and convincing that if it were not for the square of glass through which clouds tinted pink by the sunset could be seen, it would have been very easy to fall into the error of imagining that there was no roof at all. One of the walls, the north-facing one, depicted a pine grove; another, facing east, showed a shallow slope leading down to a small river and a farm; on the west-facing wall there was a meadow and two cottages standing side by side; and on the south-facing one there were bushes. It was not hard to see that the artist had reproduced the views outside his windows with astounding precision. But the scenes in Yoshihin's landscapes had turned out far richer, with more palpable space, so the originals that could be seen outside looked like pale copies of the paintings.

'In his present period he is passionately enthusiastic about landscapes,' Donat Savvich explained in a low voice, indicating the artist, who was standing by the east-facing wall with his back to his visitors and working away intently with a little brush without even bothering to glance round. 'At the moment he is painting a cycle entitled "Times of the Day". Look: this is dawn, this is morning, this is afternoon, this is evening, and the painting on the ceiling is night. The important thing is to be sure to change the canvases in time, or he will start painting a new picture straight on top of the old one. Over the years I have accumulated a substantial collection – some day I shall recover all my outlays on the clinic,' Korovin joked. 'Or if I don't, my heirs will.'

Lisitsyna cautiously approached the genius (who was working on the 'Evening' wall) from the side, in order to get a better look at him.

She saw the profile of a thin face that wore a constant grimace, with greying, dirty hair hanging down over the forehead, a greasy stained blouse and a thread of spittle dangling from a drooping lower lip.

On closer inspection the picture itself produced an equally unpleasant, although decidedly powerful, impression on the visitor. Beyond the slightest doubt it was a work of genius: the brightly lit windows of the two cottages, the moon hanging above their roofs and the dark silhouettes of the pines all emanated an air of mystery, horror and death – it was not simply an evening, it was some all-encompassing Evening, the precursor of eternal darkness and silence.

'Why is it that in art the repellent and the hideous are more compelling than the beautiful and the uplifting?' Polina Andreevna asked with a shudder. 'It never happens in nature; the repellent is present there too, but it is created only to serve as a foil for the Beautiful.'

'You speak of the creation of the Heavenly Artist, but art is produced by earthbound creators,' the doctor replied, following the movements of the brush. 'Here you have yet another confirmation that artists can trace their family tree back to the rebellious angel Satan. Konon Petrovich!' he said, suddenly raising his voice and slapping the painter on the shoulder. 'What's that you've depicted there?'

Lisitsyna saw that something strange had been painted a little to one side of one of the cottages, at the level of its roof: an unnaturally elongated figure in a black robe with a pointed hood, with long, thin legs like a spider's. The young lady instinctively glanced out of the window, but she did not see anything of the kind out there.

'It's a monk,' Polina Andreevna said in an emphatically naïve voice. 'But he looks rather strange.'

'And not just a monk, but the Black Monk, Canaan's foremost attraction,' Donat Savvich said with a nod. 'I'm sure you've heard about him already ...' He slapped the artist on the shoulder again, harder this time. 'Konon Petrovich!'

Yoshihin had no intention of turning round, but Mrs Lisitsyna tensed up in anticipation. It seemed likely that a fortunate coincidence might render her task easier. She was getting warm now, very warm!

'The Black Monk?' she asked. 'Is that the ghost of Basilisk, the one who is supposed to wander across the water, frightening everybody?'

Korovin frowned; he was beginning to lose his temper with the stubborn painter. 'Not only frightening them. He has also managed to provide me with two new patients.'

Warmer and warmer!

'Konon Petrovich, I am talking to you, and once I have asked a question, I won't go away without an answer,' the doctor said sternly. 'Is this Basilisk you have shown here? Who told you about him? You don't talk to anyone except me. How do you come to know about him?'

Without turning round, Yoshihin muttered: 'I know only what I see with my own eyes.' He touched the black figure lightly with his brush, and Polina Andreevna thought she saw it sway, as if it were struggling to maintain its balance against the pressure of the wind.

'New patients?' the visitor asked with a sideways glance at Korovin. 'I expect they are interesting too?'

'Yes, but very seriously ill. Especially one, little more than a boy. He sits in the conservatory, as naked as our ancestor Adam, so I would not dare to show him to you. Acute progressive traumatic idiotism – he is being consumed before my very eyes. He doesn't allow anyone to come near him and won't take any food from the attendants. He eats what grows on the trees, but how long can you survive on bananas and pineapples? Another week, or two at the most, and he'll be dead – unless I can come up with some form of treatment. So far, alas, nothing does any good.'

'And what about the other one?' the curious lady asked. 'Another case of idiotism?'

'No, entroposis. It's a very rare sickness, similar to autism, except that it's not innate but acquired. Science still knows no treatment for it. But he was a most intelligent man; I met him when he was still perfectly sane ... Alas, in a single day – or rather a single night – he was reduced to a ruin.'

Now she was getting hot! Ah, how well everything was working out!

Mrs Lisitsyna gasped: 'From a highly intelligent man to a ruin in a single night? But what happened to him?'

Poor Berdichevsky

'This man is the victim of a traumagenic hallucination induced by preceding events and a general morbidly susceptible nature. During the initial period the patient spoke frenziedly and at length, so I more or less know the nature of his vision. For some reason Berdichevsky (that is the man's name) decided to go to a certain abandoned house in the middle of the night, a place where a terrible catastrophe had recently occurred. Acutely sensitive people are affected in a special way by such places. I won't go into the fantastic details of that house's reputation; they are not really significant. But the substance of the hallucination is quite distinctive: Basilisk appeared to Berdichevsky, and then he had a hallucinatory vision of himself sealed inside a coffin alive. A classic case of the superimposition of a pre-pubic mystical psychosis, very common even among highly educated people, on thanatophobic depression. The stimulus for this delirious vision was obviously provided by certain real events. There actually was a coffin lying on a table in the hut – the former occupant had made it for himself, but it was never used. It was the combination of the darkness, strange creaking sounds and moving shadows with this shocking object that pushed Berdichevsky into a state of raptus.'

Mrs Lisitsyna listened most attentively to this abstruse lecture full of peculiar terminology. But the artist carried on working on his canvas, paying not the slightest attention to what the doctor was saying – it seemed unlikely that he even heard it.

'You mean he saw an empty coffin in a dark room and immediately lost his reason?' Polina Andreevna asked emphatically.

'It is hard to say exactly what happened there. There can be no doubt that Berdichevsky had something like an epileptic fit. He must have slithered across the floor, striking himself against corners and household items, writhing convulsively. The skin on his hands was torn, the nails were ripped off, his fingers were absolutely covered in splinters, there was a bump on the back of his head, the tendons of his left ankle were sprained, and he had wet himself too, which is also typical for an epileptoidal episode.'

Unable to control her agitation, his listener exclaimed: 'Let's go out into the air. These walls are oppressing me . . .

'So this poor man is quite insane?' she asked quietly once they were outside the cottage.

'Who, the artist?'

'No . . . Berdichevsky.'

Donat Savvich shrugged. 'Well, you see, in a case of entroposis, day by day a person withdraws further into himself and gradually stops responding to what is going on around him. The other name for the illness is petrosis, since it seems as if the sick person is gradually turning to stone. As a result of the shock, Berdichevsky's personality has completely collapsed. And the worst thing of all is that he is still having hallucinations during the night. He is afraid to be left alone, and I have put him in cottage number seven, where another extremely interesting patient lives. He is a scientist, a physicist by profession, and his name is Sergei Nikolaevich Lampier. He is a kind man, a positive angel, and so he does not object to sharing his home. They get on very well together. Lampier conducts some kind of strange experiments on Berdichevsky – they are entirely harmless – and they are quite content with each other.'

Polina Andreevna pretended that her capricious attention had shifted from Berdichevsky to the mad physicist: 'An extremely interesting patient? Oh, do tell me about him!'

They walked out into a meadow and stopped. The light of day had almost faded away and there were lights burning here and there in the cottages and the clinic buildings.

'I think Sergei Nikolaevich Lampier is probably also a genius, like Yoshihin. But the problem is that while Yoshihin has no need to demonstrate his genius in words – he paints a picture and everything is clear – Lampier is a scientist, and he conducts research in strange areas, bordering on quackery. And so he absolutely has to provide convincing, preferably eloquent, explanations. Unfortunately Sergei Nikolaevich suffers from a severe disorder of discursive expression.'

'From what?' Lisitsyna asked, puzzled.

'A disruption of coherent speech. To put it in simple terms, his words cannot keep up with his thoughts. It is almost impossible to understand what he says. Nine times out of ten even I cannot guess exactly he is trying to say. And other people – well, they regard him as a complete idiot. But Lampier is very far from being an idiot. He graduated from grammar school with a gold medal and was the top student in his year at university. But he didn't study in the same way as everyone else; he did written papers for all the exams: they made a special exception for him.'

'And how does his genius manifest itself?' asked Polina Andreevna, cautiously pursuing her line of enquiry. 'What kind of experiments does he perform on the other man – what's his name – Boguslavsky.'

'Berdichevsky,' the doctor corrected her. 'If Yoshihin is a genius of evil, then Lampier is undoubtedly a genius of good. He has a theory that everything around us is permeated with certain rays that are invisible to the naked eye and every person also gives off an emanation of various colours and shades. Sergei Nikolaevich spent many years on the invention of a device capable of perceiving and analysing this aura.'

'And what kind of aura is it?' asked Lisitsyna, not yet daring to turn the conversation back to Berdichevsky.

'Sergei Nikolaevich is concerned most of all with the moral emanation,' Korovin said with a smile that was benign rather than mocking. 'Certain precious orange rays, which are the sign of spiritual nobility and kind-heartedness. Lampier claims that if we can learn to see this emanation, then there will be no place for evil people in the world, and they will be left with no choice but to develop the orange spectrum of radiation within themselves.'

'He is a truly remarkable man!' the doctor's visitor declared decisively. 'I absolutely must see him, come what may. Let him study me to see if he can find an orange emanation!'

The doctor took a watch out of his pocket. 'Well, let us assume that Lampier will not actually study you. In the first place, he is not very fond of women, and in the second, he has a strict timetable. If I am not mistaken, now is his time for experiments. Would you like to take a look? Especially since it is very close by? There it is: cottage number seven.'

'I certainly would!'

'Very well, I shall grant your request. And afterwards you will grant mine – agreed?' Korovin's eyes glinted cunningly.

'What request?'

'I'll tell you later,' Donat Savvich laughed. 'Don't be frightened; I shan't ask you to do anything terrible.'

They were already approaching a lovely two-storey cottage in the alpine style – built of logs, with broad steps and a decorative chimney on its slanting roof. There was no knocker or bell-button or bell on the door. But what Polina Andreevna found strangest of all was that there was no handle – she couldn't understand how such a door could be opened.

The doctor explained: 'Sergei Nikolaevich lives according to the principle: "I don't need strangers, but I'm always glad to see friends." That is, a stranger will never get him to open the door, but his friends, who know the secret, can enter quite easily, without any forewarning.' He pressed a little concealed button at one side, and the door slid open with a jerk.

'How delightful!' Mrs Lisitsyna exclaimed as she entered the hallway.

'The entrance to the bedroom is on the left, the laboratory is on the right. The stairway leads up to the first floor. There is an observatory up there, where Mr Berdichevsky, the victim of mysticism, is living temporarily. So we should go to the right.'

The lighting in the laboratory was unusual: there was an extremely bright electric lamp burning by the wall, beside a table completely covered with complex instruments intended for incomprehensible purposes, but a long metallic shade prevented the light from spreading, so that all the other parts of the rather large room were immersed in dense shadow.

The disorder in the room was so pervasive that it seemed not to have arisen spontaneously but to have been created deliberately. The floor was littered with books, bottles and scraps of paper, several squares of carefully cut turf and some stones or other. The physicist himself, a small man with tousled hair, was sitting on a chair beside the lamp and the only armchair was occupied by a large heap of rags, so there was absolutely nowhere for the two new arrivals to put themselves.

'Yes, yes,' Lampier said instead of a greeting, glancing round. 'What for?'

He looked at the unfamiliar lady, frowned and asked again: 'What for?'

Korovin led his companion closer. 'Mrs Lisitsyna here has expressed a desire to make your acquaintance. She would like to know the spectrum of her emanation. Take a look at her through your remarkable spectacles. What if you should find orange radiation?'

The physicist muttered something incomprehensible, but he was clearly angry. 'They don't have anything. Only from the womb. Reproductive automatons. No brains. Crimson, crimson, crimson. All the brains went to one, Masha.'

'Masha? Which Masha?' asked Polina Andreevna, who was listening intently.

Lampier gestured impatiently at her and launched a verbal assault on Korovin: 'Orange later. No time. The emanation of death, I told you. And Masha and Toto! Only worse! A thousand times! Ah, but why, why?'

'Yes, yes,' Korovin said gently, as if he were speaking to a child, and nodded. 'Your new emanation. What was wrong with the last one, I wonder? At least you didn't get so excited. You already told me about the emanation of death, I remember. I hope you also remember how it all ended that time.'

The little man immediately fell silent and started back from the doctor. He put his hand over his mouth.

'Well now, that's a bit better,' said Korovin. 'How are the experiments going with your faithful Sancho Panza? Where is he, by the way – upstairs?'

Realising that the doctor meant Berdichevsky, Polina Andreevna held her breath.

'I'm here,' said a voice out of the semi-darkness – the familiar voice of Matvei Berdichevsky, except that it sounded strangely feeble.

The form that Lisitsyna had taken for a heap of old rags dumped in the armchair stirred and carried on speaking: 'Hello, sir. Hello, madam. Can you forgive me for not greeting you sooner? I did not think that my modest presence could be of any importance to anyone. You, sir, said "Sancho Panza". That is from the novel by the Spanish writer Miguel Cervantes. You were referring to me. In God's name, please forgive me for not getting up. I am absolutely exhausted. I know how impolite it is, especially in the presence of a lady. I'm sorry, I'm sorry. There is no forgiveness for me . . .'

Berdichevsky carried on apologising for a long time in the same pitiful, lost tone of voice, which Polina Andreevna had never heard from him before. She abruptly swung the shade of the lamp round, so that the circle of light took in the seated man, and gasped.

Oh, how strangely the sharp-eyed, energetic assistant public prosecutor had changed! As if there were not a single bone left in his body: he was hunched over, with his shoulders drooping and his hands lying lifelessly on his knees. The gaze of his rapidly blinking eyes held absolutely no expression, and his lips kept moving all the time, muttering endless apologies gradually fading into silence.

'Good Lord, what happened to you?' Lisitsyna cried out in horror, forgetting about all her cunning plans.

As she entered cottage number seven, Polina Andreevna had been prepared for the possibility that Matvei Bentsionovich, who had seen her previously in her role as a 'Moscow noblewoman', might recognise his old acquaintance, and she had invented a plausible explanation to meet the case; but now it was quite clear that all her concern on that account had been pointless. Berdichevsky slowly transferred his gaze to the young lady, screwed up his eyes and said: 'Something very unpleasant happened to me. I lost my mind. I'm sorry, but there is nothing to be done about it. I am really very ashamed. Please forgive me, for God's sake . . .'

Korovin walked up to the sick man, took hold of his limp wrist and felt his pulse. 'It is me – Dr Korovin. You can't have forgotten me; we saw each other only this morning.'

'Now I remember,' said Berdichevsky slowly, nodding like a sprung wooden toy. 'You are the head of this institution. I'm sorry for not recognising you straight away. I did not wish to offend you. I have never wished to offend anybody. Ever. Forgive me, if you can.'

'I forgive you,' interrupted Korovin rapidly and half-turned to explain to his fellow visitor: 'If he is not stopped, he will carry on apologising for hours. Some strange, inexhaustible abyss of guilt.' He leaned down to the patient and raised his eyelid with his finger and thumb. 'Mm, yes. You slept badly again. Was it Basilisk this time too?'

Without moving or even trying to close his extended eyelid, Matvei Berdichevsky began to cry – quietly, pitifully, inconsolably. 'Yes. He glanced in through the window at me, knocked and threatened me. He comes to steal my reason. I have almost nothing left as it is, but he keeps coming back, again and again . . .'

'At first I put Mr Berdichevsky on that divan over there,' said Korovin, pointing into a dark corner. 'But the Black Monk came knocking on his window in the night. Then I had a bed made up for him upstairs, in the observatory. Two nights passed quite calmly, but now, as you can see, Basilisk has grown wings, and reaching the first floor is no trouble to him.'

'Yes,' the assistant public prosecutor sobbed. 'It's all the same to him. I shouted out the formula and he moved away and dissolved.'

'Still the same one? – "I believe, O Lord"?'

'Yes.'

'Well then, you see you have nothing to be afraid of. Basilisk is afraid of your magic formula.'

Berdichevsky whispered in a trembling voice: 'He'll come again tonight. He'll steal all that's left. And then I'll forget who I am. I'll turn into an animal. And that will cause you tremendous inconvenience. After all, you're not a veterinary doctor; you don't treat animals. I beg your forgiveness in advance . . .'

'Mmm, yes,' Dr Korovin sighed, rubbing his chin in bewilderment. 'Of course, I could give him a sleeping draught for the night, but who knows what dreams he might have. He could dream of something even worse . . . What's to be done?'

Polina Andreevna's poor heart was breaking, she felt so sorry for the sick man, but she had no idea of how to help him.

'Sleeping draught – rubbish,' Lampier muttered. 'In my room. Very simple. Two of us. I don't mind and he's not afraid.'

'Put his bed in your bedroom? Is that what you mean?' Korovin asked, galvanised. 'Well, if he has no objection, why not? – it's one solution.'

'Hey, you!' the physicist suddenly shouted at Berdichevsky as if he were deaf. 'Want to sleep in my room? Only I snore.'

The sick man fumbled clumsily at the armrests, got up out of his chair and began waving his arms about. His tearful apathy was suddenly replaced by extreme excitement: 'Yes, I do! I should be quite exceptionally grateful! I'll have peace with you! Snore as much as you like, Mr Lampier, that's even better! I am so grateful to you, so grateful!'

'No damn gratitude needed!' Lampier shouted threateningly. 'Terrorise with politeness – I'll throw you out!'

Berdichevsky was about to start apologising for his politeness, but the physicist shouted at him even more peremptorily, and the sick man fell silent.

When the doctor and his visitor began to take their leave, the unhinged investigator timidly asked Mrs Lisitsyna: 'Have we met somewhere before? No? I'm sorry, I'm sorry. I must be mistaken. I feel so awkward. Please don't be angry . . .'

Polina Andreevna almost burst into tears.

A Scandal

On the way back to the house Mrs Lisitsyna looked sad and thoughtful, but Dr Korovin, on the contrary, was in a quite excellent mood. Every now and then the doctor glanced at his companion with a mysterious smile, and once he even rubbed his hands together, as if in anticipation of something interesting or pleasant.

Finally Korovin broke his silence: 'Well now, Polina Andreevna, I granted your request and showed you Lampier. Now it is your turn. You remember our agreement? One good turn deserves another.'

'So how am I to repay you?' asked Lisitsyna, turning to the doctor and noticing a cunning gleam in the psychiatrist's eyes.

'In a manner that could not possibly be easier. Stay and have supper with me. No, really,' Korovin added hastily, noticing the shadow that briefly clouded the lady's face. 'It will be an entirely innocent evening; in addition to yourself another lady has been invited. And I have an excellent chef, Maître Armand, brought specially from Marseilles. He does not accept the rules of monastic cuisine, and today he has promised to serve fillets of new-born lamb with *sauce délicieux*, young zander stuffed with crayfish tails, patties *mignon* and all sorts of other delicious things as well. And afterwards I will drive you into town.'

This unexpected invitation suited Polina Andreevna very well, but she did not accept immediately. 'What kind of lady?'

'A rather lovely young lady, extremely picturesque,' the doctor replied with an incomprehensible smile. 'I'm sure the two of you will like each other.'

Mrs Lisitsyna raised her face to the sky, looked at the moon creeping out from behind the trees and made some kind of calculation. 'Well now, the stuffed zander certainly sounds tempting.'

No sooner had they sat down at the table set for three than the 'picturesque young lady' arrived.

There was a faint clatter of horse's hooves outside the window and a minute later a beautiful young woman in a black silk dress came rushing into the dining room. She threw back the flimsy veil from her face and exclaimed in ringing tones 'André!' – then stopped short when she saw that there was a third person in the room.

Lisitsyna recognised the impetuous young lady as the same individual who had been waiting on the landing stage for Captain Jonah, and there could be doubt that the beautiful woman had also recognised her. Just as they had done then, on the dockside, the stranger's subtle features contorted into a grimace, but this time it was even more hostile: her nostrils quivered, her slim eyebrows bunched together over the bridge of her nose and her over-large eyes (in Polina Andreevna's opinion they were actually *disproportionate*) glittered and sparkled malevolently.

'Well, now we are all here!' Donat Savvich declared cheerfully, getting to his feet. 'Allow me to introduce you to each other. Lidia Evgenievna Boreiko, the fairest of all Canaan's maidens. And this is Polina Andreevna Lisitsyna, a pilgrim from Moscow.'

The red-haired lady nodded to the black-haired one with an extremely pleasant smile that went unanswered.

'André, I have asked you a thousand times not to remind me of my appalling surname,' Mademoiselle Boreiko exclaimed in a tone that a man would no doubt have described as *ringing*, but Mrs Lisitsyna thought unpleasantly shrill.

'What is so appalling about the name "Boreiko"?' Polina Andreevna asked with an even more friendly smile, and then repeated it, as if she were seeing how it tasted. 'Boreiko, Boreiko . . . A perfectly ordinary name.'

'That is the problem,' the doctor explained with a straight face. 'We cannot bear anything ordinary, that is vulgar. "Lidia Evgenievna" now – that has a melodic, noble ring to it. Tell me,' he said, turning to the brunette and maintaining the same polite manner, 'why are you always in black? Are you in mourning for your life?'

Polina Andreevna laughed in appreciation of Korovin's literary reference, but Lidia Boreiko seemed not to have recognised the quotation from the fashionable play of the moment.

'I am mourning the fact that there is no true love left in the world,' she said gloomily, taking her seat at the table.

The cuisine was indeed truly delightful; the doctor had been quite right there. Polina Andreevna was hungry after her long day and she did ample justice to the tartlets with grated artichokes and patties *mignon* with veal hearts and the tiny *canapés royales* – her plate, rapidly emptied in magical fashion and then refilled with hors d'oeuvres, was soon standing empty again.

However, Korovin had been mistaken about one thing: the women clearly did not like each other. This was particularly noticeable from Lidia Evgenievna Boreiko's manner. She barely even sipped her wine, did not touch her food at all and regarded the woman facing her with unconcealed hostility. In her usual persona as a nun, Polina Andreevna would undoubtedly have found a way to soften the heart of her enemy through genuine Christian humility, but her present role as a society lady justified a different style of behaviour.

Mrs Lisitsyna demonstrated a perfect mastery of the English art of *looking down* on people – in a metaphorical sense, of course, since Mademoiselle Boreiko was taller than she was. But that did not prevent Polina Andreevna from gazing at her over a haughtily raised freckly nose and from time to time indicating surprise by raising her eyebrows gently in that manner so wounding to any provincial lady's heart when it is employed by a denizen of the capital.

'Charming shoulder pads,' Lisitsyna might say, for instance, indicating Lidia Evgenievna's shoulders with her chin. 'I used to adore them myself. Such a terrible shame that everyone in Moscow has moved on to close-fitting dresses.' Or she would suddenly stop paying any attention to the brunette, leaving her to her pale-faced fury, and strike up a long conversation with their host about literature, in which Mademoiselle Boreiko either did not wish or was unable to participate.

The doctor seemed highly amused by the bloodless battle unfolding before his eyes, and he did his best to pour oil on the flames.

First he declaimed an entire panegyric in honour of red hair, which he asserted was a certain sign of an exceptional character. Polina Andreevna enjoyed listening to this, but she could not help squirming under Lidia Boreiko's intense gaze – the local beauty would probably have taken pleasure in tearing out every last hair of those 'fiery locks' extolled so highly by Donat Savvich.

Even the Moscow lady's miraculous appetite served Korovin as a pretext for a compliment. Noticing that Polina Andreevna's plate was empty yet again, Dr Korovin gestured to his servant and said: 'I have always liked women without affectation, who eat well and enjoy their food. It's a sure sign of a taste for life. Only a woman who knows how to enjoy life is capable of making a man happy.'

This remark effectively marked the end of supper, which concluded suddenly, with high words.

Lidia Evgenievna tossed down her gleaming fork, still unsullied by any contact with food, and flung her hands up like a wounded bird flapping its wings. 'Torturer! Butcher!' she screamed so loudly that it set the crystal ware on the table jingling. 'Why do you torment me? And she, she . . .'

Casting a swift glance at Lisitsyna, Mademoiselle Boreiko dashed out of the room. The doctor clearly had no intention of running after her; in fact he seemed quite pleased.

Shaken by the departing glance of the impassioned young lady – a withering glance blazing with frenzied hatred – Polina Andreevna turned enquiringly to Korovin.

'I'm sorry,' he said with a shrug. 'Let me explain the meaning of this scene to you . . .'

'Please don't bother,' Lisitsyna replied coldly, getting up. 'Spare me your explanations. I understand only too well that you foresaw this outcome and exploited my presence for some base, ignoble purpose of which I am unaware.'

Dr Korovin leapt to his feet, seeming confused now, rather than pleased. 'I swear to you, there was nothing ignoble. That is, of course, from one side I owe you an apology for—'

Polina Andreevna did not allow him to finish: 'I am not going to listen to you. Goodbye.'

'Wait! I promised to drive you into town. If . . . If my company is so repellent to you, I will not go, but at least allow me to give you a carriage!'

'I do not need anything from you. I cannot bear intriguers and manipulators,' Lisitsyna said angrily as she threw her cloak over her shoulders in the hallway. 'There is no need to drive me to town. I'll manage somehow on my own.'

'But it's late, it's dark!'

'Never mind. I have heard that there are no bandits on Canaan, and I am not afraid of ghosts.'

She turned haughtily on her heels and walked out.

Last of the Bishop's Men

Once outside Korovin's house, Polina Andreevna began walking more quickly. When she was past the bushes, she pulled the hood up over her head, drew the black cloak around her more tightly and became almost completely invisible in the darkness. It would be hard for Korovin to find his touchy guest in the autumn night now, no matter how much he might wish to do so.

In all honesty, however, Polina Andreevna was not even slightly offended with the doctor, and on closer consideration it would probably have remained unclear who had manipulated whom during the supper that had concluded in such an unfortunate manner. Undoubtedly the doctor had had some reasons of his own for provoking the black-eyed beauty, but Mrs Lisitsyna had not played the part of a metropolitan snob without reasons of her own. And everything had turned out just as she had intended: Polina Andreevna had been left completely alone in the middle of the clinic, with total freedom of movement. That was why the *talma* had been swapped for the long cloak, in which she could move through the darkness so conveniently, while remaining almost invisible.

The purpose of the comic performance that had led to the scandalous quarrel had been achieved, and the task that she now faced was less difficult – to locate among the grove of pine trees the conservatory in which the unfortunate Alyosha Lentochkin dwelt among the tropical plants: she had to see him in secret; no one else must know, especially the owner of the clinic. Mrs Lisitsyna stopped in the middle of the avenue and tried to identify some landmarks.

Earlier, when she and Donat Savvich were walking to the mad artist's house, she had glimpsed a glass dome on the right, above the hedge – that must have been the conservatory.

But where was that spot? A hundred paces away? Or two hundred? Polina Andreevna set off, peering into the gloom.

Suddenly someone came round the bend towards her, walking with rapid, jerky steps, and the spy barely managed to press herself against the bushes in time and freeze.

The lanky, stooped figure was swinging its long arms as it walked along. Suddenly it stopped only two paces away from the hiding woman and muttered: 'Right. Once again, more precisely. The infinite extent of the Universe means that the possible combinations of molecules are repeated an infinite number of times, and that means that the combination of molecules known as me is also repeated a countless number of times, from which it follows that I am not alone in the Universe, but there is a countless multitude of mes, and exactly which one of this multitude is present here at this present moment is absolutely impossible to determine . . .'

Another one of Dr Korovin's collection of 'interesting people', Lisitsyna guessed. The patient nodded to himself, pleased, and marched on by.

He hadn't noticed her: Ooph!

Polina Andreevna took a deep breath and moved on.

What was that glinting in the moonlight to her right? It looked like a glass roof – the conservatory?

It *was* the conservatory, and it was absolutely huge – a genuine crystal palace.

The transparent, almost invisible door opened with a quiet squeak, breathing a mingled scent of exotic aromas and damp heat into Lisitsyna's face. She took several steps along the path, stumbled over a hosepipe or a creeper, pricked her hand on some sharp thorns and cried out in pain.

She listened. Not a sound.

She raised herself up on tiptoe and called: 'Alexei Stepanovich!'

Nothing stirring. Not a sound.

She tried again, louder: 'Alexei Stepanovich! Alyosha! It's me, Pelagia!'

What was that rustling sound nearby? Footsteps?

She moved quickly towards the sound, parting the branches and stems as she went. 'Answer me! If you hide, there's no way I'm ever going to find you!'

Her eyes gradually grew accustomed to the darkness, which was not really so impenetrable: passing unhindered through the glass roof, the pale light was reflected from the broad glossy leaves, glinting in the drops of dew and intensifying the fantastic shadows.

'A-ah!' Polina Andreevna gasped in fright, clutching at her heart.

There, swaying gently right in front of her nose, was a human leg – entirely naked, emaciated, as white as sour cream in the wan glow of the moon. And there, only a few inches away, not in the light but in the shadow, was a second leg dangling in the air.

'Oh Lord, Oh Lord . . .' Mrs Lisitsyna exclaimed, and began crossing herself; but she was afraid to look up – she already knew what she would see: a hanged man, with his eyes bulging, his tongue lolling out of his mouth and his neck stretched.

Gathering her courage, she cautiously touched one of the legs to see if it was already cold.

The leg suddenly jerked away and Polina Andreevna heard someone giggling above her head. She gave an even more piercing howl than before and leapt back.

There was Alyosha Lentochkin, not hanging but sitting on the spreading branch of some unfamiliar tree and placidly swinging his legs. His face was flooded with bright moonlight, but Polina Andreevna could scarcely recognise the former Cherubino, he had become so thin. His limp hair was dank and matted, his cheeks had lost their childish plumpness, and his collarbones and ribs stuck out like the spokes of a taut umbrella.

Mrs Lisitsyna hastily averted the gaze that had involuntarily slipped below the permissible limit, but then immediately reproached herself for her false modesty: this was not a man she saw before her but an unfortunate, starving creature. No longer the boisterous puppy who had once snapped at the heels of the condescending Father Mitrofanii; more like an abandoned wolf cub – hungry, sick and mangy.

'That tickles,' said Alexei Stepanovich, and he giggled again.

'Come down, Alyoshenka, get off there,' she told him. Previously she had always addressed Lentochkin formally, by his first name and patronymic. But it would have been strange to stand on ceremony with a boy who was mentally ill, and naked as well.

'Come on now,' said Polina Andreevna, holding out both hands to him. 'It's me, Sister Pelagia. Surely you recognise me?'

In former times Alexei Stepanovich and His Grace's spiritual daughter had greatly disliked each other. On a few occasions the insolent youth had attempted to play spiteful tricks on the nun, but had been rebuffed with unexpected firmness, after which he had pretended not to take any notice of her. But this was no time to be thinking of old jealousies and settling stupid scores from the past. Polina Andreevna's heart was breaking out of sheer pity.

'Here, look what I've brought you,' she said gently, as if she were talking to a little child, and she began taking food out of the handiwork bag hanging round her neck: tartlets, canapés and *mignon* patties, all cunningly stolen from her plate during supper. Apparently Dr Korovin's guest did not possess such a gigantic appetite after all.

The naked faun sniffed the air greedily and jumped down to the ground. But he lost his balance, swayed and fell.

He is terribly weak, Polina Andreevna thought with a sigh as she put her arm round the boy's shoulders. 'Here, take it, eat.'

Alexei Stepanovich did not have to be asked twice. He grabbed two small patties at once and greedily stuffed them into his mouth, then reached out for more before he had even finished chewing.

One more week, two at most, and he will die – Lisitsyna

remembered what the doctor had said, and she bit her lip to avoid bursting into tears.

What good had it done for her to demonstrate such miraculous ingenuity to get here? How could she help? And it was clear that Lentochkin could not assist her in the investigation either.

'Be patient, my poor boy,' she said over and over again, stroking his tangled hair. 'If this is the Devil's work, God is stronger anyway. And if it is a cunning plot by evil people, I will unravel it. I *will* save you. I promise!'

The madman could hardly have understood the meaning of these words, but her quiet, gentle tone of voice found an echo somewhere in his lost soul. Alyosha suddenly pressed his head against his comforter's breast and asked in a quiet voice: 'Will you come back again? Do come. Or else he'll take me soon. Will you come?'

Polina Andreevna nodded without speaking. She could not speak – the tears she was struggling to hold back were choking her.

Not until she had left the conservatory, leaving its glass walls behind as she walked into the pine grove, did she finally surrender to her feelings. But then she sat down on the ground and wept for all of them at once: for Lentochkin with his mind destroyed, for Matvei Bentsionovich with his spirit extinguished, for Lagrange, driven to suicide, and for His Grace Mitrofanii, whose heart had given way under the strain. She wept for a long time, perhaps half an hour, perhaps even an hour; but still she could not calm herself.

The moon had already ascended to the centre of the vault of heaven, somewhere in the forest an eagle owl had begun hooting, the lights in the windows of the clinic's cottages had all gone out, one by one, and still the disguised nun shed her bitter tears.

The unknown enemy was fearsome; he struck with a sure aim, and every blow inflicted a terrible, irreparable loss. The valiant forces of the Bishop of Zavolzhsk, defender of Good and persecutor of Evil, had been shattered, and the general himself lay in his bed, brought low by a grave illness that could yet prove fatal. Of all Mitrofanii's warriors only she was left, a weak and defenceless woman. The entire burden of responsibility now lay on her shoulders, and she had nowhere to retreat.

But this terrifying thought did not set the tears flooding from Mrs Lisitsyna's eyes even faster, as it ought to have done. Instead, by some strange paradox, her tears suddenly dried up.

She put away her soaked handkerchief, stood up and walked on through the bushes.

Night in the Abode of Woe

It was easier to find her way through the grounds now: Polina Andreevna already had a clearer idea of the clinic's geography and the moon was shining brightly high in the sky. Her courage now recovered, the solitary warrior noted in passing the surprising mildness of the island's 'microclimate', which produced an abundance of clear, warm nights like this, even in November, and then directed her steps in the first instance towards the house of the clinic's owner. But the windows in the white mansion with its decorative colonnade were all dark – the doctor was already asleep. Lisitsyna stood there for a while and listened without hearing anything of interest, and then walked on. Now her path lay in the direction of cottage number three, the dwelling of the insane artist.

Yoshihin was not sleeping: his little house was still brightly lit and she glimpsed a shadow flitting to and fro across one glowing rectangular window.

Polina Andreevna walked round two sides of the house in order to look in from the opposite side.

She glanced in.

Konon Petrovich was running rapidly along the wall, painting in the final specks of moonlight dotted across the ground in the panel 'Evening'. The picture had reached the stage of absolute completeness and its perfection rivalled, or perhaps even surpassed, the magic of a real evening. But Mrs Lisitsyna was only interested in the section of the canvas where the artist had depicted the elongated black silhouette with spider's legs. Polina

Andreevna gazed at it for quite a long time, as if she were trying to solve some abstruse puzzle.

Then Yoshihin stuck his brush in his belt and climbed up on to the scaffolding standing in the centre of the room. The secret observer pressed her cheek and nose against the glass in order to see what the artist would do up there.

She realised that, having finished 'Evening', Konon Petrovich had moved straight on to finish 'Night' without taking even a moment's break.

Lisitsyna shook her head and stopped watching. The next point of call on her planned itinerary was the neighbouring cottage, number seven, where the physicist Lampier lived with his house-guest.

They were not sleeping either – all the windows on the ground floor were lit up. Polina Andreevna remembered that the bedroom was on the left of the door and the laboratory on the right. Matvei Berdichevsky must be in the bedroom.

She took hold of the window sill with both hands, braced one foot against the narrow step in the wall and looked inside.

She saw two beds. One was made up, but empty. A lamp was lit beside the other and there was a man half-sitting, half-lying in it on a tall heap of fluffed pillows, nervously turning his head first to the left, then to the right. Berdichevsky!

The spy craned her neck to see if Lampier was in the room, and the catch of her hood clinked against the glass – the sound was barely audible, but even so Berdichevsky started and turned to face the window. The assistant public prosecutor's face contorted in a grimace of horror. His lower jaw twitched convulsively, as if he were about to scream, but then his eyes rolled upwards and his head slumped back on to the pillow. He had fainted.

Oh, how awful! Polina Andreevna even cried out in her frustration. Why, of course, when he saw the black figure with a hood lowered over its face in the window, the poor patient had imagined that Basilisk had appeared to him again. She had to correct Berdichevsky's mistake, no matter what the risk.

No longer trying to hide, she pressed herself against the glass, to make sure that the physicist was not in the room, and then took action. The main window, naturally, was latched, but the small window at the top was slightly open, and that was enough for the teacher of gymnastics.

As quick as a flash, Lisitsyna dropped the cumbersome cloak on the ground and climbed in through the narrow opening just as quickly, demonstrating a quite miraculous flexibility. She braced her fingers against the window sill, performed a remarkable somersault through the air (her skirt inflated into a rather unseemly bell shape, but there was no one there to see it) and landed nimbly on the floor, making hardly any noise at all. Polina Andreevna waited for the sound of footsteps in the corridor – but no, everything was all right. The physicist must be too preoccupied with his strange experiments.

She moved a chair closer to the bed and cautiously stroked the sunken cheeks, the yellow forehead and the eyelids, closed as if in mourning, of the man lying there. She moistened her handkerchief with water from a glass standing on the bedside cabinet and massaged the sick man's temples. Berdichevsky's eyelids trembled.

'Matvei Bentsionovich, it's me, Pelagia,' the woman whispered, leaning right down to his ear.

The man opened his eyes, saw the freckled face with its wide, anxious eyes and smiled. 'Sister . . . What a lovely dream . . . And is the Bishop here?' Berdichevsky turned his head, evidently hoping to see Father Mitrofanii as well, and was disappointed when he didn't.

'It's terrible when I don't sleep,' he complained. 'I wish I could never wake up at all.'

'Not waking up at all would be going too far,' said Polina Andreevna, still stroking the poor man's face. 'But right now it would be good for you to sleep for a while. Close your eyes and take deep breaths. Perhaps you will dream of His Grace.'

Matvei Berdichevsky obediently closed his eyes tight and

began breathing deeply – he obviously wanted very badly to dream of the Bishop.

Perhaps things are not all that bad after all, Polina Andreevna thought, trying to console herself. If you tell him your name, he recognises you. And he remembers His Grace. Mrs Lisitsyna glanced at the door and then looked in the bedside cabinet. Nothing out of the ordinary: handkerchiefs, a few blank sheets of paper, a wallet. And in the wallet some money and a photograph of his wife.

But under the bed she discovered a travelling bag of yellow pigskin. Beside the catch there was a small bronze plate with a monogram: 'F. S. Lagrange'. And inside the bag she found the items that Berdichevsky had gathered for the investigation: the minutes of the inspection of the suicide's body, Alexei Lentochkin's letters to the Bishop, a revolver wrapped in a piece of cloth (Polina Andreevna shook her head – that was fine work by Korovin, not even bothering to check a patient's belongings) and another two items of unknown origin, a long glove with a hole in it and a dirty cambric handkerchief.

Mrs Lisitsyna decided to take the travelling bag with her – what good was it to Berdichevsky now? She looked round to see if there was anything else useful in the room and saw a thick notebook lying on the locker beside Lampier's bed. After a moment's hesitation she picked it up, carried it across to the lamp and began leafing through it.

Alas, it was quite impossible to understand a thing from all those formulae, graphs and abbreviations. And the physicist's handwriting was no more comprehensible than his way of speaking. Polina Andreevna gave a sigh of disappointment and turned to the front page. With an effort, she could just make out the epigraph that was written there:

Measure everything that can be measured, render what cannot be measured measurable.   G. Galilei

But it was time to call a halt.

The uninvited guest put the notebook back in its place and climbed back through the small window, first throwing the travelling bag out, and then squeezing through herself.

The distance to the ground was greater than to the floor of the room, but once again the somersault was a great success. The flexible young lady landed in a comfortable squatting position, straightened up and shook her head: after the light in the bedroom the darkness of the night seemed impenetrable, and by a stroke of bad luck the moon had hidden behind a cloud.

Mrs Lisitsyna decided to wait for her eyes to adjust to the gloom and leaned against the wall with one hand. But there was nothing wrong with Polina Andreevna's hearing, and when she heard a rustling sound behind her, she swung round abruptly.

Very close, only about a *sazhen* away, a slim black figure emerged from the darkness. The stupefied woman clearly saw a pointed hood with holes for the eyes and noticed the way the strange silhouette turned round its own axis; then suddenly there was the whistle of something slicing through the air, and Lisitsyna felt a blow of appalling power strike her on the side of the head.

Polina Andreevna collapsed backwards and fell across Lagrange's travelling bag.

New Sins

The victim was only able to assess the full extent of the damage that had been inflicted the following morning.

She did not know how long she had lain unconscious beside the wall of cottage number seven, until the cold had brought her round. She could barely even remember staggering back to the hotel, clutching her head in her hands. She had slumped straight on to the bed without getting undressed and instantly fallen into a state of oblivion bordering on a faint.

She woke late, just before noon, and sat down at the dressing table to look at herself in the mirror.

It was a sight worth looking at. Polina Andreevna did not know how an incorporeal phantom had managed to knock her down from a distance of a *sazhen* away, but the blow that had struck her temple and cheekbone had certainly been material in its effect: there was an immense dark-crimson bruise beside her left eye, stretching upwards and downwards across almost half her face. Even the memory of the appalling mystical event paled beside her distress at the sight of her own disfigurement.

Mrs Lisitsyna turned her undamaged profile towards the mirror and squinted sideways at it faint-heartedly: it looked perfectly respectable. But then she turned back to look at her full face and groaned. If she looked at the left side, her face would probably look like a purple aubergine.

Such is the beauty of the flesh – dust and decay: a single heavy blow is enough to destroy it, Polina Andreevna said to herself, recalling her temporarily abandoned vocation. It was a correct thought, a praiseworthy thought, but it brought her no consolation.

The main problem was: how could she go outside looking like this? She couldn't possibly just stay in her room for a week, waiting for the bruise to disappear! She had to think of something.

With a heavy sigh and a guilty feeling, Lisitsyna opened her suitcase and took out a set of make-up – another complimentary gift from the Cook and Kantorovich travel agency, received at the same time as the handiwork bag already mentioned. Naturally, the pilgrim had not intended to use the make-up – unlike the bag, which was very useful. She had intended to make a present of it to some laywoman, but this was an emergency!

A fine nun I am, Polina Andreevna thought mournfully as she powdered the hideous mark. She felt envious of brunettes – they had thick, dark skin that healed quickly; but for the white skin of a redhead a bruise was an absolute catastrophe.

Even with the make-up it still looked awful. In debauched St Petersburg or frivolous Moscow she could perhaps have gone out looking like that, especially if she hid behind a veil: but in pious Ararat she could not even think of it – they would probably stone her, like the loose woman in the Gospels.

What could she do? She couldn't go out wearing powder and she couldn't go out without it, displaying the bruise. And she couldn't afford to waste any time, either.

She thought very hard, and eventually she thought of something. She put on a very simple dress of black Tibet, then tied her pilgrim's headscarf round her head, pulling it tight right down to the corners of her eyes. She covered the visible part of the bruise with white powder. If you didn't look too closely, it was all right, almost unnoticeable.

Covering the cheek with her handkerchief, she slipped through to the exit, taking the yellow travelling bag with her – she couldn't risk leaving it in her room. Everyone knew what the staff in hotels were like, always poking their noses into everything and rummaging in people's things. God forbid that they should find the revolver or the minutes. It was not such a heavy burden; her arms could manage it.

Once out in the street the pilgrim lowered her eyes meekly and walked along like that until she reached the main square, where the day before she had noticed a shop selling monks' garments.

For three roubles and seventy-five kopecks she bought a novice's outfit from the monk minding the shop: a skullcap, a moiré cassock and a fabric belt. To avoid rousing any suspicion, she said that she was buying them as a donation to the monastery. The shop monk was not at all surprised – pilgrims often made gifts of vestments to the brethren; that was what the shop was for.

And now she had to embark on a new masquerade, even more indecent and blasphemous than the first. What else could she do?

But then again, walking about in the guise of a modest young monk promised a certain additional advantage that Polina Andreevna had only just thought of. She pondered this new idea while she searched for a suitable place to change her clothes, looking around as she walked along the streets where there were fewer passers-by.

Perhaps as a consequence of the blow, or perhaps because she was upset about the disfigurement of her appearance, Mrs Lisitsyna was in a strange state of nervous agitation that day. From the moment she left her guest house, she was haunted by a strange feeling that was hard to put into words, as if she were *not alone*, as if there were someone else there beside her, invisible, either watching her or following her; and this attention was clearly malevolent and hostile. Though she rebuked herself all the while for being such a superstitious and impressionable female, Polina Andreevna glanced round several times, but she did not notice anything unusual: nothing but some monks going about their usual business, someone standing beside a stone post, reading a newspaper; someone else bending down to pick up the matches they had dropped. People in the street, doing perfectly normal things.

But after a while Lisitsyna forgot this disturbing feeling, because she found an excellent place to change her appearance and, what was more, it was only five minutes' walk from the Immaculate Virgin. Standing on a corner at the waterfront there was a closed and shuttered pavilion with a sign that read: 'Holy water. Automatic dispensers'. Its front façade overlooked the promenade, and its back wall faced a blank fence.

Polina Andreevna walked round to the back of the large wooden booth, ducked into the gap and saw that she was in luck: the door was only secured with the very simplest of padlocks. After poking and prodding it for a while with a knitting needle (O Lord, forgive this transgression also!), the enterprising lady slipped inside.

There were bulky metal boxes with little taps standing along the walls, but the space in the centre was empty. Light percolated through the gaps between the boards and she could hear the voices of the public strolling along the waterfront. It really was an absolutely perfect spot.

Lisitsyna quickly pulled off her dress. She hesitated, wondering what to do about her drawers. She left them on – the cassock was long, they wouldn't be visible, and it would be warmer that way. This was not July, after all.

Her shoes were rather masculine, with blunt toes, as the latest fashion required, but they were still a bit too foppish for a novice. Polina Andreevna sprinkled them with dust and decided they would do. Women knew nothing about the peculiarities of monk's garments, and monks were men – which meant they were not very observant of such details and would probably not notice anything.

She left the bag with her knitting hanging round her neck. What if she had to wait somewhere or spend hours in surveillance? Many of the monks consoled themselves by knitting, so it would not look suspicious, and the regular clickety-clack of the needles made it easier to think.

She stuck the little bag inside her cassock. Let it hang there.

Then she hid the travelling bag between two of the automatic dispensers, pulled her long hair out from under her cap, tugged down the cassock and wiped the powder off her face with her sleeve.

In short, she entered the holy-water pavilion as a modest young lady and ten minutes later emerged as a skinny, red-headed young monk with nothing unusual about him – unless, of course, you took note of the massive bruise on the left side of his face.

Nothing but Riddles

Up to this point the actions of the female investigator have been more or less comprehensible, but now, if some stranger were to decide to follow Lisitsyna's movements, he would be thrown into a state of total bewilderment, since the pilgrim's further behaviour seemed to lack any logic whatsoever.

At this point, in order to avoid any ambiguity, we shall be obliged once again to bring our heroine's name into conformity with her new appearance, as we have already done once. Otherwise it will be impossible to avoid ambivalent phrases such as, 'Polina Andreevna called into the brothers' cells' – for it is well known that women are strictly forbidden to enter the monks' inner chambers. Therefore, from this point on we shall not follow Sister Pelagia, or the widow Lisitsyna, but a certain novice monk who, as we have already said, was behaving very strangely on that day.

For about two or two and a half hours, beginning from midday, the young monk could be seen in various parts of the town: within the confines of the monastery itself and even – alas – in the aforementioned brothers' cells. His lazy gait suggested that he was simply wandering about without anything particular to do, apparently out of pure boredom, stopping here for a moment and listening, stopping there for a moment and looking. Several times the idly wandering youth was stopped by senior monks, and once even by the peace-keepers, who asked him sternly who he was and how he had come by the bruise – had it been a drunken incident or some bout of fisticuffs? The youth humbly replied in a thin voice that his name was Pelagius, that he had come to Ararat from holy Valaam as a work of penance, and the bruise on his face had been give to him by the father cellarer for his carelessness. This explanation satisfied everyone, for the harsh manners of the father cellarer were well known and young monks who had been 'taught a lesson' – some with bruises, some with bumps, some with a red, swollen ear – were a common sight on the streets and in the monastery. And so the young monk bowed and carried on along his way.

Shortly before three in the afternoon Pelagius wandered out of the town and found himself close to Lenten Spit, opposite Outskirts Island. In recent weeks this place had acquired a disquieting reputation among the pilgrims and local residents, and so the shore was completely deserted.

The novice walked along the spit until he reached its very end and then began skipping from one boulder to another, moving ever closer to the island. Here and there, for some incomprehensible reason, he thrust a stick that he had picked up into the water. Beside one of the boulders he squatted down on his haunches for a long time and fumbled in the cold water with his hands – as if he were catching fish. Although he lifted nothing out of the water, he seemed quite delighted about something and even clapped his chilly hands together.

He came back to the beginning of the spit, sat down on a rock beside an old boat that was moored there, and began working away with a pair of knitting needles, looking around him every now and then; and quite soon the person for whom the youth had apparently been waiting put in an appearance.

The monk walking along the path leading from the old chapel did not appear particularly meek and mild: a matted beard, bushy eyebrows and a bluish nose with open pores, set in a large, crumpled face.

Pelagius jumped up and greeted him with a low bow. 'Would you perhaps be the venerable holy elder Kleopa?'

'Indeed I am,' said the monk, squinting gloomily at the young lad. He scooped up some water out of the lake with his broad palm and drank it. 'What do you want?'

Heaving a sigh full of suffering that scalded the novice's nostrils with the sour smell of stale alcohol, he began taking his oars out of the bushes.

'I have come to implore your holy blessing,' Pelagius chirped in a shrill tenor.

Brother Kleopa was surprised at first, but his spiritual and bodily state at that moment were more conducive to irritability than astonishment, and he raised his massive, heavy fist as if to strike the boy. 'Come here to play jokes, have you? I'll give you a blessing, you red-haired pup! I'll blacken your other eye for you!'

The young monk moved back a few steps, but did not run away. 'But I was thinking of offering you fifty kopecks,' he said, and then he took the silver coin out of his sleeve and showed it to Kleopa.

'Give that here.' The boatman took the coin, bit on it with teeth yellow from smoke, and seemed satisfied. 'Well, what do you want, tell me.'

The novice babbled shyly: 'I have a dream. I want to be a holy elder.'

'A holy elder? You will be,' said Kleopa, mellowed by the silver. 'In about fifty years for certain, you will be, you can't avoid it. Unless, of course, you die before then. And as for holiness, you're already standing there in a cassock, even though you're no more than a spring chicken. What's your name?'

'Pelagius, holy Father.'

Kleopa pondered for a moment, obviously trying to recall his saints.

'After St Pelagius of Laodicea, who persuaded his faithful wife to honour brotherly love above the love of a husband? Why, St Pelagius was getting well on, and you still haven't seen anything at all of life. What made a brainless young thing like you become a monk? Live a bit, sin to your heart's content, then atone for it all by prayer – that's the way the wise ones do it. The holy elder Israel, over there in the hermitage' – he nodded in the direction of the island – 'now there's a prudent man for you. He had his fun and plucked plenty of young chicks, and now he's the abbot. He lived well here on Earth, and now he's prepared a fine little place for himself in Heaven, close to the Father and the Son. That's the way to do it.'

The little monk's brown eyes lit up. 'Ah, if only I could just get a little glimpse of the holy elder!'

'Sit here and wait. He comes out on to the shore sometimes, only not very often – not got the strength he used to have. I reckon he'll be ascending soon.'

Pelagius leaned down towards the boatman and whispered: 'Couldn't I take a closer look, eh? Take me over to the island, Father, and I'll remember you in my prayers for ever.'

Kleopa pushed the boy back as he untied the mooring rope. 'Oh, don't want much, do you! You know what you'd get for that?'

'Is it absolutely impossible?' the ginger novice asked in a quiet voice, showing the corner of a piece of paper protruding from his white fist.

Brother Kleopa looked closely – it looked like a rouble all right.

'It's not allowed,' he sighed regretfully. 'If they find out, it's the punishment cell for sure. A week, or even two. And I can't live on bread and water; water makes my head swell up.'

'But I've heard tell that these days none of the brothers except you will dare take a boat to the island anyway. They won't put you in the punishment cell, Father. And how will they find out? There's nobody here, is there?'

And he stuffed the note into Kleopa's hand, the little tempter.

Kleopa took the bribe, looked at it and started thinking.

Then another note appeared, as if out of nowhere.

The red-headed imp forced it into the boatman's reluctant fingers. 'Just a quick glimpse, with one eye, eh?'

The monk turned both notes over, stroked them lovingly and shook his grey locks. 'Well, you won't be able to see him with two, heh-heh!' Kleopa laughed, delighted with his own joke. 'Who fixed your fizzog for you, eh? Had a ding-dong with some workmen, I bet? As quiet as they come, but I can see you're a rascal! Over some girls, was it? Oh, you won't last long as a novice, Pelagius. They'll throw you out. Tell me, was it the workmen, then? Over some girls?'

'It was girls,' the young monk confessed, lowering his eyes.

'I knew it. "I want to be a holy elder",' Kleopa mimicked as he tucked the fifty-kopeck coin and the notes in behind his belt. 'And you want to see the island for the sake of a bit of mischief, I suppose? Don't lie; tell me the truth!'

'I'm just curious, that's all,' said Pelagius with a sniff, entering fully into his role.

'And where did you get so much money from? Did you pilfer it from the donations?'

'No, Father, of course not! I have an uncle who's a merchant. He feels sorry for me and sends me money.'

'A merchant – that's good. Was it him put you in the monastery for your pranks? Never mind; if he feels sorry for you, he'll be merciful and take you back, just wait and see. Right, I'll tell you what, Pelagius.' The boatman looked round at the deserted shore and made his mind up. 'There was this one time last year, you see. I flayed the skin off my finger on Father Martini's face – the stinking dog stuck his teeth in the way of my fist. My hand swelled up so bad I couldn't row with it. So I struck a deal with Ezekiel the street-sweeper to help me out: me on one oar, him on the other . . . We rowed the boat three days like that. Anyway, that's an old story now. But if they see us, I'll say my hand's hurting again. Climb in!'

Then he tore a strip of cloth off his undershirt and wound it round his hand. They laid into the oars and moved off.

'Only you look here,' Kleopa warned Pelagius sternly. 'Don't you set one foot out of the boat on to the island! I'm the only one who's allowed to go there. And keep your ears open for what the elder says – I've got a memory like a sieve nowadays and he won't say it twice. To be honest, sometimes I forget before I get back to the father steward. Then I tell him any nonsense that comes into my head.'

As he rowed, Pelagius kept glancing over his shoulder at Outskirts Island slowly drifting closer. It was deserted, with no movement at all: black rocks, pale-grey grass, straight pines jutting up from the top of the hill, like hair standing on end.

The boat nudged against the sand; Brother Kleopa picked up the basket of provisions and jumped out on to the shore. He wagged his finger at his partner, as if to say: Stay there and don't move.

The little novice turned round on his bench, propped his chin in his hands and opened his eyes as wide as he possibly could – in short, he got ready.

And then he saw one of the black boulders suddenly start to move: it seemed to break into two parts, one larger and one smaller. The smaller part straightened up and became a featureless black sack, pointed at the top and broader at the bottom.

The sack slowly moved downhill, to the edge of the water. Pelagius could make out two hands, a staff, a white border along the edge of the abbot's robe and, just below the top of the cowl, a skull and crossbones. The boy raised his hand to cross himself at the sight.

The boatman set down what he had brought on a flat rock in a habitual manner: three small loaves of bread, three earthenware pots, a little bag of salt. Then he walked up to the elder, pressed his lips against the bony yellow hand and was blessed in reply with the sign of the cross.

Pelagius sat in the boat, shuddering. The skull and crossbones certainly looked terrifying, but the worst thing was the holes in the covering of the face, and the two glittering eyes looking out through them, straight at the novice; and even that was not enough for the faceless holy elder Israel. Moving his feet with difficulty, he walked right up to the boat, stood facing the quailing young monk and stared steadily at him for a while – he was probably not used to seeing any emissaries from the outside world apart from Kleopa.

The boatman explained: 'I hurt my hand. I couldn't row on my own.'

The ascetic nodded, still looking at the novice.

Then Kleopa cleared his throat and asked: 'What will the phrase be today?'

Pelagius thought he saw the black figure start, as if awakening from a state of reverie or trance. It turned towards the monk and a low, hoarse voice spoke very clearly, with gaps between the words: Today – dost – Thou – release – Thy – servant – the death.'

'Oh, my Lord,' Kleopa exclaimed, taking fright at something and starting to cross himself frantically. 'Now we're for it . . .'

He hastily clambered back into the boat and pushed off from the shore with his foot.

'What's wrong, uncle?' the boy asked, looking back at the holy elder (he was standing quite still, leaning on his staff). 'What was that he said about death, eh?'

'I'll give you uncle,' Kleopa snapped, absorbed in his own thoughts. 'Lay into that oar there, lay into it! Well, now, there's a fine trip we've made!'

They had almost reached the shoreline of Canaan before he explained: 'If the words are "Today dost Thou release Thy servant", one of the hermits has passed away. Tomorrow I'll bring another one to take his place. Father Ilarii's been waiting a long time. They'll sing his requiem this evening, take him to the Farewell Chapel to take his leave of the world all alone, sew up his cowl and cut holes in it. And at first light I'll take a living man to join the dead . . . Ah, why can't people be happy to live in the world?' Kleopa shook his shaggy head. 'But how do you like that holy elder Israel! That makes seven he's outlived now. He must have sinned in real style; the Lord still won't take him to Himself yet. Which one of them's passed on, then? Holy elder Theognost or holy elder David? What was it that he said, exactly?'

'Today dost Thou release Thy servant, the death,' Pelagius recited. 'But why was "the death" added at the end?'

Kleopa moved his lips, remembering the words. He answered

the question with a shrug, as if to say: That's none of our business.

What else should be told about the events of that day? Probably what happened at the buoy-keeper's hut, although it won't make any sense at all.

When he left the boatman, Pelagius did not go straight back to the town; first he strolled along the shore as far as a solitary log hut – the self-same ominous hut that has already featured in our narrative several times. It was hardly any distance to walk from Lenten Spit: a hundred paces to the Farewell Chapel, and then another hundred and fifty.

The novice walked round the outside of the plain little dwelling and glanced inside through the small dusty window. He pressed his cheek against the glass and started running his finger over the eight-pointed cross crudely scratched into it. He said just one word: 'Aha.' Then he suddenly squatted down on his haunches and started rummaging in the weeds with his hands. He picked up some small object and held it close to his face (the light of the autumn day was already fading and it was hard to see). He said 'Aha' a second time. And then the boy set off with remarkable fearlessness towards the boarded-up door and tugged on the handle. When it creaked open quite easily, he looked at the nails protruding from it and nodded to himself.

He went inside. In the semi-darkness he could see a table with an open coffin lying on it and the lid of the coffin lying on the floor. The novice felt the wooden box from this side and that; then for some reason he set the lid in place and slapped it gently. The coffin closed tightly, with a quiet crunch.

The youth went over to the window, where there were two sacks of straw lying on the floor. For some reason he set one on top of the other. Then, with an anxious glance through the window at the rapidly failing light, he got up on a bench and began running his hand along the smoothly trimmed logs of the wall. He started at the top, just under the ceiling, then checked the next row down, then the next, and the next. Having finished these mysterious manipulations on one wall, he moved on to the next and continued with this strange occupation for some time.

When the windowpane was already tinted pink by the final glow of sunset, Pelagius uttered the word 'Aha' for a third time, in a louder and happier voice than before. He took a knitting needle out from inside his cassock, poked at the beam with it for a moment and then extracted something really tiny, no bigger than a cherry, with his fingers.

He didn't stay in the hut any longer after that. He strode off rapidly along the deserted path to New Ararat and half an hour later he was already on the waterfront, near the automatic dispensers of holy water.

First he strolled past (there were rather a lot of people), then he seized his chance and slipped nimbly into the crack between the pavilion and the fence.

Ten minutes later a modest young lady in a black pilgrim's dress emerged on to the promenade, wearing a headscarf pulled right down to her eyes – a precaution that was probably unnecessary, for the bruise was in any case invisible in the evening twilight.

A Few Things are Made Clear

That evening Polina Andreevna wrote a letter in her room.

To His Grace Mitrofanii light, joy and strength.

If you are reading this letter of mine, Father, it means that I have been overtaken by disaster and was not able to tell you everything in person. But then, what is 'disaster'? Perhaps what people are accustomed to calling disaster is really cause for joy, because when the Lord calls one of us to himself, what is bad about that? Even if he does not call us, but subjects us to some terrible test, that also is no cause for sadness, for after all, that is why we are born into the world: to be tested.

Ah, but why am I preaching to you, my pastor, about what is obvious? Forgive my stupidity.

But above all, forgive my deception, my wilfulness and my flight. Forgive me for stealing all your money and for irritating you so often with my obstinacy.

And so, now that you have forgiven me (for how could you not forgive me if I have been overtaken by disaster?), let me move straight on to the essential matter, for I have a lot to write and I have more business to deal with tonight. But I shall tell you about that business at the very end. First I shall recount everything in the proper order, as you like things done (in other words, not the 'woman's way' but the 'man's way'): what I have heard from others; what I have seen with my own eyes; what conclusions I draw from all this.

What I have heard

Many people have already seen the Black Monk on Canaan during the night. Basilisk frightens some with his sudden appearance and others take fright themselves when they see him in the distance, creeping or hurrying along. I must have overheard a dozen or so such stories in the town and the monastery. The general opinion among the monks and the local people is that Basilisk's Hermitage is an evil spot, because one of the ascetics has sold his soul to the Enemy of Man, and so the place is cursed and the holy elders should be removed from there; Outskirts Island should be declared an uninhabitable wilderness and it should be prohibited to land there or even come close in a boat.

Let me say immediately that all this is absolute nonsense. St Basilisk has not descended from heaven, but remains serene in his place beside the Throne of the Lord, which is where he should be. There is nothing mystical about this story; it is only a matter of malicious deception. Today, as the end of my second day on Canaan approaches, I have become absolutely convinced that the appearances of the Black Monk are nothing more than a cunning and ingenious performance.

What I have seen

The secret of the 'walking on water' is very easily explained. Between the fourth and the fifth rocks that jut up out of the water beyond the end of the Lenten Spit I discovered an ordinary wooden bench under the surface of the water. It is hidden in the shallows, lying on its side. When it is stood on its iron-bound feet, the board is one inch below the surface of the water. At night, even from close up, anyone walking along this bench would certainly appear to be walking on the water. I cannot say anything definite about the 'unearthly glow' that is supposed to envelop Basilisk; however, I expect that if you were to hold a powerful electric torch behind your back and suddenly switch it on, it would produce more or less the same effect: it would give a sharp outline to your silhouette and the light would spread out, dissipating into the darkness. This simple trick should produce a great impression on monks who are frightened to death by the 'walking on water' and are unlikely ever to have seen an electric light. And possibly also on anybody who has a lively imagination or is inclined towards mysticism. Imagine a moonlit night, an unnaturally bright light, a black figure with no face hovering above the water. I encountered it on dry land, and my blood still ran cold! No, I am skipping ahead, and that is the 'woman's way'. I shall write about my encounter with 'Basilisk' later.

Now for the buoy-keeper's hut that you know from Alyosha's letter, the place where Felix Stanislavovich died and Alexei Stepanovich and Matvei Bentsionovich lost their reason. There our malefactor carried off a more cunning trick than on the spit, but there was still nothing mystical about it.

The cross was scraped on the glass with an ordinary iron nail – I found it in the grass under the window. It is hardly surprising that when the criminal displayed a hermit's hood with holes in it at the window in the middle of the night and scraped on the glass with the nail, the buoy-keeper's poor wife was so frightened that she had a miscarriage.

And the villain dealt with your emissaries as follows.

He hid in the dark room. Possibly, in order to distract attention, he placed a dummy dressed in a pointed cowl at the window – in any case, I discovered two sacks of straw in the hut, and there is no reason for them to be there. When the victim entered and noticed the motionless silhouette, he turned his entire body in that direction and the bandit struck him on the head from behind with some heavy object. Hence the 'bump one inch to the right of the top of the head' that I read about in the report of the inspection of Felix Stanislavovich's remains. It is not at all a matter of convulsive blows of the head against the floor, as Matvei Bentsionovich assumed when he wrote his description. Berdichevsky himself, and no doubt Lentochkin before him, when he came running to the clinic, also bore the traces of blows to the head, but Dr Korovin did not attach any great importance to the fact, since they both also had numerous other injuries: grazes, scratches and bruises. In speaking about Berdichevsky the doctor mentioned his skinned fingers and broken nails. That was what helped me to reconstruct the picture of the villainous deed.

Having stunned his victim, the criminal placed him in a coffin (there is a coffin lying on the table; the buoy-maker made it for himself, but it has remained unused, since the drowned man's body was never found) and shut him in with the lid. I tried putting the lid on and saw that the nails sat loosely in their holes – someone had beaten the lid off with powerful blows from below. I assume that it happened twice: the first person who was entombed alive in the coffin and forced his way out was Alyosha, and the second was Matvei Bentsionovich.

No mind, not even the very strongest, can withstand such an ordeal – the criminal was correct in that assumption. But he did not let things rest at that, as I shall tell you later.

First about Lagrange. In Felix Stanislavovich's case the attacker's plans evidently misfired. Either the police chief's head proved too hard, or something else went wrong, but the colonel did not lose consciousness and evidently tussled with the villain. Then the criminal killed him with a shot at point-blank range.

Yes, yes, Lagrange did not commit suicide; he was an innocent victim, which should gladden your heart. That is the explanation of the strange path that the bullet followed, upwards and from the left to the right. It is the path that a bullet would follow if someone whom the colonel was holding tight by the shoulders or the throat were to fire upwards with his right hand.

Remembering that no bullet was found in the body, which

meant that it had passed straight through, I searched the upper sections of the walls and found what I was looking for. We now have incontrovertible proof that it was murder.

The bullet that I extracted from the log was not forty-five calibre, like the police chief's Smith and Wesson, but thirty-eight calibre, and as I discovered from my textbook on ballistics, it was fired from a Colt revolver. After the murder, the criminal fired his victim's gun in the air and put the Smith and Wesson in the colonel's hand to make the death look like suicide.

Now let me return to our friends, whom the villain did not kill but drove insane, which is perhaps even more terrible. If only you had seen into what a pitiful parody of a man the sharp-witted Alexei Stepanovich Lentochkin has been transformed, and how little remains of the highly intelligent Matvei Berdichevsky's intelligence! It is a sin to say it, but I believe it would have caused me less pain to see them dead ...

The most abominable thing about the false Basilisk is that he is not content with his violent savagery and has not left the poor madmen in peace. From Alyosha Lentochkin's troubled words it seems clear that the 'phantom' continues to appear to him even now. And as for Berdichevsky, I myself witnessed and even fell victim to another attempt by the criminal to extinguish the final spark of reason barely glowing in his soul.

Last night I saw the Black Monk with my own eyes. Ah, how terrifying it was! Of course, he did not appear in order to frighten me – it was Berdichevsky that he wanted. Having stunned me with a blow to the head (delivered with some skill) the villain fled, and I failed to recognise him. But the blow knocked some sense into my head, so that I began searching, not for a devil but a man, though one who is little different from the Evil One.

I did not realise straight away what he could have struck me with when he was standing so far from me. But then I recalled a story that the doctor had told me and a certain painting by an artist who lives here (now there is someone you ought to talk to, someone for you to bring to their senses!) and I understood everything straight away.

'Basilisk' struck me with a stilt – the kind that you see at fairgrounds. It would take too long and there is no point in explaining here how fairground stilts came to be in the clinic, but one thing is certain: the criminal used them to look in at the first-floor window where Berdichevsky used to sleep – with the same purpose: to frighten him and finish him off. Yesterday night, however, Matvei Berdichevsky was moved from the first floor to the ground floor, but Basilisk still had his stilts with him – so the Black Monk was unaware of the move? But then what kind of supernatural force is he?

And now the conclusions

I do not know who is concealed beneath the disguise of the enraged Basilisk, but I do have a conjecture concerning the goal of his evil actions.

This person (definitely a person, and not a being from another world) wishes to have Basilisk's Hermitage abolished and has almost succeeded in his intentions.

Why? That is the most important question, and as yet I do not have any answer, only possible explanations. Some of them will seem quite incredible to you, but perhaps even they might prove useful if you have to bring this matter to a conclusion without me.

Let me begin with the father superior himself, Father Vitalii. For him the hermitage is a vexatious encumbrance, since it has lost all importance in the economic sense (forgive me for writing in such terms, but I believe that this is more or less the way the archimandrite himself thinks), and in terms of the ambition that His Reverence possesses in abundance, the hermitage actually hinders him by overshadowing his achievements as the ruler of New Ararat, which are quite genuinely substantial. The income from the rosary beads, on which the brethren formerly supported themselves, is laughable these days and can in no wise be compared with the other sources of revenue. The hermitage has also ceased to be the main attraction for pilgrims, for the well-to-do among them, whom Father Vitalii welcomes especially, are more interested in the healthy air, the restorative waters and picturesque boat rides. In the archimandrite's opinion, Outskirts Island and its holy inhabitants merely serve to sow confusion in the brethren's minds, distracting them from useful labour and indirectly undermining the authority of the archimandrite's position by constantly reminding them that there is another Authority, incomparably superior to that of the archimandrite. Vitalii is a man of harsh and even cruel disposition. How far his love of power and his ambition extend, God only knows.

Another possible explanation is a conspiracy among the monks who are dissatisfied with Vitalii's frenzied economic activity at the expense of spiritual service and the saving of their souls. There is no doubt that a secret party of those opposed to His Reverence exists among the senior brethren. It is possible that some of these 'mystics' might have decided to frighten the pilgrims away and undermine Vitalii's authority with the Church hierarchy – for instance, with you. In that case the play-acting with the Black Monk might be intended to rid New Ararat of the vain, bustling throng. The depths of perfidy and even barbarity to which perversely understood piety can lead are well known – the history of religion is full of sad examples.

It is also possible that the culprit is one of the hermits living on the island. I will not even attempt to surmise why and to what end, since as yet I know nothing about the life of the holy elders. However, all the mysterious events are connected in one way or another with the hermitage and revolve around it. And so this possibility will also have to be investigated. I was at Outskirts Island today (yes, yes, do not be angry) and the abbot Israel posed a riddle, the meaning of which is not clear to me. I shall have to go visiting again.

And now two possibilities of a quite different type, with no religious connotations.

Donat Savvich Korovin, the owner of the clinic, is a curious individual. This millionaire philanthropist is far from straightforward, an enthusiast of all kinds of games and experiments with living people. He might possibly be expected to engage in this kind of mystification for the purposes of some kind of research: studying the effect of mystical shock on various psychological types, for instance, or something else of that kind; and afterwards he could publish an article in some 'Heidelberg Psychiatric Yearbook' in order to maintain his reputation as a luminary of science, which, to my unenlightened eyes appears none too well deserved (he keeps treating his patients, but somehow never seems to cure them).

Finally, it could be one of Korovin's patients who is playing the part of Basilisk. They are all unusual people, and they are free to come and go as they wish. There are twenty-eight in all (with Lentochkin and Berdichevsky the number has risen to thirty), and I have only seen a few of them. They should be studied more closely, only I do not know how to set about it. Donat Savvich and I have fallen out, a state of affairs that I deliberately provoked. That, however, is not where the difficulty lies – it would not be hard to bring about a reconciliation. But until the after-effects of my encounter with the Black Monk disappear from my face, it would better for me not show myself to Korovin. For him I am an ordinary, attractive woman (no doubt the local waters offer poor fishing), but just how attractive would I be with half my face swollen up? Men are constituted so that they will not even talk to an ugly-looking woman.

At this point I can see the ironic smile that has appeared on your face. I shall not prevaricate. You can see through me. Yes, I find it unpleasant to think that Donat Savvich Korovin, who has looked on Polina Andreevna Lisitsyna in a special way and showered her with compliments, might see her in such a shocking state. I repent of my sinful vanity.

Now I am writing the last few lines before I leave.

It is a moonlit night – exactly as required. Precisely the kind of night when 'Basilisk' appears near the Lenten Spit. My plan is simple: I shall conceal myself on the shore and attempt to track down the hoaxers.

If my excursion is in vain, tomorrow I shall start investigating the abbot and Outskirts Island. And if it should happen that my excursion ends in the aforementioned disaster, my only hope is that Your Grace will receive this message from me.

Your loving daughter Pelagia

A Terrible Vision

After she finished writing this letter Pelagia looked out of the window and frowned in concern. The sky, only recently clear and flooded with tranquil moonlight, was changing colour: the north wind was driving a dark curtain of cloud across it from the horizon to the centre, shrouding the infinite depths of the astral sphere. She had to hurry.

Lisitsyna had intended to leave her letter to the Bishop on the table, but then she remembered the curiosity of the hotel staff. She thought hard and finally put the letter in the handiwork bag hanging round her neck, reasoning that if she did suffer the same fate as Lagrange or – God forbid! – Lentochkin and Berdichevsky (Polina Andreevna shuddered at the very thought), the letter would not in any case get lost. It would reach His Grace even sooner. And if the Bishop was not destined to rise from his sick bed (she sighed bitterly), then the senior levels of the police could look into things.

After that she acted quickly. She threw on the cloak with the hood, grabbed the travelling bag and set off into the night.

The waterfront was quite deserted now and the investigator had no difficulty slipping into the closed pavilion. Soon after that a skinny young monk was walking along the path leading from New Ararat to the Lenten Spit, shuddering as his black cassock billowed in the freezing-cold wind.

The sky was darkening with increasing rapidity. Pelagius lengthened his stride and walked faster, but the blank curtain was moving closer and closer to the serene face of the lamp of night. The implacable advance of darkness raised two concerns in the novice's mind: would his sortie not be in vain, would the criminal not change his mind about impersonating Basilisk tonight? And if he did appear in any case, ought Pelagius not to have taken Lagrange's revolver? What good was it doing, lying in the travelling bag between the bulky iron chests in the pavilion? He would have felt much safer on the dark, deserted shore if he had had it with him.

Nonsense, Pelagius told himself. The weapon would be no use. He could not fire at a living soul in order to save his own life, could he? The young monk stopped thinking about the revolver, and now the only thing that concerned him was the moon, which had hidden behind a cloud.

Any long-time resident of Canaan would have told Pelagius that when the wind was from the north the moon was doomed and it would never peep out again now, except perhaps for a few brief moments, and even then not at full strength but only shining through some thin cloud. However, the novice had not had occasion to discuss the caprices of the moon over the Blue Lake with individuals more experienced than he, and so he continued to gaze up at the silver-shrouded vault of heaven with a certain hope.

At the beginning of the spit Pelagius bent down and pressed himself against the surface of the earth. He settled down beside a large rock and sat quietly, looking towards the spot where the murderer had concealed his bench so cunningly.

With every minute that passed the night grew darker. At first the surface of the lake was still visible, its wrinkled surface frowning up at the violent rage of the north wind, but soon the gleams of light on its surface disappeared and the only indication of a large body of water was the sound of splashing and a fresh, damp smell, as if somewhere close by someone had sliced up an immense number of cucumbers.

The young monk sat there, hugging himself round the shoulders and sighing in disappointment. A fine chance there was of seeing Basilisk now! How could he go walking on the water, if it wasn't lying smoothly, but splashing about? The entire effect would be destroyed.

The sensible thing would have been to leave and go back to the guest house. But Pelagius lingered on and couldn't bring himself to go. Perhaps it was sheer obstinacy, or perhaps he had intuitively sensed something. Because just when the boy was chilled right through to the marrow and was on the point of giving up, his patience was rewarded. A rent appeared in the curtain over the sky as the moon finally found a thin cloud and lit up the lake for a few instants – only dimly, but still brightly enough to reveal a sinister vision to the observer's gaze.

In the middle of the narrow gulf separating the large island from the small one, Pelagius saw the narrow form of a boat swaying among the waves, with a black figure in a pointed cowl standing upright in it. The figure bent down, picked up something soft and light-coloured and tumbled it over the edge of the boat.

The novice cried out, for he had quite clearly seen two naked, emaciated legs dangling lifelessly. The water closed over the body, and a moment later the rent in the sky also closed.

Pelagius himself could not tell if he had imagined this hellish scene. It would have been easy, with the uncertain light and the surrounding darkness. But then the young monk was struck by an idea that made him shriek out loud. He picked up the hem of his cassock, revealing the white frills of a pair of lady's drawers, and set off at a trot away from the shore towards the centre of the island.

As he ran, he muttered the words of a confused, hastily com-posed prayer: 'Preserve, O Lord, Thy lamb from the teeth of the wolf and men of blood. God shall arise and scatter all before him, and his enemies shall flee from His face!'

Soon the young monk's shoes were clattering on the bricks of a paved road, but it was no easier to run – the ground was gradually rising upwards, and the further he went, the steeper it became.

At the edge of the pine grove where Korovin's land began,

the runner slowed to a walk, for he was completely exhausted. The windows of the little houses were dark; the mentally ill patients were sleeping. Sensing rather than seeing the glass roof of the conservatory above the dense wall of bushes, Pelagius set off at a run again.

He burst in and shouted in a despairing, faltering voice: 'Alexei Stepanovich! Alyosha!'

Silence.

He rushed this way and that through the luxuriant thickets, breathing in the intoxicating tropical aromas through his open mouth. 'Alyoshenka! Answer! It's me, Pelagia!'

There was a cold draught coming from the corner. The young monk turned in that direction, peering into the darkness. First there were shards of glass crunching under his feet, and then Pelagius made out the immense hole broken in the transparent wall of the conservatory. He sat down on the ground and covered his face with his hands.

Oh, disaster!

Gulliver and the Lilliputians

'Will you come again? Do come. Or else he'll come to take me soon. Will you come?' Alyosha Lentochkin's childish voice and the intonation in which he had spoken those words, so full of timid hope, had imprinted themselves indelibly on Pelagius' memory, and now, when it was already too late to change anything, they tormented his very soul. Pelagius put his hands over his ears, but it didn't help.

He ought not to have been tracking the criminal but trying to save poor Alexei Stepanovich; he ought to have been beside him all the time, protecting him, reassuring him. It had been clear (and the letter to Mitrofanii had said so) that the malefactor would not leave his victims in peace, that he would hound them to death. How could Pelagius have failed to hear a plea for help in Alyosha's pitiful babble?

After grieving for a while to ease his remorse, Pelagius got up off the ground with a sigh, shook off the crumbs of glass that had stuck to his cassock and set off back the way he had come.

Korovin could find out about his patient's disappearance in the morning – from his gardener. There was no time to waste on unnecessary explanations now, and it was still not clear what role the doctor was playing in this whole business. And there was no point in Pelagius racking his brains over what had happened either; his poor head was already bursting. He needed to go to bed and sleep on things. Or try to.

Sighing and sobbing, the novice made his way along the dark road to the town and stole into the pavilion to make the reverse transition from a male state to a female one. He had just removed his skullcap and cassock and taken the folded dress out of the travelling bag, when suddenly something incredible happened.

One of the cumbersome iron cupboards magically detached itself from the wall and moved straight towards Polina Andreevna. Squatting down on her haunches, she gazed up at this miracle, so dumbfounded that she quite forgot to feel frightened. But there was good reason to be frightened. The automatic dispenser had blocked off the light patch of the door, and now Mrs Lisitsyna could see that that it was not a cupboard at all, but an immense silhouette in a black monk's cassock.

Pressing her hands against her chemise (at that moment Polina Andreevna was not wearing anything else apart from her underwear and drawers), she said in a trembling voice: 'I'm not afraid of you! I know you're not a ghost, but a man!' And she did something that she would hardly have dared to do, if she had been wearing humble monk's garb: she drew herself up to her full height, stood on tiptoe and struck the nightmarish vision with her fist at the point where its face should have been, and then again and again.

Although Mrs Lisitsyna's fist was not large, it was firm and sharp, but the blows produced no effect whatever. Polina Andreevna merely scratched her knuckles against something rough and prickly. A gigantic pair of hands seized the female warrior's slim wrists and pressed them together. One hand clutched them both while the other wound string around them with incredible dexterity.

Even without her hands, Polina Andreevna did not surrender: she began lashing out with her feet, endeavouring to catch her enemy on the knee or, if possible, even higher.

The attacker squatted down, which made him much lower than the standing lady, and with a few swift movements he hobbled her ankles. Lisitsyna tried to jump back, but she could not move her feet and fell over on to the floor.

Now she was obliged to resort to a woman's ultimate weapon: screaming. Perhaps that is what she should have done at the very beginning, instead of lashing out with her fists.

She opened her mouth wide to call for help – in case there might be a detachment of peace-keepers patrolling the waterfront or simply someone out late walking by; but an invisible hand thrust a coarse, repulsive, sour-tasting rag between her teeth, and then tied her own scarf round her mouth to prevent her from spitting the gag out.

Then the strongman picked up his helpless captive with an easy movement, holding her by the neck and her bound feet, as if she were a sheep, and threw her on to a sheet of sackcloth spread out on the floor, which Polina Andreevna had failed to notice. The well-prepared villain rolled her body over and over, wrapping the sackcloth round it at the same time, and in a second Mrs Lisitsyna was transformed from a half-dressed lady into a shapeless bundle.

Mumbling and wriggling, the bundle was raised into the air, thrown across the nape of a neck as broad as a horse's back, and Polina Andreeevna felt herself being carried along. Swaying in rhythm to the long, even strides, at first she carried on struggling and uttering sounds of protest, but a tightly bound bundle does not allow much scope for movement, and it was unlikely that anyone could hear her groans, muffled as they were by the gag and the coarse sackcloth.

Soon she began feeling unwell – from the rush of blood to her dangling head, from the sickening swaying and, most of all, from the cursed sackcloth that prevented her from getting her breath properly and was impregnated with dust. Polina Andreevna wanted to sneeze, but she could not – it is not so easy with a gag in your mouth!

The worst thing of all was that her abductor seemed determined to carry his victim away to the very ends of the earth. He kept walking and walking without stopping or pausing for breath even once, and the agonising journey seemed to go on for ever. The semiconscious captive was sure that the island of Canaan must have been left behind long ago, because it was not big enough to accommodate such vast distances, and the giant was already marching across the waters of the Blue Lake.

Just as Mrs Lisitsyna, exhausted by nausea and the lack of air, was on the point of losing consciousness completely, the hollow thud of the villain's footsteps was replaced by creaking and a new swing was added to the sway of his walk, as if the very ground itself had begun to heave. Could it really be water, Polina Andreevna wondered fleetingly, her reason fading. But then why the creaking?

Here the oppressive journey finally came to an end. The sackcloth bundle was dumped unceremoniously on to a hard surface – not the ground; more likely a wooden floor. There was a clang and the creak of rusty hinges. Then the captive was lifted up again, not horizontally this time, but vertically, with her head downwards, and lowered into some kind of hole or pit – in short, into some place a lot lower than the level of the floor. The top of Polina Andreevna's head struck something hard, and then the entire bundle was dropped with a crash on to another flat surface. There was more creaking and grating from above and the sound of a door slamming, followed by the hollow echo of receding footsteps, as if someone were walking across the ceiling, and then silence.

Lisitsyna lay there for a while, listening. Somewhere nearby there was water splashing, an awful lot of it. What else could she tell about her place of incarceration (for, to judge from the clang of the door, the captive had surely been incarcerated)? Probably that she was not on dry land, but on a ship of some sort, and the water was splashing against its side, or perhaps against the dockside. Straining her ears again, Polina Andreevna caught a quiet squeaking that she did not like the sound of at all.

Having assembled her initial impressions, she began to act.

The very first thing she had to do was to free herself from the disgusting sackcloth. Lisitsyna turned over from her back on to her side, then on to her stomach, again on to her back and – alas – came up against a wall before she had had managed to free herself completely. Polina Andreevna was still tightly swaddled, but the outer layer of sackcloth had unrolled, giving her the opportunity to use another two senses: smell and vision. Unfortunately, the latter was of little use to the captive, for her eyes could not make anything out in the pitch-darkness. As for the former, her dungeon smelled of stagnant water, old wood and fish scales. And perhaps rusty iron as well. All in all, things had not become very much clearer.

But ten minutes later her eyes had become accustomed to the darkness, and she discovered it was not so impenetrable after all. There was scanty light of a kind, little better than the darkness, seeping in through long, narrow cracks in the ceiling, and after a while this dark-grey illumination allowed Polina Andreevna to grasp that she was lying in a narrow, cramped space with walls of wooden boards – most likely the hold of a small fishing vessel (otherwise what explanation could there be for the pervasive smell of fish scales?).

The old tub appeared to be completely decrepit. There was light coming in not only through the ceiling but also in places at the top of the sides. In a high sea a proud vessel like this would probably take on water by the ton and perhaps even sink.

However, just at the moment Mrs Lisitsyna was more concerned with her own lot than with the decrepit vessel's navigational prospects; and meanwhile the situation, already desperate, was taking an unexpected and extremely unpleasant turn.

The squeaking that she had heard earlier grew louder and a little dark shadow moved up on to the sackcloth, followed by a second, and a third.

With her eyes wide in terror the captive watched as a procession of mice crept across her chest towards her chin.

These denizens of the hold must have hidden at first, but now they had decided to come out and reconnoitre: they wanted to know what this gigantic object was that had come tumbling out of nowhere into their mouse universe.

Polina Andreevna was by no means a coward, but the small, nimble, rustling inhabitants of this twilight underworld filled her with revulsion and a strange, inexplicable, mystical horror.

If not for her bonds, she would have leapt up with a shriek and been out of this loathsome hole in an instant. But she had only two possible choices: either to lie there moaning in shameful fear, shaking her head pointlessly, or to call on the assistance of her reason.

They're only mice, Mrs Lisitsyna told herself. Perfectly harmless little beasts. They'll just take a sniff and go away.

At this point Polina Andreevna remembered Gogol's rats sniffing at the mayor and comforted herself with the thought that mice were not rats, they didn't attack people, they didn't bite. It was really rather funny – she could see that they were desperately afraid too, barely even crawling along, like Lilliputians on Gulliver's bound body.

A drop of cold sweat slithered down her temple. The boldest of the mice had crawled very close now. Polina Andreevna's eyes had grown so used to the darkness that she could make out every detail of her visitor, right down to its stumpy little tail with the end gnawed off. The abominable creature tickled the rationalist's chin with its whiskers, and reason immediately capitulated.

Choking on her own shriek, the prisoner tensed her entire body and rolled back into the middle of the hold. This rid her of the mice, but it wrapped the sackcloth round her again. But it was better that way, Lisitsyna told herself as she listened to the wild pounding of her own heart.

Alas, no more than five minutes had passed before those prehensile little claws were rustling across the sackcloth again, this time directly above her face. Polina Andreevna imagined what would happen when the one with the short tail crept inside the bundle, and rolled quickly back to the wall again. She lay there, drawing in the air through her nostrils and waiting.

Soon it happened all over again: first the squeaking, then the cautious expedition across her chest. Then another roll across the floor.

After a while it developed into a routine, with the prisoner alternately wrapping and unwrapping the sackcloth as she threw

273

off her uninvited guests. The mice seemed to take to this amusing game and the interludes between their visits gradually grew shorter. Polina Andreevna began feeling as if she had been transformed into a train in some mathematical puzzle, moving from point A to point B and back with ever shorter halts.

When Lisitsyna heard footsteps above her (presumably on the deck), she was not frightened, but delighted. She was glad of anything that might bring this nightmarish waltz to an end!

There were two people: the heavy, bear-like tread that Polina Andreevna had heard earlier had been joined by a lighter, clattering stride. The trapdoor clanged open, and the prisoner screwed up her eyes, so bright did the blue-grey light of night seem to her.

The Empress of Canaan

An imperious female voice spoke: 'All right, show her to me!'

Polina Andreevna was just making a stop at point B, by the wall, so her face was uncovered, and she saw a ladder being lowered down into the hold. A huge pair of boots came clattering down the rungs, heels first, with the hem of a black cassock swaying above them.

The blinding light of a kerosene lamp flooded across the ceiling and the walls. The gigantic figure, which occupied almost half of the hold, turned round, and Lisitsyna recognised her abductor.

Brother Jonah, the captain of the steamship *St Basilisk*!

The monk put the lamp on the floor and stood beside his prone captive, clasping his hands across his stomach.

The woman, whose face Polina Andreevna could not see, squatted down beside the open trapdoor. There was a rustle of fine fabric and a voice that now seemed terribly familiar ordered: 'Unwrap her, I can't see a thing.'

Lidia Evgenievna Boreiko, Dr Korovin's hysterical guest!

Mrs Lisitsyna had no time to understand anything or make sense of what was happening. With a single jerk, rough hands shook the prisoner out of her sackcloth shroud on to the floor.

Polina Andreevna struggled to her knees and then moved across on to the low wooden shelf surrounding the entire cramped space. That was what she had kept running into, not the wall, when she was rolling to and fro across the floor. It was a hard seat, but still more dignified than lying on the floor. But then, what talk could there be of dignity, when you were dressed in nothing but your underwear, with your hands and feet tied and your mouth stopped with a dirty rag?

Mademoiselle Boreiko came down the rungs of the ladder, but not all the way to the bottom, halting in an elevated position. Under her black cloak she was wearing a silk dress, also black, and there was a string of large pearls gleaming on her neck. Polina Andreevna noticed that Korovin's acquaintance was dressed far more spectacularly today than when they had met the previous evening: she had rings with precious stones sparkling on her fingers and bracelets on her wrists; even her veil was not the usual one, but a golden cobweb – in short, Lidia Evgenievna Boreiko looked like a real queen. The captain gazed at her in rapture – no, not in rapture, in reverential awe, the way the pagans of old must have gazed at the golden-faced goddess Ishtar.

Mademoiselle Boreiko surveyed her contemptible captive with a disdainful eye and said: 'Take a look at yourself and at me. You are a pitiful, filthy slave trembling with fear. And I am a queen. This island belongs to me, it is mine! I rule over this kingdom of men, and my rule is absolute! Every man who lives here and every man who sets foot here becomes mine. *Will* become mine, if I wish it. I am Calypso, and the Northern Semiramis, and the Empress of Canaan! How dare a common ginger cat like you try to steal my crown? Usurper! False pretender! You came here deliberately to take my throne from me! I realised that immediately, the first time I saw you there on the landing stage. Women like you don't come to this place – only quiet, pious little mice come here, but you are a fiery-red vixen, and you wanted my hen house!'

At the mention of mice Polina Andreevna squinted briefly down at the floor, but the little partners in her recent nightmarish game had obviously taken refuge from the light and noise in their dark nooks and crannies.

'You are not here to see Ararat's holy shrines!' said Mademoiselle Boreiko, continuing her astounding speech in a ferocious voice. 'My slave' – here she pointed at Jonah – 'has been following you. You have not visited a single church, not a single chapel! Of course not, since that is not what you came here for!'

So this was what it was all about; this was the answer to the riddle, the bold investigator realised too late. All the theories, both plausible and incredible, were wrong. The truth was fantastic, quite unbelievable! Who could ever have imagined that one of the island's female inhabitants would want to declare herself Empress of Canaan! So this was why the brilliant Mademoiselle Boreiko had settled on this remote island; this was why she stayed here! It was certainly true that she was lovely, elegant, even majestic in her own way. But in St Petersburg she would have been one among many; in a provincial city, one of a few; even in a remote district town, she might have had a rival. But here, in this little male world, there was no one to compete with her. There was no local female society at all; women of the common classes did not count. And the female pilgrims who came here were of a special kind, pious women who walked around with glum faces, wrapped themselves in black shawls and did not look at the men – and why should they, when they had more than enough admirers in the place they had left behind in order to come here and atone for their sins in prayer?

Boreiko had established her very own state here on the island. And she had her own genie, her faithful slave: Captain Jonah. There he was, the Black Monk in person! Standing there with an idiotic smile of bliss on his weathered face. A man like that would carry out any whim of his sovereign without a murmur, no matter how criminal it might be. If she ordered him to frighten her subjects and strike mystical terror into their hearts, Jonah would do it. If she ordered him to kill someone, drive them mad, abduct them, he would do that too, without a moment's hesitation.

Just at that moment the astounded Polina Andreevna had no time to untangle all the possible motives behind this monstrous idea, but she knew one thing quite certainly: female ambition is more extreme and more absolute than its male equivalent; if it senses a threat from someone, it is capable of any perfidious and cruel act. The infuriated empress had to be disabused concerning the false pilgrim's intentions (for Polina Andreevna certainly had no interest in the men of New Ararat, or any men at all, come to that), or in her spite Lidia Evgenievna would commit another heinous crime. What would it matter to her, after all the others that had gone before!

Mrs Lisitsyna tried to reach the gag with her hands, which were tied together at the wrist, but she could not: the sailor's deft fingers had fastened the bonds on her hands to those on her feet, making it impossible for her reach the tight knot at the back of her head.

The prisoner began moaning plaintively, making it clear that she wanted to say something. The effect was pitiful, but Boreiko's heart was not softened.

'You wish to provoke my pity? Too late! I would have forgiven you for the others, but for him – never!' Her eyes glinted with such fierce hatred that Polina Andreevna realised she would not have listened anyway; she had already decided everything.

Lisitsyna never did learn who was the man for whom Lidia Evgenievna would not forgive her: her accuser haughtily set one hand on her hip, extended the other downwards in the gesture of a Roman empress condemning a gladiator to death and declared: 'Your sentence has already been pronounced and now it will be carried out. Jonah, will you be true to your oath?'

'Yes, my queen,' the captain replied in a hoarse voice. 'For you, anything you desire!'

'Then get to work.'

Jonah rummaged in a dark corner and pulled out an iron crowbar from somewhere. He spat on his hands and took a firm grip on it. Was he really going to beat her brains out? Polina Andreevna screwed her eyes tight shut.

There was a crunch and the crack of breaking boards.

Opening her eyes, she saw that with a single blow the giant of a man had smashed a hole in the side of the vessel – and it was below the waterline, because water was gushing into the hold. The captain took a swing and struck again. Then again and again. And now there were four streams of black, oily, glistening water running in through holes in the wall and splashing down on to the floor.

'Enough,' said Lidia Boreiko, halting the demolition. 'I want this to last as long as possible. Let her howl in terror and curse the day and the hour when she dared intrude into my realm!' And, having pronounced her terrible verdict, the empress climbed up the ladder and out on to the deck. Jonah clattered up after her.

Polina Andreevna could not see the floor any more – it was completely covered with water. She lifted her feet up on to her seat and then straightened up with difficulty, pressing her back against the side of the boat. How disgusting! The water had driven the mice out of their holes, and they were squeaking in fright as they clambered up the condemned woman's drawers.

Lisitsyna heard a malevolent laugh from above her head: 'Behold a genuine Princess Tarakanova! Close it!'

The ladder rose up through the trapdoor, the door slammed shut and the hold was suddenly dark.

She could hear the murderers' conversation through the boards.

The woman said: 'Wait on the shore until it sinks. Then come. Perhaps you will receive a reward.'

The answer was a roar of ecstasy.

'I said perhaps,' said Lidia Evgenievna, cutting short Jonah's triumph.

Receding footsteps. Silence.

In Mrs Lisitsyna's world, now shrunk to the dimensions of a wooden cage, there was nothing but darkness and the splashing of water. The thing that Polina Andreevna found most annoying as she prepared to die was that her letter to the Bishop – which she now knew to be mistaken in its deductions – would drown together with her, and no one would ever know that Basilisk was not a phantom or a chimera but a malevolent game played by a criminal mind.

And yet she must not give in – not until the very final moment. Only when every last human resource had been exhausted was it permissible to accept the inevitable and entrust herself to the Providence of the Lord.

However, Polina Andreevna was bound and shut in a trap,

and the resources available to her were precious few. She could not remove the gag, nor could she untie her hands. So I have to try to free my feet, she told herself. She squatted down, and found her fingers could feel the string on her ankles.

But alas, the knots were complicated, and some especially cunning – no doubt sailors' knots – and they were pulled so tight that her nails could get no purchase on them.

From the sound of splashing she guessed that the water had already risen to the level of her seat. A mouse was squeaking somewhere very close at hand, but Polina Andreevna had no time now for female phobias. If only she could tackle the knots with her teeth! Doubling up as tightly as she could, she took a firm hold on the piece of cloth tied tightly across her face and jerked it downwards – she almost dislocated her lower jaw and the sudden blow drove something sharp into her chest.

What was that?

Needles, knitting needles. She was wearing the handiwork bag under her chemise.

Lisitsyna quickly thrust her hands up under the chemise and located the little bag with her fingers. It only took her a second to pull out a needle.

Now she could use the sharp metal point to pick at the knot, pull it open and loosen it.

There was cold water lapping at the soles of her shoes, gradually seeping through.

That was it! Her feet were free.

She would not be able to untie her hands, but at least now she could reach up with them.

First she untied the headscarf and pulled the repellent gag out of her mouth. Then she stood up on tiptoe and pushed against the ceiling with her clenched fists

Ah! The trapdoor was bolted shut. Even now she could not get out of the hold! But Polina Andreevna did not despair for long. Dropping to her knees and splashing water up all around her, she leaned down and began fumbling on the floor.

There was the crowbar, lying where Jonah had dropped it.

She straightened up to her full height again, swung the crowbar back and struck at the roof with all her might.

The iron bar broke right through the rotten wood of the trapdoor. A few more blows, and the bolt shot out of its groove. Lisitsyna threw back the door and saw the early-dawn sky above her head. The air was stale and dank, but it smelled of life.

Clutching the edge of the hole with her fingers, Polina Andreevna pulled herself up, bracing first one elbow and then the other on the edge – it was all not so very difficult for a teacher of gymnastics.

When she was already sitting on the deck, she glanced down into the hole. The black, dead water was heaving and swaying, rising faster and faster – the holes must have been widened by the pressure.

What was that little spot on the surface?

She looked closer and saw it was a mouse, the only one that had survived – the others had all drowned; and this one was floundering, its strength almost exhausted.

After her own miraculous escape Polina Andreevna leaned down with a grimace of disgust and scooped up the little grey swimmer in the palm of her hand (it was her close acquaintance with the stub tail) then flung it on to the deck, as far away from herself as possible.

The mouse shook itself like a dog and immediately, without even giving its rescuer a second glance, set off at a run down the gangplank to the shore. It had made the right choice: the deck had already settled almost to the level of the lake.

Mrs Lisitsyna looked round and saw half-sunk boats, masts protruding from the water, wooden hulks rotting in the shallows. A graveyard of small fishing boats and smacks – that was what it was, this place where the love-crazed Captain Jonah had brought his victim to die.

And suddenly, there was the man himself, a massive black figure looming up over the shoreline, swaying from side to side as he moved slowly towards her.

A Long-distance Run

Polina Andreevna watched in horror as the monk's hands rolled up the sleeves of his cassock with slow deliberation. The meaning of the gesture was so obvious that the newly resurrected victim even stopped breathing in the blessed smell of life and followed the example of her spry little friend by making a dash for the gangplank. She ran down the rickety plank on to dry land, ducked under a monstrous clutching hand and then darted off across the gravel and rocks, on to a path that she calculated must lead to the town.

Glancing round, she saw that Jonah was plodding after her, his boots clattering heavily over the ground. But how could he possibly overtake his fleet-footed quarry! And there was another circumstance that was against him – his long cassock; and yet another – the lightweight drawers that allowed Lisitsyna complete freedom of movement. There could be no possible doubt that if the events taking place at that moment had been part of that new-fangled European amusement, the Olympic Games, then the gold medal for sprinting would not have gone to the pursuer, but to his intended victim.

Mrs Lisitsyna opened up a lead of twenty paces, then fifty, then a hundred, until she could hardly even hear the tramping of boots behind her. But even so, every time she looked round she saw the obstinate captain still running, running and refusing to give up. The path was completely deserted, and on both sides of it there were empty meadows, with not a single house – nothing but squat farming buildings, all dark and abandoned. Polina Andreevna could count on nobody and nothing except her own two feet. She breathed in time to the pounding of those feet against the resilient earth: one-two-three-four-in, one-two-three-four-out, but the further she ran, the more of a hindrance her hands became. According to the English science of sport, correct running required a reverse-symmetrical swing of the arms, involving the energetic employment of the elbows and shoulders, and what swing could she make, how could she employ her elbows, with her bound wrists pressed against her breast?

Later, as the path started to rise a little, she began to run out of breath. In total violation of the correct method, Polina Andreevna was already breathing with both her mouth and her nose, and not at every fourth step, but in any way she could manage. Several times she stumbled and barely kept her feet.

The tramping of the boots drew a little closer, and Lisitsyna remembered that, apart from sprinting – that is, short-distance running – the latest Olympic charter also provided for long-distance running events. It seemed likely that in a long-distance race the victory would be Brother Jonah's.

The mist melted away and the dawn gradually grew brighter, until the distance that had to be covered was finally made clear. There on the left, one, or perhaps one and a half versts away, lay the sleepy town with its grey bell towers. Exhausted as she was, Polina Andreevna would never be able to run that far; her only hope was that she might meet someone who would save her. But what if she didn't?

On her right, no more than three hundred paces away, there was a solitary white tower standing on the cliff top, obviously a lighthouse. There had to be someone there! She made a dash for the slim stone structure, half-running and half-walking, gasping for breath. She ought to have shouted for help, but she didn't have the strength.

When she had almost reached the lighthouse, Lisitsyna saw that the windows were boarded up with crossed planks, the yard was overgrown with grass and weeds, and the fence was dilapidated and tumbling down.

The lighthouse was empty, deserted!

By sheer inertia she ran on a little further, even though it was pointless. Then she stumbled over a tussock and fell, right in front of the lopsided gate that was standing ajar.

She did not have the strength to get to her feet – and what was the point? Instead, she propped herself up on her elbows, threw back her head and shouted out loud. Not to call for help (who would hear her in this?) but in sheer despair: Here I am, Lord, the nun Pelagia, in the secular world Polina Lisitsyna. I'm done for! And having purged all her fear, she turned to face the approaching tramping of boots.

The pursuit had not greatly shortened the captain's breath, he was simply somewhat redder in the face than usual.

Pressing her hands to her breast, so that she looked as if she were begging for mercy, Polina Andreevna said piteously: 'Brother Jonah! What have I done to you? I am your sister in Christ! Do not destroy a living soul!'

She did not think he would answer. But the monk halted, standing over the woman on the ground, wiped his forehead with his sleeve and rumbled: 'If I've doomed my own soul, why should I spare yours?'

He glanced round, picked up a large, rough stone from the edge of the path and raised it above his head. Mrs Lisitsyna did not screw her eyes tightly shut; she looked upwards, but not at her killer – at the sky: it was stern and overcast, but suffused with light.

'Hey, dear fellow!' she suddenly heard a clear, calm voice say.

Polina Andreevna, already reconciled to the fact that her ginger head was about to be shattered like an eggshell, stared at Jonah in astonishment. Still holding the cobblestone up over his head, he turned towards the lighthouse, where the voice had come from.

The door of the tower, which had been closed, was wide open. Standing on the bottom step was a gentleman in a silk dressing gown with tassels and brightly patterned Persian slippers. He had clearly only just risen from his bed.

Lisitsyna recognised the gentleman straight away. How could she possibly not have! How could anyone forget that bold face, those blue eyes and that lock of golden hair tumbling across the noble forehead? It was he, the saviour of kittens and perturber of women's hearts.

What strange delusion was this?

The Temptation of St Pelagia

'Put the stone down, servant of God,' said the handsome devil, surveying the doughty monk and the young woman lying at his feet with keen interest. 'And come here; I'll box your ears, to teach you how to treat a lady.'

He was simply magnificent as he pronounced those defiant words: slim and elegant, with a mocking smile on his thin lips. David hurling his challenge at Goliath – that was the comparison that immediately came to Mrs Lisitsyna's mind as she struggled to absorb this rapid turn in events.

However, in this case, unlike the biblical combat, the stone was not in the hands of the handsome hero but of the giant, and with a dull roar he swung his arm back and hurled the missile at this witness who had appeared out of nowhere.

The heavy stone would probably have knocked the blond-headed young man off his feet, but he dodged it nimbly and the cobble struck the open door of the lighthouse, splitting it in two, then fell on to the porch and clattered down the three steps, one at a time, before burying itself in the mud.

'Ah, so that's how it is! All right then, brother long-skirt!'

The valiant knight's mocking expression changed to one of determination, his chin jutted forward and his eyes took on a steely gleam. The miraculous intercessor dashed at the monk, assumed an elegant pugilist's pose and began peppering the captain's vast physiognomy with precise, crushing blows which, unfortunately, produced no effect whatever on Jonah.

The monstrous hulk shrugged off his energetic opponent's punches as if they were no more than flea-bites, then seized him by the shoulders, lifted him up and tossed him a good two *sazhens* away. Lisitsyna could only watch and gasp.

The handsome blond immediately jumped to his feet and tore off his dressing gown, which, given the situation, was rather inappropriate. Since there was no shirt under the dressing gown, this gesture revealed to Polina Andreevna's gaze a lean stomach and a muscular chest overgrown with golden hair – now the bold warrior was even more like the biblical David.

Evidently realising that his bare hands were not enough to deal with such a huge bear of a man, the inhabitant of the lighthouse turned his gaze to the left and the right in search of some form of weapon. Fortunately, it lit upon an old axle-shaft lying in the grass beside a decrepit shed with a sagging roof full of holes.

In two swift bounds David was there beside it. He grabbed it with both hands and swung it round above his head in a whistling circle. The chances of the two opponents appeared to have been evened out now. Polina Andreevna's spirits rose; she got up off the ground and sank her teeth into the string that bound her hands. She had to untie them as quickly as possible and help!

Captain Goliath was not intimidated by the axle-shaft; he walked straight at his enemy, with his fists clenched and his head down, making no attempt to dodge, and when the improvised club smashed into his temple, he merely swayed slightly on his feet. But the axle snapped in two like a matchstick.

Again the captain seized his opponent by the shoulders, took a run and flung him hard, this time not on to the ground but against the wall of the lighthouse. It was simply amazing that the handsome young fellow was not knocked unconscious by the sheer impact!

He staggered as he scrambled up on to the porch, intending to retreat into the house, where he very probably had some other defensive weapon, something more effective than the rotten axle-shaft. But Jonah guessed the handsome gentleman's intentions and dashed forwards with a roar to overtake him.

The outcome of the duel was no longer in doubt. The monk

pressed the poor paladin against the door frame with one hand and drew the other back slowly, clenching it into a fist as he prepared to strike a crushing, probably fatal blow. But at that moment Mrs Lisitsyna finally managed to untie her bonds. Leaping to her feet with a piercing shriek, she dashed to save her defender. Moving at full speed, she leapt up on to the captain's shoulders, flung her arms around him and bit him on his neck, which tasted salty and was as tough as dried Caspian roach.

Jonah shook off the weightless lady as easily as a bear shakes off a dog: he swung his trunk round sharply, and Polina Andreevna went flying off into the air. But the captain was standing on the edge of the porch, and the sudden jerk made him lose his balance: he swayed, with his arms waving above his head, and the hero David seized this precious opportunity that would surely not be repeated – he butted the hulking brute on the chin as hard as he could with his forehead.

The giant's fall from what was a rather low height had a monumental grace to it, like the toppling of the Vendôme column (Polina Andreevna had once seen a painting showing the communards of Paris felling Bonaparte's pillar). Brother Jonah collapsed flat on to his back, and the back of his head struck the very same irregular stone which he had only recently intended to use as a weapon of murder. The impact was accompanied by a terrifying crunch: the giant lay there with his mighty arms flung out wide and did not move again.

'Thank you, Lord,' Lisitsyna whispered fervently. 'That is just.'

But instantly she felt ashamed of her bloodthirsty fervour. She walked over to the man lying on the ground and raised his limp eyelid to see if he was still alive. 'He's alive,' she exclaimed with a sigh of relief. 'How could anyone have a skull that thick!'

'Damn him. I wish he were dead,' said the hero.

He surveyed the lady dressed in muddy underwear with a leisurely glance. Polina Andreevna blushed and covered her shameful bruise with her hand.

'Ah, the widow-bride,' said the handsome fellow, recognising her nonetheless. 'I knew we would meet again, and here we are.'

He moved her hands aside and whistled. 'What delicate skin you have! You have only just fallen, and already there is a bruise.'

He ran his finger cautiously (or perhaps even tenderly?) over her blue skin. Mrs Lisitsyna did not move away. She did not tell him that the bruise was not fresh and had been made the day before.

The amazing young blond gentleman looked straight into her eyes and attempted to extend his lips into a jolly smile, in which he was not entirely successful, because there were scarlet drops of blood trickling from the corner of his mouth. 'You are brave; I like women like that.'

'Turn round,' Polina Andreevna said quietly, transferring her gaze from his face to his badly scratched shoulder. 'There, your back is all scraped raw. It's bleeding. It needs to be washed and bandaged.'

He laughed at that, paying no attention to his split lip. The gaps between his white teeth were also red with blood. 'A fine nurse you are. You should take a look at yourself.'

He stood up, put one arm round the lady's shoulders and the other under her knees, then swept her up in his arms and carried her into the house. Polina Andreevna tried to resist, but after all her nervous and physical ordeals she had absolutely no strength left, and pressing herself against the warm, firm chest of this resolute man of action gave her a calm, comforting feeling. Only a minute earlier, everything had been bad, absolutely terrible, but now everything felt good and right – that was more or less the feeling that came over Mrs Lisitsyna. She did not have to think about anything else or worry about anything. There was someone there who knew what had to be done and was prepared to take all the decisions.

'Thank you,' she whispered, remembering that she had not yet thanked her rescuer. 'You saved me from certain death. It's a genuine miracle.'

'Yes, it is a miracle,' replied the handsome blond, setting her down carefully on a trestle bed covered with a bearskin. 'You were lucky, my lady. I only took up residence here a week ago.

The lighthouse has not been inhabited for a long time. That is why it is so neglected, so please do not be too critical.'

He gestured round the room, which to Polina Andreevna, in her present blissful condition, seemed quite exceptionally romantic. In the only window the missing half of the glass had been replaced by a rolled-up sheepskin cloak, but the other half revealed a superb view of the lake with the bluish profile of Outskirts Island in the distance. The only furniture in the room was a rickety table covered with a magnificent velvet tablecloth, a soft Turkish armchair with a heap of cushions lying on it and the aforementioned trestle bed. A few logs surviving from the previous day's fire were crackling in the soot-blackened hearth. The only decoration on the bare stone walls was a brightly coloured oriental carpet, with a gun, a dagger and a long, fancy chibouk hanging on it.

'Do you really live here all alone? Why?' the rescued woman asked, not entirely politely. 'Ah, I'm sorry, we have not been introduced. I am Polina Andreevna Lisitsyna, from Moscow.'

'Nikolai Vsevolodovich,' her host replied with a bow, without mentioning his surname. 'I find living here quite splendid. And as for the reason . . . There are no people here, just the wind and the waves. But we can talk later.' He poured hot water from a samovar into a basin and picked up a clean handkerchief from the table. 'First we shall deal with your injuries. Be so good as to raise your chemise.'

Of course, Polina Andreevna declined to raise her chemise, but she did allow her companion to wash her face, the grazes on her elbows and even her ankles where the string had scraped the skin. Nikolai Vsevolodovich did not make a very skilful male nurse, but he was painstaking. As she watched him carefully remove her wet shoe from her foot, Mrs Lisitsyna fluttered her eyelashes and felt no resentment when his finger pressed painfully against a bruised bone.

'I simply cannot tell you how grateful I am to you. Especially for the way you did not think twice about dashing to the rescue of a complete stranger.'

'Nonsense,' her host said dismissively as he washed a scratch on her ankle. 'It's not even worth mentioning.' And it was clear that it was no pose – he really did not attach any importance to his own remarkable actions. He had simply acted in the way that was natural to him, just as he had that other time with the kitten. And that was the most captivating thing about him.

Polina Andreevna tried not to turn the disfigured side of her face towards the hero, and so she was obliged to squint sideways at him all the time.

Ah, how attractive she found him! If Nikolai Vsevolodovich had exploited the intimate nature of the situation in which they found themselves and permitted himself even a single playful glance, even a single immodest touch, Mrs Lisitsyna would immediately have recalled her duty to vigilance, but her host's concern was purely fraternal, and so her heart missed the moment when it should have manned its defences.

When Polina Andreevna realised that Nikolai Vsevolodovich's glance was no longer entirely what it ought to be, and took fright, it was already too late: her heart was beating a lot faster than it should have been, and the touch of the impromptu healer's fingers was spreading a dangerous languor through her body. This was the very moment to pray to the Lord to strengthen her spirit so that she could overcome temptation, but there was not a single icon in the room, not even the very smallest.

'Well now,' Nikolai Vsevolodovich said with a nod of satisfaction. 'At least there will not be any inflammation. And now your turn.' And he turned his naked back, covered with scratches, towards the recumbent lady.

Then an even worse ordeal began. Sitting up on the trestle bed, Polina Andreevna wiped down her saviour's white skin, barely managing to prevent herself from stroking it with her hand. Especially difficult were the breaks in the conversation that arose from time to time. In years of monastic life she had forgotten that they were the most dangerous thing, those pauses when you could suddenly hear your own rapid breathing and feel the pounding in your temples.

Polina Andreevna was immediately embarrassed by her state of undress and glanced around for something to cover herself with, but she could not see anything.

'Are you cold?' Nikolai Vsevolodovich asked without turning round. 'Why don't you put on the cloak? – there isn't anything else anyway.'

Mrs Lisitsyna walked across the cold floor to the window and wrapped herself in the heavy, smelly sheepskin. She began feeling a bit calmer, and the wind from the hole in the window was pleasantly cool on her flaming face.

In the distance, at the beginning of the Lenten Spit, she saw a group of monks waiting for something. Then the door of the Farewell Chapel opened and a man with no face came out, dressed in black with a pointed cowl covering his head. The monks bowed to him from the waist. He made the sign of the cross over them and walked towards the shoreline. It was only then that Polina Andreevna noticed the boat and the oarsman sitting in it. The black man sat in the stern with his back towards Canaan, and the bark began moving towards Outskirts Island, where two other men without faces, wearing hermit's cowls, were standing waiting at the water's edge.

'Brother Kleopa is taking the new hermit to the hermitage,' Lisitsyna said to Nikolai Vsevolodovich, who had come across to her. She was squinting, because her spectacles and their case had been left behind on the floor of the closed pavilion, together with her dress. 'His name is Father Ilarii. He is in great haste to quit this earthly vale. A learned man who studied theology for many years and yet failed to understand the most important thing of all about God. What God wants from us is not death, but life . . .'

'A most timely remark,' Nikolai Vsevolodovich whispered in her very ear, and then suddenly took her by the shoulders and turned her to face him.

He looked down at her and asked mockingly: 'Now, whose

widow are you, and whose bride?' Without waiting for an answer, he put his arms round her and kissed her on the lips.

For some reason at that moment Polina Andreevna remembered a terrible scene she had seen a long time before, when she was still a child. Little Polinka was on her way to visit the neighbouring estate with her parents. They were hurtling along like the wind over the snow-covered ice on the River Moscow, with the sleigh carrying the presents ahead of them (it was Christmas time). Suddenly there was a dry cracking sound, a black fissure appeared in the smooth white surface and an irresistible force pulled the whole leading team down into it – first the sleigh and the driver, then the snorting horse, flailing with its front hooves . . .

And now once again Polina Andreevna heard that same sudden crack, etched for ever into her memory; and once again she saw something dark, terrible and implacable moving closer from beneath the pure white surface, spreading wider and wider.

She trembled, pressed her hands against the seducer's chest and implored him: 'Nikolai Vsevolodovich, my dear, have pity . . . Do not torment me so! I must not do this. It is quite impossible!'

It was said so sincerely, with such childish artlessness, that the sweet-lipped seducer released her from his embrace, took a step backwards and bowed facetiously. 'I respect your devotion to your bridegroom and will not encroach on it again.'

Then Polina Andreevna kissed him, not on the lips, but on the cheek. She sobbed: 'Thank you, thank you . . . for . . . for being merciful.'

Nikolai Vsevolodovich sighed regretfully. 'Yes, it is a great sacrifice on my part – for you, my lady, are extremely seductive, especially with that bruise of yours.' He smiled on seeing the lady hastily turn her face sideways and squint to look at him. 'However, in gratitude for my heroic restraint, at least tell me who this fortunate man is. To whom do you remain so implacably faithful, despite the isolation of this place, the feeling of genuine gratitude that you have already mentioned and –

begging your pardon – your experience, for you are not a virgin, are you?'

Despite his light tone, she could tell that the handsome blond's self-esteem had been wounded. Therefore – and also because at that moment she did not wish to lie – Polina Andreevna confessed: 'My bridegroom is He.'

When Nikolai Vsevolodovich raised his eyebrows in puzzlement, she explained: 'Jesus. You have seen me in secular dress, but I am a nun and His bride.'

She was prepared for anything except what happened next.

The handsome man's face, which had so far remained derisively calm, suddenly contorted: his eyes blazed, his eyelashes began to flutter and pink blotches appeared on his cheeks.

'A nun?' he exclaimed. 'A bride of Christ?' A scarlet tongue flickered agitatedly across his upper lip. The strangely transformed Nikolai Vsevolodovich gave an ominous laugh and moved closer to her.

'I would have yielded you to anyone at all. But not to Him! Well now, we shall see! I would be able to protect my bride, but will He?' And he threw himself on the startled lady without the slightest trace of tenderness, with nothing but crude, violent passion. He tore open the flimsy chemise and began showering kisses on her neck, shoulders and breasts. The treacherous sheepskin cloak instantly slid to the floor.

'What are you doing?' Mrs Lisitsyna cried out in horror, throwing her head back. 'This is villainous!'

'I adore villainy!' he purred, stroking her back and her sides. 'It is my trade!' He laughed again. 'Allow me to introduce myself: the Satan of New Ararat! I was sent here to stir up the waters of this quiet millpond and release all the demons lurking in its depths!' Nikolai Vsevolodovich was greatly amused by his own joke. He burst into a peal of spasmodic, maniacal laughter, and Polina Andreevna shuddered, struck by a new realisation.

What, after all, was this entire business with the resurrected Basilisk, if not a monstrous, blasphemous deception for impressionable idiots? A woman was not capable of such play-acting for the sake of strangers unknown to her. A woman always needed someone more specific, not a chance audience or mere chance victims; but in all this she could sense genuine impersonal male cruelty, the impulse of perverted male ambition. And what adroit cunning and ingenuity had been required to arrange the spectacle of the apparitions and the walking on water! No, the 'Empress of Canaan' and her slow-witted slave had had nothing to with it.

'So it was all you?' Polina Andreevna gasped. 'You ...! What a terrible, pitiless joke! What great evil you have worked, how many people you have destroyed! And all for nothing, out of sheer boredom? You truly are Satan!'

Nikolai Vsevolodovich's cheek began twitching nervously, so that his face seemed to be dancing a wild devil's cancan.

'Yes, yes, I am Satan!' his thin scarlet lips whispered. 'Give yourself to Satan, bride of Christ!' He lifted the woman up lightly in his arms, flung her on to the bearskin and threw himself on top of her. Polina Andreevna raised her hand to scratch at the rapist's eyes with her nails, but suddenly felt she could not do it – and that was the most shameful and terrible thing of all.

Give me strength, she prayed to her patron, St Pelagia. The noble Roman woman, promised in marriage to the Emperor's son, had preferred a fearsome, savage death to sinning with the handsome pagan. It was better to writhe in agony in a red-hot copper bull than to submit to the shameful embrace of a seducer!

'Forgive me, forgive me, save me,' poor Mrs Lisitsyna babbled, confessing her accursed womanly weakness to her Eternal Bridegroom.

'Gladly!' Nikolai Vsevolodovich chuckled, tearing at her drawers.

But it turned out that the Heavenly Bridegroom was able to protect the honour of his betrothed after all.

Just as Polina Andreevna felt that all was lost and there could be no salvation, she heard a loud voice calling from outside: 'Hey, Childe Harold! Are you not frozen to death in there? Your door's split in two. I've brought you a warm rug and a basket with your breakfast from Maître Armand. Hey, Mr Terpsichorov, are you still asleep?'

A hurricane blast seemed to tear Nikolai Vsevolodovich off the body of his victim. For a second time the face of the tower's inhabitant changed beyond all recognition: from being demonic it became frightened, the face of a little boy who has been up to mischief.

'Ai-ai! Donat Savvich!' the amazing theomachist keened as he pulled on his dressing gown. 'Now I'll really get it in the neck!'

Interesting People – 2

Still not quite believing in this miracle, Polina Andreevna quickly stood up, adjusted the tattered remnants of her torn underwear as best she could and dashed for the door.

Doctor Korovin was standing by the crooked fence, tying the bridle of a sturdy pony to the gatepost. The pony was harnessed to a two-seater English gig and the doctor was wearing a straw boater with a black ribbon and a light-coloured coat. He took a large bundle out of the carriage and turned round, but did not immediately notice the tormented lady (she had instinctively ducked back inside the building). He stared at the unconscious figure of Brother Jonah lying on the ground.

'Did you get the monk drunk?' the doctor asked, shaking his head. 'Are you still blaspheming, then? I must say, that's not a very substantial piece of sacrilege; you still have a long way to go before you're a real Stavrogin. Really, Mr Terpsichorov, you should drop this role, it simply doesn't suit . . .'

At this point Korovin spotted the woman in her underwear peeping out from behind the door frame and stopped speaking. First he stared blankly, and then he frowned. 'Aha,' he said sternly. 'That too. It was to be expected. Of course, Stavrogin is a great womaniser. Good morning, madam. I'm afraid I shall have to explain something to you . . .'

Donat Savvich spoke these words as he walked up the steps on to the porch, but then he stopped short again, because he had recognised his guest of the previous day. 'Polina Andreevna, you?' the doctor exclaimed, stunned. 'I would never have . . .

Good Lord, what has happened to you? What has he done to you?'

Korovin glanced at the lady's battered face and pitiful attire and went rushing through into the room. He tossed the basket and the rug aside, grabbed hold of Nikolai Vsevolodovich's shoulders and shook him so hard that his head bobbled backwards and forwards.

'This, my good fellow, is vile and infamous! Yes, sir! You have gone too far. The torn chemise I can understand. Seduction, African passion and all the rest, but why beat a woman on the face? I tell you, you are not a brilliant actor, you are simply a scoundrel!'

The blond man whom Donat Savvich had called Terpsichorov exclaimed plaintively: 'I swear I didn't beat her!'

'Silence, you villain,' Korovin shouted at him. 'I shall deal with you later.'

He dashed back to Polina Andreevna, who had only understood one thing from this strange dialogue: fearsome as Nikolai Vsevolodovich might be, the owner of the clinic was clearly even more so. Otherwise, why would the Satan of New Ararat be so afraid of him?

'Yes, this is bad,' the doctor sighed as the lady backed away from him in fright. 'What's wrong, my dear Polina Andreevna – it's me, Korovin. Do you not recognise me? I don't need another patient just at the moment! Allow me to put this round you.' He picked the rug up off the floor and solicitously wrapped Mrs Lisitsyna in it, and she suddenly burst into tears.

'Ah, Terpsichorov, Terpsichorov, what have you done?' Donat Savvich muttered, stroking the weeping woman's red hair. 'Never mind, my dear, never mind. I swear I'll rip his head off and bring it to you on a plate. But first I'll take you back to my house, give you a tonic infusion to drink and a sedative injection.'

'I don't want an injection,' Polina Andreevna sobbed. 'Just take me to the guest house.'

Korovin shook his head and replied with gentle reproach, as if he were speaking to a foolish child: 'In that condition? I won't hear of it. I have to examine you. What if you have a broken bone or a contusion somewhere? Or even, God forbid, concussion? Oh no, my dear, I took the Hippocratic oath. Now, let's go. Where's your dress?' He looked around and even glanced under the trestle bed.

Lisitsyna said nothing, and neither did the limp, miserable Nikolai Vsevolodovich.

'All right then, damn the dress. We'll find something for you there.' He put one arm halfway round Polina Andreevna's shoulders and led her towards the door. She had no strength to resist, and anyway, how could she possibly appear in the town in such a state of undress?

For some reason Dr Korovin began by apologising. Setting the pony moving at a light trot, he said guiltily: 'Such an appalling thing to happen. I don't even know what excuse I can make. I have never had anything like it happen before. Naturally, you are entitled to complain to the authorities, take me to court and so on. It will mean trouble for my clinic, perhaps even closure, but *mea culpa*, so I must be held responsible.'

'What have you got to do with it?' Polina Andreevna asked in surprise, pulling up her frozen feet: her shoes had been left in the lighthouse, and what good would they have been anyway – they were soaked through. 'Why must you take responsibility for this man's crimes?' She was on the point of revealing the whole truth about the Black Monk to the doctor, but before she could, Korovin gestured angrily and began speaking in a rapid, agitated manner.

'Because Terpsichorov is my patient and cannot stand trial. He is in my care and my responsibility. Ah, how could I have been so mistaken in my diagnosis! It is absolutely unforgivable! To fail to notice latent aggression, and such violent aggression! Using his fists on a woman – it's absolutely scandalous! In any case, I shall send him back to St Petersburg. There is no place in my clinic for violent cases!'

'Who is your patient?' Lisitsyna asked, unable to believe her ears. 'Nikolai Vsevolodovich?'

'Is that what he said his name was – Nikolai Vsevolodovich? Why, of course! Oh, I can guess who gave him that vile filth!'

'What filth?' asked Polina Andreevna, totally confused.

'You see, Laertes Terpsichorov (naturally, that is his stage name) is one of my most interesting patients. He used to be an actor, and a brilliant one – a gift from God, as they say. When he acted in a play, he was completely transformed into the character he played. The public and the critics adored him. Everybody knows that the very finest actors are those with a weak sense of their own individuality, whose own personality does not prevent them from mimicking every new role. Well, Terpsichorov has no distinctive personality of his own at all. If he is left without any roles to play, he will just lie on the divan all day long from morning till night, staring up at the ceiling, like a puppet lying in the puppet-master's trunk. But the moment he enters into a role, he comes to life, he is charged with life and energy. Women fall madly, ecstatically in love with Terpsichorov. He has been married three times, and each time the marriage lasted for only a few weeks – on the longest occasion for a couple of months. Then every time the latest wife realised that her chosen one was a zero, a nonentity, she had not fallen in love with Laertes Terpsichorov but some literary character. Owing to his pathologically under-developed personality this actor used to immerse himself so deeply in his latest role that he even carried it with him into everyday life, extending the author's ideas, improvising, inventing new situations and lines. And he carried on like that until he was given the next play to learn. And so his first wife married Griboedov's Chatsky and then suddenly found herself the lifetime companion of Gogol's Khlestakov. The second one was wild about Cyrano de Bergerac, but soon ended up with Pushkin's Miserly Knight. The third one fell in love with the melancholy Prince of Denmark, but then he turned into Beaumarchais's foppish Count Almavive. It was after the third divorce that Terpsichorov came to me. He loved his third wife very much and despair had driven him almost to the point of suicide. "I'll give up the theatre," he said; "help me to become myself!"'

'And did it not work?' asked Polina Andreevna, enthralled by this strange story.

'Oh yes, it worked. The genuine, unadulterated Terpsichorov is a pale shadow of a man. He spends the whole day in a state of passive depression and is profoundly unhappy. Fortunately, I happened to acquire a Russian translation of a certain book, a collection of stories that describes a similar case. It also proposes a remedy – naturally, as a joke, but it seemed like a productive idea to me.'

'What idea was that?'

'A perfectly sensible one from the psychiatric point of view: it is not always the right thing to straighten out a crooked psyche – that can crush the individual personality. What is needed is to transform a weakness into a strength. After all, turn any depression through a hundred and eighty degrees and it becomes an elevation. If a man cannot live without play-acting, and only lives a full life when he is playing some part or other, he should be provided with a permanent repertoire. And the roles chosen should be ones that positively glitter with the finest, most exalted qualities of the human soul. No Khlestakovs, Miserly Knights or – God forbid – Richard the Thirds.'

'So "Nikolai Vsevolodovich" is Nikolai Vsevolodovich Stavrogin from Dostoevsky's novel *The Possessed*,' Lisitsyna gasped. 'But why did you choose such a dangerous part for your patient?'

'I didn't choose it at all,' the doctor exclaimed in annoyance. 'I follow his reading very closely, I know what kind of role can enthral him, and so for a year now the only book he has been allowed to read is another one by Dostoevsky: *The Idiot*. Of all the characters in that book the only one suited to Terpsichorov is Prince Mishkin himself. And Laertes really took to the role. He was transformed into the absolutely inoffensive and extremely conscientious Lev Nikolaevich Mishkin, the very best of men in the entire world. Everything was going really well until some hooligan gave him a copy of *The Possessed* and I failed to notice. Well, of course, Stavrogin is far more impressive than Prince Mishkin, and so Terpsichorov switched roles. In dramatic terms Byronism, theomachism and the poeticisation of Evil are far more attractive than feeble Christian compassion and forgiveness for all. When I realised what had happened, it was too late – Laertes had already become someone else, and I had to adapt as best I could. For the period of crisis I moved him as far away as possible from the other patients and tried to choose some reading even more dramatic than *The Possessed* for him. But I must say, that is by no means easy. I had not suspected that Stavrogin could be so dangerous, and I had underestimated the strength of Laertes' own creative fantasy. But even so, the idea of Stavrogin beating a woman is too bold an interpretation of the character. He is an aristocrat, after all.'

'He didn't beat me,' Mrs Lisitsyna said in a quiet voice. She had guessed where the poor madman had acquired the detrimental novel: Father Mitrofanii had given it to Alyosha to read on his journey, for pedagogical purposes – and now look what it had led to!

Feeling almost like an accomplice to the crime (for it was she who had induced the Bishop to start reading novels), Polina Andreevna said: 'Do not throw Nikolai Vsevolodovich out; he is not to blame. I shall not make a complaint.'

'Really?' Korovin asked in a more cheerful voice. He wagged a threatening finger at an invisible Terpsichorov. 'Well, now I shall have you learning the part of the Sugar Loaf in Maeterlinck's *Blue Bird*!' But then he immediately hung his head in dejection again. 'I have to confess that I am not a very good healer of souls. The people I am able to help are too few. Terpsichorov's case is serious, but not hopeless, but how to save Lentochkin I have not the slightest idea.'

Lisitsyna shuddered as she realised that Alyosha's disappearance had not yet been discovered, but she said nothing.

The gig was already rolling through the pine grove, between the gaily coloured little houses of the clinic in their various styles. The doctor's mansion appeared from round a corner: standing in front of it was a low black carriage with a gold crest on its door, harnessed to a four-in-hand.

'His Reverence has come calling,' Korovin said in surprise. 'Why would he do that? He usually invites me to call on him, with advance warning. Something out of the ordinary must have happened. I'll show you through to my private apartments, Polina Andreevna, and see that you are taken care of. And if you will pardon me, I'll go through to the study to see the master of the island.'

However, things did not work out as Korovin had proposed. The archimandrite must have seen the carriage approaching through the window and he came out into the hallway to meet it. In fact he came flying out, a black figure of fury, beating his staff menacingly on the ground. He glanced briefly at the tormented creature of the female sex with a grimace of disgust and turned his eyes away – as if he were afraid of defiling his gaze by contemplating such obscenity. It was not clear whether he had recognised the generous pilgrim or not. Even if he had, there was no need to worry, Mrs Lisitsyna reassured herself: he would simply think that the extravagant woman had had another crocodile dream.

'Good morning, Father,' said Korovin, inclining his head as he regarded the wrathful father superior with jovial puzzlement. 'To what do I owe this unexpected honour?'

'You are violating our contract!' Vitalii cried, slamming his staff against the floor. 'And a contract, sir, means more than mere money! Did you or did you not promise me that she would leave the brethren alone? And now what has happened?'

'Yes, what has happened?' the doctor asked, not frightened in the least. 'What is this terrible thing that has happened?'

'The *Basilisk* did not sail this morning! The captain has disappeared! He is not in his cell, he is not on the landing stage, he is not anywhere! The passengers are complaining, there is an urgent cargo of monastery sour cream in the hold, and there is no one to captain the ship!' His Reverence grabbed hold of the cross hanging round his neck – clearly in order to remind himself of the Christian virtue of meekness. It did not help. 'I conducted an inquiry! Yesterday Jonah was seen with your Whore of Babylon!'

'If you are referring to Lidia Evgenievna Boreiko,' Dr Korovin replied calmly, 'then she is by no means a whore; her diagnosis is quite different: pathological quasinymphomania with obsessive compulsional delusions and chronic libidinal deficiency. In other words, she is one of those inveterate coquettes who turn men's heads, but would never, under any circumstances, allow them to touch their bodies.'

'We had an agreement!' Vitalii roared in a deafening voice. 'She was not to go near the monks! She could practise her wiles on the visitors if she wished! Did we or did we not have an agreement?'

'We did,' the doctor admitted. 'But perhaps your Jonah himself behaved with her in a manner not entirely becoming to a monk?'

Brother Jonah is a simple, artless soul. I take his confession myself. I know all his ingenuous sins inside out!'

Korovin screwed up his eyes. 'A simple soul, you say? I found a packet of cocaine in Lidia Evgenievna's bedroom here, and another two empty packets, with traces of the powder. Do you know who brings this filth from the mainland for her? Your sailor.'

'Lies! Whoever told you that is nothing but a liar and a spreader of slander!'

'Lidia Evgenievna admitted it herself,' said Donat Savvich. He gestured in the direction of the lake. 'And at this moment your fallen lamb, the simple soul, is lying, blind drunk, over there, beside the old lighthouse. You can go and see for yourself. And so it is not Miss Boreiko's fault that the steamer did not sail on time.'

The archimandrite's eyes flashed, but he did not argue any more. Like a black tornado he hurtled outside to his carriage, slammed the door and shouted: 'Let's go! Come on!'

The carriage started with a sudden jerk, scattering the gravel from under its wheels.

'So Boreiko is one of your patients too?' Polina Andreevna asked, nonplussed.

The doctor frowned as he listened to the wild clatter of hooves retreating into the distance. 'I'm not so sure now that it is Terpsichorov who gets the captain drunk ... I beg your pardon? Ah, Boreiko. Why, naturally she is one of my patients. Can you not tell just from looking at her? A rather common accentuation of the female personality, usually referred to as a *femme fatale*, but in Lidia Evgenievna Boreiko's case it has developed to an extreme degree. The girl constantly needs to feel that she is the object of desire of the greatest possible number of men. She derives her sensual satisfaction from others' lust. She used to live in the capital, but after several tragic stories that ended in duels and suicides, her parents entrusted her to my care. The island life is good for Lidia Evgenievna: far fewer stimuli, almost no temptations and – most importantly – a total absence of competitors. She feels that she is the most beautiful woman in this isolated little world and so she is calm. Sometimes she tries out her charms on one of the visitors to convince herself that she is irresistible, and she is satisfied with that. I can see nothing dangerous in these little pranks. Miss Boreiko promised not to experiment on the monks – and strict sanctions are envisaged for any violation of trust. Evidently this Jonah really is to blame himself.'

'Little pranks?' Mrs Lisitsyna echoed with a sad laugh. And she told the doctor about the 'Empress of Canaan'.

Korovin listened and clutched his head in his hands. 'That's awful, simply awful!' he said, sounding crushed. 'What an appalling relapse! And once again it's entirely my fault. My experiment with supper for three has to be acknowledged a total failure. You did not give me a chance to explain at the time ... You see, Polina Andreevna, a psychiatrist's relations with patients of the opposite sex are constructed according to several models. One of them, the most effective, uses infatuation as its instrument. My power over Boreiko, my lever of influence on her, is that I provoke her vanity. I am the only man who remains entirely indifferent to all her cunning charms as a *femme fatale*. If not for my inaccessibility, Lidia Evgenievna would long ago have fled from the island with some admirer or other, but until she has managed to conquer me, she will not go anywhere; her vanity will not allow it. Every now and then some salt needs to be rubbed into this wound, which is what I attempted to do with your help. Alas, the effect produced far exceeded my expectations. Instead of feeling slightly envious of the marks of attention that I paid to my attractive guest, Boreiko relapsed into a paranoidal-hysterical state and interpreted your arrival here as a conspiracy. And you almost paid with your life as a result. Ah, I shall never forgive myself for this!'

The doctor was so upset that the kind-hearted Mrs Lisitsyna had to console him again. She even went so far as to say that she was to blame for everything, because she had deliberately taunted the poor psychopath (which was partly true). And as for the doctor's mistake – who did not make mistakes, especially in such subtle matters as healing a sick soul? On the whole, she seemed to succeed in setting the despondent doctor's mind at rest.

Korovin rang to summon the duty doctor to his study and told him glumly: 'Bring Lidia Evgenievna Boreiko to me immediately. Prepare an injection of tranquilium – a nervous fit is quite likely. Have the head nurse choose some shoes and clothes for Mrs Lisitsyna. And make sure she has a relaxing massage and a lavender bath.'

Blue, Green, Yellow, Straw-coloured

And so the summary result of all the shocks of the night and the morning was that Polina Andreevna Lisitsyna had arrived right back where she started.

She had made not the slightest progress with the main business that had brought her to New Ararat. And the most annoying thing of all was that twice already in a short space of time she had believed with all her heart first in one theory and then in another, and now she could not have said which of them was the more absurd. Never before had the perspicacious Sister Pelagia suffered such an embarrassing fiasco. Of course, there had been special circumstances interfering with the smooth process of her thought, but even so, now that she was rested and her head was clear, she felt ashamed.

The results of the investigation into the Black Monk presented a sorry picture.

First of all, there were the people who had died untimely deaths: the barrister Kubovsky, terrified into having a stroke; then the buoy-keeper's wife, who had miscarried her baby; the buoy-keeper, who had drowned; Lagrange, who had been shot; and finally, poor Alyosha Lentochkin.

Kubovksy had been taken away on the steamship in a zinc-bound coffin; the unfortunate mother and her lifeless child had been buried in the ground; Felix Stanislavovich was lying in the morgue, packed in blocks of ice; and who knew where the bodies of those who drowned were carried away to by the dark underwater currents?

And was Matvei Bentsionovich's lot any happier, with his reason clouded?

During the last few days, bearing in mind Alexei Lentochkin's fate (the attendants from Korovin's clinic had searched the whole of Canaan, but failed to find him), Mrs Lisitsyna had visited Berdichevsky frequently but found nothing to console her – he was deteriorating steadily. He either did not recognise his visitor, or took no interest in her at all. They sat facing each other without speaking, and then Polina Andreevna went on her way with a heavy heart.

That terrible night filled with fateful events had concluded in total farce – and also, of course, in the strict punishment of the guilty parties.

His Reverence Vitalii had demoted Brother Jonah from captain to stoker and immediately put him in the punishment cell for a month on nothing but bread, water and prayer.

Dr Korovin had dealt with his own charges no less severely. Lidia Evgenievna had been forbidden (also for an entire month) to use powder, perfume or pomade, and to wear black. The actor Terpsichorov had been placed under house arrest with a single solitary book, another work by Fyodor Dostoevsky but a harmless one, the short novel *Poor People* – to make him forget his dangerous role as 'the gentleman from the canton of Uris' and adopt the image of the sugary-sweet, retiring Makar Devushkin. Two days later Polina Andreevna had visited the prisoner and been amazed by the change that had taken place in him. The former seducer had regarded her with a sincere, gentle smile and called her 'dear friend' and 'little mother'. To be quite honest, his visitor was actually rather upset by this metamorphosis – Terpsichorov had been far more interesting in his previous role.

Other events that are worthy of mention here had included the appearance in a certain liberally inclined Moscow newspaper of an article about the incredible happenings at New Ararat and the negative rumours concerning Outskirts Island. One of the pilgrims must have reported everything. For the first time ever, the rosary beads carved by the hermits had been left unsold in the monastery shop. Father Vitalii had ordered a special cheap sale to be held, reducing the price first to nine roubles and ninety-nine kopecks, and then to four roubles and ninety-nine kopecks. At that point some of the beads had been bought, but not all. It was a bad sign. In the town, people were already saying openly that the hermitage had become unwholesome and unclean, that it should be closed for the time being and no one should be allowed to visit Outskirts Island for a year – to see if St Basilisk's fury would abate.

The monastery's patron, however, seemed to have quietened down already: he was no longer walking on water or frightening people in the town – but possibly that was only because the nights had become dark and moonless.

As for Mrs Lisitsyna, during this period of calm she spent almost all of her time deep in thought and took very little action. In the morning she studied her battered face in the mirror for a long time, noting the changing coloration of the bruising. Apart from that, there was nothing to distinguish any particular day from all the others. In her own mind she even named them after the colour of her face.

Well, the first of these quiet days, the one following the night when Polina Andreevna was first almost drowned and then almost dishonoured, did not count – one might almost say that it had never even happened. After a bath, a massage and an injection to relax her nerves, the long-suffering Mrs Lisitsyna had slept for almost twenty-four hours and only returned to the guest house the following morning, refreshed and invigorated. On looking at herself in the dressing-table mirror, she had noted that the mark on her face was no longer crimson and blue, but merely blue. And so that was the name she gave that day.

On the afternoon of the 'blue' day Polina Andreevna changed into her novice's garments in the pavilion (they and her other things had lain undisturbed on the floor ever since the evening of two days previously), all the while glancing round warily at the dark silhouettes of the automatic dispensers. From there the short, skinny little monk set off for the Lenten Spit to wait for the boatman. Brother Kleopa appeared on time, at precisely three o'clock, and was delighted to see Pelagius there – less for the novice's own sake than for the baksheesh he anticipated. He asked briskly: 'Well, are you sailing today or not? My hand still hurts.' And he winked.

After receiving a rouble, he told Pelagius how he had taken the holy elder Ilarii across to Outskirts Island the day before and the two hermits had greeted their new brother: one had kissed him – that must mean he had pressed his own cowl against the other man's – and the abbot had declared in a loud voice: 'Thine are the most glorious heavens of Theognost.'

'Why "Theognost"?' Pelagius asked in surprise, '– when the holy father is called Ilarii?'

'I didn't understand that myself at first; I thought Israel had become completely infirm and was confusing the names. That was what his fellow hermits were called: Theognost and David. But when I told the father steward what the abbot had said, he gave me a real scolding for being disrespectful and explained what the words meant. The first six words – "Thine are the most glorious heavens" – are canonical, the promise of the Kingdom of Heaven from the psalm of Efamov. That is how the head of the hermitage is always supposed to greet the new hermit. And the last two words are free, for the monastery's information. The father steward said the holy elder was letting us know which of the brethren had ascended to Heaven. Not David, in other words, but Theognost.'

Pelagius thought for a little while. 'Father, you've been the boatman for a long time. So I suppose you must have taken the last hermit to the island as well?'

'At Easter, the holy elder David. And before that, at Assumption last year, the holy elder Theognost. And before that the holy elder Amfilokhii, before him Gerontii ... or was that Agapit? No, Gerontii ... I've taken a lot of our intercessors across; you can't remember everyone.'

'So I suppose the abbot greeted the new holy elder like that every time, telling you who had died. You simply forgot.'

'I didn't forget anything!' Brother Kleopa said angrily. 'I remember "Thine are the most glorious heavens" – that was there all right. But he never mentioned anyone's name after that. It was only afterwards, from all kinds of indirect clues, that we found out which of the hermits had surrendered his soul to God. And as far as we, the living, are concerned, they're already dead; they've had their funeral and been seen off to the Farewell Chapel. Israel had no need to say it. I think he can sense his own end is near and his heart's softened.'

They set off for the island: Kleopa on one oar, Pelagius on the other.

The holy elder Israel came out to meet them, handed over the rosary beads that had been carved since the previous day and said: 'And then David's heart did tremble is obscure.'

Pelagius thought the abbot seemed to pronounce the final words more slowly and loudly, looking not at Kleopa but at his young assistant – but then how could you see, through those holes?

As soon as they set off on their way back, the novice asked quietly: 'What was that he said? I can't make any sense of it.'

'"And then David's heart did tremble" – that's about the holy elder David. He must be having problems with his heart again. Ever since David was put in the hermitage, the abbot has often taken phrases from the First Book of Kings, where there's a lot written about King David. The name's the same, and that can save an extra word. And what was that last bit? "Is obscure"? Well, the father steward can guess that; he's got a good head on his shoulders.'

That was all for the 'blue' day. Its other events were far too insignificant even to mention.

The next day was 'green'. Not entirely green, that is – not the colour of a green leaf; more like a sea wave – the dense blue coloration of the bruise had begun to fade, becoming paler and acquiring a greenish tinge.

At three o'clock Pelagius handed Brother Kleopa two fifty-kopeck pieces and they set off in the boat.

The boatman gave the abbot some medicine for the holy elder David. Israel took it and waited for something else. Then he heaved a deep sigh and said something that was extremely strange, looking straight at the young red-headed monk: 'Let him who has ears hear cuckoo loose.'

'What was that?' Pelagius asked when the holy elder had hobbled away.

Kleopa shrugged. 'I managed to make out "Let him who has ears hear" – that's from the Apocalypse, though I don't understand why he said it, and I couldn't make out what it was he added on at the end. Something about a "cuckoo". See, I was right about Israel; the father steward was wrong to tell me I'm an ignoramus. It's the holy elder who's touched.' He twirled a finger beside his temple: 'Cuckoo, cuckoo.'

Pelagius's raised eyebrows suggested that the young monk thought differently, but he did not argue; all he said was: 'Let's go again tomorrow, all right?'

'You keep sailing just as long as your uncle's roubles last.'

Then came the 'yellow' day, when the green bruise began turning yellowish.

On that day the holy elder declared: 'Thus the leach creates a mixture nonfat sit.'

'Yet more senseless twittering,' Brother Kleopa remarked. 'He'll start talking nothing but the language of the birds of heaven soon. I'm not going to bother remembering that nonsense; I'll invent something for the father steward.'

'Wait, Father,' Pelagius put in. 'That part about the leach – I think it's from the Book of Jesus, son of Sirakhov. A leach is a doctor, and "mixture" means medicine; it's a scientific term. But what "nonfat sit" means here, I don't understand.' He repeated it several times – 'nonfatsit, nonfatsit' – then fell silent and made no more conversation with the boatman after that.

When they parted he said: 'Until tomorrow then.'

The following day Polina Andreevna's face was almost entirely respectable again, with only a slight hint of a pale straw colour; and the day itself was the same colour: gentle sunshine with a fine mist.

Pelagius was so impatient to reach Outskirts Island as soon as possible that he kept moving his oar too fast and rowing harder than necessary, making the prow of the boat swing round. Eventually he received a clip round the ear from Brother Kleopa for his muddle-headed zeal and moderated his ardour somewhat.

The abbot was waiting on the shore. Pelagius had been right about the mixture, of course – the holy elder took the bottle and nodded. Then he said the following to the novice: 'Mourn not, for he is well, mona koom.'

The young monk nodded, as if he had been expecting to hear these very words.

'Well, the Lord be praised; it seems the sick man's a bit better,' Brother Kleopa said on their way back. 'But that was a strange name he called David: "mona koom". The holy elder's getting odd all right . . . What about tomorrow – are you coming?' the boatman asked the boy, who was strangely silent now.

But the boy did not hear him.

So that was the straw-coloured day, and then came the final day, when everything drew to a conclusion.

So many different things happened on that final day, God grant that we do not grow confused and omit anything.

The Final Day: Morning

Let us make a proper start, beginning with the morning.

Between eight and nine, when it was still not really light, there was a long, drawn-out hoot from the lake – the steamship *St Basilisk* had arrived from Sineozersk with its newly hired captain. By this time Mrs Lisitsyna had already drunk her coffee and was sitting in front of the mirror, contemplating her entirely clear face with great satisfaction, turning it this way and that, unable to get enough of the joyful sight. Although she heard the steamship's whistle, she did not attach any importance to it.

But she should have.

A period of about an hour had passed since that doleful, lingering signal; Polina Andreevna had already breakfasted and dressed and was preparing to go out to visit Berdichevsky when there was a knock at the door of her room. It was the archimandrite Vitalii's lay-brother assistant.

'His Reverence the father superior requests you to come to him,' the monk said with a bow, adding in a tone that was polite but brooked no denial: 'Immediately. The carriage is waiting.'

He replied evasively to the surprised pilgrim's questions. In fact, you could say his answers were not really answers at all – nothing but words of a single syllable. However, from the messenger's manner Lisitsyna assumed that something out of the ordinary must have happened at the monastery. But if he did not wish to tell her, so be it.

She hesitated for a moment over whether to take the

travelling bag with her, but decided to leave it behind. To go to a monastery with a lethal weapon smacked of sacrilege. In order to protect the revolver from prying eyes, she wrapped it in a pair of lacy drawers and put it right at the bottom of the bag, under everything else. But whether that would help or not, God only knew.

They reached the monastery quickly, in only ten minutes. When Polina Andreevna got out of the carriage and glanced around the courtyard of the monastery, she was certain that something had happened.

The monks were not walking sedately, waddling like ducks as they did at any normal time, but running. Some were sweeping the pavement, which was already clean in any case; others were carrying feather mattresses and pillows; but the most surprising sight of all was the singers of the archimandrite's choir, holding up their cassocks as they trudged into the cathedral church, led by the pompous, pot-bellied precentor.

What strange wonders were these?

The lady's guide led her not into the archimandrite's residence but into the hierarchical chambers, which were intended for highly important guests and usually stood empty. Polina Andreevna felt a sudden premonition stir in her heart, but immediately suppressed it as impossible and certain to lead to disappointment.

But her premonition had not deceived her after all! As Lisitsyna entered the refectory, the sun was shining in through the windows behind the backs of people sitting at a long table covered with a white cloth, and straight into her eyes, so she could only distinguish the outlines of several men sitting in dignified immobility.

As she bowed respectfully from the doorway she heard Father Vitalii's voice: 'There she is, Bishop, the person whom you wished to see.'

Polina Andreevna quickly pulled her spectacles out of her case, screwed up her eyes and gasped. Sitting there in the place of honour, surrounded by the senior members of the monastery, was Mitrofanii – alive and well, although he looked a little drawn and pale.

The Bishop looked the 'Moscow noblewoman' over from head to toe with a glance that boded nothing good and chewed on his lips. He did not bless her or even nod.

'Let her break bread with us, and I'll talk to her later.' He turned back to the father superior to continue his interrupted conversation.

Lisitsyna sat on the very edge of her chair, overwhelmed by her joy and also, of course, her fear. She noticed that there were more grey hairs in His Grace's beard than there had been, that his cheeks were hollow and his fingers had become thin and were trembling slightly, which had never happened before. She sighed.

The Bishop's eyebrows rose and fell sternly. It was clear that he was angry, but just how angry she could not tell by looking at him. Polina Andreevna gazed imploringly at her spiritual father, but was not rewarded with any attention. She concluded that he was very angry indeed.

She sighed again, but less bitterly than the first time, and began listening to what the Bishop and the archimandrite were talking about. It was an abstract conversation, about the community of the blessed.

'In my actions, Your Grace, I proceed out of the conviction that a monk should be like a dead man among the living. Ceaseless labour for the good of the community and prayer – that is his life, and nothing else is needed,' Vitalii said, evidently responding to some question or, perhaps, reproach. 'That is why I am stern with the brethren and do not allow them any liberty. When they took monastic vows, they abandoned their own will to the greater glory of God.'

'But I cannot agree with Your Reverence,' Mitrofanii replied with animation. 'In my opinion, a monk should be more alive than any layman, because he lives the genuine life – that is, the spiritual life. And you must treat those in your care with respect, for each of them possesses an exalted soul. But here they are put in a dungeon, tormented with hunger and even, so they say, beaten around the face.' At this point the Bishop cast a rapid glance at the burly monk who was sitting on the archimandrite's right – Polina Andreevna knew that he was the fearsome Father Triadii, the monastery's cellarer. 'I cannot turn a blind eye to such laying on of hands.'

'Monks are like children,' the father superior protested. 'For they are detached from the usual earthly cares: suspicious, inquisitive, intemperate in their speech. Many have been saving their souls in monasteries since they were children, and so they have remained children in their souls. They cannot be managed without strict paternal discipline.'

His Grace replied in a restrained tone: 'Then do not accept into the order of monks those who have not yet experienced life and come to know themselves. There are, after all, other paths to salvation open to a man apart from serving God as a monk. Indeed, there is a countless multitude of such paths. A simpleton might well believe that the monastic life is the most direct route to the Lord, but in God's world a straight line is not always the shortest route between two points. Let me appeal urgently once again to Your Reverence: do not become infatuated with excessive strictness. The Church of Christ must inspire love, not fear. But as things are, observing the way our clerics manage things, one feels like repeating Gogol's famous words: "It makes me sad that there is no kindness in goodness."'

Father Vitalii listened to this admonition with his head inclined stubbornly. 'I will answer Your Grace not with the words of a lay author, but with the saying of the most devout holy elder, Zosima Verkhovsky: "If we are not with the saints, then we shall be with the devils; for there is no third place for us." The Lord winnows mankind, deciding who shall be saved and who shall be doomed. The choice is stern and terrible, so how can we manage without sternness?'

Polina Andreevna knew that the Bishop held the deceased holy father Zosima Verkhovsky of Optinsk in special esteem, and the archimandrite's objection had hit the target.

Mitrofanii said nothing. The other monks looked at him, waiting. Suddenly Mrs Lisitsyna began feeling awkward: she was the only one there in lay costume, the only bright spot among all the black cassocks – like a blue-tit or a canary that had accidentally flown into a flock of ravens.

No, Polina Andreevna told herself. I am the same breed. And they are not ravens at all; they are talking about important things, concerned for the good of mankind. What would Mitrofanii say to the father superior?

'Catholicism accepts the existence of Purgatory, because there are not many people who are entirely good or entirely bad,' the Bishop said slowly. 'Of course, Purgatory has to be understood in a spiritual sense – as a place for cleaning away the dirt that has adhered to the soul. But our Orthodox faith does not acknowledge Purgatory. I pondered the reason for such intransigence for a long time until I found an answer. It comes not from sternness but from greater compassion. For, after all, there are no absolutely black, unwashable sinners; in every villain, even the most inveterate, there is still a spark of life glowing. And our Orthodox Hell, unlike that of Catholicism, does not deprive anyone, even Judas himself, of hope. It is my opinion that the torments of our Hell are not intended for all eternity. The Orthodox Hell is also Purgatory, because the time every sinful soul will spend there is fixed. It cannot be that God, in His mercy, would punish a soul for all eternity, with no forgiveness. What then is the point of the torments, if not to purge?'

The holy fathers of New Ararat exchanged glances and said nothing in reply to this opinion, but Polina Andreevna shook her head. She knew that, in talking of religion, the Bishop often expressed ideas that might be regarded as freethinking or even heretical. This was perfectly safe among his close companions. But in front of these dogmatists? They would report him; they would complain.

But Mitrofanii had not yet finished his commentary. 'And I

must reproach Your Reverence yet again. I have heard that you pay excessive attention to earthly rulers when they visit you. I have been told that last year, when the young grand duchesses were brought here on pilgrimage, you laid a carpet runner to each holy site, and your choir performed an entire concert for the visitors. For under-age girls! And why did you go in person to bless the Governor General's dacha in Sineozersk, and even take a wonder-working icon with you?'

'For the sake of a matter pleasing to God,' Vitalii explained passionately. 'For on earth we live in the body and walk on the ground! Because I obliged their imperial highnesses, the monastery received a plot of land for a church from the court department in St Petersburg. And in his gratitude the Governor General sent us a five-hundred-*pood* bronze bell. This was not done for me, the sinful Vitalii, but for the Church!'

'Oh, I fear that our Church will have to pay a great price for its close embrace of temporal power,' the Bishop sighed. 'And perhaps that time is already none too distant ... Well, all right,' he said and paused briefly, then suddenly smiled. 'I have only just arrived and already I am arguing – that does not seem very friendly. Father Vitalii, I would like to look round your famous island. I have been dreaming of it for a long time.'

The archimandrite inclined his head respectfully. 'I had been wondering how I could have provoked Your Grace's anger, and why you never favour Ararat with a visit. If you had informed us beforehand, we would have prepared a worthy reception for you. But as things are, please do not judge us too harshly.'

'That does not matter; I am no great lover of ostentation,' the Bishop said good-naturedly, pretending not to have noticed the hidden reproach in the father superior's words. 'I wish to see everything, just as it is on an ordinary day. And I shall begin straight away.'

'But will you not dine?' the father cellarer asked in alarm. 'Our Blue Lake fish, pasties, preserves, honeycakes?'

'Thank you, but my doctor forbids it.' Mitrofanii struck

himself on the left side of the chest and stood up. 'I drink broth and eat plain gruel, and I am well fed.'

'Well then, I am willing to accompany you wherever you wish,' said Vitalii. He got to his feet, followed by the others. 'The carriage is ready and waiting.'

The Bishop said in an affectionate tone: 'I am well aware how very busy Your Reverence is. Do not waste your time on idle respect for rank; it is not flattering to me, and not pleasant for you.'

The archimandrite frowned: 'Then I shall assign Father Siluan or Father Triadii to Your Grace. You cannot go with no guide at all.'

'They are not needed either. I have not come here for an inspection, as you no doubt must have thought. I have long dreamed of simply spending time here, like an ordinary pilgrim. A simple visit, not in my role as your superior.'

The Bishop's voice sounded sincere, but Vitalii frowned even more intensely – he did not trust the simplicity of Mitrofanii's intentions. He believed that the Bishop wished to look around the territory of the monastery without anyone to prompt his thoughts or spy on him. And he was right.

It was only then that His Grace looked at Polina Andreevna. 'This lady, Mrs ... Lisitsyna, will go with me. She is an old acquaintance of mine. Polina Andreevna, do not refuse to keep an old man company.' The glance he shot at her from under his thick eyebrows was so intense that Lisitsyna immediately jumped to her feet. 'We can talk about the old days, you can tell me how life has been treating you, and we can compare our impressions of the holy monastery.' The tone in which this was said was ominous, or at least it seemed so to Polina Andreevna.

'Very well, Father,' she muttered, lowering her eyes.

The father superior stared hard at her with an expression of profound suspicion. He laughed darkly and asked: 'And what of the crocodile, Mother? Is it not bothering you any more?'

Lisitsyna said nothing and merely hung her head even lower.

They drove out of the gates in the same carriage that had brought Polina Andreevna from the guest house. As yet nothing had been said. In her agitated state, the criminal did not know how to begin; whether she should repent or try to justify herself, or talk about the progress she had made.

Mitrofanii deliberately remained silent, to impress on her the seriousness of the situation. He looked out of the window at the tidy streets of Ararat, clicking his tongue approvingly. When he began to speak it was so unexpected that Mrs Lisitsyna actually started.

'Well now, this crocodile – what is that? Yet another piece of mischief?'

'I am at fault, Father. I deceived His Reverence,' Polina Andreevna confessed humbly.

'Indeed you are at fault, my little Pelagiushka. And that's not all you have been up to ...'

This was it; it had begun. She sighed repentantly and lowered her eyes.

Mitrofanii bent down his fingers one at a time as he counted off all her guilty acts: 'You broke an oath given to your spiritual father when he was sick and almost at death's door.'

'I did not swear!' she said quickly.

'Don't play games with words. You understood my unspoken request not to go to Ararat perfectly well; you nodded your head and kissed my hand. Is that not an oath, you perfidious snake?'

'I am a snake, verily, a snake,' Polina Andreevna agreed.

'You have arrayed yourself in forbidden dress and brought disgrace on the vocation of a nun. Your neck is uncovered – pah, the sight is shameful.'

Lisitsyna quickly covered her neck with her headscarf, but attempted nonetheless to refute this point of the accusation. 'There were times when you gave your blessing for me to do such things.'

'But this time not only did I not give my blessing, I explicitly forbade it,' Mitrofanii snapped. 'Is that not so?'

'It is ...'

'I thought of reporting you to the police. And it was quite inexcusable of me not to do so. You stole money from your own pastor! You could not possibly fall any lower than that! You should be sent to do hard labour; that's where thieves belong.'

Polina Andreevna did not object – there was no point.

'And if I did not report you, a fugitive nun and bandit, as wanted by the police throughout the empire – with your red hair and freckles, they would have found you soon enough – then it was only out of gratitude for curing me.'

'For what?' Lisitsyna asked in amazement, thinking that she had misheard.

'As soon as I heard from Sister Christina that you had gone away somewhere, allegedly at my request, I realised what your intentions were and my health immediately took a turn for the better. I felt ashamed, Pelagiushka,' the Bishop said quietly, and it was suddenly clear that he was not angry at all. 'I felt ashamed of my weakness. What was I doing lying in bed like a snivelling old woman, with doctors feeding me decoctions by the spoonful? I had abandoned my poor children in their misfortune, shrugged off my burden on to a woman's shoulders. And I began to feel so ashamed that a day later I started sitting up, on the fourth day I started walking, on the fifth I took a little drive round the town in a carriage and on the eighth I packed for the journey here – to see you. Professor Schmidt, who came from Peter to look after me, says that he has never in his life seen such a rapid recovery from a ruptured cardiac muscle. The professor went back to the capital feeling very proud of himself – now people will pay him more money for his visits and consultations. But it was you, not he, who cured me.'

Polina Andreevna sobbed and kissed His Grace's thin white hand. He kissed the parting of her hair.

'Phew, what powerful perfume you're wearing,' the Bishop growled, no longer pretending to be angry. 'All right, tell me about our case.'

Lisitsyna took out a letter and handed it to him. 'It would be best if you read this. All the most important things are in it. I have been adding to it every evening. That will be briefer and clearer than telling you myself. Or would you prefer me to tell you?'

Mitrofanii put on his pince-nez. 'Let me read it. If there's anything I don't understand, I'll ask.'

With all the additions that had been made to it in the course of an entire week, the letter was long – very nearly ten pages. In places the words were blurred where they had got damp.

The carriage stopped. The monk driving them removed his cowl and asked: 'Where would you like to go? We are out of the town already.'

'To Dr Korovin's clinic,' Polina Andreevna said in a low voice, in order not to disturb the Bishop at his reading.

They drove on.

Her heart was wrung as she examined the changes brought about in the Bishop's appearance by his illness. Oh, he had risen from his bed too soon – if only that did not provoke another disaster! But, on the other hand, lying there doing nothing would have been even worse for him.

At one point His Grace cried out as if in pain. She guessed that he had just read the part about Alyosha Lentochkin.

At last the Bishop laid the sheets of paper aside and fell into a morose reverie. He did not ask her any questions – she must have presented everything clearly. He muttered: 'And there was I, like a useless old man, swallowing pills and learning how to walk ... Oh, I am ashamed.'

Polina Andreevna was impatient to talk about the case. 'Your Grace, I cannot get the holy elder Israel's mysterious words out of my mind. What they add up to ...'

'Wait a while with your riddles,' said Mitrofanii, holding up his hand. 'We'll talk about that later. First the most important thing: I want to see Matvei. Is he in a bad way?'

'Very bad.'

The Final Day: the Middle

'Very bad,' Dr Korovin confirmed. 'Every day it is harder to get through to him. The entroposis is progressing. From one day to the next the patient becomes more feeble and passive. The nocturnal hallucinations have stopped, but I see that as a turn for the worse, rather than the better: the psyche no longer has any need for stimulation. Berdichevsky has lost the ability to experience even powerful feelings, like fear, and the instinct of self-preservation has grown weak. Yesterday I carried out an experiment: I ordered him not to be taken any food until he asked for it. He never asked. He spent the entire day without eating anything. He has begun to forget who people are if he has not seen them since the day before. The only person who has been able to involve him in coherent conversation is his house-mate, Lampier, but he is also a rather unusual individual and no master of eloquent speech – Polina Andreevna has seen him, she knows. All my experience suggests that from now on things will only get worse. If you wish, you can take the patient away, but even in the most fashionable Swiss clinic, even if he is with Schwanger himself, the result will be the same. Alas, in such cases modern psychiatry is powerless.'

The three of them – the doctor, the Bishop and Lisitsyna – entered cottage number seven together. They looked into the bedroom and saw two empty beds – one of them, Berdichevsky's, dishevelled, the other neatly made up. They walked through into the laboratory. Despite the fine day, the curtains were closed and the light was not on. It was quiet.

There was the balding top of Matvei Berdichevsky's head

protruding above the back of an armchair. In former times it had always been concealed by a slick of precisely combed hair, but now it was exposed and defenceless. The sick man did not turn round at the sound of footsteps.

'But where's Lampier?' Polina Andreevna asked in a whisper.

Korovin did not bother to lower his voice. 'I have no idea. Whenever I come, he's not here. I suppose it must be several days since I last saw him. Our Sergei Nikolaevich is an independent character. He must have discovered some new emanation and got carried away with his "field experiments" – that's one of his special terms.'

The Bishop stopped by the door and looked at the back of his spiritual son's head, blinking very rapidly.

'Matvei Bentsionovich!' Mrs Lisitsyna called.

'Speak louder,' Donat Savvich advised her. 'He only responds to powerful stimuli now.'

She shouted at the top of her voice: 'Matvei Bentsionovich! Look who I've brought to see you!' Polina Andreevna had just a faint hope that when Berdichevsky saw his beloved mentor he would rouse himself and come back to life.

The assistant public prosecutor looked round, searching for the source of the sound. He found it. But he only looked at the woman and paid no attention at all to her companions. 'Yes?' he asked slowly. 'What do you want, madam?'

'He used to ask about you all the time!' she whispered despairingly to Mitrofanii. 'And now he's not even looking ... Where's Mr Lampier?' she asked cautiously, moving closer to the seated man.

He answered in a dull, indifferent voice: 'Under the ground.'

'You see,' Korovin said with a shrug. 'He only reacts to the intonation and the grammar of a question, with a nonsensical response. It is a new stage in the development of his psychological illness.'

The Bishop took a step forward, decisively moving the doctor to one side. 'Let me see him. Physical damage to the brain is definitely a matter for medicine, but a diseased soul, a soul, as they used to say in the old days, that has been possessed by the devil – that, doctor, falls into my department.' He raised his voice imperiously and said: 'I tell you what: why don't you leave Mr Berdichevsky and me alone together? And don't come back until I call you. If I don't call you for a week, then stay away for a week. Nobody must come, not a single person. Do you understand?'

Korovin laughed: 'Oh, Bishop, this is not your domain, believe me. You can't drive this demon out with prayers and holy water. And I won't allow any medieval nonsense in my clinic.'

'You won't allow it?' the Bishop said, screwing up his eyes as he looked round at the doctor. 'But you allow sick people to wander around among the healthy? Just what sort of muddle have you created here in Ararat? There's no way of telling which members of the public are sane. In the world we live in, it's hard enough to tell which of the people around you are mad and which aren't, but here on your island there is nothing but temptation and confusion. It's enough to make a sane man have doubts about himself. Why don't you just do as you are told? Or I'll forbid you to keep your institution on Church land.'

Korovin did not dare to carry on arguing. He shrugged and spread his hands, as if to say: Do as you wish. Then he turned and walked out.

'Come along, Matiusha.' The Bishop took the sick man gently by the hand and led him out of the dark laboratory into the bedroom. 'Don't you come with us, Pelagia. I'll call when you can come.'

'All right, Father, I'll wait in the laboratory,' Lisitsyna replied with a bow.

The Bishop sat Berdichevsky down on the bed and moved up a chair for himself. They sat in silence for a while. Mitrofanii looked at Matvei Bentsionovich, who looked at the wall.

'Matvei, do you really not recognise me?' His Grace could not help asking.

It was only then that Berdichevsky turned his eyes to look at him. He blinked several times and asked uncertainly: 'Are you a

328

cleric then? You have an icon hanging on your chest. Your face seems familiar. I must have seen you in a dream.'

'Touch me. I am not a dream. Are you not glad to see me?'

Berdichevsky obediently touched his visitor's sleeve and replied politely: 'Of course I am, very glad.' He looked at the Bishop again and suddenly began to cry – quietly, without any sound, but with copious tears.

Mitrofanii was glad to see a demonstration of feeling, even of this kind. He began stroking the wretched man's head, repeating over and over again: 'Cry, cry, tears wash the poison out of the soul.'

But Berdichevsky apparently intended to cry for a long time. His tears kept streaming down in a way that was oddly monotonous; and the way he cried was strange too, like the endless drizzle of autumn. His Grace's handkerchief was completely soaked through from wiping his spiritual son's face, and it was a very big handkerchief indeed.

The Bishop frowned. 'Well now, you've had a cry and that will do. I've brought you some good news, very good news.'

The sick man batted his eyelids obediently and his eyes immediately dried up. 'It's good to have good news,' he remarked.

Mitrofanii waited for a question, but it did not come. Then he declared solemnly: 'Your promotion to the next rank has arrived. Congratulations. You have been waiting for a long time. You are now a state counsellor.'

'I can't be a state counsellor,' Berdichevsky said in a thoughtful voice, wrinkling up his brow. 'Madmen can't be state officials of the fifth level; it is forbidden by law.'

'Oh yes, they can,' said the Bishop, trying to joke. 'I know officials of the fourth rank and even, Lord help us, the third, who ought to be in an asylum.'

'You do?' asked Matvei Bentsionovich, slightly surprised. 'And yet the articles of the state service absolutely forbid it.'

Again they sat in silence for a while.

'But that is still not my most important news,' said the Bishop. He slapped Berdichevsky on the knee – the assistant public prosecutor started and winced tearfully. 'You have a son, a fine baby boy! He is healthy, and Masha is well too.'

'It's very good when everybody is well,' Berdichevsky said with a nod. 'Without health nothing brings any happiness – neither fame nor riches.'

'We've even chosen the name already. We thought for a long, long time and decided to call him ...' Mitrofanii paused. '... Akakii. So he'll be Akakii Matveevich. Doesn't that have a fine ring to it?'

Berdichevsky approved the name as well.

Silence descended again. This time they said nothing for about half an hour at least. It was clear that Berdichevsky did not find the silence irksome. He hardly even moved, and just looked straight ahead. Once or twice, when Mitrofanii stirred, he looked at him and smiled benevolently.

Unsure of how to break through this blank wall, the Bishop began a conversation about Berdichevsky's family – he had brought some photographs from Zavolzhsk for this purpose.

Matvei Bentsionovich looked at the photographs with polite interest. He looked at his own wife and said: 'A pretty smile, only rather stern.' And he liked the children too.

'You have charming little ones, Father,' he said. 'And so many of them. I didn't know that individuals of the monastic vocation were allowed to have children. It's a shame that I cannot have any children, because I am mad. The law forbids those who are mad from entering into marriage, and if someone has already done so, then the marriage is declared null and void. I think that I used to be married too. There's something I can rem—'

At this point there was a cautious knock and Polina Andreevna's freckled face appeared round the door – at just the wrong moment. The Bishop waved one hand at his spiritual daughter: Go away, don't interfere – and the door closed. But the critical moment had been lost and, instead of exploring his memories, Berdichevsky became distracted by a cockroach that was crawling slowly across his bedside locker.

The minutes passed, and the hours. The day began growing

dark and then faded away completely. No one knocked at the door again or dared to disturb the Bishop and his insane charge.

'All right then,' said Mitrofanii, getting up with a quiet groan. 'I'm feeling a bit tired. I'm going to settle down for the night. Your physicist is not here anyway, and if he turns up, the doctor can put him somewhere else.' He lay down on the second bed and stretched out his numb legs.

For the first time Berdichevsky showed signs of concern. He switched on the lamp and turned to his recumbent visitor. 'You're not supposed to sleep here,' he said nervously. 'This place is for madmen, and you are sane.'

Mitrofanii yawned and crossed his mouth so that the evil spirit would not fly into it. 'What kind of madman are you? You don't howl or roll around on the floor.'

'I don't roll around on the floor, but I howl sometimes,' Berdichevsky confessed. 'When I feel very afraid.'

'Well, I'm going to be with you.' His Grace's voice was serene. 'From now on, Matiusha, I am never going to leave you. We shall always be together. Because you are my spiritual son and because I love you. Do you know what love is?'

'No,' replied Matvei Bentsionovich, 'I don't know anything now.'

'Love means always being together. Especially when the one you love is suffering.'

'You can't stay here! Why can't you understand? You're a bishop!'

Aha! Mitrofanii clenched his fists in the semi-darkness. He has remembered! Come on then, come on!

'That's all the same to me, Matiusha. I'm going to stay with you. And you won't be afraid any more, because two people together are never afraid. We can both be madmen together, you and me. Dr Korovin will take me in; it's an interesting case for him: a provincial prelate who has gone barmy.'

'No!' Berdichevsky said suddenly. 'Two people can't go mad together!'

This also seemed a good sign to the Bishop – previously Matvei Bentsionovich had agreed with everything.

Mitrofanii sat up on the bed and hung his legs over the edge. He began speaking, looking his former investigator straight in the eye: 'But I, Matvei, do not think that you have gone mad. You've just gone a little crazy. It happens to very clever people. Very clever people often want to squeeze the whole world into their heads. But it won't all fit in. It's God's world. It has a lot of corners, and some of them are very sharp. They poke out through your head, they squeeze your brain, they hurt you.'

Berdichevsky pressed his hands to his temples and complained: 'Yes, they do squeeze. Do you know how badly it hurts sometimes?'

'But of course it hurts. If you clever people can't fit something inside your brain, you start to get frightened of your own brain and you go out of your mind. But there is nowhere else for you to go, because apart from his mind a man can only have one other support: faith. Matvei, no matter how often you repeat "I believe, O Lord," you still won't really believe. Faith is a gift from God that is not given to everyone, and it is ten times more difficult for clever people to attain it. And so it turns out that you have gone out of your mind but not arrived at faith, and that is all there is to your madness. Well, I cannot give you faith; that is not in my power. But I will try to lead you back into your mind. So that you can fit God's world between your ears again.'

Berdichevsky listened suspiciously, but very attentively.

'You haven't forgotten how to read, have you? Here, read what another clever person writes, someone even cleverer than you. Read about the coffin, about the bullet, about Basilisk on stilts.' The Bishop took Sister Pelagia's letter out of his sleeve and held it out to the other man.

Berdichevsky took it and moved it closer to the lamp. At first he read slowly, to himself, moving his lips laboriously at the same time. On the third page he shuddered, stopped moving his lips and began batting his eyelids. He turned to the next page and began ruffling up his hair nervously.

Mitrofanii watched hopefully and also moved his lips – he was praying.

When he reached the end of the letter, Matvei Bentsionovich rubbed his eyes furiously. He shuffled the pages in the reverse direction and began reading them again. His fingers reached up to seize the tip of his long nose – in his former life this had been a habit of the assistant public prosecutor's that he indulged at moments of stress.

Suddenly he jerked bodily, put down the letter and swung round to face the Bishop.

'What do you mean – "Akakii?" My son – Akakii? What sort of name is that? And Masha agreed?'

The Bishop made the sign of the cross, whispered a prayer of gratitude and pressed his lips fervently against his precious *panagia*.

He began speaking in a light, happy voice: 'I lied, Matveiushka. I wanted to shake you up. Masha hasn't give birth yet; she's still carrying the child.'

Matvei Bentsionovich frowned. 'And was it a lie about the state counsellor?'

At the sound of peals of laughter mingled with breathless panting and sobbing coming from the bedroom, the door opened without a knock, but it was not Mrs Lisitsyna who looked in, it was Dr Korovin and his assistant, both wearing white coats – they must have just got back from their rounds. They stared in fright at the crimson-faced Bishop wiping away his tears and their tousle-headed patient.

'I had never imagined, dear colleague, that entropic schizophrenia was infectious,' Korovin muttered.

His assistant exclaimed: 'That, my dear colleague, is a genuine discovery!'

When he had finished laughing and wiped away the tears, Mitrofanii told the confused assistant public prosecutor: 'I didn't lie about the new title; that would have been an unforgivable sin. So congratulations, Your Honour.'

Donat Savvich took one look at the expression on his patient's face and dashed towards him.

'Permit me if you will.' He squatted down by the bed, took Matvei Bentsionovich's pulse with one hand and began pulling his eyelids up with the other. 'What miracle is this! What did you do to him, Bishop? Hey, Mr Berdichevsky! This way! Look at me!'

'Why are you shouting like that, doctor?' the new state counsellor asked, frowning and moving away. 'I don't believe I'm deaf. And by the way, I've been meaning to tell you for a long time: you are mistaken if you believe that the patients don't hear those "asides" of yours when you and the doctors, nurses or visitors are talking to each other. You're not on a stage in a theatre.'

Korovin's jaw dropped, which looked rather strange in combination with the mask of supercilious self-confidence that the doctor had adopted so firmly as his own.

'Donat Savvich, do you serve supper here?' His Grace asked. 'I haven't had a bite since this morning. How about you, Matvei – aren't you hungry?'

Berdichevsky replied rather uncertainly, but without a trace of his former dreariness: 'I suppose something to eat would be quite nice. But where is Mrs Lisitsyna? I don't remember very clearly what happened here, but she visited me, I didn't dream it, did I?'

'Supper later! Afterwards!' Korovin shouted in great agitation. 'You must tell me immediately what exactly you remember about the events of the last two weeks! Every last detail! And you, dear colleague, take down every word in shorthand! This is of great importance for science! And you, Your Grace, you must reveal your method of treatment to me. You employed shock, didn't you? But of what kind exactly?'

'Oh no,' Mitrofanii snapped. 'First supper. And send for Pela— For Polina Andreevna. Where has she disappeared to?'

'Mrs Lisitsyna went away,' the doctor replied absent-mindedly and began shaking his head again. 'No, I have definitely never heard or read about anything like it! Not even in the *Jahrbuch für Psychopathologie und Psychotherapie*.'

'Where did she go to? When?'

'When it was still light. She asked to be taken to her hotel. She wanted to tell you something, but you would not let her in. Oh yes. Before that she wrote something in my study. And she asked me to give you an envelope and a bag of some kind. I have the envelope here; I put it in my pocket. But which one? And the bag is outside the door, in the hall.'

Without waiting to be asked, the assistant carried in the bag, which was large and made of oilcloth, but obviously not heavy.

While Korovin was patting all the numerous pockets of his white doctor's coat and frock coat, the Bishop looked into the bag. He took out a pair of tall rubber boots, an electric torch of unusual design (screened with sheets of tin to produce a small aperture) and a piece of black cloth rolled into a bundle. When he unrolled it, it proved to be a cassock with a cowl, the edges of which had been crudely sewn together with coarse thread. There was a slit in the chest, so that it could be thrown back over the head of the person wearing it, and there were two holes in it for the eyes. Puzzled, Mitrofanii stuck his finger first into one hole and then the other.

'Well, doctor, have you found the letter? Give me it.' He put on his pince-nez and muttered as he opened the sealed envelope: 'We've been doing nothing all day but read letters from a certain individual ... Look at that scrawl – like a chicken writing with its claw. She was clearly in a great hurry ...'

Another Letter

I came dashing to you, but realised it was not the right time. I have important news, but your business is a hundred times more important. May God assist you to return Matvei Bentsionovich's lost reason to him. If you succeed, then you are a genuine magician and miracle-worker.

Forgive me for not waiting and acting wilfully once again, but I do not know how long your cure will take. You said it could be a whole week, and it is quite definitely not possible to wait that long. Indeed, I believe I cannot wait at all, for God alone knows what is on this man's mind.

I am writing in haste, but nonetheless I shall try not to deviate from the correct order of exposition.

While I was waiting for you and trembling for the outcome of your difficult (perhaps even impossible?) task, I could not think what to do with myself. I began wandering round the house – at first the laboratory, and then the other rooms, which, of course, was improper on my part, but I could not get out of my head what Donat Savvich had said about not having seen Lampier for several days. Of course, the patients in the clinic are free to come and go, but even so it is rather strange. And at the same time I realised that in concentrating too much on Father Israel and Outskirts Island I had almost completely neglected the clinic – that is, the theory that the criminal might be one of its inhabitants, whereas when I recall the night when the Black Monk attacked me, my attention is directed to precisely that line of enquiry.

In the first place, who could have known about the stilts belonging to the patient who is obsessed with cleanliness and where they could be found? Only someone well informed on the habits of the clinic's residents and the arrangement of the buildings.

In the second place, who could have known where exactly Matvei Bentsionovich was being kept, so that they could frighten him at night? The answer is the same.

And the third thing. Yet again, only someone involved with the clinic could have repeatedly visited Lentochkin in the conservatory without hindrance (it is clear from what Alexei Stepanovich told me that the Black Monk used to appear to him), and then killed the poor boy and carried away the body. That is, to be absolutely precise, an outsider could have done this – after all, I was able to get into the conservatory without anyone noticing – but it would have been easier for one of the inmates.

I began to worry that something might have happened to the physicist. What if he had seen something he should not have seen and now was also lying on the bottom of the lake? I recalled disjointed statements by Lampier in which he had spoken passionately about a mystical emanation of death and some terrible danger.

And so I decided to look into the cloakroom to see if his outer clothing was there, after first asking an attendant what Mr Lampier usually wore. Apparently it was always the same: a black beret, a checked cloak with a hood, galoshes and, without exception, a large umbrella, no matter what the weather.

Imagine my alarm when I discovered all of these items together in the cloakroom! I squatted down to take a closer look at the galoshes – sometimes dried lumps of mud can tell you a great deal: how long it is since the person was last outside, what kind of soil they walked across and so forth. And then my eye was caught by the oil-cloth bag, squeezed into a dark recess behind the galosh stand.

If you have not yet had time to look inside the bag, then do so now. There you will find a full set of material evidence: the Black Monk's cassock; boots suitable for 'walking on water'; a special torch with its beam directed sideways and upwards. As you no doubt recall, I had suspected something of the kind.

For a moment I thought the things had been left there deliberately, that the criminal had planted them. But then I measured Lampier's galosh against the sole of a rubber boot and saw that they were the same size. The physicist has small feet, almost like a woman's, so there could be no mistake about it. It was as if my eyes had suddenly been opened. Everything fitted perfectly!

Well of course, the Black Monk is Lampier, the insane physicist. There is not really anyone else it could be. I ought to have guessed a lot sooner. I suspect that what happened was this.

Obsessed by a maniacal idea about some 'emanation of death' supposedly emitted by Outskirts Island, Lampier decided to scare everyone away from the 'accursed' place. We know that frequently it is only madmen's basic ideas that are insane, while in putting them into practice they are capable of truly miraculous skill and cunning.

First the physicist invented the trick with Basilisk walking on water – the bench hidden under the water, the cowl, the cunning torch, the sepulchral voice telling the frightened witness: 'Go and tell everyone. This place shall be cursed' – and other things in the same vein. This device was effective, but not effective enough.

Then Lampier moved his performance on to dry land and even committed an act of undiluted villainy in the death of the buoy-keeper's wife and then of the buoy-keeper himself. Insanity of this kind is prone to grow worse, impelling the maniac to ever more monstrous actions.

I have already described to you how the attacks on Alyosha, Felix Stanislavovich and Matvei Bentsionovich were carried out. I am sure that is precisely how everything happened.

However, Lampier was afraid that Lentochkin or Berdichevsky might recover from their terrible shock and remember some detail or other that could lead back to the criminal. So he continued to frighten them even in the clinic.

Lentochkin was in a truly pitiful state; it did not require much to deal with him. But Lampier paid especial attention to Berdichevsky, who had retained the rudiments of memory and coherence. He arranged for Matvei Bentsionovich to be moved into his cottage, where Basilisk's victim would be under constant surveillance by the Black Monk himself. Nothing could have been easier for the physicist than to frighten Berdichevsky at night. All he had to do was go outside, get up on the stilts, and knock on the first floor window.

I also remembered that when I stole into Matvei Bentsionovich's bedroom, Lampier's bed was empty. I thought that he was working in the laboratory, but in fact he was outside, dressed as Basilisk and preparing for another performance. When I surprised him by suddenly climbing out through the window and jumping down to the ground, he had no choice but to stun me with a blow from a wooden stilt.

This is what I wanted to tell you when I dared to glance into the room. You drove me away, and you were right to do so. It has worked out for the best.

I began thinking again. Where had Lampier got to? And why had he not taken his outer clothing? He had not been seen for several days – did that perhaps mean since the very night that Alexei Stepanovich was killed?

I recalled that appalling scene: the boat, the silhouette of the Black Monk, the naked, emaciated body thrown overboard. And I suddenly realised – a boat! Lampier had a boat!

What for? Could it have been for making secret visits to Outskirts Island?

I sat down at the desk and quickly wrote down all of the holy elder Israel's utterances, six in all. In my previous letter, I informed you I had sensed that these words contained some secret message, but I simply could not decipher its meaning.

Here are these brief phrases as they were spoken day by day:

'Today dost Thou release Thy servant – the death.'
'Thine are the most glorious heavens – of Theognost.'
'And then David's heart did tremble – is obscure.'
'Let him who has ears hear – cuckoo loose.'
'Thus the leach creates a mixture – nonfat sit.'
'Do not mourn, for he is well – mona koom.'

I have separated off the final words of each phrase, because they were added to Holy Scripture by the abbot himself. What if the secret message is only contained in the conclusion of each utterance? I thought.

I wrote out the final words in a single line, and this is what was produced: 'The death – of Theognost – is obscure – cuckoo loose – nonfat sit – mona koom.'

At first I thought it was nonsense, but I read it a second time, and a third, and a fourth, and the light dawned.

There is not one message here, but two, each in three parts! And the meaning of the first is perfectly clear! The death of Theognost is obscure.

That is what the holy elder wished to communicate to the senior brothers in the monastery! – that the circumstances of the death of the hermit Theognost, whose place became free six days ago, were suspicious. Then after that he added this from the Apocalypse: 'Let him who has ears hear' – the monks had not heard; they had not understood.

What exactly does 'his death is obscure' mean? Could it

possibly be a reference to murder? And if so, then who killed the holy elder and for what end?

The answer was given in the second message, which I puzzled over for a long time. Then I realised 'mona koom' is 'monachum', the Latin for 'monk'. It was in Latin! 'Cuckoo loose' was *cucullus* – a cowl. And 'nonfat sit' was *non facit*. The complete phrase was: *'Cucullus non facit monachum'* – or, 'Not everyone in a cowl is a monk'!

But why in Latin? I asked myself, before I realised the full meaning of these words. The father steward, to whom all the abbot's utterances were reported, was hardly likely to understand a foreign language, and the ignorant Brother Kleopa would only mangle gibberish of that kind. The holy elder Israel must have understood that.

So the Latin phrase was not addressed to the brother monks, but to me. On the last three days the hermit had only looked at me, as if he wished to emphasise that.

How could he know that a modest novice with a black eye knew Latin? It is a mystery! But one thing is certainly clear: Israel wanted me alone to understand him. He evidently did not trust the father steward's acumen.

Then my thoughts turned back again to the most important point and I discovered the meaning of the Latin riddle. I realised what the holy elder had wanted to say! The new wearer of a hermit's cowl was not Father Ilarii! It was the criminal, Lampier! That was where he had disappeared to; that was why he was nowhere to be seen; that was why all his clothes were still at the house!

The physicist had crossed over to Outskirts Island! And in that case, on that night he must have committed not one murder but two; and there must have been two dead bodies! It was simply that the moon had peeped out from behind the clouds too briefly and I had only seen half of the terrible ritual. The villain has stopped Lentochkin's mouth for ever, but God only knows why he has spared Berdichevsky. Perhaps not all feelings die, even in a heart that is hardened by insanity, and Lampier had become attached to Matvei Bentsionovich during the days he spent together with him under the same roof.

That night the maniac crept into the Farewell Chapel, where Father Ilarii was preparing alone for his heroic feat of asceticism, praying and sewing up his cowl. A murder was committed. And in the morning the person who came out to the boat in a black shroud was not the holy elder, but the criminal.

I do not know and I cannot even guess what monstrous fantasies govern this clouded reason. Perhaps he intends to kill the other two hermits as well?

Having arrived at this idea, I almost came dashing to your room again. After all, it was a matter of people's lives, you would have forgiven me! We had to go to the hermitage immediately and unmask the pretender!

I already had my hand on the door handle, but then I was overcome by doubt.

What if I were mistaken? What if Lampier was not on Outskirts Island and I induced you to violate the seclusion of the holy hermitage? The consequences of such an act would be appalling. No outsider had set foot there for eight centuries! A bishop would not be forgiven for such sacrilege. You would be trampled into the dirt, hounded and defiled – Father Vitalii would do his best to make sure of that. What a loss that would be for the province! And not only the province – for the whole of the Orthodox Church!

But what could they do to a stupid, curious woman? The worst they could do to her would be to send her away in disgrace on the next sailing of the steamer.

So I decided to act as follows. I shall go into the town and change into my novice's clothes. Then I shall make my way to Lenten Spit, where Brother Kleopa's boat is moored. As soon as it is dark (and it gets dark early these days), I shall row across to Outskirts Island – God grant that no one sees me from the shore.

I shall verify my assumptions in the hermitage and come back. If I am mistaken, there will be no harm done. The holy elder Israel would need to recite the entire Bible to expose my unprecedented audacity – at a rate of one or two words a day. And those slow-witted monks in Ararat will never understand anyway.

It is very possible that I might return before you have left Matvei Bentsionovich's room. I hope to find him resurrected to life through the grace of God and the wisdom of your heart.

Do not be angry with me.

Your daughter Pelagia

The Final Day: Evening

Mitrofanii read the final lines of the letter with his beard clutched in his hand, and when he finished reading, he began rushing round the room. He dashed to the door, stopped and turned to Berdichevsky.

'Disaster, Matvei, disaster! Ah, that wild hothead has gone to the hermitage! She was afraid for me! Afraid they would accuse me of sacrilege! It's not sacrilege we need to be afraid of, it's that he will kill her!'

'Who will kill whom?' Berdichevsky asked in amazement, still not thinking too clearly for lack of practice – and indeed, how could he think clearly, when he had not read the latest letter?

His Grace thrust the letter into his hand and went running to the doctor: 'Quickly, quickly, we must go! What is one more murder to him!'

'And just who is "he"?' asked Korovin, also unable to understand.

'That physicist of yours, Lampier! He is the Black Monk; it has been definitely proved now! And he is a murderer too! He has hidden on Outskirts Island! And Pelagia – I mean Lisitsyna – has taken a boat there! Straight into the wolf's jaws!'

Meanwhile the assistant public prosecutor shook his head doubtfully before he had even read very much of the letter. 'Lampier on Outskirts Island! What do you mean, Father? That's not where he is!'

'Where, then?' asked Mitrofanii, swinging round.

'There,' said Berdichevsky, gesturing downwards with his hand. 'Under the ground.'

The Bishop froze. Had his cure not been complete? Or had the ravings begun again?

'I mean to say, he's in the basement,' Matvei Bentsionovich explained. 'He set up another laboratory for himself some time ago, and he's working there now. I helped him to carry some sheets of metal down there; he tore them off the roof. Sergei Nikolaevich told me something about some emanation and some dangerous experiments of his, but I didn't understand a thing – I was still in a trance. And the instruments are all in the basement now. He hardly ever comes out of there. He might just pop out once a day, eat a piece of bread and then go back down.'

The assistant public prosecutor spoke slowly, choosing his words with difficulty – he had clearly not yet recovered completely, but he did not seem like a madman.

'Where is this basement?' the Bishop asked the doctor, not knowing if he should believe what he had just heard. Perhaps the basement did not even exist.

'Over this way, follow me.'

Dr Korovin led the others out into the hallway and into a closet, and from there down a stone stairway. It was dark, and his assistant struck a match.

'There is the door. But it was empty, and there was no laboratory . . .' Without finishing what he was saying, Korovin pulled the handle of the door towards him, and an unearthly reddish light streamed out through the opening. They could hear a quiet clicking and the tinkling of glass vessels.

Mitrofanii glanced inside and saw a small figure in a loose blouse leaning over a long table crowded with instruments and tools. The lamp glowing on the ceiling was shrouded in a red scarf – hence the strange light.

The man hunched over the table was looking through some complicated kind of microscope at a small vice holding a black plate of metal in a vertical position. There was an empty flask standing on a special stand behind the plate. But no, it was not empty – there was a tiny pile of some kind of powder, or perhaps fine sand, glittering inside it.

The researcher was so absorbed in his observations that he did not hear the sound of footsteps. His appearance was strange: he had a fireman's helmet on his head and a zinc basin tied to his chest – the ordinary kind that is used for washing laundry.

'So that's where the helmet from the fire panel got to,' the assistant said in a low voice. 'Frolov came to me and complained, but I didn't want to bother you over such a trifle, Donat Savvich.'

Without answering his assistant, Korovin stepped forward and said in a loud voice: 'Mr Lampier! Sergei Nikolaevich! What are all these underground mysteries?'

The little man glanced round and waved his arms at his visitors: 'Out, out! You mustn't! Nothing can stop it! Nothing! Tried iron, tried copper, steel. Not zinc – like a knife through butter. Going to try tin plate.' He gestured towards a piece of roofing metal lying on the edge of the table. 'Then lead, then silver! Something must contain it!' Lying beside the tin plate there was another sheet of metal with a dull sheen and a much brighter silver tray.

'I see,' Korovin said. 'The tray was stolen from my pantry. Lampier, I see that in addition to all your other pathological conditions you are a kleptomaniac too! Shame on you, Sergei Nikolaevich. And you such an apologist for morality.'

The physicist was embarrassed and he began muttering inarticulately: 'Yes, not good. But where? Time! No one, not anyone! All myself! And gold as well. Very hopeful. And noble metals! Or straight to platinum, like with like? But where, where?'

Mitrofanii moved forward and looked down at Lampier's puny frame. 'Sir, I am going to ask you some questions. And you answer me clearly, with no concealment.'

The scientist looked the Bishop up and down with his head on one side. Then he suddenly jumped up on the chair and tugged the red material off the lamp and the light in the room became normal.

Even standing on the chair Lampier was not much taller than the Bishop. The strange man put his hand into the pocket of his blouse, took out a large pair of spectacles with violet lenses, set them on his nose and began inspecting the Bishop again, this time more thoroughly.

'Ah, ah,' he cackled, 'so much light blue! And orange, orange! Never so much! A wonderful spectrum! Ah, if only sooner! You can! Tell them! They're such! Even this one!' he said, pointing to Korovin. 'I tell, and he jabs me! Others are worse! Crimson, all crimson! Must do something! Quick! Can't stop it!'

The Bishop frowned, waiting for Lampier to calm down.

'Don't play the holy fool. I know everything. Are these yours?' He gestured to Berdichevsky, and the assistant public prosecutor, who had positioned himself under the lamp in order to read Pelagia's letter, took the cassock, boots and torch out of the bag, then stuck his nose back in the sheets of paper again. He seemed entirely uninterested in the interrogation.

At the sight of the incontrovertible proof, Lampier started blinking and sniffing loudly – in short, he was embarrassed, but not as greatly as before, when the doctor had discovered his theft. 'Mine, yes. How else? No one! Invented. All crimson. Don't understand, then not interfere. Shame.'

'Why did you act out this sacrilegious performance?' asked the Bishop, raising his voice. 'Why did you frighten people?'

Lampier pressed his hands to his chest and began jabbering even more rapidly. It was clear that he was struggling as hard as he could to explain something very important to him, and he simply could not comprehend why they refused to understand him: 'Ah, yes, me! All crimson, impenetrable. I tried. That faceless one! Not a word! Told him!' he said, pointing at Korovin again. 'Injected me! Rubbish! My head two days! Don't hear! Voice in wilderness!'

'He's talking about the soporific injection that I was obliged to prescribe for him,' the doctor explained. 'Well, he really bears a grudge – that was three months ago. He was seriously over-excited at the time. Worse than now. But afterwards he slept for twenty-four hours, he was calmer. He kept trying to give me a notebook so that I could read his notes. How could I – there was nothing in it but formulae. And crooked scribblings in the margins with thousands of exclamation marks, about the "emanation of death".'

'Make clearer!' Lampier shouted despairingly, with saliva spraying from his mouth. 'Need other way. Thought! Not matter of death! Can't be stopped! Perhaps "penetration"? Goes through everything! But "penetrating emanation" is unpronounceable!'

'So you don't deny that you dressed up as Basilisk and walked on the water, shining this complicated torch from behind your back?' the Bishop interrupted.

'Yes, superstition with superstition. Since they don't hear. Oh, very cunning.'

'And you threatened the buoy-keeper through the window and scratched the glass with a nail? And then you attacked Lentochkin in the hut, and Lagrange, and Matvei Bentsionovich?'

'What hut?' Lampier muttered. 'Nail on glass – brrrr, repulsive!' he shuddered. 'To hell with hut! Most important thing! Everything else nonsense!'

'And you didn't knock on Matvei Berdichevsky's window, wearing stilts?'

The physicist was astonished: 'Why stilts? Why knock?'

The assistant public prosecutor finished reading the letter and said in a quiet voice: 'Bishop, it could not have been Sergei Nikolaevich. She is mistaken. Judge for yourself. Sergei Nikolaevich knew that I had been moved from the first floor down to the ground floor that night. Why would he have needed the stilts? No, it was someone else. Someone who was not aware that I had been moved to the ground-floor bedroom.'

Berdichevsky's capacity for logical thought had apparently been restored, and His Grace was glad of it. But this meant . . .

'Then there was another Basilisk?' The Bishop shook his head sharply so that he could think clearly. 'A violent one? – who struck

Pelagia, and before that attacked you, Alyosha and Lagrange in the same way. But that is absurd!'

Berdichevsky remarked cautiously: 'I am not prepared to draw any conclusions as yet. But take a look at Sergei Nikolaevich. Would he have had the strength to lift up an unconscious body and put it in a coffin, while standing on a chair? He might have managed Lentochkin, although it's doubtful, but he definitely could not have lifted me. I have heavy bones, I weigh more than five *poods*.'

Mitrofanii looked at Berdichevsky as if he were assessing his weight, and then at the skinny physicist. He sighed. 'Very well, Mr Lampier. But where were you that night! When Matvei Bentsionovoich was moved into your bedroom?'

'Where? Here.' The scientist gestured round the walls of the basement and then jabbed his finger at the instruments. 'Brought everything important here. Stone walls after all. Never mind me, researcher. But he' – Lampier nodded at Berdichevsky – 'mustn't. Dangerous.'

'Just what is so dangerous?' the Bishop exclaimed in exasperation, tired of listening to these ravings. 'What is this danger you keep talking about all the time?'

Lampier said nothing, squinting at the doctor and licking his lips nervously.

'Word?' he asked His Grace in a quiet voice.

'What word?'

'Honour. Not interrupt. Or inject.'

'Word. I won't interrupt and I won't allow anyone to give you any injections. Speak, only slowly. Don't excite yourself.'

But this was still not enough for Lampier. 'On this,' he said, pointing to His Grace's chest and the Bishop, having apparently learned to understand the little man's speech a little, kissed his *panagia*.

Then Lampier nodded in satisfaction and began his explanation, struggling with all his might to speak as clearly as possible.

'Emanation. Penetrating rays. My name. Masha wants a different one. But I like this one.'

'Rays again!' Donat Savvich groaned. 'No, gentlemen, say what you will, but I have not kissed the cross, so come, dear colleague, let us go out into the fresh air.' The two medical men walked out of the basement and Sergei Nikolaevich immediately became calmer.

'I know. Speak wrongly. Always ahead. Words too slow. More advanced communications system. Convey thoughts. Thought about it. Electromagnetism? Or biological impulses? Then all understand me. Thoughts directly – eye to eye – that would be best. No, eyes are bad.' He suddenly became agitated. 'Pluck eyes out! They only confuse! But I mustn't. Everything by sight. Sight is deception, false information. What doesn't exist, yes – but important things missed. Wretched instrument.' Lampier pointed to his eye with his finger. 'Only seven colours in the spectrum! But there are a thousand, a million, countless!'

Then he suddenly shook his head and clasped his hands together in front of himself. 'No-no, not about that. About penetration. I'll try. Slowly. Word!' The physicist gave the Bishop a frightened look, in case he might stop listening or turn away. But no, Mitrofanii was listening closely, patiently.

'Outskirts is there, yes?' Lampier asked, pointing to the right.

'Yes,' said the Bishop, although he had no idea in which direction the hermitage lay from there.

'Legend, yes? Basilisk. Fiery finger from heavens, burning pine.'

'Yes of course, that is a legend,' the Bishop agreed. 'Religion includes many magical traditions; they reflect the human longing for the miraculous. We have to interpret these stories allegorically, not in the literal sense.'

'Precisely literal!' Lampier cried. 'Literal! Happened. The finger, the pine! There are coals. Fossilised, clearly a trunk!'

'Wait, wait, my son,' Mitrofanii put in. 'How could you have seen the scorched trunk of that pine? Have you . . .' The Bishop's eyes opened wide. '. . . Have you been on Outskirts Island?'

Lampier nodded as if that was nothing out of the ordinary.

'But . . . but what for?'

'Needed good emanation. Plenty of bad, grey-coloured. Not rare. Pure orange, like yours, almost never. Not even precise shade. Needed it – for science. Thought and thought. Eureka! Hermits righteous, yes? So powerful moral emanation! Logic! Test and measure. Yes? Very simple. Took boat at night and went.'

'You took a boat to the hermitage to measure the hermits' moral emanation?' the Bishop asked in a dubious tone of voice. 'With those violet spectacles of yours?'

Lampier nodded, delighted to have been understood.

'But that is absolutely forbidden!'

'Nonsense. Superstition.'

His Grace was about to wax indignant and he even knitted his brows in a frown, but curiosity proved stronger than righteous wrath.

'And what is there on the island?'

'Hill, pines, cave, kingdom of death. Bald. Repellent. Not important, sphere the main thing.'

'What?'

'Sphere. Like this. Passage, chambers along sides. Inside, under summit – round.'

'What is round?'

'Cave. Fell in. Through roof. Then hole, roots, grass, earth, not visible now. But trunk still. Eight hundred years, visible! Coals. Sphere, like big, big pumpkin. Even bigger, like …' – Lampier looked around – 'like an armchair.'

'In a round cave below the summit of the hill, there is a sphere,' Mitrofanii summed up. 'What sort of sphere is it?'

'I just. From above. Broke ceiling. When Basilisk. Meteorite. Fell, broke through, set pine on fire. Visible night faraway. He saw.'

'Who, Saint Basilisk?' The Bishop wiped his forehead. 'Wait. You are trying to tell me that eight hundred years ago he saw some kind of heavenly body fall to earth. He took it for the finger of God pointing the way, walked across the water and found the island at night because of the burning pine tree?'

'You can't walk on water,' the physicist observed with unexpected coherence. 'Relative density won't permit it. He didn't walk. He had a boat or something. That's not important. What's important is what's there. In the cave I fell into.'

'And what is there?'

'Uranium. Heard of it? You know it? Pitchblende. Deposit.'

His Grace thought for a moment and nodded. 'Yes, yes, I read something in the *Physics Herald*. Uranium is a natural element that possesses unusual properties. Together with another element, radium, it is presently being studied by the finest minds of Europe. And pitchblende, if I am not mistaken, is a mineral with a very high content of uranium. Is that right?'

'Cleric, but you follow. Good,' Sergei Nikolaevich said approvingly. 'Light-blue aura. Good head.'

'Never mind my head. What about this pitchblende of yours?'

Lampier drew himself upright. 'My discovery. Nucleus starts to divide. Spontaneously. Special mechanism required. Invented a name: "Nuclear Factor". Incredibly difficult conditions. So far impossible. Theoretically can in nature. Very rare conditions. But there it was! A unique instance.' He dashed across to the table and began rustling the pages of a plump notebook. 'Look, look! It splits! Look! Meteorite, extremely high temperature – one. Deposit of pitchblende – two! Underground sources – three! That's all! The factor! Natural! Worked it out! Energy of the nucleus, a chain! Once started, can't be stopped Eight hundred years! I sent Masha and Toto a letter! No, they don't believe! Think I'm mad! Because I write from a madhouse!'

'Wait a moment, will you!' Mitrofanii implored him. The strain had brought beads of sweat out on the Bishop's brow. 'The fall of the meteorite into the deposit set off some kind of natural mechanism that started giving out energy. I don't understand anything about it, but assume everything is just as you say it is. But where is the danger in all this?'

'Don't know. Not doctor. Didn't write in notebook, because don't know. But am certain. Absolutely. I was there a few hours – nausea, then fever. Hermits always there. So they die. Six months, a year, death. A crime! Should be closed! But no one. Don't listen! Went to one with the skull. He raised his hand...'

'What skull?' His Grace asked, confused again. 'Who are you talking about?'

'On forehead. Right here. One with no face, with holes. There.' And once again the physicist gestured in the direction of Outskirts Island.

'A hermit. The holy elder Israel? With a skull and crossbones embroidered on his cowl?'

'Yes. The head. Went to Korovin, injected me. Notebook, didn't read it.' Sergei Nikolaevich's voice began to tremble as he recalled the old injury. 'Thought and thought. Invented Black Monk. Frighten. Cursed place. Then research in peace. No interference.'

'But how did you discover the emanation? I remember reading that radiation of that kind cannot be perceived by the sense organs.'

Lampier smiled proudly. 'Not immediately. First sample sphere. Realised straight away, meteorite. Fused surface. Rainbow colours. Especially with torch. Mystery of hermitage. Sacred. Holy elders' secret. Eight hundred years. Reason for silence. Couldn't give it away. Sample one way, another. No good. Exceptionally hard. Came back. Tempered steel file. No use. Then diamond file. From Antwerp by post. It worked. Quarter of an hour – look, three grams.' He pointed to the little pile of powder in the flask. 'Enough for analysis.'

'You ordered a diamond file by post from Antwerp?' Mitrofanii asked, mopping up his sweat with his handkerchief and feeling that his head, no matter how blue its aura might be, could not take in so much astounding information. 'But surely that must have been very expensive?'

'Possibly. No matter. Korovin has lots of money.'

'And Donat Savvich did not even ask why you needed such a strange instrument?'

'He asked. I was glad. Explaining – waved his arms about. "I don't wish to hear about the emanation, you'll have your file.' Let him think. I got it.'

The Bishop cast a curious glance at the table. 'But where is it? What does it look like?'

The scientist shrugged casually. 'Disappeared. Ages ago. Never mind, not needed now. Don't interrupt with stupid questions!' he said angrily. 'You kissed the cross! Listen!'

'Yes, yes, my son, forgive me,' His Grace said reassuringly, and turned to see if Berdichevsky was listening. He was, very attentively, but to judge from his wrinkled brow he did not understand very much. Unlike the Bishop, Matvei Bentsionovich did not take any great interest in the latest news of scientific progress; he read almost nothing apart from legal journals and, naturally, he had never heard about the mysterious properties of radium and uranium.

'So what did the analysis of the meteoritic material show?' the Bishop asked.

'Platinum-iridium nugget. From up there.' Lampier jabbed his finger towards the ceiling. 'Sometimes from space. Rare, never so huge. Of course steel file useless. Density of twenty-two! Only diamond. No way to move it. Hundred and fifty, two hundred *poods*.'

'Two hundred *poods* of platinum!' the assistant public prosecutor gasped. 'But that is immensely valuable! How much is an ounce of platinum worth?'

Sergei Nikolaevich shrugged. 'No idea. But no value, only danger. Eight hundred years, penetrated through. Found them: rays.' He nodded at the flask. 'Pass through everything. Exactly as Toto wrote. About photographic film. And Masha wrote. Earlier. Korovin wrote a letter. Said I'm in a madhouse. They don't write now.'

'Yes, yes, I read about the experiments with radium radiation in Paris,' the Bishop recalled. 'They were carried out by Antoine Becquerel, and a married couple, the Curies. Pierre and Marie.'

'Pierrot is crimson-head,' Lampier snapped. 'Not good. Masha shouldn't have. Better an old maid. But Toto Becquerel is clever – blue. Talk about them all the time: Masha and Toto. Ignoramuses! And Korovin too! Fine island! I went to quayside, looked through spectroscope. Find someone intelligent. Who could help. Explain to them. I couldn't. Good you're here. You understand, yes?'

He looked at the Bishop in fear and hope. 'You understand?'

Mitrofanii walked over to the table, cautiously picked up the flask and looked at the filings glinting dully inside it. 'So the nugget is polluted with harmful rays?'

'Through and through. Whole cave. Eight hundred years! Even six hundred, all the same. Not island, a gallows.' Sergei Nikolaevich grabbed hold of the sleeve of the Bishop's cassock. 'You are their superior! Forbid it! So that no one! Not one! Bring those back! If it's not too late. But no, too late to bring them. I heard, a new one just sent. Hasn't been in the round cave, not long. Can be saved. Not the earlier two. But this one. How long is he there? Five days? Six?'

'He means the new hermit, the one that Pelagia was mistaken about,' Berdichevsky explained to the Bishop, who was frowning perplexedly. 'Well, well, the idea never even entered my head that your nun and Mrs Lisitsyna were the same person.'

'I'll explain to you about that,' Mitrofanii said, embarrassed. 'You see, according to the monastery's charter, it is absolutely impermissible, scandalous even, but—'

'Stop this stupid nonsense,' said Lampier, tugging unceremoniously at the Bishop's cassock. 'Take those out. Don't let any more in. Only me. Need screening material. Looking. Nothing so far. Copper no, steel no, tin plate no. Perhaps lead. Or silver. You're intelligent. I'll show you.'

He pulled the Bishop over to the table, leafed through the pages of the notebook and began running his finger over the calculations and formulae. Mitrofanii watched with interest and sometimes even nodded – either out of politeness or because he really did understand something.

Berdichevsky looked as well, peeping over Sergei Nikolaevich's narrow shoulder. He sighed. Something jingled four times in his waistcoat pocket.

'Good Lord! Your Grace!' the assistant public prosecutor exclaimed. 'Four o'clock in the morning! And Polina Andreevna, Pelagia, still isn't back! Could something have happened . . .'

He choked and stopped without finishing his question when he saw the sudden change in Mitrofanii's face as it contorted into a grimace of alarm and guilt. Pushing aside the fascinating notebook, the Bishop abruptly gathered up his cassock and dashed out of the basement and up the stairs with his shoes clattering.

The Cave

When Polina Andreevna called in to the Immaculate Virgin on her way from the clinic, to collect the things she needed for her expedition, there was an unpleasant surprise waiting for her in her room.

The precautionary measures taken to protect Lagrange's dangerous legacy from curious members of staff had failed. While still in the vestibule Lisitsyna noticed the attendant on duty looking at her in a rather strange way – with either suspicion or fear. And when she glanced into the travelling bag, she discovered that someone had been rummaging in it: the glove with the bullet-hole was not lying in the same way as before, and the revolver was also wrapped rather differently in the drawers.

Never mind, Polina Andreevna told herself. She might as well be hanged for a sheep as for a lamb. If she got away with her nocturnal expedition, then the matter of the gun could be managed somehow. The Bishop would smooth things over. But she could deal with it even more simply than that. When she was changing in the pavilion she could take the revolver out of the travelling bag and hide it there, and if the monastery's peace-keepers came calling, she could tell them the half-witted maid had imagined it. Come now, what would a pilgrim want with a gun?

In any case, one way or another she had to take the travelling bag with her. She put several candles and some matches into it. What else did she need? Nothing, really. She sat down for a moment before her journey and crossed herself. Then she set off into the gathering twilight.

She had to wait a long time on the waterfront by the pavilion. It had been a clear, windless evening and there were so many people still out strolling that she simply had no chance to slip in behind the little wooden structure without attracting attention to herself. Polina Andreevna walked to and fro, huddled up in her long cloak, burning with impatience, but still there were as many people in the street as ever. A group of elderly women had stopped right in front of the pavilion and launched into a discussion of the provincial prelate's arrival – a colossal event by the standards of New Ararat. Numerous suppositions and guesses were voiced, and it was clear that the pilgrims' animated discussion would continue for a long time yet.

Do I really need to change? Polina Andreevna suddenly thought. A novice and a woman were prohibited alike from visiting Outskirts Island. And she would be held doubly responsible for the masquerade. For a woman to dress up in monk's robes was not simply blasphemous, it was probably a criminal offence as well. And so she abandoned her wait and went as she was, in her woman's clothes and carrying the travelling bag.

As we have already observed, it was a bright, moonlit night and Lisitsyna found Brother Kleopa's boat very quickly. She looked along the Canaan shoreline – all was quiet; not a single soul. As she embarked, she whispered a prayer and then started pulling on the oars.

Outskirts Island came drifting towards her out of the darkness, round and overgrown with pine trees that made it look like a prickly hedgehog. The keel of the boat scraped repulsively on the bottom and the prow nudged into the gravel.

Polina Andreevna sat there and listened. The only sounds were the splashing of the oars and the sleepy rustling of the pine needles.

She weighed the boat's chain down with a heavy stone and

set off to walk round the island, moving in a gentle upwards spiral. If not for the moon, she would have been unlikely to find the hermitage: a small dark door of oak surrounded by an uneven border of moss-covered stones.

The little door was set straight into the slope on the side facing towards the lake, not Canaan – the side on which the sun rose in the morning.

Mrs Lisitsyna was anything but timid, but she had to summon up her courage before she took hold of the bronze ring.

She pulled on it gently, prepared to discover that the hermitage was bolted shut for the night. But no, the door yielded easily. And indeed, who was there to lock the door against here?

The creak was not loud, but in the absolute silence it sounded so clear that the sacrilegious trespasser shivered. But she only paused for a brief moment before tugging on the ring again.

Beyond the door there was darkness. Not like the darkness outside, permeated with a silvery glow, but genuine pitch-darkness that smelled of something musty and something else very specific – either wax or mice or old wood. Or perhaps it was simply the dust that had accumulated over the centuries?

When the spy stepped forward and closed the door behind her, God's world seemed to disappear, swallowed up by the gloom and the silence, leaving nothing but the strange smell as a reminder of itself.

Polina Andreevna stood there and sniffed, waiting a while for her eyes to grow accustomed to the darkness. But they did not – evidently no light at all penetrated into this place, not even the tiniest amount.

She took the matches out of the travelling bag, struck one and lit a candle.

A wide gallery led into the depths of the hill, its high vaulted ceiling lost in darkness. Its walls were uneven and a vague white colour – lined with blocks of limestone, or perhaps shell rock. Mrs Lisitsyna raised her candle higher and screamed.

And with good reason. These were no blocks of stone, but dead bodies laid one on top of another in a stack taller than the height of a man. Not skeletons, but remains desiccated with age, mummies with tautly stretched skin, sunken eyelids and mouths, their hands folded devoutly on their chests. When she saw the bony fingers of the upmost body, with its long, curved nails, Polina Andreevna gave a quiet gasp. How terrifying!

She wanted to get past the terrible place as quickly as possible – no matter where she might come to. The rows of the dead stretched on and on; there were hundreds and hundreds of them. The ones lying closest to the entrance were almost naked, barely covered by scraps of rotted clothing – they were obviously the most ancient burials. After them the walls gradually grew darker as the hermits' robes were better preserved. But the cowls that had covered the faces of the holy elders in life had all been slit open, and Mrs Lisitsyna was struck by the incredible similarity between all of these dead heads: smooth cranium, no eyebrows, no moustache, no beard, not even any eyelashes – the pious hermits were all as alike each other as brothers; and this discovery suddenly dissipated the fear that had been driving Polina Andreevna to turn and run as fast her legs could carry her away from this kingdom of death.

It was not a kingdom of death at all, she told herself, but the gateway to Heaven. Something like a cloakroom, where pure souls left their outer clothing before entering into their bright dwelling. There were the clothes, no longer needed. Lying there and decaying.

But in fact they were not even decaying very fast, the intrepid investigator told herself. All these bodies had not belonged to ordinary people, but to holy elders. And therefore their remains were incorruptible. There should have been a stench of dead flesh and decay, but if anything had decayed here, then it was Time itself. That was what the smell was: the decay of Time.

She walked on between the walls of heaped-up bodies, no

longer afraid of anything. And then the remains came to an end. Polina Andreevna saw a bare stone wall on her left, and on her right the row of bodies was incomplete, with only three bodies lying one on top of the other.

Leaning down over the top body, she saw that this man had died recently. A bald head gleamed between the folds of the slit cowl: the hairless, wrinkled face seemed to be sleeping, not dead.

The holy elder Theognost. It was a week since he had passed on, and there was no smell of decay at all. Or could the composition of the air be different here, in the cave? Polina Andreevna decisively dismissed this last thought as sacrilegious and undoubtedly prompted by the Eternal Doubter and Enemy of Man. He was a holy elder – that was why he was not decaying.

The gallery led on further, into the pitch-darkness and up a gentle incline. And from up ahead, out of the very heart of the hill, she suddenly heard a faint sound, alarming and terribly unpleasant, as if somewhere in the distance someone was scraping an iron claw across a sheet of glass.

Mrs Lisitsyna shuddered. She took a few steps forward, and the sound disappeared. Had she imagined it?

No, a moment later the claw set about its scraping once again. Her heart skipped a beat: bats! Oh Lord, give me strength and protect me from stupid womanish fears. What was wrong with bats? There was nothing dangerous about them. And it wasn't true that they sucked blood; that was just a childish fantasy.

She halted in indecision, peering into the ominous darkness, and then suddenly took several quick steps forward: the gallery continued onwards, but at this point she could see the vague outlines of three doors in its walls, two on the right, one on the left. There was a thin strip of light under the door on the left.

The hermits' cells! Her timid fear of loathsome flying creatures was immediately forgotten. She had no time for such nonsense when there in front of her was the goal for which she had risked all these horrors!

Lisitsyna crept up to the door with the light seeping from under it. Just like the outer door, it had no bolt, but its hinges were well oiled, and when Polina Andreevna pulled it gently towards her it did not creak or squeak.

She had to blow out her candle.

Pressing her eye to the narrow crack, she saw a crude table, illuminated by an oil lamp and a man leaning over a book (she heard the rustle of a page being turned). The man was sitting with his back to her and his head was as perfectly smooth and shiny as the head of a pawn on a chessboard.

Lisitsyna opened the door a bit further to get a better look at the cell – only the tiniest little bit, but this time it betrayed her and squeaked.

The chair scraped on the floor and the sitter swung round sharply. Against the light she could not see his face, but there was a double white border on the front of his cassock, the sign of the rank of abbot. The holy elder Israel!

Polina Andreevna panicked and slammed the door, which was stupid. She was suddenly left in pitch-darkness and in her fright she even forgot in which direction the exit lay. But how could she run anyway, when she could not see a thing?

She froze there in the absolute blackness, where there was nothing but that stealthy, harrowing scraping sound: kshi-ik, kshi-ik, kshi-ik. Any moment now she would feel a webbed wing brush against her cheek!

But she was only left standing there for a few seconds. The door opened, lighting up the gallery.

The abbot of the hermitage was standing in the doorway, holding a lamp. His cranium was as naked as the deceased Theognost's had been, and he also had no beard or moustache – but at least he had eyebrows and eyelashes, or the sight would have been absolutely terrifying. Set at the centre of his naked face was a large, aristocratic nose, above a plump-lipped mouth; and Polina recognised the piercing gaze of those black eyes, even though she had only seen them through the holes in a cowl.

The holy elder shook his bald head and spoke in a familiar voice – low and slightly husky. 'So you did come. You guessed the riddle. You are a brave one.' He did not seem very surprised at the appearance of an uninvited guest in the hermitage in the middle of the night.

But that was not why Polina Andreevna was taken aback. 'Holy father, do you talk?' she gasped.

'Not with them,' said Israel, nodding towards the doors on the other side of the gallery, 'but to myself, when I am alone. Come in. It is not permitted to be in the Approach at night.'

'Where? The Approach? The approach to what?' Mrs Lisitsyna looked further along the gallery. 'And why is it not permitted?'

Israel did not answer the first question. To the second he replied: 'The charter forbids it. From sunset until dawn, we must be in our cells, devoting ourselves to reading, prayer and sleep. Come in.'

He moved aside, and she stepped into the cell, a narrow chamber cut into the rock, its only furnishings a table, a chair and a palliasse lying in the corner. There was a dark icon hanging on the wall, with a flickering icon lamp, and in another corner there was a small stove, with its chimney running straight into the low ceiling, where there was also a dark slit, no doubt an air duct.

So this is how salvation is attained, Lisitsyna thought mournfully as she surveyed the squalid dwelling. This is the place where prayers are offered for the whole of mankind.

The hermit looked at his nocturnal visitor in a strange manner, as if he were waiting for something or perhaps wished to make sure of something. His gaze was so intense that it made Polina Andreevna shudder.

'Lovely ...' the holy father said in a barely audible voice. 'Beautiful. Even better than beautiful – full of life. And there is nothing, nothing at all.' He crossed himself with sweeping movements and declared in a different, joyful voice: 'Saved! Delivered! The Lord has freed me!'

His eyes were no longer alert and probing – they seemed to be filled with light, they glowed. 'Sit on the chair,' he said gently. 'Let me take a better look at you.'

She sat down on the very edge and glanced in apprehension at this strange hermit. 'You seem to have been expecting me, Father.'

'I was,' the abbot confirmed, putting the lamp down on the table. 'I was hoping you would come. And praying to God that you would.'

'But ... But how did you guess?'

'That you were not a novice, but a woman?' Israel carefully pulled the hood back off her head, but immediately took his hand away. 'I have a special intuition for the female sex; I can't be deceived. All my life I have been able to recognise a woman from her smell, her skin, her body hair. Almost all of mine has fallen out now, it is true,' the holy elder said with a smile, 'but never mind that – I knew straight away who you were. And I realised that you were daring. You weren't afraid to dress up as a novice and come to the island in the boat. It was obvious that you were intelligent, too – with that keen, inquisitive look. And when you came the second time, I could see quite clearly that you had caught the special meaning in my words. Not like those dimwits in Ararat. On the last few occasions I spoke only for you, I put all my hope in you. I hoped you would guess.'

'Guess what? About Theognost's death?'

'Yes.'

'What did happen to him?'

Israel looked away from her face and wrinkled up the skin on his forehead. 'He was killed. At first I thought he had passed on in the ordinary way, that his time had come ... He had not come out of his cell by midday and I decided to look in. I saw him lying on his pine twigs (Theognost would have no truck with palliasses). He was quite still and not breathing. He had been weak and unwell, and so I was not at all surprised. I was about to close his mouth when I saw threads between his teeth – threads of red wool. Theognost had a red knitted scarf to wrap round his throat. Well, the scarf was lying a little distance away, on the table, neatly folded. How could that be? I thought. I unfolded it and saw that in one spot the wool was torn and there were threads sticking up ...'

'Someone came in the night,' Mrs Lisitsyna interrupted hastily, 'covered Theognost's face with his own scarf and smothered him? It's the only possible explanation. As he was choking, the holy father gnawed the wool with his teeth – that's why there were threads between them. And afterwards the killer folded the scarf and left it on the table.'

The abbot nodded approvingly. 'I was right about you: you are intelligent. You saw everything straight away. I had to think a lot longer than you did. When I finally realised what had happened, I shuddered inwardly. Who could have committed such an appalling deed? It wasn't me. Then who? Could it have been the holy elder David? Perhaps a devil had possessed him and incited him to commit evil? But David was even more infirm than Theognost; his heart was so bad that he hardly ever rose from his bed. He couldn't have done it! So it was an outsider. A fourth person. Isn't that right?'

'Yes,' said Polina Andreevna, and nodded. She was still in no hurry to share her own theories with the holy elder – she had the impression the hermit had not yet told her everything.

'Three months ago someone came. At night, like you. He came into my cell,' said Israel, confirming her guess.

'A little man, dishevelled and fidgety?' she asked.

The holy elder screwed up his eyes. 'I see that you know him. Yes, a little man. What he said was incomprehensible; he slavered as he spoke. He was like a holy fool. But he did not kill Theognost.'

At those words Lisistyna took her spectacles out of their case, put them on her nose and looked attentively at the abbot of the hermitage. 'You seem very sure of that. Why?'

'He is not that kind of man. I know people very well. And

I saw his eyes. People with eyes like that do not kill, let alone kill a sleeping man, in secret. I did not understand what he tried to tell me when he was here. About some kind of rays. He kept trying to inspect my bald head more closely. I drove him out. But I did not complain to the monks in Ararat. It is hard to explain anything to them, with one or two words a day, and the holy fool did no harm ... No, my daughter, it was someone else who smothered Theognost. And I believe I know who.'

'*Cucullus non facit monachum*,' Polina Andreevna said with an understanding nod.

'Yes. I said that just for you, so that the boatman would not understand.'

'But how did you know that I understand Latin?'

The holy elder laughed, parting the plump lips that were so out of keeping with the taut skin of his ascetic face. 'Do you think I can't tell an educated woman from a cook? You have a mark from your spectacles on the bridge of your nose – it's just barely visible, but I am observant when it comes to details. Wrinkles here' – he pointed to the corners of her eyes with his finger – 'that's from reading a lot. You know, my dear, I know everything there is to know about women. I only need one glance and I can tell any woman her life story.'

Mrs Lisitsyna could not tolerate such self-assurance, not even from a holy elder. 'Any woman! Then what can you tell me about my life?'

Israel inclined his head to one side, as if he were checking something that he already knew in part. He spoke without hurrying.

'You are thirty years old. No, more likely thirty-one. Not an innocent young lady, but not married either. A widow, I think. You have no sweetheart and you do not want one, because ...' He took his startled listener's hands in his own and looked at her nails and her palms. 'Because you are a nun or a novice. You grew up in the country, on an estate in the central region of Russia, but later you lived in the capital and were accepted into high society. What you want above all else is to live an exclusively spiritual life, but it is hard for you, because you are young and there is still a lot of strength in you. And above all – there is a lot of love in you. You are filled with this unexpended love. You are overflowing with it.' The holy elder sighed. 'I used to value women like you more than anything else. There is nothing on earth more precious than they are. And some time ago, five or six years, you suffered a great disaster, an immense grief, after which you decided to leave the world behind. Look into my eyes. Yes, that's right ... I see, I can see what that grief was. Shall I tell you?'

'No!' Polina Andreevna exclaimed with a shudder. 'Don't!'

The holy elder smiled a gentle, otherworldly smile. 'Don't be surprised; there is no magic in this. You have probably heard that before I became a monk I was an inveterate sensualist. Women were the entire meaning of my former life. I loved the tribe of Eve more than anything else on Earth. No, that's wrong: apart from women there was nothing that I loved. For as long as I can remember, I was always like that, from my earliest childhood.'

'Yes, I have heard that you used to be an outrageous Don Juan, that you had a thousand women and even compiled an atlas of their bodies.' She looked at the wizened old man with a fearful curiosity that was far from appropriate for an individual of the conventual calling.

'The idea of the atlas is a stupid, cynical joke. And as for sleeping with a thousand women – that's nonsense. No great prowess is required to rack up the numbers. Anyone can do that, if he is not disgusted by three-rouble whores. No, my dear, the body alone was never enough for me; I wanted to possess the soul as well.'

As he spoke about women, the hermit was transformed. His eyes became gentle and pensive, his mouth twisted into a sad smile, and even his speech became freer, as if it were not an ascetic monk talking, but some ordinary man.

'After all, what is the most magical thing about women?

Their infinite variety. And with every woman I loved, I became different from the way I was before. Like a frog taking on the temperature of his surroundings. And for that, every one of them loved me. For the way that I existed only for her – perhaps not for long, but still I was hers alone. And how they loved me! I lived on their love, I was nourished by it, as a vampire is by living blood. It was not lascivious passion that set my head spinning, but the knowledge that now she would sacrifice her immortal soul for my sake! That I meant more to her than God himself! Only women know how to love like that.' The abbot lowered his head and sighed repentantly. 'But once I had taken possession of the body and the soul, drunk my fill of blood, I soon began feeling bored. One thing I could never do and regarded as a base deception was pretend to love. And I had no pity at all for those I had ceased to love. It is a great sin to make a heart your own and then simply smash it against the ground. A heart-breaker – the word may sound beautiful, but there is no greater crime on Earth ... and I always knew that. Drop by drop, year by year this poison accumulated within me. And when my cup was full and began to overflow, I was suddenly enlightened – I cannot say if it was a blessing or a punishment. Probably both. I repented. There was one story ... I will tell you it later, but first let me finish about myself ... I entered a monastery to find salvation, but I did not find it, for there is much vanity in monasteries too. Then I conceived the desire to come here, to Basilisk's Hermitage. I waited four years until my turn came. Now I have been trying to save my soul here for two years, and still cannot. Of all those who have ascended to Heaven from this place, I am the only one who has been tested for so long – for my sins. Do you know what torment I have suffered as a monk?' The holy father gave Polina Andreevna a doubtful glance, as if he were not sure whether to tell her or not. 'I will tell you. You are not some dim-witted virgin. Desires of the flesh have tormented me. Incessantly, through all my years as a monk. By day and especially by night. That was the ordeal I was given – according to my deeds. The monks used to whisper – I do not know how they found out – that in Basilisk's Hermitage the Lord first of all granted release from sensual yearnings, in order to purge his lambs' thoughts and bring them closer to himself. And it was true, the other hermits were quickly released from desires of the flesh; but there was no release for me. Every night was filled with voluptuous visions. Everyone here loses the hair on their head and body; it soon falls out – it is in the nature of the place. But I kept my hair longer than anyone else. It was only when I had become abbot and outlived everyone else that my hair fell out.'

'But why does the hermits' hair fall out?' Mrs Lisitsyna asked, looking compassionately at the holy elder's bald cranium.

He explained: 'It is a special mercy from God and a deliverance from the flesh. During the first few weeks the holy fathers are greatly tormented by lice and fleas – the charter does not allow us to wash. But without hair the torment is far less, and our hands are freed from shameful scratching to be clasped in devout prayer.' He clasped his hands piously in front of himself to demonstrate. 'I was tormented by the insects for more than a year. There was no end to my suffering, and I repeated after Job: 'I decay, hounded in spirit, begging for death but not receiving it.' There was no death and no forgiveness for me. Things have only improved recently. I can feel that my body has grown weaker. It is hard to walk, my belly will not hold my food and when I rise in the morning everything inside my head is spinning.' Israel smiled triumphantly. 'That means it is close already. I do not have long to wait for deliverance. And just recently, I have been granted relief from my greatest torment. God has called off the demon of fleshly desire. And now I have bright, joyful dreams. When I saw you, so young and beautiful, I listened to my feelings – and nothing stirred within me. The Lord has purged me. Purged me and forgiven me.'

Polina Andreevna was glad for the holy elder, glad that now it would be easier for him to save his soul; but it was time to turn the conversation back to urgent matters.

'Tell me, Father, what were you trying to tell me with your Latin riddle? That your new colleague is not Ilarii but someone else who has gained admission here by deception?'

Israel was smiling brightly, still rapt in thoughts of his own imminent bliss.

'What, my daughter? Ah, about Ilarii. I don't know, after all we don't show our faces to each other, and we are not allowed to talk. When necessary, we explain ourselves with signs. I saw the learned brother Ilarii once in the monastery, but that was a long time ago. I don't remember his figure or even how tall he was. So I don't know if it is him or not, but one thing I do know for certain: the new holy elder has not come here to save his soul. He does not carve rosary beads and during the day he does not even put his nose outside his cell. I went in to beckon him to a session of joint prayer and meditation (we pray silently, of course). He was lying there, asleep. He just waved his hand at me, turned over on his side and carried on sleeping. In the middle of the day!'

'But what does he do at night?' Lisitsyna asked quickly.

'I do not know. At night I am here, in my cell. The charter is very strict; it forbids us to go out.'

'But you have broken the vow of silence with me! Have you never gone out into the gallery at night?'

'Never,' the abbot replied sternly. 'Not even once. And I will not. And I have a special reason for speaking so much to you ...'

He hesitated, then suddenly covered his face with his hands and fell silent.

Polina Andreevna waited for as long as her patience would allow and asked: 'What special reason is that?'

'I wish to ask your forgiveness,' the holy elder answered faintly through his closed fingers.

'My forgiveness?'

'I shall never see another woman again ...' He took his hands away from his face, and Polina Andreevna saw that his eyes were wet with tears. 'The Lord has tested me and forgiven me – that is God's way. But I have sinned heinously against you, my sisters. How can I leave this world if I have not been forgiven by Woman? I will not relate all of my abominable deeds to you – that would be a long tale. Only the story that I have already mentioned, the story that weighs heaviest of all on my heart. The story with which my enlightenment began. Listen to it and tell me one thing – if a woman's soul can forgive me. That will be enough ...'

The Heart-breaker's Confession

And so he began.

'This is only one story, but there were two women. The first was no more than a little girl. A slim, fragile creature who barely even came up to my elbow. But girls like that are quite common there.

'I was just completing my round-the-world trip that had lasted four years. I had begun in Europe and I was finishing at the other end of the world, in Japan. I had seen a lot – I won't say "all sorts of different things" – "all sorts of different women" would be more accurate.

'In Nagasaki, and later in Yokohama, I saw plenty of their local geishas and *djoros* (that's what they call loose women). And just as I was about to sail on without anything in Japan having caught my fancy, I found myself in the house of a Japanese official and saw his daughter there. The way she looked at me with her narrow little eyes, as if I were some kind of animal, like a gorilla, piqued my unfailing sense of adventure. Now that would be interesting, I thought. I've never had anything quite like that.

'She had been raised very strictly, the samurai way; she was only half my size and about a quarter of my age. In her eyes I was a hairy monster, and I also lacked my most important weapon, language – there was absolutely no way at all that we could understand each other.

'Well, I stayed on in Tokyo, and begin visiting the official's home more and more often. We became friends. I talked politics, drank coffee with liqueur and studied his daughter. She had clearly only been allowed to see guests very recently – she was very shy. How can I find the key to fit this little lacquer box? – I wondered.

'Well, I managed to find one. I had plenty of experience and, more importantly, I knew the workings of women's hearts.

'I could not make myself pleasing to her in the usual way; I was too much unlike the men she was used to seeing. But that meant I could exploit the dissimilarity.

'Her mother once told me jokingly that her daughter used to compare me to a bear – I was so very big, with such huge sideburns.

'Well then, a bear it would be.

'I bought a live bear cub from some sailors in the port – a brown bear from Siberia – and brought him to her as a present – so that she would grow used to his hairiness. He was a fine little fellow, mischievous and affectionate. My Japanese girl played with him from morning till night and came to love him greatly: she stroked him and kissed him, and he licked her with his tongue. Excellent, I thought. She loves the bear, and she will love me too.

'And indeed, she began to look at the man who gave her the bear in a different way, with curiosity instead of apprehension. As if she were comparing me with her favourite. I deliberately began waddling as I walked, fluffing out my sideburns and speaking in a gruffer voice.

'And after that, things happened in the usual way. A young girl languishing in idleness as her body blossoms. She wants something, new, untried, unusual. And here is an exotic foreigner. He shows her all sorts of interesting things, brought from all over the world. Postcards with views of Paris and St Petersburg, the skyscrapers of Chicago. And most importantly, after the young bear's fur, she was no longer squeamish about touching me. She would take hold of my hand, or stroke my moustache – out of curiosity. And a young girl's curiosity is highly inflammable material.

'I won't tell you all the details; they are not interesting. The main problem, to put it in scientific terms, was for me to become a member of the same biological species as her, so that cross-breeding became possible. And once we were no longer a Japanese girl and a foreign bear, but an innocent virgin and an experienced man, everything followed the ordinary route that I had taken many times.

'Well then, when I sailed from Japan, the Japanese girl was with me – she herself had asked to come. I suppose her parents never even knew where their daughter had disappeared to.

'As far as Vladivostok my love for her remained strong. And afterwards too, when we were travelling on the railway. But in the middle of Siberia her childish passion began to pall. I couldn't even talk to her about anything. She, on the contrary, only became all the more inflamed with love. I would wake up at night and she would not be asleep, but propped up on her elbow, just looking at me through her slit eyes. Women's love flares up more brightly than ever when they feel you beginning to grow cold – that is a well known fact.

'As we came closer to St Petersburg, I could no longer bear the sight of her and I racked my brains, wondering how I could get rid of her. Send her back to her parents? But they were no ordinary *papa* and *maman*, they were samurais. They might do away with the girl. I felt sorry for her. Pay her off? She wouldn't have taken the money, and she would never have left me in peace, she was too clinging. She didn't know how to do anything, except what I had taught her so assiduously in the ship's cabin and the railway compartment.

'That was the thought that gave rise to my decision. I had heard from one of our travelling companions in the train that while I had been away a new establishment had appeared in St Petersburg, owned by a certain Madame Pozdnyaeva. A fashionable bordello with young ladies brought from many different countries: there were young Italian girls and Turks and Annamites – anything you could want. It was very popular with the men of St Petersburg.

'I paid a visit to Pozdnyaeva to make her acquaintance and

make sure that the girls were well treated. The mistress of the house told me that she put part of the income in the bank for each of them, in a special account. The very next morning I handed my little girl over to her in person. And for a start I put a thousand roubles in the bank in her name.

'But the Japanese girl never used the money. When she realised where I had brought her and that I was not going to take her back again, she threw herself out of the window and landed head first on the pavement. She floundered for a few moments, like a fish thrown up on a river bank, and then lay still.

'When I heard about it, of course, I felt sad, but not excessively so, because by that time I was already obsessed with a new goal, the most unattainable of all.

'This goal was none other than Madame Pozdnyaeva herself, the owner of the establishment. When I held negotiations with her about the Japanese girl, she had made a great impression on me. She was no longer young – about forty – but she was smooth-skinned and took very strict care of herself. I could tell from her eyes that she had seen everything there was to see. She could see straight through any man and cared not a jot for any of them. Her heart was stone, her soul was ashes and her mind was an arithmetical calculator.

'As I looked at this terrifying creature I gradually became inflamed. All sorts of women had loved me, but never one so cold and cruel. Or was she not capable of love at all? That only made it all the more enticing to rummage around in those ashes to find a coal that was not yet completely dead and blow on it gently and carefully, heating it into an all-consuming flame. If I could manage it, it would be a genuine labour of Hercules.

'I spent more than one month on the siege of that Troy. The first thing that was needed, I reasoned, was for her to see me in a different light from other men. For Madame Pozdnyaeva all men were divided into two categories: those from whom she could not profit, owing to their age, poverty or ill health, and those who wished and were able to pay for debauchery. Men of the former category did not even exist for her, while she despised the latter and fleeced them mercilessly. As I later discovered, she even stooped to blackmail (there were all kinds of cunning devices in her establishment for spying on customers and photographing them).

'And so I had to occupy a position between the two categories of male: someone from whom there was profit to be made, but who had no interest in venal love. And then again, women like that, who have been through hell and high water and achieved everything for themselves, are very susceptible to subtle flattery.

'I got into the habit of going to her den of vice almost every day. But I did not visit the young ladies; I sat with the madam and made clever, cynical conversation of a kind that she might enjoy. And every time I left her money – a generous amount, twice the usual charge.

'She was perplexed. She simply could not assign me to a definite category. Then she began to imagine that I was in love with her, and immediately conceived an even greater contempt for me than for her other clients. One day she laughed and said: "Why are you being so sloppy? I'm surprised at you. You don't seem like the shy type. And, God knows, I'm certainly no ingénue. If you want to get into my bed, then say so. You've paid out so much money that it would be too discourteous to refuse you." I thanked her gratefully, accepted the invitation and we went to her bedroom.

'It was a strange assignation; both of us wanted to impress the other with our skill, and both of us were cold: she because she had burned out long ago; I because what I wanted from her was something different. Eventually, when she was worn out, she said: "I can't understand you." And that was the first step towards my victory.

'I didn't stop going to see her after that, but I didn't ask to be allowed into her bedroom, and she didn't invite me. She watched me closely, as if she were trying to find something that she had forgotten long ago.

'I began asking her a little about her past. Not as a grown woman, God forbid. About her childhood, her parents and her friends at grammar school. I needed her to remember a different time, before her heart and her feelings had grown cold. At first Madame Pozdnyaeva replied curtly and unwillingly, but after a while she became more talkative, and all I had to do was listen. And one thing I certainly knew how to do was listen.

'So now I had overcome the second barrier and won her confidence, and that in itself was no small achievement.

'When she invited me into her boudoir for the second time, a few weeks later, she behaved quite differently, without any mechanical tricks; and at the end she suddenly burst into tears. She was terribly surprised herself – she said she hadn't been able to shed a single tear for thirteen years, and then suddenly this had happened.

'Never before had I known the kind of love that Pozdnyaeva gave to me – as if a dam had burst, and I was caught up in the current and swept away. It was a genuine miracle – to observe a dead soul coming back to life. As if springs of pure, clear water had suddenly broken through the sand of a parched desert, up through the cracked earth, and lush green plants had sprung up, putting out flowers of incredible beauty.

'She closed her bordello, distributed the money accumulated from her pandering among the girls and set them all free to go their own way. And she herself changed beyond all recognition. She became younger and fresher and looked just like a girl. Every morning she sang and laughed. And she cried a lot too, but without any bitterness – it was simply the tears that she hadn't shed in all those years coming out.

'And I loved her. I was absolutely overjoyed at what my efforts had achieved.

'I was happy for a month, two months. And then in the third month my happiness came to an end.

'One morning (she was still sleeping) I left the house, got into a fiacre, drove to the station and took a train to Paris. I left her a note saying that the apartment was paid for until the end of the year, there was money in the casket, goodbye and forgive me.

'They told me later that when she woke up and read the note, she dashed out of the house wearing nothing but her chemise, ran off along the street and never came back to the apartment again.

'I returned from abroad six months later, when it was already winter. I rented a house and began living in my former manner, but something was happening inside me; the old familiar amusements no longer brought me any joy.

'Then one day I was riding through Ligovka on my way to a certain country villa and I saw her, Pozdnyaeva, lying in the ditch by the side of the road – dirty, louse-ridden, with grey hair and almost no teeth. She could not see me, because she was lying there blind drunk.

'That was the very moment when my invisible cup ran over. I began trembling, I came out in a cold sweat all over my body and I saw the pit of hell gaping open before me. I was terrified and my conscience was awoken.

'I ordered the tramp to be picked up and put up in a decent room. I went to see her and beg her forgiveness. But my former beloved had changed again. There was no love left in her, nothing but malice and greed. The flowering garden had withered, the miraculous spring had dried up. And I realised that the most evil of all deeds is not to destroy a living soul, but to resurrect a soul that is dead and then annihilate it utterly.

'I transferred all my fortune to the unfortunate woman's name, and I became a monk in order to piece the fragments of myself back together and purge myself of filth. And that is my story.

'And now tell me, my sister, is there any forgiveness for my transgressions or not?'

Polina Andreevna was so shaken by this story that for a while she said nothing.

'That is known only to God ...' she said, avoiding looking at the repentant sinner.

'God will forgive me. I know. Perhaps he has even forgiven

me already,' Israel said slowly. 'But you tell me, as a woman –
can *you* forgive me? Only tell the truth!'

She tried to avoid an answer: 'What would my forgiveness
mean? You have not done me any harm.'

'It would mean a great deal,' the abbot said firmly, as if speaking of something he had decided a long time ago. 'If you forgive
me, then they would have forgiven me.'

Polina Andreevna wanted to speak words of consolation to
him, but she could not. That is, it would have cost her no effort
to speak them, but she knew the holy elder would sense her
insincerity, and that would only make things worse.

The hermit's face darkened when there was no answer. 'I
knew it . . .' he said in a quiet voice, and put his hand on the
seated woman's shoulder. 'Get up. Go. Back to the world. You
should not be here. I have another confession to make. I deliberately lured you here, to the hermitage. Not because of Theognost, and not because of Ilarii. That is all idle vanity – who killed
whom, and why they killed them. The Lord will render unto
each according to his deeds, and not a single deed, either good
or evil, shall be left unrewarded. And I spoke those mysterious,
enticing words to you because before I die I wanted to see a
woman one last time and ask for her forgiveness . . . I have asked
and I have not received. And that is how it must be. Go.' So
impatient was he for his guest to go away and leave him alone
that he began pushing her towards the door.

Stepping out into the gallery, Lisitsyna heard the faint, repulsive scraping sound again.

'What is that?' she asked with a shudder. 'Bats?'

Israel replied indifferently: 'There are no bats here. And what
happens in the cave at night, I do not know. It is the kind of place
where anything might happen. After all, it contains a piece of
the sphere of Heaven.'

'What?' Polina Andreevna asked in amazement. 'A piece of
the sphere of Heaven?'

The holy elder frowned, seeming annoyed that he had said
something he should not have. 'You are not supposed to know

about that. Go now. And tell no one what you have seen here. But you won't: you are an intelligent woman. Only do not lose your way. Go right to reach the way out.'

The door slammed shut, and Polina Andreevna was left alone in total darkness. She lit a candle and listened closely to the mysterious sound. Then she set off, but not to the right. She went to the left.

Basilisk

The gallery that the holy elder Israel had called the Approach gradually rose higher and higher as it led on. The walls on both sides were bare now, and Polina Andreevna saw that there would be enough room for many hundreds more dead bodies.

The sound was clearer now and harder to bear – an iron claw scraping, not against glass but against a naked, defenceless heart. At one point, when Lisitsyna could stand it no longer, she set the travelling bag down on the ground and put her hands over her ears, despite the risk that her hair might catch fire from the burning candle clutched in her fingers.

Her hair did not catch fire, but a drop of wax fell on to her temple, and the sudden hot sensation settled Polina Andreevna's nerves.

She went further.

Thus far the gallery had been almost straight, or at least there had not been any visible bends, but now it suddenly turned a ninety-degree corner. Mrs Lisitsyna peeped round the corner and froze.

There was dull light glimmering up ahead. The explanation for the strange scraping sound must be very close now.

Polina Andreevna blew out her candle, pressed herself flat against the wall and took a cautious step round the corner. She crept forward on tiptoe, without making a sound.

The passage widened out into a round cave with its high ceiling lost in darkness. But Polina Andreevna did not even glance upwards – she was so stunned by the picture that opened up to her eyes.

Lying in the middle of the cave was a perfectly round sphere, with its bottom third sunk into the ground. It was about the same size as one of those large balls of snow that children use as the base for a snowman. The surface of the sphere shimmered with shifting rainbow patterns in violet, green and pink. The sight was so wonderful, so unexpected after wandering so long in the dark, that Lisitsyna gasped.

There was a lantern standing beside the sphere, illuminating the smooth, glittering surface, setting it flashing and sparkling, and she could see a black shadow hunched over between the lantern and the sphere, swaying in a steady rhythm, like a pendulum. The sickening scraping sounds matched its movements perfectly.

Polina Andreevna took another short step forward, but just at that moment the sound broke off and in the sudden silence the gentle rustle made by the sole of her shoe sounded deafening.

The crouching figure froze, as if it were listening. It made a careful movement, as if stroking the sphere or gently sweeping something off it.

What should she do? Freeze stock-still and hope that it would be all right, or make a run for it?

Mrs Lisitsyna was standing in a most uncomfortable position, with one foot extended in front of her and supporting all her weight, and the other foot poised on its toes. And then she felt an irresistible tickling in her nose. She suppressed the sneeze by pressing a finger against the base of her nose, but she could not suppress the sudden intake of breath.

The black man (if, of course, it was a man) made a quick movement that puzzled Polina Andreevna at first, but when the rounded upper part of the silhouette suddenly became pointed, she realised he had pulled a cowl up over his head.

There was no point in hiding any longer, and Mrs Lisitsyna did not try to run away. She walked straight towards the standing hermit (she could see now that it was a hermit) and he backed away.

When she had almost reached the slim black shadow, Polina

Andreevna was halted by the terrible glint in the eyes behind those holes. That must be the way the eyes of a basilisk glinted. Not the righteous St Basilisk's eyes, but those of that appalling, nightmarish emissary of Hell with the body of a toad, the tail of a snake and the head of cock. The monster whose death-dealing gaze cracked stones, withered flowers and struck people dead on the spot.

'So this is what you are really like, Alexei Stepanovich,' Polina Andreevna said with a shudder.

The Black Monk did not budge, and so she continued – in a low voice, without hurrying. 'Yes, it is you, I know it. There is nobody else it could be. At first I suspected Sergei Nikolaevich Lampier, but now, after walking through the Approach alone in the darkness, I have seen the light. That often happens: when the eyes are blind, the sight of the mind and the soul becomes keener; they are not distracted by false appearances. Sergei Nikolaevich could not have carried you all the way from the conservatory to the lake. He is not strong enough, he is too puny, and it is a long way. And then, I could not get that saying of Galileo's about measuring the immeasurable out of my head: I found it in the notebook with all the formulae, but where had I seen it before? I have remembered now, only a moment ago. It was in your third letter. So by that time you must already have been in Lampier's laboratory and looked at his notebook. After that everything fell into place very quickly. Everything became clear. It's just a shame I did not realise sooner.' Polina Andreevna paused to see if the hermit would reply to that, but he said nothing. 'On the very first day you found the bench hidden under the water and hinted at this "piquant circumstance" in your letter, promising to reveal all the next day and present a simple answer to the riddle. That night you went to track down the "Black Monk" – and you succeeded. You followed the hoaxer to the clinic to discover who he was. You saw the laboratory and you were intrigued. You pried into his notes ... I could not understand a thing from those formulae, but you could. They were right at the university when they predicted you would be another Faraday. There was something written there about this cave and this sphere that changed all your plans and you began playing out your own nocturnal performance.' She glanced fearfully at the mysterious, glimmering sphere. 'What is so special about this sphere that could make you do such terrible things and destroy so many people's lives?'

'Enough,' said the hermit, pulling off the cowl that was no longer needed and shaking his head of curly hair. 'This sphere contains everything that I could ever desire. Absolute freedom, fame, riches, happiness! Firstly, this object consists of at least six hundred thousand *zolotniks* of the most precious metal in the world, and every *zolotnik* is a month of life without any limitations. Secondly, and most importantly, that half-witted midget has given me the idea for a great project, a great idea! I am the only one who can appreciate it and understand it! When they threw me out of the university, I thought it was the end of everything. But no, behold, here is my future.' He gestured around the cave. 'No need for degrees, no need to spend years as an assistant to some provincial luminary of science. I shall set up my own laboratory, in Switzerland. I shall develop the theory of emanation myself! No one can tell me what to do; I have no need to beg for money from anyone! Oh, the world shall know the name of Lentochkin!' He leaned down and stroked the shimmering surface lovingly. 'It is a shame that I have not managed to file off more platinum-iridium. But never mind, what I have already will suffice for my purposes.'

He turned to face Polina Andreevna, and the sunken cheeks wrinkled up into the semblance of a smile, with no trace of their former dimples.

'You tracked me down a bit too soon, Sister. But at least now I can speak out after mumbling to myself for so long. Much more of that and my brains might really have addled. You have a quick mind, you are able to appreciate my scheme. Well conceived, was it not? Especially the primordial nakedness? I had to maintain a foothold in Canaan somehow, while I prepared everything. During the day I relax in Eden, eating pineapples (ah, how sick I am of those damn things!), at night I take my cassock out from under a bush and go striding off round the island to frighten the locals. And the best thing is that I am absolutely beyond suspicion. Mr Lampier and I made an excellent pair of Basilisks – we frightened all the curious and pious pilgrims away from the shoreline. Ah, one more month and I would have filed off not five pounds, but fifty or a hundred. Then I could have set up an entire research centre, not just a laboratory. The conditions in which the natural factor comes into effect have been determined and confirmed in Lampier's experiments,' he said in a low voice, no longer talking to Polina Andreevna, but to himself. 'Now I can try to create an artificial factor – there will be enough money to make a start, and then the blockheads will shell out . . .'

'What is this factor?' Lisitsyna asked guardedly.

Lentochkin started and beamed another withered smile at her. 'You wouldn't understand that. But you can appreciate the elegance of my solution to the problem. I arranged everything quite beautifully, didn't I? A quiet idiot sitting in his glass palace and talking in riddles, luring the stupid carp to the right spot – that empty hut. Then hook them, bash them over the head, and into the bucket with them! I know that you, Mam'selle Pelagia, could never stand the sight of me, but you must agree it was all wonderfully well planned.'

'Yes, it was ingenious,' Polina Andreevna conceded. 'But absolutely ruthless. It was your cruelty that first made me dislike you so much. I did not like the hideous revenge you took on the vice-chancellor to settle your grudge.'

Lentochkin started walking round the cave, shaking his work-weary fingers.

'Oh yes, of course. Prince Bolkonsky would not have acted like that. That's why he never became a Bonaparte. But I shall. There is my Toulon!' He nodded at the miraculous sphere again. 'With this fulcrum I can overturn that other, far more voluminous sphere. Ah, I should have smacked you harder that time, with the stilt. I have only had six nights with the sphere, and now I shall have to leave. Never mind, what I already have will suffice for my idea.'

He slapped himself on the chest and halted beside the gaping black maw of the gallery. Raising one hand to his mouth, he licked the palm – it was covered with bloody, broken blisters. However, it was not the blisters that caught Mrs Lisitsyna's attention, but the strange long blade glittering in Lentochkin's fingers.

'What's that you have there?'

'This?' He held up a narrow strip of metal covered with brilliant points of light. 'A diamond-grit file. It's the only thing that will touch platinum-iridium. I borrowed it from the good Mr Lampier. Of course, he is an absolute blockhead, but I am grateful to him for his idea of a nuclear factor and his analysis of the material of the meteorite.'

Polina Andreevna did not understand about the idea, or about the 'material of the meteorite' either, but she did not ask any questions – she had only just realised that after his apparently random movements around the cave, Lentochkin was now blocking her only route of escape.

'Are you going to kill me too?' she asked quietly, gazing mesmerised at the glittering file. 'Like Lagrange, like Theognost, like Ilarii?'

Alyosha pressed one hand to his chest, as if he were trying to justify his actions. 'I do not kill anyone unnecessarily, only if I have to. It's Lagrange's own fault that he had such a hard head – I couldn't stun him, so I had to shoot him. Theognost was preventing me from moving into the hermitage; he was occupying my place. And the monks had already held Ilarii's funeral, so he was already as good as dead anyway. . .'

His white teeth suddenly glinted in the light of the lantern, making it clear that the ingenious youth was not trying to justify himself at all: he was joking. But then his smile instantly disappeared and he spoke in a serious, puzzled voice. 'There's just one thing I don't understand? What were you counting on when you came in here? You already knew you would find me here, not that weakling Lampier! Were you hoping I would take a chivalrous attitude towards a lady? That was foolish! Really, Sister, I simply cannot let you live, no matter how much I might wish to. I need at least one day to get away from the archipelago.' He sighed regretfully, then winked and bared his teeth – he had only been playing the fool again.

'To tell you the truth, regardless of that consideration, I would still kill you anyway. I don't feel any pity for you, you skulking little mouse. And why should I want a witness like you around when I am a world-famous scientist?'

Alexei Stepanovich lifted up the hand holding the file, and it flashed and sparkled with points of multicoloured light, like a magic wand in some fairy tale.

'Just look, Mam'selle Pelagia. It is a beautiful dream – to receive your death from a thing of such beauty; Cleopatra herself would envy you. And it is so sharp that it will quite easily run through your ginger head from one ear to the other. I'll put you in the pile, under some dried-out righteous holy man,' said Alyosha, screwing up his eyes dreamily. 'The hermits won't notice you straight away. Only when you start to rot. You're not a saint, are you? – so you're not guaranteed incorruptibility.' He laughed. 'And you'll enjoy it. At least when you're dead, you'll be lying under a man.'

Polina Andreevna backed away, covering her chest with the travelling bag like a shield. Her fingers fumbled in panic at the catch.

'Go away, Alexei Stepanovich. Do not take another sin on your soul; you have already committed more than enough atrocities. I swear to you in Christ's name that I will do nothing until tomorrow, until three o'clock in the afternoon. You will have time to leave the island on the morning ferry.'

She clicked the small nickel-plated balls apart and thrust her hand into the travelling bag. Lagrange's revolver was in there, wrapped in her drawers. She would not shoot, of course, but it would be enough to frighten him. Then Alyosha would understand what she had been counting on when she entered the cave and put herself in danger.

Lentochkin took a few quick steps forward, and Polina Andreevna suddenly realised that she would not have enough time to unwrap the thin silk. She ought to have taken the gun out sooner, while she was walking along the gallery. She pressed her back against the uneven wall. She could retreat no further.

The false hermit was in no hurry. He stopped in front of the cringing woman as if he were contemplating where to strike – at the ear, as he had threatened, at the neck or at the stomach. The lantern had almost run out of oil and was giving almost no light at all. The darkness behind Alyosha's back was impenetrable.

'Why have you got your head down like that?' Lentochkin laughed. 'Would you like to butt, but God didn't give you any horns? If that's the case, you shouldn't have meddled in the corrida, my little hornless cow.' He suddenly raised the file above his head like a toreador's sword and sang a phrase from the latest fashionable opera: *"Toréador, prends garde à toi—"'*

The melody was suddenly choked off as he collapsed under the blow from a knotty staff that came smashing down on his curly head. There, standing just behind the spot where Alyosha had been, was a black shadow in a pointed cowl. Polina Andreevna tried to scream, but her mouth would not draw in the air.

'I have violated the charter for you,' the holy elder Israel said in a peevish voice. 'I have left my cell at night. Defiled myself with the sin of violence. And all because I knew that women like you are obstinate and curious to the point of foolhardiness. There was no way you would ever go back to the world until you had sniffed out every last detail with that freckled nose of yours. Well then, look, since you are already here. There it is, the heavenly fragment that we hermits have guarded for hundreds of years. It is the sign sent down to our founding father, Saint Basilisk. Only be sure not to say a word of this to anyone. Agreed?'

Mrs Lisitsyna nodded without speaking, for after all these horrors she had not yet recovered the gift of speech.

'And who is this boy?' the abbot asked, leaning on his staff as he bent down over the body on the ground.

Before she could answer, Alyosha suddenly lifted himself up and thrust the file deep into the centre of the hermit's chest. Then he pulled it out and struck again.

Israel fell on top of his murderer. His hands fumbled at the ground, but he could not get up, or even raise his head.

It took Lentochkin only a few moments to toss the holy elder's body aside and get to his feet, but that was enough for Polina Andreevna to run from the wall to the middle of the cave, grab the revolver out of the travelling bag and free it from the slippery silk. She threw the bag down on the ground, clutched the fluted handle of the revolver in both hands and aimed it at Lentochkin.

He looked at her without any sign of fear. His mouth twisted into a crooked sneer as he rubbed the bruised back of his head and tugged the blade out of the hermit's chest without the slightest effort – like pulling a knife out of butter.

'Do you know how to use a firearm, Sister?' Lentochkin asked mockingly. 'Do you know which little thingamajig to press?' He walked casually straight towards her, strutting. The diamonds on the file were dull now; the blood had dimmed their sparkle.

'Yes! This is a Smith and Wesson forty-five six-shooter, central-firing with a double-action trigger,' Mrs Lisitsyna replied, blurting out the information she had gleaned from the ballistics textbook. 'The bullet weighs three *zolotniks*, its initial velocity is a hundred *sazhens* a second and it can puncture a pine board three inches thick from a distance of twenty paces.'

It was a shame that her voice was so unsteady. But even so the required effect was achieved.

Lentochkin stopped dead and looked at the black hole of the muzzle, perplexed. 'And where's the thirty-eight calibre Colt?' Polina Andreevna asked, hoping to reinforce the impression she had made. 'The one you used to shoot Lagrange? Give it to me, but slowly, with the handle first.'

When Alyosha failed to respond, she did not say anything else to him, but simply cocked the trigger. The click was not really all that loud, but in the silence of the cave it sounded most impressive.

The murderer shuddered, dropped the file on the ground and held his hands out, palms upward. 'I haven't got it! I threw it in the water that night! I couldn't hide it in the conservatory, could I? What if the gardener had found it?'

Emboldened now, the investigator jerked the long barrel menacingly: 'You're lying! You weren't afraid to hide Basilisk's clothing, were you?'

'Of course not – just an ordinary cassock and an old pair of boots. If anyone had found them, they wouldn't have taken any notice. Ah!' Lentochkin suddenly screeched, throwing his hands up in the air and gazing in horror at something behind Polina Andreevna's back. 'Ba-Ba-Basilisk!'

Alas, Mrs Lisitsyna fell into his childishly simple trap. Even the wise stumble. She swung round in confusion, peering into the darkness. What if the shade of the hermitage's holy founder really had appeared to protect his treasure?

But there was no phantom, and meanwhile the crafty Alyosha had seized his chance to duck down and make a dash for the gallery.

'Stop!' Polina Andreevna shouted in a terrible voice. 'Stop, or I'll fire!'

She was about to rush into the Approach after him when she heard a groan – a terrible groan, full of excruciating suffering.

She swung round and saw the holy elder Israel propping himself up on one elbow and reaching to her with a trembling, emaciated hand,

'Don't go, don't leave me like this . . .'

She only hesitated for a moment. Let him get away. Compassion was more important than vengeance, even than justice. And what point was there in pursuing the villain anyway? What if he didn't stop? She couldn't shoot him for that. And then again, where could he go in Kleopa's little boat with its puny oars?

Well, he could get as far as Canaan. But he would still never reach the mainland. And so, casting aside all lesser considerations, Polina Andreevna walked across to the dying man, knelt down on the ground and put the holy elder's head on her knees. Carefully removing his cowl, she saw his eyelids trembling feebly and his lips moving soundlessly. The lantern gave one last bright flash of light and went out. She had to light a candle and stick it to a stone.

Meanwhile the holy elder had prepared his soul to be set free and folded his hands across his chest. Then suddenly he raised his eyebrows piteously and looked at Polina Andreevna with fear and entreaty in his eyes. His lips whispered a single, short word: 'Forgive . . .'

And this time she did forgive him – without the slightest struggle, she simply forgave him because she could. And she leaned down and kissed him on the forehead.

'Good,' the holy elder said with a smile, and closed his eyes.

A few minutes later they opened again, but they were already empty and lifeless.

When Mrs Lisitsyna went down to the shore to see if Lentochkin had already reached Canaan in Kleopa's boat, there were two surprises waiting for her. Firstly, the boat was still where she had left it, completely undamaged. And secondly, she saw an entire flotilla of boats with their oars raking the water in unison, heading towards Outskirts Island from the opposite shore, rowlocks creaking, oarsmen gasping, torches blazing brightly.

And there, standing in the prow of the leading boat and shaking his crosier belligerently as his long beard fluttered in the fresh breeze, was His Grace Mitrofanii.

Joy to All Who Sorrow
and Grieve

That self-same breeze was blowing on the other side of Outskirts Island, not merely fresh, as it was in the gulf, but gusting powerfully.

A young man dressed in a cassock, with his cowl thrown behind his shoulders, pulled a boat out from its hiding place between two boulders, got into the 'rocker' and pushed off with an oar. When he had rowed a little way from the shore, he threw the oar into the bottom of the boat and raised a slim mast, on which he hoisted a white sail to catch the fair wind, and his light bark began skimming fleetly across the waves – perhaps moving even faster than the steamship, especially since the steamship had to follow the twisting fairway, but the 'rocker' had nothing to fear from the shoals.

The traveller had a compass, which he checked occasionally, evidently afraid of running off course in the darkness. From time to time he turned the rudder or trimmed the sail, but when the scarlet rim of the rising sun appeared over the mist-wreathed lake, the young man stopped worrying.

And the reason for this was that as the first timid ray of sunlight traced out a line to the horizon, it lit up a golden spark at the edge of the sky that did not fade away again. It was the dome of the bell tower of the Church of Joy to All Who Sorrow and Grieve, the main church of the town of Sineozersk, which on a clear day could be seen from thirty versts away. So the boat had not gone astray in the night; it was still exactly on course.

The helmsman set the bow of his 'rocker' directly in line with the Church of Joy and began humming a jolly little tune. Things could not possibly have been going better. Two more hours, and the voyage would be over – the wind did not look likely to change. It was a shame, of course, that he had not managed to collect more of the precious filings, but in any case, he already had five pounds or so. The small, but heavy bag was hanging under his cassock, against his iliac bone. The string had chafed his neck a bit, but that was nothing. Five pounds – almost five hundred *zolotniks*, each worth ...

His calculations were cut short by a sudden attack of nausea. The young man leaned over the side, groaning and gurgling as the spasms shook his body. Then he slid down, exhausted, into the bottom of the boat, wiped the sweat from his brow and smiled light-heartedly. The bouts of sickness and weakness had become frequent recently – no doubt because of the poor food and the nervous strain. All he needed was a rest and a few good meals, and it would pass.

He massaged his temples furiously to suppress the pounding of the blood. A lock of wavy hair came away in his fingers, and that upset the youth far more than the preceding fit. But not for long. I should think so, he told himself. I haven't washed my hair in a month. It's a miracle I'm not riddled with lice. Never mind, I'll travel third class to Vologda, in modest style, and then I'll get dressed up and book into a good hotel, with a bathroom, and a restaurant, and a hairdresser's.

And it would be better to set up the laboratory in America, not Switzerland. Less trouble. Naturally, I shall take another name. How about 'Mr Basilisk' – what's wrong with that?

He tried to laugh, but the attempt failed – it turned into a long, painful fit of coughing. He wiped his lips and wrapped the black cowl more tightly round his neck. Perhaps it was a good thing that he hadn't stayed on the island any longer. The cold season would set in any time now; the autumn had already lasted for an unusually long time. It would have been awkward to catch a chill in his lungs. He had no time to be ill.

The new radiation physics opened up prospects that the half-witted Lampier and those laboratory rats in Paris were not capable of appreciating, with their pitiful little intellects. 'Death rays!' Only an idiot could possibly have come up with such stupid nonsense. It was simply a new form of energy, no more dangerous than magnetic or electrical radiation. The incalculable power of the atomic nucleus – that was the key. The first person to realise that would rule the world. And he was the perfect age: twenty-four, just like Bonaparte.

A bright ray of sunlight lit up the top of the triumphant victor's head, revealing a round bald spot that looked very much like a tonsure.